jackie cassada

court of all kings

a
changeling: the dreaming
novel

White Wolf
Publishing

court of all kings	jackie cassada
book design & layout	larry s. friedman
cover illustration	joshua gabriel timbrook

White Wolf Publishing
780 Park North Boulevard
Suite 100
Clarkston, GA 30021
World Wide Web page: www.white-wolf.com

For Nicky, for believing in me and sharing the dreams that became this book.

Special thanks to Erin Kelly, for her patience, encouragement and incisive criticisms; to Carla Hollar, for her constant friendship; to Stephen Herron, for his insights and his Irish wit; to Ian Lemke, for his invaluable assistance; and to my family, for everything they have given me.

> When sleep it comes, the dreams come running clear
> The hawks of morning cannot reach you here
> Sleep is a river, flow on forever...
> —Christy Moore, "John O'Dreams"

4   The young woman in the picture held a baby in her arms. Both mother and child looked vaguely familiar to the old man, but it was the child in particular who held his attention. Unlike most infants, whose baby-cute faces bear only hints of the persons they will one day become, this wide-eyed, heart-faced child contained an unadulterated spirit, a wholeness that gazed out at the world—defined by a pair of sheltering arms and a mother's face—with a sweet confidence that spoke of utter self-possession. The old man blinked back an unexpected wetness from his eyes.

He flipped the clear plastic page of the small maroon leather photo album. On the left-hand page, the same child—now perhaps three years old—sat beneath a Christmas tree. An enormous pile of stuffed animals, dolls, picture books, educational gadgets and other less identifiable toys surrounded her. Her chubby arms clutched a large brown stuffed rabbit. A fairy-tale princess doll, complete with wings of organdy and glitter, lay across her lap. Beneath her mop of dark, curly hair, a pair of too-wise, too-sad eyes looked, not at the unseen camera, but at the rabbit in her arms.

The right-hand page held a photo taken outdoors, in the front yard of a two-story, mock-Tudor house. The little girl, now a raven-haired cherub in a white playsuit and a beribboned straw hat, straddled a bright red tricycle, its out-of-focus pedals a distorted blur in an otherwise perfect shot. Her head was turned to one side, as if intent on someone just out of the camera's range. In profile, her features were as delicate as if drawn by an artist's ink-brush. Below the handlebars of the tricycle hung a small vanity plate proclaiming the name MORGAN in a florid, curlycued script.

Morgan. The old man felt his jaws tighten suddenly as a hard ache filled his throat. He turned the page quickly, closing his eyes and leaning back against the palm tree that provided a small circle of shade along the gleaming white beach.

"Anything?" The speaker, a Hawaiian man in his late twenties dressed in a white cotton shirt and shorts, placed his hand gently on the older man's shoulder, leaning over him to look at the photographs.

The old man shook his head. He struggled to his feet, dusting the sand from his faded trench coat—much too hot a garment for Hilo's tropical climate, even in late December.

"I thought the pictures might bring something back," he said, tapping the album against his broad palm. "But all I get is the feeling that I should know these people—and then, nothing."

The younger man fingered the silver cross at his throat. He nodded sympathetically. "The doctor who examined you when you first came to the mission said that you were suffering from a slight concussion and that your memories should return over time. Maybe if you keep trying, Mr.—"

"Larssen," the older man muttered, his voice a low growl. "Torvald Larssen. That much I know." He patted the pocket of his coat, feeling for the wallet that contained a few dollars and a crumpled birth certificate, currently his only identification.

"Mr. Larssen," his friend repeated, looking at his watch. "I came down here to tell you that the mission is serving lunch in about twenty minutes and Sister Beatrice has some furniture she wants moved, if you wouldn't mind—"

all kings

The two men turned away from the beach and began walking toward the Mission of Refuge, a large, two-story stucco building on Hilo's outskirts.

The younger man smiled. "If you're technically employed by the mission, it's possible to bend the three-day rule and let you stay here longer. I think Sister Beatrice likes you."

Larssen grunted. "I'm too old for her," he said.

His companion chuckled. "She says you remind her of her father." His dark eyes suddenly grew serious and the smile disappeared from his face. "When she was fourteen, Sister Beatrice's father died of exposure in an alley in Detroit. She believes that God has called her to save the fathers of other children from the same fate."

"Is that why you're a priest, Father Kalepa?"

The younger man shook his head. "I come from a long line of *kahunas*—the old word for priests..." he paused as he saw Larssen's head bob up and down. "You know the term?" he asked.

The old man nodded. "I heard it somewhere," he admitted.

"Most *haoles*—nonnatives—never bother to learn anything beyond *aloha*," Father Kalepa said. "When the white men came with their new religion, my ancestors wanted to make sure that the new god did not forget the Hawaiians. My uncle was a priest, and his uncle before him."

"As simple as that?" Larssen asked.

"There are other reasons," Father Kalepa said, "why I remain a priest. And those are more important than why I became one in the first place."

"So what are those other reasons?" Larssen asked.

"To help men—and women—like you remember," the priest said.

court of

all kings

part

chapter

one

one

10   Morgan hung up the phone in the hotel lobby and
burst into tears. Leigh stooped down and put her arms
around the sidhe childling, looking over Morgan's
head at Valmont, who sat on a nearby sofa casually
flipping through the pages of a magazine. He raised
his eyebrow questioningly.

"I lied to them," Morgan sobbed, her words muffled
by Leigh's shoulder. "I told them that we were all fine
and that they shouldn't worry and then I wished them
a Merry Christmas and..." Her words dissolved into
more tears. Leigh patted the childling's back.

"Maybe we should call your parents back and level
with them," she said, again looking at Valmont for
some kind of confirmation.

"No!" Morgan drew back from Leigh, her young
voice unexpectedly vehement. "They'd just come out
here and try to make everything all right, only they
wouldn't be able to. We'd have to tell them all about
the Dauntain and how Grandpa maybe killed a man
and—"

"Let's take this conversation somewhere else,"
Leigh suggested, cutting off Morgan's words with a
stern look and a small shake of her head.

The childling clapped a hand over her mouth, her
tears forgotten in her embarrassment. She looked
around her wildly, trying to see if her hasty outcry had
drawn stares from the other people in the lobby. A
bored-looking desk clerk on the other side of the room
passed a pair of keys over to an elderly couple,
motioning them toward the elevator as he did so.

"I don't think we were overheard," Valmont said
quietly, putting down his magazine and coming over

to join his companions. "But we don't need to stay here any longer than we have to."

"Where's Rasputin?" Morgan asked, sounding concerned. "We shouldn't have left him out on the street."

"It's all right," said Leigh, standing up and taking Morgan by the hand. "He is keeping an eye out for Tor."

"Why do we have to keep staying at different hotels?" Morgan asked. "Why can't we go back to the Seacrest in case Grandpa remembers that we were staying there?"

"Because the Dauntain might be looking for us," Valmont said. "We were very lucky to escape them once, but I don't think they will be so easily put off our track. Staying in the same place would be like sending out invitations."

"Valmont's right," said Leigh. "The best we can do is keep moving and hope that we run across Tor before—" she stopped herself from continuing her thought. *Before the Hunters find him*, were the words that had almost slipped from her mouth. Still holding Morgan's hand, she started out the door of the hotel. Valmont glanced around the lobby once more, assuring himself that no one was paying any particular attention to them before he joined Leigh and Morgan.

Rasputin was waiting for them a few buildings away. The lanky young pooka tried to summon up a smile for his dispirited friends.

"I saw him everywhere I looked," he said. "Of course I expected to run into him while you were gone."

"That's all right," Morgan said. "I didn't really believe you would find him."

"Did you see anyone else?" Valmont asked quietly, falling into step with Rasputin behind Leigh and Morgan.

all kings

"I wasn't looking for anyone else. Especially not the Dauntain who were after us."

Valmont shrugged. "I don't know whether I feel comforted or not," the eshu remarked. "Where are we going?" he called to Leigh.

"I thought we'd find a place to have some dinner," she replied. "A good, crowded restaurant should give us enough privacy to talk a few things over." She brushed her short red hair out of her eyes and looked at Morgan. "I think we should discuss whether to seek help from the duke—or from your parents."

The graceful black swan ship sailed onward through the faerie trod, its prow cutting a path through a tideless ocean in a space just beyond mortal perceptions.

Aboard the ship, Yrtalien held the three glowing gems in the palm of his hand, feeling their dormant power as a resonant tingle that hovered between pain and pleasure. The stones vibrated, alive with their own eerie music, a rich choral tapestry that contained all the songs of Arcadia and the mortal realm. Even with his eyes closed, the sidhe lord could sense the individual Eyestones. The emerald, the Keystone or Eye of Opening, was warm in his hand, a gentle heat that suggested growth and healing. The black opal, the Shadowstone, radiated a cold that, he knew, could burn with an intensity greater than flame. The sapphire pulsed like a living thing, its throbbing rhythms sending ripples of heat and cold through his palm.

I wonder what the fourth stone will feel like, he thought, letting his mind drift along the currents of Glamour that crackled within him. Fragmentary pictures exploded in his head, a cacophony of visions that passed by too quickly to seize, leaving only their fading afterimages. For an instant he seemed to feel the presence of a fourth stone, a phantom weight that hinted of fire. In that moment, he opened his eyes, half expecting to see the missing stone—a ruby—lying with its sister gems. He shrugged aside a feeling of disappointment when his eyes dispelled the haunting illusion. It was too much to hope for.

"Hey, Prince!" A shrill young voice pierced Yrtalien's reveries. The dark-haired sidhe arranged his face into a careful mask of cold benevolence.

"Yes, Edmund?" he asked the redcap childling whose boldness had intruded on his meditations.

"Do you know where we're going?" Edmund gestured vaguely around him at the eerie landscape that surrounded the ship. "For that matter, do you know where we are?"

Yrtalien arched an eyebrow inquisitively.

"Is it important that you know our destination?" he asked mildly.

Something in his tone of voice sounded an alarm. *Glynnis warned me not to piss him off*, the childling thought.

From her place near the ship's stern, where she had been enjoying a respite from the demands of her companions, Lady Glynnis felt the tension in the air increase. It had fallen to her to act as mentor and babysitter to the young redcap whose betrayal of his companions had brought him into Yrtalien's sphere of influence. Unfortunately, Edmund's insatiable curiosity and his lack of concern for protocol had made her task assume herculean proportions. She stared at Edmund, willing the childling to glance in her direction.

As if he had heard her silent command, Edmund turned his head, catching sight of her. Breathing a sigh of relief, Glynnis shook her head, her brows furrowed in dismay.

"I was just curious," Edmund replied, backing down from the prince's challenge. "I mean I thought that you and Glynnis and me were in this together, so I thought it was all right to ask if you knew where we were going. But if you don't want to tell me, that's okay, too, you being the prince and all." He stared up at Yrtalien's face, trying to figure out whether he had said enough to placate the sidhe lord.

Yrtalien held out his hand to Edmund, displaying the three gems that nestled in his palm.

"Do you see these?" he asked.

Edmund nodded mutely.

"How many are in my hand?"

"Is this a test?" Edmund asked. *Bad answer*, he told himself as soon as the words were out.

"I asked you a question," Yrtalien said, his voice still soft but laced with an icy persistence that belied his mild demeanor.

"Three," Edmund replied, trying unsuccessfully not to sound sullen.

"Good," the prince said. "Now, how many gems of this kind exist?"

"Four." Edmund gritted his teeth. *I'm not a baby*, he thought furiously.

Yrtalien nodded. "Right again." He closed his hand around the gems. Turning his back on the childling, he walked toward the prow of the ship. Suddenly, he paused and looked back over his shoulder at Edmund.

"Now do you know where we are going?" he asked.

"Huh?" Edmund shook his head. "I think I missed something," he mumbled.

Yrtalien's answering laugh held more cruelty than mirth.

"Perhaps one day you will learn the fine art of reading between the lines," he said, shrugging. "The three gems that we possess will lead us to the one we still lack. That," he added, "is where we are going. Now, if you will excuse me, I have other things to do."

Edmund shoved his hands in his pockets and tried to look nonchalant.

"Why didn't I think of that?" he muttered to himself.

Sister Beatrice ran her hand through her cropped dark hair, silently offering up a prayer of thanks that she had never had to wear the confining habits that once served as the mark of a nun. The homeless men and women who depended on the Mission of Refuge cared more for the services she and Father Kalepa provided than for the outward trappings of their faith.

She watched from the veranda of the rambling mission building as Father Kalepa and Larssen, the new man, a muscular fellow with graying blond hair, struggled with a large recliner, a gift to the mission from one of the city's wealthy residents. The two men were having trouble finding the right angle for maneuvering the bulky object through the front door of the mission. Finally, Larssen mumbled for the smaller man to step aside. Heaving the chair onto his massive shoulders, he bore it on his back into the building. Father Kalepa raised an eyebrow at the impressive feat of strength.

"Mr. Larssen," Sister Beatrice called after him, "would you be so kind as to carry it into the recreation room?" She thought she heard a muffled "Yes, ma'am," from somewhere inside the house.

"I'll go and help him get it into place," Father Kalepa volunteered, following Larssen into the building and leaving Sister Beatrice alone on the porch. It was past time to serve the midday meal, but the arrival of the free furniture had necessitated a delay. As she got ready to go inside, Sister Beatrice noticed a wiry-looking young man with strong Latin features approaching the mission. She turned to him expectantly.

"Sister?" His voice was polite and bore only the slightest trace of hesitation, as if he were unsure of how to address her.

"Yes?" she responded. "How can I help you?"

"I am looking for someone," the man answered, coming up to stand next to her on the porch. "I was hoping you might have seen him or that he might be staying here." He went on to give a description of a tall, blond, middle-aged man that immediately reminded Sister Beatrice of Torvald Larssen. The intensity of his gaze made her feel slightly uneasy.

"Is he a relative?" she asked.

The man hesitated, then nodded his head.

He's lying, she thought. *Otherwise he wouldn't have had to think about his answer.*

"I'm Sister Beatrice," she said, stalling for time. "Who are you?"

"My name is Vargas," the man replied. "May I come in?"

"I didn't know that so many people went out to eat on Christmas," Morgan said, staring around her at the packed dining room.

"Most of them are tourists," Valmont said. "People who decide to spend their holidays away from home usually have to eat in restaurants." He smiled at the childling. "Just like us."

"Yes," agreed Rasputin, toying with a stray piece of pineapple that had fallen off his plate of Hawaiian turkey. "This whole restaurant is just full of people on failed quests."

Leigh nudged the pooka's leg with her knee and when he turned to look at her she shook her head in warning. Rasputin shrugged and speared the pineapple chunk with his fork and popped it into his mouth.

"There has to be something we can do to find Tor on our own," Leigh said. "I'm not sure that either the duke or your parents," she nodded to Morgan, "can do anything from San Francisco."

"But what can we do?" Morgan asked. "I just keep thinking about how Grandpa must be so confused wandering around without any idea of how he got to Hawaii or why he's here." She bit her lip to keep the tears back.

"We could try the obvious places," Valmont said. "Why don't we see if Hilo has any shelters for the homeless."

"I don't know," Morgan said, sounding dubious. "Grandpa never stayed at shelters. He always had a place to stay at the Toybox and didn't need to sleep on the streets."

"He may not have a choice," Valmont said. "In some cities, it's illegal to be homeless."

"Do you mean he might be in jail?" Morgan asked, her voice suddenly filled with panic.

"That's a comforting thought," Rasputin mumbled. "It's exactly what I might have said." The pooka looked sideways at Leigh.

"I think we need to consider all the possibilities," Leigh said, "but I think it's more likely that he's taken shelter somewhere than that he's been arrested."

"I don't suppose hiring a detective is in order," Rasputin said.

Valmont chuckled. "That's a thought," he said. "It's too bad we don't know anyone who might be in touch with what's going on in the streets—"

"The sluagh!" Leigh said suddenly. "Remember the tokens Ellen gave us before we left San Francisco?"

"Oh, yeah!" cried Morgan, her face brightening with a glimmer of hope. "They were her Yule gift to us so that other sluagh, even ones we don't know, will trust us."

"So, shall we step outside and go sluagh-hunting?" Rasputin asked.

"Not until night," Valmont said. "Our furtive cousins dislike bright lights almost as much as they shun loud noises."

"Do you think we can find any of them?" Leigh asked.

Valmont looked thoughtful for a moment, then nodded. "I think that I might be able to locate one," he said. "After all, I am an eshu."

"Then why can't you just concentrate on where Grandpa is and find him?" Morgan asked.

"I wish I could," Valmont said. "But if he has lost touch with his faerie nature, the Banality that surrounds him makes it difficult, if not impossible. Glamour is unpredictable, as magic goes," the eshu added. "I can usually find my way to where I need to be, but that path is not always the most direct."

"So you might be able to find Tor by leading us to someone who can tell us where he is?" Leigh prompted.

Valmont nodded. "Something like that," he said.

Sister Beatrice led her visitor to a small sitting room just inside the mission's doorway, then excused herself on the pretext of bringing a tray of iced tea from the kitchen and hurried to the dining room at the rear of the building. Standing in the doorway, she scanned the room, quickly locating Larssen and Father Kalepa, who sat together at the end of one of the long tables. She made her way across the room and stopped just behind Larssen's chair.

Tor looked up as he sensed her presence.

"Is something wrong, Sister?" he asked, his voice a low rumble.

Sister Beatrice smiled at the haggard-looking man who, even seated, seemed to loom over her.

"I don't know, Mr. Larssen," she said. "There's a gentleman in the parlor who seems to be looking for you. At least he gave me a fairly accurate description of you." She hesitated. "He claims you are a relative of his."

"That's wonderful!" Father Kalepa exclaimed, his broad face breaking into a smile of genuine enthusiasm.

Sister Beatrice's return smile was slow in coming. Tor felt an icy chill down the back of his neck.

"So where is he?" he asked. "Do you want me to go check him out for you?"

"I left him in the sitting room," Sister Beatrice replied. "Mr. Larssen," she said, "are you in any kind of trouble?"

"You mean with the police?" Tor's heavy brows creased in thought as he tried to penetrate the haze that blotted out his memories of the recent past.

The warrior gave Tor a beseeching look, holding out the hand that was the source of his agonizing pain. Around them the air glowed an eerie red with sulfurous fumes and behind them a slow blackish-red river of molten lava flowed sluggishly down the mountainside. Tor understood what his erstwhile enemy was asking of him. Raising his battle axe and taking aim at the juncture of hand and wrist, he brought the weapon down—

Tor shook his head, uncertain whether the vision was a memory or simply the product of his tired, befuddled mind.

"I don't think so," he replied. "I thought you said this man was a relative of mine," he added.

Sister Beatrice nodded, her face still somber. "He doesn't look at all like you," she said.

"Perhaps he's an in-law," Father Kalepa said. "Are you married?" the priest asked Tor.

Tor started to shake his head, then stopped. "I—I think I might have been, once," he said, "but not anymore."

"Why are you so suspicious, Sister Beatrice?" Father Kalepa asked. "Usually this would be a cause for celebration here at the mission."

The young nun nodded. "Usually," she said. "But this time, I'm not so certain that Mr. Vargas is on the level."

"Vargas?" Tor asked, feeling a stab of recognition at the sound of the name.

"Do you remember something?" Father Kalepa heard the change in Tor's voice.

The iron manacles sent a wave of nausea through his body as the van lurched around a curve. He and the others—his companions—were being taken someplace where their captors would subject them to—to what? A woman with a gun and the keys to their chains sat in the back of the van with them. Vargas was at the wheel—

"I don't think he's a friend—or a relative," Tor said. This time his voice held a trace of menace.

"Neither do I," said Sister Beatrice. "I just wanted to see what your reaction was." She placed a hand comfortingly on Tor's shoulder. "Why don't you and Father Kalepa stay here and finish your meal, while I return to Mr. Vargas and tell him that he had better search elsewhere for his missing relative."

On the way back to the sitting room, she stopped in the kitchen and prepared a small tray with two glasses of iced tea.

Vargas stood up as she entered the room and placed the tray on a low coffee table.

"I'm sorry to keep you waiting," she said, handing her guest one of the glasses and taking the other one for herself.

"That's quite all right," Vargas said. He looked around at the sparsely furnished room before taking a sip from his glass. "I understand that you provide shelter for the city's homeless."

Sister Beatrice nodded. "More and more dislocated people seem to come to the islands every day. We aren't the only shelter in Hilo, you know," she added.

Vargas nodded. "I know," he said. "I have been to two others already searching for my—uncle."

Sister Beatrice took a deep breath. *Forgive me, dear God*, she prayed silently. *I may be making a mistake, but I feel this man means only trouble to one who has come here seeking help.*

"The man you are looking for doesn't seem to be here," she announced.

"Are you certain?" Vargas put his glass down on the coffee table. "Do you mind if I look for myself?" He started to get up from his seat. Sister Beatrice stood up quickly, nearly upsetting her own glass as she hastily placed it on the tray.

"It is not our policy to allow outsiders to roam around the building," she said firmly. "We try to respect our residents' desire for privacy, as much as they have here. I think you had better leave."

α l l k i n g s

Vargas rose slowly from his chair and gave Sister Beatrice a curt nod.

"I have no desire to cause any trouble, Sister," he said, giving her title an emphasis that approached a sneer. "I have one or two other places to check, but if I cannot find my uncle in any of those places, I may ask you to look again."

"That is certainly your right, Mr. Vargas," Sister Beatrice replied.

"I do not think you want trouble with the authorities," he continued, making his way toward the mission's outer door. "Many communities dislike having havens for society's castoffs in their midst."

Sister Beatrice felt her face grow pale. "I think you have said quite enough, Mr. Vargas," she said, moving forward to herd him more quickly toward the door and onto the street.

When he had gone, she placed a hand on the wall to steady herself. Her legs felt suddenly weak. *Torvald Larssen*, she thought, *I hope you're worth it.*

Valmont breathed a sigh of relief as he left the small hotel where the companions had chosen to spend the night and made his way through the streets of downtown Hilo. Since becoming a member of the oath circle sworn to find and open Silver's Gate, he had had precious few moments to himself.

The handsome eshu drew a few approving glances from passers-by. To mortal eyes, he appeared as a tall, slim, dark-skinned young man, impeccably dressed for an evening on the town. Only to other Kithain and to those few mortals with faerie sight was his true nature revealed. Taller and even more slender, with darker skin and eyes like bottomless pools of blackness,

Valmont radiated a mesmeric quality enhanced by his graceful movements. Clad in a flowing desert robe fashioned from the Glamour of his faerie magic and wearing a scimitar at his side, he strode toward his destination—the abandoned house on the edge of the city which was once Yrtalien's freehold and the center of the Forsworn Prince's Shadow Court.

Only a few days ago, he and his friends had been guests of their adversary. Yrtalien had been a generous host, lavishing the companions with hospitality in the hope of winning them to his cause. Valmont was never quite sure what that cause was. Yrtalien had sometimes claimed that he wanted only a return to the old traditions of power sharing between Seelie and Unseelie. At other times, the prince had hinted at a darker purpose. At the heart of his designs, however, had been the legendary eyestones, four powerful faerie gems which, together, could locate and reopen Silver's Gate, one of the last portals between the mortal world and Arcadia.

It was the hope of many children of faerie to someday find a way to return to the realm which was the source of their power and the lifeline of their existence. The companions had been on their way to achieving that goal. They had acquired the Keystone, the emerald gem of opening. They had discovered that the native faeries of Hawaii, the elusive menehune, possessed a second gem, the Shadowstone, an opal which seemed to negate the baneful effects of Banality. Yrtalien, however, had preceded them to Hawaii and gotten the gem for himself. That had been the beginning of their difficulty.

Valmont slowed his steps as he approached the mansion on the hill. The house stood dark and silent, apparently deserted. Yrtalien and his court had dispersed in the wake of recent events; and the

all kings

Glamour that had once transformed the dilapidated building into a palatial structure full of lavish displays of faerie magic was dissipating, eroding from the lack of imagination that once gave it substance for those with the ability to touch the Dreaming.

The eshu studied the building carefully, his faerie sight attuned to catch even the slightest traces of Kithain presence. A cool December breeze carried with it the faint scent of orchids from the gardens at the rear of the house. Valmont inhaled the fragrant aroma, wrinkling his nose at the presence of another scent, a trace odor of decay, as if something vaguely rotten had wormed its way into the otherwise heady bouquet. He smiled to himself. *Gotcha*, he thought. *I knew that one of you would probably find the dark mansion an ideal place for shelter. Now to keep from alerting you to my presence long enough to catch and hold your attention.* The sluagh were known for their furtive ways and their tendency to isolate themselves, even in a crowd. They were also notorious as gatherers of information. For some reason, unknown perhaps even to themselves, a faint stench of mustiness and decay clung to them, leading some faerie lorekeepers to suspect that the sluagh had once trafficked with the world of the dead. Few Kithain actively sought close relationships with the sluagh, except when they needed something from them, as Valmont did now.

Focusing his own faerie magic on remaining unseen and unheard, Valmont crept closer to the house, his steps making a circuitous path toward the gardens. Once inside the complex maze of riotous foliage, now brown and desiccated with neglect, the eshu allowed his thoughts to roam unfettered, using the faint impressions they sent him as a guide to where he wanted to go. One pull, stronger than the others, led him to what he recognized as the center of the garden, where a small, brackish pond lay choked with sodden leaves and crumpled blossoms.

This was Kanani's place, he thought. A pang of regret coursed through him as he remembered the graceful daughter of the menehune chief who had given Yrtalien the Shadowstone, believing the Forsworn Prince to be its rightful owner. Kanani had come to Yrtalien's freehold as an ambassador from the menehune. It had been the prince's plan to use her as a sacrifice to some ancient creature from the world's beginning, a dragon that slept within the bowels of Kilauea. The companions had saved Kanani, but had paid a high price.

Valmont blinked hard, pushing away the memories that interfered with his purpose for returning to the garden. *Kanani is safe with her own people now*, he told himself. *It is pointless to speculate on what might have been if there had been more time to share with her. I did not come here to wallow in lost possibilities.* A slight rustle in the bushes behind him caught Valmont's attention. He smiled to himself. *This is what I came for.*

He stepped backward quickly and thrust his arm into the bushes where he had heard the noise. His hand snagged a handful of cloth. He thought he heard a muffled cry of pain and surprise.

"Don't struggle," he said calmly, trying not to sound threatening. "I mean you no harm. I only want to ask you a few questions."

"Lemme go," a nearly inaudible voice responded. "Whatever it is, I don't know nothin'." Valmont tightened his grip and pulled the figure toward him, noting with grim satisfaction that it was, indeed, one of the sluagh. This particular specimen appeared to be a young man still in his teens, with wispy colorless hair falling into a wizened face that was none too clean. Valmont shifted positions so that he was no longer downwind of his captive before reaching into his pocket with his free hand and drawing out a small, rounded piece of malachite.

"Do you recognize this?" he asked, holding the token a few inches from the young sluagh's watery eyes. The young man nodded.

"If I let you go, will you stay here and talk to me?" Valmont asked. After a few seconds' hesitation, the sluagh nodded again. Valmont released his hold and took a step away from the sluagh. For a moment, the young Kithain looked as if he were going to bolt. Then he shrugged and flopped to the ground next to the pond.

"Where did you get that?" he whispered, staring at the token.

"From a friend," Valmont said. "My name is Valmont."

"Germ," the sluagh mumbled. "I've seen you before."

"Were you here at Yrtalien's court?" Valmont asked.

The sluagh nodded. "Sort of," he answered. "I tried to stay out of the way."

"Probably a wise choice," Valmont observed wryly. "Why did you come back here?"

"I figured when everyone else split, after the rite on the volcano, that no one would be using this old house again."

"I'm looking for a friend of mine who has disappeared," Valmont said. Briefly he described Tor, giving the sluagh details on the troll's mortal guise as well as his faerie seeming. "I'm fairly certain that he has lost much of his faerie self," the eshu added, "and that he is probably wandering around somewhere in the city trying to remember why he came here."

Germ thought for a minute. "I remember seeing him on the beach," he whispered. "Some guys he was hanging with told him about a homeless shelter called the Mission of Refuge."

"Do you think that's where he went?" Valmont asked.

Germ shook his head. "I dunno," he said. "Maybe. I left when the sun got too bright. I didn't hear the rest of the conversation." He looked around him furtively. "Did anyone follow you here?" he asked, a nervous quaver in his soft voice.

"I don't think so," Valmont said, but he, too, glanced around the dark garden. "Why?"

"There are a couple of other people in town looking for him—for the rest of you, too—but mostly for him."

"What do they look like?" Valmont asked.

"One's a small guy, a mortal. He looks Spanish or Italian or something. The other's a woman. If you look really hard, you can see that she's a troll, but I think she's not aware of it."

Valmont shook his head. "She's aware of what she is," he replied. "But she's trying to suppress it. She's one of the Dauntain," he added. "So is the man."

"Hunters?" Germ asked, his pale skin whitening to an almost luminescent pallor as he squeaked out the word. Of all the enemies of the Kithain, the Dauntain were perhaps the most feared. Most of them were children of the Dreaming, faerie changelings who had for one reason or another turned against their own natures, either forgetting or denying their true selves in order to hunt down and destroy other Kithain.

Germ scrambled to his feet. Valmont slapped a hand on the sluagh's shoulder to keep him from running.

"Not yet," Valmont said. "I told you I wasn't followed." *I hope*, he thought. "There was a third Dauntain who traveled with them," he said. "She is an eshu. Have you seen her as well?"

Germ lowered his head and shook it. "I haven't seen that one," he said.

"Good," Valmont replied. *Perhaps Signe was able to get away.* When the Dauntain had ambushed them on the mountainside, Signe had agreed to suspend hostilities long enough to help Valmont rescue Kanani from a horrible death. Later, Valmont and Rasputin had been able to convince Signe to help them escape from her Dauntain friends, Vargas and the troll Diana. *She was never really one of them,* Valmont thought.

"Are you in touch with the other Kithain in Hilo?" Valmont asked.

Germ swallowed hard before answering. "What do you think?" he replied.

"If you are," Valmont continued, noting the ambiguity in the sluagh's response, "you might warn them that both Vargas and Diana—those are their names—are dangerous to everyone, not just us. Anyone who hopes to profit by turning us in to them will be sorely disappointed by their idea of a fitting reward." He hoped his words sounded cautionary rather than threatening.

Germ nodded. He raised his head and glared at Valmont. "They came here for you and your friends," he said, "and maybe they'll leave when you do."

"If someone tells them when we go," Valmont said. "But I wouldn't be surprised if they came back, or sent others here in their stead."

The sluagh considered Valmont's words. "That's probably true," he replied. A canny look came over him. "Are you suggesting something?"

Valmont gave the sluagh a small smile. "A certain misdirection might be in order," he said. "Something to get them off all our backs."

"What's it worth?" Germ asked.

Valmont named a price in both money and Dross,

the Glamour-infused objects that served as collateral among Kithain. After a few minutes of haggling, the eshu and the sluagh came to an agreement.

"This might not work," Germ said. "All we can do is try."

"We?" asked Valmont.

Germ nodded. "I have some friends," he said, "who might be willing to help remove some scum from the city."

"Thank you for your help," Valmont said. "I'll arrange for your payment as soon as I can."

"Just leave it in a package under that bush," Germ said, pointing to his former hiding place near the pond. "And remember that nothing happens for free."

Valmont looked in the direction of Germ's outstretched finger and nodded. When he turned back, the sluagh was gone.

"The Mission of Refuge," Valmont mused as he left the garden by a different path. "It's a place to start." Making his way back to the hotel, he tried to listen for indications that someone might be following him. At the same time, he calculated the effort it would take to accumulate the price he and Germ had agreed upon. The money would be simple. Several possibilities occurred to the eshu almost immediately—with gambling high on the list. Coming up with Dross presented a more difficult, though not insurmountable, problem. He reached inside his shirt and fingered the small sea-shell that hung from a thong around his neck. A gift from the menehune, the shell had allowed him to communicate with the native faeries, translating his words into their language. He had hoped to keep it both for its sentimental and its practical value, but he needed it now for the Glamour it contained. *I wonder if I can get the others to contribute their own shells,* he thought, then shook his head ruefully as he tried to imagine explaining to Leigh and Morgan why he wanted them to give up their menehune treasures. *Maybe Rasputin would understand.*

"That's the fourth time in the last ten minutes you've gotten up to look out the window," Leigh said, a half-smile on her face.

"I just keep hoping I'll see Grandpa if I look hard enough," Morgan said wistfully as she let the curtains fall back into place. Flopping down on the double bed that occupied most of the small motel room she was sharing with Leigh, she reached over the side of the bed to retrieve her backpack, rummaging around inside it until she found her diary, a Yuletide gift from Leigh. She grimaced as she leafed through its pages, noticing that although she had intended to keep a faithful record of her quest, she had filled only a few pages with her precise penmanship. She toyed with the idea of making another entry, but as she considered the events she would have to describe, she felt her eyes threaten to fill up with tears again.

"Shouldn't Valmont be back soon?" she asked, looking at the door as if expecting it to open.

"He's only been gone for a few minutes," Leigh said, ruffling her red hair and settling herself deeper in the overstuffed armchair in the corner of the room. The leather-bound journal that Ellen, one of the regulars at the Toybox Coffee Shop, had given to the companions, rested in her lap. She had begun reading it a few weeks ago, when they had first arrived in Hilo, but her encounters with Yrtalien and his Shadow Court had prevented her from making much progress. Ellen, a reclusive sluagh who collected information on the noble Kithain of San Francisco, had intimated that Leigh might find some useful trivia in its pages. *At least it will pass the time*, Leigh thought.

She glanced toward the open door that connected her and Morgan's room with the one shared by Valmont and Rasputin. After Valmont had set out upon his search for one of the sluagh, the pooka had announced that he needed to "rehearse," and had disappeared into the bathroom. She could barely hear his voice over the sounds of the shower.

"I hope it wasn't a mistake to let him go off by himself," she muttered, only aware after the fact that she had spoken loudly enough for Morgan to hear. The childling looked up from her diary, her face filled with instantaneous concern.

"Do you think he'll leave us, too?" she said, her voice tremulous.

"No, of course not," Leigh replied, hoping that she sounded confident enough to forestall Morgan's fears. *That was stupid*, she berated herself. *Morgan may be mature for her years, but she is still a child and has a child's terror of being abandoned.* "Valmont swore an oath to all of us, and he takes that sort of thing very seriously."

"Not like Edmund?" Morgan asked, bitterness coloring her words.

Leigh shook her head vigorously. "Not at all like Edmund." She put the journal on the desktop next to her chair and got up from her seat to join Morgan on the bed. Impulsively, she reached out to stroke the childling's dark curls. She had never thought of herself as a motherly sort, but Morgan's obvious need evoked in her a desire to protect and comfort the sidhe childling. *Her world has been turned upside down with her grandfather's disappearance. Valmont and Rasputin and I are all she has right now.*

"Why did he do it?" Morgan asked.

"I don't know," Leigh said. "Maybe he was jealous."

"Of me?" It was obvious from the incredulity in Morgan's voice that the thought had never occurred to her.

"Of you, of all of us," Leigh responded. "I don't think Edmund has ever been close to anyone, not like you and Tor."

"Or you and Valmont?"

Leigh felt her face redden and quickly lowered her head.

"It's not what you think," she said. "Valmont and I are friends, but that's all." Or is it? she asked herself. While they had been guests at Yrtalien's freehold, the Unseelie prince had courted Leigh, attempting to resurrect a relationship the two sidhe had once enjoyed in Arcadia, when she—as the Princess Eleighanara—and Yrtalien had led a youthful rebellion against their parents' rigid rule of the faerie homeland. She had been exiled to earth, but Yrtalien had been imprisoned in a pocket of Glamour between Arcadia and the mortal realm. She had been changed by her assumption of a mortal body. Yrtalien, however, had remained untouched by the years of his imprisonment. He had tempted her with a vision of a world in which the fae assumed what he considered their rightful place as rulers over pitiful humanity. She had rejected that vision, having come to realize that the sidhe were wrong to assume superiority over mortals, just as they were wrong to claim dominion over the other Kithain. Valmont had taught her that.

She and the eshu had often disagreed about the role of the sidhe since the return of faerie nobility to earth in 1969. Valmont's opposition to the assumptions of the faerie elite had placed him among the ranks of the Unseelie, although he always took great pains to avoid being so easily pigeon-holed. Leigh had never really questioned the established order of Kithain society until Valmont forced her to look at the gaping differences between the sidhe, who occupied the highest niches in the faerie community, and the other Kithain, who were expected to bow before the unquestioned authority of their noble cousins. Leigh's association with Valmont, Rasputin, Tor—and even Edmund—had taught her that nobility was not the prerogative of any one faerie race. *I wonder if all eshu are teachers and subversives at heart*, she thought. But Valmont had taught her something else, as well, she realized as she felt a stirring deep within her at the thought of the handsome eshu. *Because of him, I know what loyalty means.*

"He will come back, won't he?" Morgan asked, jarring Leigh out of her reverie.

"Of course he will," she assured the childling. "Valmont cares very deeply for all of us. I think if he had to, he would willingly sacrifice himself to make sure that we were safe."

"I know I would," a voice from the doorway adjoining the two motel rooms startled both Morgan and Leigh. They looked up to see Rasputin, his soft brown hair still damp from the shower, standing just inside their room. The pooka cocked his head at his two companions and tugged on one of his elongated, rabbitlike ears. "At least, I'd like to think that was true," he added. "Anyone for a game of charades?"

chapter

t w o

36

"I thought Morgan and Leigh and the others all treated me like I was some kind of dumb dog," Edmund muttered fiercely. Near the prow of the black swan ship, Yrtalien and Glynnis were involved in another of their interminable arguments—one which, as usual, Yrtalien seemed to be winning. Time moved differently within the confines of a faerie trod, a gateway made of dream-stuff linking the few enchanted places of the mortal realm. Although he hadn't had the urge to sleep, it seemed to Edmund that they had been traveling for ages, and he was getting bored with being alternately ignored and berated by his traveling companions. Huddled in the stern, he had decided to risk spending enough of his own Glamour to transform Mr. Dumpy from a three inch figure of a clown to a full-blown chimeric creature. The boat itself radiated enormous amounts of Glamour, so Edmund felt reasonably certain that the addition of a little more from Mr. Dumpy's presence would not be noticed.

"These bozos think I'm a grasshead," he moaned. He looked over his shoulder again to make sure that he was still out of the line of sight of the quarreling sidhe.

As if he understood the need for secrecy, the clown hunched down, allowing Edmund's wiry body to screen him from prying eyes.

"I'm not dumb," Edmund said.

Mr. Dumpy nodded sympathetically and reached up a white-gloved hand to pat Edmund's shoulder.

Edmund gave him a grateful look.

"I thought it would be different with them," he confided in a harsh whisper. "I thought that since the prince made such a big thing out of being Unseelie, that he'd be different. He said he wanted to change things."

Mr. Dumpy looked at Edmund patiently, a sad frown on his pasty white face. "He's no different from the others," the redcap continued. "In fact, he's worse. He promised me that he'd make me a knight and give me a real horse if I got Leigh's stone for him. I not only kept my end of the bargain, I got him the third stone for nothing.

"I still don't understand why Chevalier let Tor cut his hand off," Edmund said to Mr. Dumpy. The black-armored knight had seemed to be in a lot of pain from the gem in his palm and, to Edmund, it looked as if he had wanted Tor to take an axe to his hand. "But I'm glad I was there when it happened."

Edmund chuckled softly, remembering the look of undisguised disgust on Yrtalien's face when presented with the still-glowing sapphire embedded in Chevalier's grisly, bloodless hand.

Mr. Dumpy's shoulder's shook silently, as if sharing Edmund's amusement.

"Anyway," Edmund said, "I thought that the prince would be pleased, but a lot of good it did." He leaned closer to Mr. Dumpy and lowered his voice to a nearly inaudible whisper. "I sorta hoped he'd give me one of the gems to carry around. I wouldn't have cared which one."

The clown grimaced.

"Yeah, I know," Edmund said. "He won't even let Glynnis have one. So much for power sharing, huh?"

Mr. Dumpy nodded.

Edmund's keen ears noticed a change in the voices of Yrtalien and Glynnis. The two sidhe had stopped arguing and were talking quietly.

"Uh oh," he whispered. "They're probably going to

wonder what I'm up to and come looking for me," he told Mr. Dumpy. "I think you'd better get small again."

Mr. Dumpy shrugged and quickly obliged. Edmund felt a pang of regret as he saw the clown's chimeric form shimmer and fade, leaving in its wake only a tiny painted figurine. He scooped up the clown and shoved it into a small leather pouch. He scowled, remembering that the pouch had been a Christmas gift from Morgan, almost as if she had known about Mr. Dumpy.

I hope you're feeling as shitty as I am, Miss Morgan the Perfect.

"What have we here?" Yrtalien's mocking voice sent a chill through the crouching redcap.

Edmund opened his gaping mouth and yawned conspicuously, making sure that the prince got a good look at his oversized mouthful of blunt teeth.

"Nothin'," Edmund said, trying to sound bored. "I must have fallen asleep while you guys were talking. Are we there yet?"

Yrtalien laughed mirthlessly.

"Hardly," he said. "I believe it will be obvious— even to you—when we reach our destination."

Edmund squelched the retort that came to his mind in response to Yrtalien's slur.

"Where's Glynnis?" he asked instead.

Yrtalien motioned toward the prow of the ship. Edmund looked beyond the prince to where he could just barely see Glynnis' kneeling form.

"Is she praying or what?" he asked.

The prince shook his head, a thin smile hardening on his handsome, angular face. "She is contemplating the consequences of her constant opposition to me," he said softly. "And she will continue to do so until I give her leave to do otherwise."

Edmund shuddered. Yrtalien leaned down and placed a delicate hand on Edmund's shoulder.

"Get up," the prince said sharply. Edmund scrambled to his feet. Yrtalien's hand gripped the redcap's shoulder firmly. "I think it's time we had a talk, you and I." The too-casual tone of Yrtalien's voice did not sound promising.

"Oh?" Edmund said, trying to match Yrtalien's diffidence. "About what?"

"Obedience, for one thing," the prince said, tightening his hold on Edmund so that he winced with pain. "And respect," Yrtalien added.

Edmund gritted his teeth. *Maybe this wasn't such a good idea after all,* he thought as he let Yrtalien lead him toward the prow of the ship, where Glynnis knelt in motionless submission.

"Sit," Yrtalien ordered, shoving Edmund. The redcap landed with a thump and pulled himself into a cross-legged position on the deck a few feet away from Yrtalien and Glynnis. The prince looked at Edmund and arched an eyebrow.

"Consider this an object lesson," said the prince, reaching for the small velvet pouch that hung from his neck and tipping out the three Eyestones. "Watch," he whispered to Edmund, "and learn." He turned to Glynnis and his face narrowed in concentration as the gems in his hand began to glow. Edmund watched in sick fascination as Glynnis began to scream.

Malacar's eye was burning again. The satyr tried to ignore the pain as he made his way through the crowded streets, buffeted by the press of faceless mortals who surrounded him. Despite the blurred vision in his jeweled eye, he plunged ahead, fearful of what would happen if he stopped moving for even an instant. He grasped at a few scattered

memories that persisted in his mind, serving as a barrier against the overwhelming onslaught of Banality that poured in waves from the multitude of common, small-minded humans that seemed bent on blocking his progress. He concentrated on the recent results of his wanderings throughout the freeholds of Concordia, the faerie kingdom on the American continent. His myriad disguises, enhanced by the Glamour of the Changestone, the ruby gem that rested in his right eye socket, had given him entry to the most prominent Kithain courts, allowing him to appear as an itinerant bard or lorekeeper and giving him access to the libraries of faerie nobility. Among the priceless tomes, he had searched for the clues that would further his private quest, providing him with hints as to his next destination.

He cursed as someone jostled him. It had been a mistake to leave the protected environs of the Glamour-filled freeholds. If he did not soon find his way out of the crowds that sapped his faerie nature and threatened to plunge him into forgetfulness, he would lose all he had so painstakingly accumulated. Even now, he was finding it difficult to remember just what his quest was. It had something to do with the jewel in his eye and other, similar jewels.

The person in front of Malacar suddenly collapsed, and the satyr stumbled as he tried to avoid the fallen figure. Behind him, the crowd kept moving and Malacar felt a hard shove at his back. He went down to one knee. An elbow caught him in the side of his head and the satyr felt the ruby in his eye come loose from its socket and tumble to the street. He screamed and dove for the precious gem and—

—awoke with his hand cupped over the right side of his face. Around him the air was cold and crisp, with a few brilliant stars like icy pinpoints in the December

court of

sky. Malacar sat up, trembling from the aftershock of his dream. He had thrown off the heavy velvet cloak that served as his blanket, and his shivering body had responded by creating images of a frantic descent into the cold realm of Banality. *At least, I hope that is the case,* Malacar told himself as he pulled his cloak around him once more. *I have come too far and learned too much to lose it all now.*

The satyr looked around at the small faerie glen to which his latest research had led him. Since his banishment from the Kingdom of Pacifica, his travels had led him steadily eastward. That much of the dream was true. Unlike the pitiful creature who struggled through the crowds, however, Malacar had no trouble remembering the nature of his goal. He had only to touch the ruby in his right eye and tap its potent Glamour to remember that he possessed one of the keys to a legendary gateway to Arcadia. *Once I had two of the gems,* he thought bitterly, as his hand strayed to the empty socket that had held the emerald gem known as the Keystone. He had been a fool to believe in the promises that the dark-haired sidhe lady had given him. At the time, however, she had seemed to be a powerful ally, one with knowledge that Malacar needed. Now he realized that she had only been interested in the gems in his possession, and particularly in the Keystone.

Her intimations of the existence of a cache of faerie treasures in a lost freehold in Golden Gate Park had led him to a disastrous attempt to open the portal. His actions had drawn a group of Duke Aeon's toadies to him and he had been forced to surrender the Keystone to the sidhe bitch who called herself Dame Eleighanara. He shuddered from the memory of the voice inside his head that had compelled him to rip the emerald gem from his left eye socket. It had come from somewhere beyond the mortal realm, and was almost certainly the real purpose behind the schemes of his sidhe mentor.

Never again will I be played for a fool, he swore to himself. That encounter had taught him a hard lesson, but it had also become the seed of his present quest. He had lost the Keystone, but the Changestone—the ruby gem—was still his. It possessed the power to alter his appearance, making him seem taller or shorter, younger or older as it suited him. That ability—along with his own knowledge of faerie magic and his talent for acquiring bits and pieces of ancient lore—had made it possible for him to pose as a bard—as many bards—and move among the Kithain, asking questions and accumulating knowledge about Silver's Gate and, more importantly, the ancient freehold known as the Court of All Kings, said to be its home.

Legends differed as to what that Court was. Some manuscripts he had studied maintained that once, long ago, before the mortal realm was sundered from the realm of the Dreaming, the kings and queens of all the noble houses of Arcadia had held court together in a grand palace located in the center of an enchanted isle. Other, more obscure writings, hinted that the origins of the Court of All Kings predated the dominion of the sidhe. There, each faerie race was represented by a king or queen, and all fae were equal within its boundaries.

The passing of time had not been kind to the reputation of satyrs. In ancient Greece, they were considered demi-gods, children of Pan and deities of the forest. They were worshipped with music and dance and lovemaking. Now the word satyr had become synonymous with lecher, and their lust for life's experiences denigrated to gross carnality and lewdness. Even among Kithain, satyrs were seen as lascivious gadabouts, unable to contain their passions and unworthy of noble status.

If this Court of All Kings is what I hope it is, Malacar mused as he prepared to make another stab at sleep under the chill December sky, *I will wrest from these ancient kings the right to call myself the new King of the Satyrs and will prove to them by my diligence and scholarship that I belong among them in the halls of power.* His mind churning with these grandiose dreams, the aging satyr drifted off into sleep, not noticing when the boundaries of his faerie glen began to shimmer and part, revealing an open portal through which a watery trod could be seen. Sailing upon the waters of that faerie dreampath, a black swan ship silently landed a few yards from the satyr's sleeping form.

"Is this the place?" Morgan tried not to betray the anxiety she felt as she stood with her friends in front of the two-story stucco house at the edge of the city.

Valmont nodded, pointing at the small hand-lettered sign. "Mission of Refuge," he said. "This is where the sluagh I spoke with last night said Tor might be."

"What if he's not?" Morgan asked.

"We won't find out anything if we don't try," Leigh said, taking Morgan's hand and walking toward the house. Valmont and Rasputin followed, stopping at the bottom of the stairs that led up to the wide front porch.

Morgan looked over her shoulder. "Aren't you coming?" she asked.

Valmont glanced around, noting the nearly empty streets that surrounded the building. *Even Hawaii has its poor sections*, he thought, as his keen eyes took in the general dilapidation of the houses in the neighborhood.

"I think Rasputin and I will wait here," he said, "at least until you find out whether Tor is staying at the mission."

"Do you think there might be a problem?" Leigh asked. Valmont had come in very late last night, after she and Morgan had gone to bed. The soft sounds of conversation between the eshu and Rasputin had tempted her to join them in their room to find out what the results of Valmont's visit had been, but she had been afraid that Morgan might wake up before she returned. The last thing she wanted was for the childling to awaken alone in a strange room.

"Not inside," Valmont said. He traded looks with Rasputin, who smiled and shrugged at Leigh and Morgan.

"It's nothing you need to worry about," the pooka said nonchalantly.

Realizing she was not going to get any more information from the pair, Leigh turned her back on the two Kithain and knocked on the door. It opened almost immediately, revealing a young Hawaiian man with a pleasant face.

"Good morning," he said, smiling at Leigh and Morgan. "How may I help you?"

"We're looking—" Leigh began.

"We're looking for my grandfather," Morgan said. "Is he here?"

Father Kalepa looked from the tall red-haired woman to the raven-tressed child who accompanied her and who had so insistently taken charge of the conversation. His heart thudded once, loudly, as he regarded the child with surprise and recognition.

It's her! he thought, remembering the little girl who had figured so prominently in the photos that were

Torvald Larssen's only connections with his elusive past. She was older, certainly, but the heart-shaped face and innocent, determined expression were the same.

"My name is Father Kalepa," he replied. "I think I might have some good news for you. Won't you come inside?" He held the door open and gestured for Leigh and Morgan to enter the mission.

"Can our friends come, too?" Morgan turned her head and indicated Valmont and Rasputin. Father Kalepa seemed to see them for the first time.

"Of course," he said. "Everyone is welcome here."

Valmont hesitated, but could think of no reason for declining the priest's invitation. He and Rasputin had spoken about the possibility that Vargas might be looking for any or all of them, and the two had decided to try to maintain a discreet watch as the group searched for Tor.

"You go in," Rasputin said. "I'll stay here." The pooka waved to Father Kalepa. "I'm allergic to stucco," he called up to the priest as Valmont joined Leigh and Morgan at the mission's door.

Father Kalepa gave the young, sandy-haired man a puzzled look, but said nothing. He had long ago stopped questioning the idiosyncrasies of the people around him. Many of the inhabitants of the mission had developed strange mannerisms, and he had learned to accept even odder explanations than the one just given to him.

He ushered the three visitors into the sitting room and made them comfortable. Morgan perched on the edge of her chair. "Let me find Sister Beatrice and see if she knows where your grandfather might be," he said.

"I thought you said he was here!" Morgan replied plaintively. Leigh reached from where she sat on the room's battered sofa and patted the childling's hand.

"Sister Beatrice is the director of the mission," Father Kalepa said. "I will tell her that you have come for someone who might be your grandfather. She will probably want to speak with you for a few minutes before you see him."

"Don't you need a description?" Leigh asked.

Father Kalepa shook his head. "I believe I know what your grandfather looks like. He's a large gentleman with light-blond hair and a face that has seen many troubles."

"And he always wears a trench coat," Morgan added.

Father Kalepa's face broke into a wide grin. "I'll be back in a few minutes," he said, and hurried off to find Sister Beatrice.

Outside the mission, Rasputin shifted his weight from one foot to the other as he tried to keep a lookout in all directions without seeming to do so. Valmont's report of his conversation with Germ the night before worried him. Although only a few people were on the streets, Rasputin studied each stranger carefully, halfway expecting to see one of them turn into either Vargas or Diana. The brief time he had spent as the Dauntains' captive weighed heavily on him.

He tried to maintain the pose of a carefree jester, even with his friends, but sometimes the fear that lurked always just within his mind's reach surfaced to torment him. Discovering that he was one of the Kithain had been his salvation. As a child, the pooka's inability to tell the truth had earned him the hatred of his father, an autocrat who tried to beat the feyness out of his wayward son. Rasputin had run away from one of those beatings, and since then he tried to forget the torture that associated itself with life in the world of reason and normality. He had managed to communicate this fear to Signe, the eshu who had turned against her Dauntain companions to help Rasputin and his friends escape, but the hopelessness he had felt while in their power still haunted him.

Unconsciously, he rubbed his wrists, as if to erase the memory of the iron shackles the Dauntain had used to ensure that their captives could not connect with their faerie natures. Without his ties to the Dreaming, Rasputin was only the adult version of the battered child once known as Raphael. *Never again*, he thought. *I'd die first.*

His sharp hearing caught the sound of paired footsteps seconds before he saw two familiar shapes turning the corner and approaching the mission. All his nightmares came rushing headlong into his mind as he recognized Vargas and Diana. His instincts cried out to him to run away from them, as far and as fast as possible, but even as he felt his muscles tense in preparation for a quick sprint behind the building before they could catch sight of him, he realized that his oathmates would have no warning of the Dauntain's approach.

Before he could reconsider the wisdom of his actions, Rasputin dashed quickly into the middle of the street and waved his hands in the air.

"Can't catch me!" he called to the pair of Dauntain. He began running at an angle toward them, hoping to draw both of them away from the mission in pursuit of him.

"There's one of them!" he heard Vargas shout, and even as his terror added a burst of speed to his flight, Rasputin felt a grim satisfaction as he heard both Vargas and Diana running to catch up with him.

αLL kings

Malacar started as a sharp pain in his side woke him from his sleep. Instinctively, he reached for the dagger he carried at his waist. His arm would not move, trapped, like the rest of him, in a tangled growth of long grasses and tree roots.

"You're awake," a familiar voice said, its mock-soothing tones sending a chill of fear through his immobilized body. He looked up into the face of the dark-haired sidhe lady he once served. Beside her stood another of the noble kith, one whose arrogant features and cruel smile made Malacar wish that he could be anywhere else but where he was. He struggled again, but the entangling vegetation held him fast.

"Don't bother," the sidhe lord said, his voice laced with disdain. "I have no intention of releasing you until you have heard what I have to say."

"I'm listening," Malacar managed to croak.

"You have undoubtedly met Lady Glynnis."

Malacar tried to nod and found that, with great effort, he could move his head just enough to signify agreement. Until recently, he had not known her name, but he had worked to accomplish her plans in San Francisco, plans he once thought would elevate him to a position of power. For his efforts, he had suffered both the loss of the Keystone which had served as his left eye and the sentence of banishment from the Kingdom of Pacifica. She had hinted to him that she, in turn, served one even greater. Looking again at the figure that loomed over him, Malacar knew he was in the presence of that greater personage.

"My name is Yrtalien," the sidhe noble continued, pacing around Malacar's prone form as he spoke. "In Arcadia, I am a prince. Here, in this mortal realm, I hope to become much more."

"What do you want from me?" Malacar asked, fearful of the answer but unable to keep himself from voicing the question.

Yrtalien laughed. "First of all," he said, "I suppose I should thank you for providing the means of freeing me from my prison." Suddenly, he dropped to one knee and held a hand in front of the satyr's face. Malacar could see a glowing emerald caught securely between the prince's thumb and index finger.

"Do you recognize this?" the prince asked.

Again Malacar nodded.

"Good," Yrtalien said. "It is one of four such gems. I have two others and lack only the final one to possess them all. Can you guess which gem I need?"

Malacar's face grew pale. Yrtalien palmed the emerald. Extending one finger, the prince touched the ruby gem that rested in the satyr's right eyesocket. Malacar flinched as a jolt of pain lanced his skull from the contact. He felt the ruby begin to glow.

"Shall I take it from you?" Yrtalien asked. "Or will you agree to come with me, so that you and your treasure need not be separated?" He lifted his finger away from Malacar's face and the satyr breathed a broken sigh of relief.

"What choice do I have?" Malacar replied. "Without the gem—"

"Exactly," Yrtalien said. "Without the gem, you are nothing but a blind old man, lost to the Dreaming through the weight of your years."

"It is all I have," Malacar said, trying to sound as pitiful as possible.

Glynnis laughed softly. "He is very good at cringing, my lord," she said. Even in his fear, Malacar wondered at the humble tone of her speech. The lady he served had not been so meek.

"As are you, my love," Yrtalien said blandly. Once more, he turned his attention to the captive satyr. "Well?"

Malacar swallowed hard before he spoke.

"I will gladly go with you," he said, trying to keep his voice from trembling.

"I thought you would see reason." Yrtalien rose to his feet and gestured with his hands. Malacar's bindings fell away from him.

The satyr started to rise, but the prince's booted foot shoved him back onto the ground. Malacar identified the source of the pain that had wakened him.

"First, we must ensure that you will not try to betray me," Yrtalien said. "I will have you kneel and swear an oath before two witnesses, binding yourself to my service until such time as I see fit to release you."

Malacar nodded. Gingerly, he struggled to his knees and looked around. "I see only one witness," he said. "Is someone else here?"

Yrtalien turned and motioned to someone behind him.

Recognizing his cue, Edmund stepped out from behind the tree where he had been watching the prince's performance with fascination. He marched forward and took his place at Yrtalien's side, giving Malacar a broad, toothy grin.

"Hi!" he said. "Remember me?"

Malacar looked at the childling and groaned.

"Your grandfather has been staying with us," Sister Beatrice explained to Morgan, "but he isn't here right now."

"Why not? Where is he?" Morgan bit her lip to hide her disappointment.

"Mr. Larssen has probably gone down to the beach," the mission director said. "He likes to watch the ocean. That's where Father Kalepa first came across him, yesterday morning."

"Then that's where we need to go," Morgan said, her young voice emphatic with urgency.

Leigh smiled at the nun. "We're anxious to find Morgan's grandfather," she said. "I hope you'll forgive our hastiness."

Sister Beatrice nodded. Like Father Kalepa, she recognized Morgan from the pictures Mr. Larssen had shown her. She wondered briefly about the relationship the child bore to the red-haired young woman and the handsome, dark-skinned man who accompanied her, but decided that it was none of her business.

"We are very grateful to you for caring for Mr. Larssen," Valmont said, reaching for his wallet and withdrawing some bills from a carved moneyclip. "I hope we can express our thanks by contributing something to the upkeep of this mission." He handed the money to Sister Beatrice.

"It isn't necessary," she said, but accepted the donation.

"Can you point us in the direction he went?" Leigh asked. "Hilo seems to have a surfeit of beaches."

Sister Beatrice smiled. "Go out the front door and head west. There is a beach about a quarter of a mile from here. That's probably where he went."

She watched the trio leave and offered a silent prayer that the child would be reunited with her grandfather. They were out of sight before she remembered that she hadn't told them that they were not the first to ask about Mr. Larssen.

Rasputin ran blindly, his only thought to put as much distance between his pursuers and the mission as possible. Behind him, he could hear that Diana, at least, was catching up with him. The female troll had a greater stride than the fleet pooka, and endurance was on her side as well. A quick glance over his shoulder revealed that Vargas was not far behind.

"Give it up!" he heard Diana yell. Rasputin ran faster, trying to ignore the stitch in his side that would soon force him to slow his pace. He swerved suddenly, and struck a course that would take him toward the beach that lay just outside the city.

If I can make it to the water, he thought, *maybe I can swim out of reach.* Barring that, maybe I'll drown. The prospect was not a comforting one, but to his mind, anything was preferable to being caught by those who would rip him away from his true self and condemn him to a life of stark, colorless mundanity.

He reached the white sands and stumbled slightly as the soft footing threw him off stride. Cursing, he drove himself onward, heading in the direction of the ocean. Ahead of him, outlined against the sky, Rasputin saw a lone figure standing near the water's edge. The silhouette was unmistakable, and the pooka nearly stopped in panicked recognition.

I've led them right to Tor, he despaired. *The others will be so pleased.*

As he stared out at the endless expanse of glistening ocean, Tor felt as if he were on the verge of remembering something. There had been a sea voyage, and a large white ship with a shape like—like nothing he had ever seen. Tor shook his head. He was reaching into the pocket of his long coat for the small album of pictures, hoping one of them would jar his memory, when he caught movement out of the corner of his eye. He turned in the direction of the disturbance and saw a young man running toward him, pursued by a muscular woman. In the distance, a smaller man struggled to keep pace.

The lead runner stopped abruptly, still some distance from Tor, and looked wildly about, like a rabbit trapped by a pack of dogs. Tor shoved the fanciful notion out of his mind as he watched the tableau unfold. For a moment he felt a strong urge to go to the aid of the fleeing young man. *He looks familiar, somehow,* Tor thought.

The young man wheeled around to face his closest pursuer, trying at the same time to dodge her grab for him. The unsteady surface of the sand pulled him off balance and he stumbled. The woman caught him by one arm.

"I've got him!" she called.

Before he could think about what he was doing, Tor found himself lumbering toward them. Oathmate. The word flashed quickly into Tor's consciousness. It felt right. He quickened his pace, reaching as he ran for—for something that should have been at his side. I had a weapon, he thought, and the image of a large, two-handed axe jogged his memory.

The young man was struggling in the woman's grasp, twisting his body about in a frantic effort to break her hold. Her companion was nearly upon them.

"Let him go!" Tor shouted. The small man looked up.

Vargas. His name is Vargas. Tor knew this with a certainty that left no room for questions. *And hers is Diana.*

A fierce call to battle sounded in his ears and he lunged toward the dark-haired man.

all kings

Rasputin was nowhere to be seen. Leigh looked worriedly at Valmont, who returned her glance with a nearly invisible nod in Morgan's direction.

"I thought Rasputin was going to wait here for us," Morgan said. Valmont smiled at the childling.

"I'm sure he's not far away," the eshu said mildly, trying to keep from betraying his concern at the pooka's absence.

"Should we stay here until he comes back?" Morgan asked. She fidgeted restlessly, shifting her weight from one foot to the other, her eyes straying in the direction of the ocean.

"I think we should go ahead to the beach," Leigh said. "If we don't go now, we might miss Tor. I'd hate to think of us arriving there after he'd left." Suddenly, Leigh felt the urgent need to follow Sister Beatrice's directions. "Valmont?"

The eshu ignored her. He stood, statuelike, his head thrown back as if he heard something audible only to himself.

"What is it, Valmont?" Morgan said, reaching for his hand to get his attention.

Valmont started.

"We need to go, now!" He was moving toward the beach before he finished speaking. Without hesitating, Leigh and Morgan followed him, quickening their paces to keep up with his lanky strides. Soon all three were running toward the ocean, propelled by a growing sense of panic.

They had to slow down as they approached a small rise, all that separated them from the white sand beach and the roar of the ocean. For a moment, the three oathmates stood looking at the expanse of sand and water.

"There he is!" cried Morgan as she spotted the unmistakable figure of her grandfather. "Where's he going?" she asked, as Tor turned and began running along the water's edge.

Leigh put a hand up to block out the glare of light on water. "There's a fight going on down there," she said. "I see three people—and one of them is Rasputin!"

Without stopping to see if the others were behind her, Leigh began running down the sloping hillside. Ahead of her, Tor lowered his head and launched his massive bulk at one of Rasputin's assailants. She recognized both of them at once, and her heart grew cold with dread as she saw the wiry man pull a knife from his belt and stab viciously upward at Tor. Feeling deep sickness well up inside her, she knew the knife was made of iron.

"No!" she screamed, and pushed herself to run faster.

Vargas saw the old man make his move and braced himself for the impact. His right hand snaked to his side and pulled out his iron knife. *Let him come,* he thought, bringing the weapon around to meet the oncoming attack. *This will burn the evil presence from him.* Suddenly he felt a hand grasp his wrist, twisting it away from his body. The knife fell from his grip and thudded onto the sand just as Tor barreled into him, knocking him on his back.

Having appeared from nowhere, Valmont released his hold on Vargas' wrist as the Dauntain went down under Tor's crushing weight. Then he turned his attention to Rasputin. The pooka was in desperate need of assistance. The muscular woman, whom Valmont recognized as Diana, had forced Rasputin onto his stomach, both his arms twisted painfully behind his back.

all kings

The eshu took a step toward her, but stopped as she grasped the pooka's hair with her free hand.

"One step and I'll snap his neck," she hissed, raising her head to stare first at Valmont, and then at Leigh, who arrived just in time to hear the threat.

"She's only bluffing," Rasputin said, his voice muffled by the sand. "Don't listen to her."

"Call off your friend," Diana ordered, motioning with her head toward Tor, who had Vargas pinned beneath him and was pounding his fist into the small man's ribs with a vicious intensity. "Now, before he kills Vargas, too."

Valmont nodded once and stepped slowly backward.

"Tor," he called gently. "Let him go."

The soft command pierced the fog of battlelust that surrounded the troll warrior. Tor blinked and shook his head. *I nearly killed him,* he thought. Slowly, he raised himself, allowing Vargas to roll out from under him to lie, gasping for breath, on the sand.

No one noticed Morgan's soft approach. It's *now or never,* the childling thought, seeing her friends and the pair of Dauntain locked in a battle of wills. Clutching the Glamour-filled silver locket she wore around her neck, a gift from her grandfather on the day of her Chrysalis, she felt herself surrounded by the stuff of faerie magic. *I hope this works.*

She concentrated on thoughts of the duke's court back in San Francisco, where she was known as Baroness Morgania. *I am a noble sidhe of House Eiluned,* she told herself, calling up all she knew of the grandeur of her kith. She paced forward, deliberately, an icy expression on her heart-shaped face. As she moved, she felt the Glamour crackle with power, enveloping her in an aura of undeniable authority.

She sensed the moment when the others became aware of her. Diana looked up, a puzzled expression on her face.

"Let Rasputin go!" She spoke slowly, her young voice delivering the force of a command.

Diana reeled as the Glamour that seemed to roll off Morgan touched her own buried faerie nature. She could feel her grip on reality weaken as her troll-self began to respond to the childling's overwhelming presence, and she let go her hold on Rasputin's hair. Even Valmont, taken aback, felt the urge to bow before the young baroness, seeing her resplendent in a dark blue court gown formed from the gossamer threads of the Dreaming. Behind him, Tor stared at the radiant image that was at once the child from his treasured album of photos and something utterly alien and terrifyingly beautiful.

Vargas, struggling to regain his feet, looked at Morgan and whimpered softly, crossing himself and trying to scramble away from the unnatural child.

Leigh saw her opportunity and dove for Diana. Her knuckles caught the troll just under the jaw while her knee found its target in her midsection. With a whuff of pain and surprise, Diana toppled backward, unconscious, onto the sand next to Rasputin's prone form. The sudden movement stirred Valmont into action and he wheeled around to face Vargas. This time, there was no knife in the Dauntain's hand. Valmont's fist slammed into Vargas' face just before Tor bludgeoned the wiry young man from behind, using his interlocked hands as a club. Vargas slumped to the ground.

Still glowing with Glamour, Morgan stepped shyly toward Tor.

"Grandpa?" Her voice trembled as she spoke.

Tor dropped to one knee and enfolded the child. As he touched her, Tor felt a flood of memories rush through him. Morgan hugged her grandfather fiercely,

all kings

willing her Glamour outward to encompass Tor's human form. Ignoring the unconscious Dauntain, Leigh and Valmont joined in the embrace, adding some of their own faerie magic to the infusion.

"Look!" Morgan breathed. "It's working." Before their eyes, Tor's features began to change as his troll nature emerged. Visible only to the companions' faerie sight, Tor once more resembled a craggy, blond giant, clad in the leather armor favored by warriors of his kith.

"Welcome back," Valmont said, his voice filled with relief.

"Oh, good," Rasputin mumbled faintly, as he tried to sit up. "I'm glad we're all safe and sound once more." Valmont had to move quickly to catch the pooka as his legs buckled beneath him.

"We need to leave quickly," the eshu said, "before they wake up."

"Rasputin's hurt," Morgan said, noticing the bruises on the pooka's face.

Valmont nodded. "I'll deal with it," he said. Closing his eyes, the eshu began to chant softly, using the sound of his voice as a conduit for the Glamour that powered his healing ability. The pooka brightened visibly as Valmont's faerie magic soothed his bruised flesh and aching ribs.

Leigh and Morgan, with Tor in between them, led the way back to the city. "Valmont's right," Leigh said, as the group neared the motel where they were staying. "We need to put as much distance between us and the Dauntain as possible."

"But where are we going to go?" Morgan asked. "And how?"

As they started back toward their hotel to gather their things, Leigh turned to Valmont.

"That instant transport trick of yours *does* come

in handy," she said, trying not to sound envious at being upstaged. "You saved Tor's soul—and his life."

Valmont shrugged.

"It's not that difficult a trick," he said. "It puts me where I want to be when I want to be there—when it works."

Leigh shuddered, knowing the fickleness of faerie magic. "I'd prefer not to think about it failing," she said.

chapter

three

62 *Dear Layla, I feel like I haven't written you in a very long time, but when I look back at the last time I wrote to you, it was really only a few days ago.* Morgan looked up from her diary as she tried to set in order the things she wanted to record. Valmont and Leigh stood together at the prow of the swan ship, their attention focused on the ever-changing swirl of colors and almost discernable images that surrounded the faerie trod through which they sailed. Rasputin sat in the stern of the ship, his hands occupied with a pair of brass meditation balls, his Yule gift from Leigh, just as the diary had been Leigh's gift to her. Tor lay near him on the deck, deep in slumber, his hand clutching the hilt of a large battleaxe. Morgan felt a lump in her throat as she watched her grandfather's slow, regular breathing. Even more than she loved her parents, Morgan felt a fierce affection for the man who was, like herself, a faerie trapped in human flesh. *I'm glad Rasputin saved Grandpa's battleaxe to give back to him,* she thought. *Maybe its enchantment will help him remember who he is.*

She looked down at what she had written, and sighed. So much had happened since her last entry, when she and her companions had been the guests of Prince Yrtalien at his freehold in Hilo. Edmund had not yet turned traitor and Yrtalien had not made the pact with the Dauntain to set up the ambush that had led to Tor's disappearance. It was impossible to write about things at the moment they were happening, but by the time events had calmed down enough so that she could write, she had trouble deciding where to start. Another sigh escaped her. She brushed back a

stray strand of curly black hair from her face before
continuing her chronicle.

*We left Hawaii as soon as we found Grandpa, because
Leigh was afraid that the Dauntain would try to find us
again after we left them on the beach. Valmont said that*
*he didn't think that would be a problem, but he wouldn't
explain what he meant. I tried to ask him, but he just said
that he had taken care of things. I have to trust him because
he's my oathmate, but I hope that nothing really terrible
has happened to Vargas and Diana, even if they do want
to hurt us and make us forget what we really are.*

*We traveled from Hilo back to the hidden beach where
we left the swan ship. Leigh said that the first thing we
needed to do was return it to the selkies at Point Reyes,
and that from there we could decide whether or not to
continue with the quest. I wanted to go back to the palace
and ask Duke Aeon and Lady Alyssa for their advice, but
Leigh said that there were some problems we had to solve
by ourselves. Personally, I think she just didn't want to
admit to the duke that we had lost the Eyestones and that
Edmund had turned traitor.*

*The swan ship took us back to the selkies' freehold,
almost as if it knew that was where we wanted to go. I
wish I knew more about how faerie trods worked.
Rasputin says it's done with mirrors, so I know that's
wrong. Ondine and her kithmates were waiting for us,
just as if they knew we'd be coming. I think that Valmont
was hoping that Ondine would tell us another story like
the one she told us about the legend of Silver's Gate and
the two brothers whose eyes became the Eyestones. We
spent the night at the freehold, and that was when things
started to happen. First, I had a dream about a forest
with golden and silver trees and something very ancient
in its center. It was very beautiful and sad all at the same
time, and I woke up crying.*

"I hope you don't think that all that huffing and

puffing will make this ship move any faster." Rasputin's voice startled Morgan, and she looked up to see him standing over her, a wry look on his expressive face.

"I wasn't sighing that loud," Morgan said, defensively. The pooka cocked an ear. "Was I?" This time, Morgan sounded concerned. She glanced toward the boat's prow to see if either Valmont or Leigh had taken any notice of her. "*They* didn't hear me," she said, "and neither did Grandpa."

"I guess it's just my big ears," Rasputin said, sitting down next to Morgan. The childling bit back the impulse to cover the page of her diary. *After all*, she thought, *it's not like he's Edmund. Rasputin's not a snoop.*

"I'm not disturbing you, am I?" the pooka asked. Morgan opened her mouth to inform her companion that yes, he was interrupting her narrative, but realized that she felt more like talking than writing.

"I was trying to figure out what happened at the selkies' freehold," she said. "I had just gotten to the part about my dream when you—"

"When I provided you with a welcome distraction?"

Morgan giggled. Somehow, Rasputin managed to take the sting out of words that would sound cold or sarcastic coming from anyone else.

"Do you mind if I ask you something?"

"The thought of your asking me anything, Lady Morgania, makes me tremble."

"Good," Morgan replied, thankful that she was used to his contradictory style of speaking and hoping that she would be able to understand his answer.

"That night in the freehold, did everyone have a dream? Or was it just me?"

Rasputin turned his head away from Morgan before answering. "I'm reasonably certain it was just you," he mumbled.

"I thought so," Morgan said. "I know Leigh heard a voice that told her to look in the journal Ellen gave us for the answer to where we should go, and I know that Grandpa had a dream he couldn't remember." Like most aging Kithain, Tor was beginning to lose touch with the Dreaming, the tenuous connection that was all that was left to the faeries on earth to remind them of the glorious realm of Arcadia. "But I don't know if those count as dreams."

Rasputin shrugged.

"Did you have a dream, Rasputin?"

"I slept like a baby all night," Rasputin said softly.

"I guess that means you had one, too," Morgan said. "Will you tell me about it?"

Ahead of him a bright doorway opened, revealing a swirling pathway of iridescence that beckoned his spirit to venture forth upon its sparkling surface. "This is your home," a voice within him said. "This way lies the source of dreams and the wellspring of your spirit."

Just then, a twisted shadow lurched toward the shining gate, clutching a smaller figure in its gnarled arms.

"Help me!" Morgan screamed, beating frantically at her captor. "Don't let him take me through! He'll destroy it!"

He looked behind him and saw a great battle raging around him. He alone had no one to fight.

Morgan cried out again, and without further hesitation, he threw himself at the blurry form now beginning to breach the gateway. Light and sound and pain exploded around him—

"It was just wishful thinking," he mumbled. "I've forgotten it already." Before Morgan could respond, Rasputin got to his feet and wandered off toward the stern of the ship. Morgan watched him go and felt a sudden concern for the lanky pooka. *Something's bothering him*, she thought, trying to remember the last time his normal carefree nature had asserted itself. *Not since we fought the Dauntain on the side of the volcano and lost.*

She shook her head and turned back to her diary. *I think Rasputin had a dream that he doesn't want to talk about*, she wrote. She grimaced as she imagined a sneering Edmund responding to her commentary with "Well, duh." There were times, even now, when she missed the scruffy redcap's unconscious rudeness.

Leigh got up the next morning and found Ellen's journal in her backpack and curled up outside the freehold on a ledge overlooking the ocean. She spent the whole morning reading it and hardly took notice of anything else. Grandpa and I walked along the beach and collected seashells while Valmont and Rasputin spent some time with Ondine and the other selkies.

Just before noon, Leigh called us all together and announced that she had found something in the journal. "According to the this," she told us, "Silver's Gate was somewhere off the western coast of Ireland."

So now we're on the swan ship again. After Leigh said that we needed to go to Ireland, she and Valmont had a long discussion with the selkies. Valmont asked me if I had a passport. I told him that my parents took me with them to England when I was five or six, but I didn't remember much about it except a long plane flight and watching some soldiers in funny hats parade around. Now I know those were the Buckingham Palace guards.

I asked Valmont why we needed passports, and he said we probably wouldn't since we would be traveling there by another sea trod, but that we might as well cover all the bases. Then he and Rasputin went into town. They were gone for most of the day.

Ondine took me for a walk along the cliffside and showed me some of her favorite places, really wild places where no one goes except the selkies. She took me swimming with her and even though it's winter, the water around us wasn't even cold. I got to play with some real seals—not selkies, but the actual animals. I tried to ask Ondine about the merfolk who figured in her story about Silver's Gate, but she only said that maybe I'd meet them myself one day.

By the time we got back to the freehold, Valmont and Rasputin were back. Valmont said that everything had been taken care of and that we could leave anytime we were ready. I guess he made some more connections.

Ondine told us that there were more selkies in Ireland, at the other end of the sea trod, and that they would help us get to where we needed to go. I remembered that the last time we left the freehold at Point Reyes to sail to Hawaii, we had to pass by a guardian beast so I asked Ondine if there would be another one waiting for us between here and Ireland.

She laughed and went round to each of us and kissed us on the forehead. She said the beast would recognize the selkie's blessing on us and let us pass by without challenge.

"It's opening up ahead!" Leigh's voice interrupted Morgan's writing. The childling looked toward the swan ship's prow and saw an archway looming ahead. Behind her, Tor roused himself and began lumbering toward Leigh and Valmont. Rasputin stopped next to Morgan and held out his hand to her.

More later, Morgan scribbled hastily, before shutting her diary and stuffing it, along with her pink ballpoint pen, into her backpack and taking Rasputin's hand.

"Shall we jump ship now and swim for our lives?" the pooka asked, something of the old sparkle evident in his voice.

all kings

Morgan stared at the sight that unfolded in front of her as she and Rasputin joined the others at the prow. "I think we should land first," she said as she gazed upon a vista of gray-blue water and steel-colored sky separated by a line of rocky cliffs.

"Is that Ireland?" she asked Valmont as the swan ship broke free of the sea trod and headed, as if by instinct, for an inlet nestled between the junction of two massive walls of rock.

The eshu nodded, not taking his eyes off their approach. "I believe so," he said.

"I thought it would be green," Morgan whispered.

"It will be," Leigh said, "once we get past the coast."

The swan ship glided to a stop against a narrow strip of beach. One by one, the companions stepped from the ship onto the shore, picking their way across the pebbled sand until they stood in a sheltered place beneath an overhanging rock.

Still clutching Rasputin's hand, Morgan reached out for Tor with her free hand. A light, cold drizzle filled the air and she shivered.

"It's cold," she said, huddling next to her grandfather for warmth. Tor let go of Morgan's hand and removed his trenchcoat, draping it like a blanket over Morgan's head so that it covered her entire body and pooled on the ground around her.

"Is that better?" he asked.

Morgan nodded and held out her hand again for her grandfather to take.

"I just thought of something," she said. "If we don't have any of the Eyestones, how are we going to find Silver's Gate?"

"I'm not sure," Leigh answered. "But we're a lot closer to it now than we were in California."

"Of course, once we find it, and I have no doubt that doing so will be an easy task, the small matter of opening it without the stones should be simple," Rasputin said.

"That's right!" said Morgan. "Even if we do find it, we can't open it without all four stones and we only had three to begin with. We don't even know where the fourth one is." Her voice was small and quiet. Tor pulled her closer to him and wrapped an arm around her shoulders.

"I know where the fourth stone can be found," Valmont said quietly, his low, mellow voice clearly audible beneath the gusting wind that surrounded them.

"Where?" Morgan asked.

"I remembered something this morning when I woke up in the selkies' freehold," the eshu said.

"You *did* have a dream," Morgan said.

Valmont nodded. "Something like that, I think," he said. "I dreamed about our last encounter with Malacar, when we forced him to give us the Eye of Opening."

Morgan frowned. "He took it out of his own eye socket," she said. "It was gross."

"He had a gem in his other eye, as well," the eshu replied. "A ruby."

"The fourth stone!" Morgan said, her voice trembling with excitement as well as from the cold.

"I believe so," Valmont replied.

"But that just means we have to find Malacar, too," the childling said.

"Or let him find us," Leigh observed. She stepped away from the group, feeling overwhelmed with the enormity of the task that faced them and wanting only to be alone with her thoughts. Feeling the cold wind penetrate her thin jacket, she bowed her head and closed her eyes. *This is like the moment before a battle*, she thought as she tried to find a center of calmness within the turmoil of uncertainty that filled her mind. *Only the enemy is my own fear that we have come here to no avail.*

"It's not as if we're stranded here or anything," Rasputin said suddenly, pointing toward the swan ship, which had begun to drift slowly back toward the still-open sea trod.

"The boat's leaving us!" Morgan exclaimed. "It's never done that before. Now what do we do?"

"We wait," Tor said. "That's the only thing we can do."

"We could always get lost," Rasputin said, his voice full of false cheer.

"There they are, Kieran, just like in your dream."

The slim brown-haired woman emerged from the water and finished tying her hair back with a long, gray scarf. Her companion, a young man with dark hair clipped close to his head, had just unfastened the neck of the close-fitting body suit he wore. He flexed his webbed fingers and shook himself dry before he responded to the woman's words.

"I see them, Emer," he replied. "They look like a bundle of wet landrats."

"They haven't noticed us yet," Emer replied. "You'd think they'd be looking about and moving to warm themselves instead of huddling up in a clutch like that. They'll catch their deaths."

"Don't say that," Kieran said sharply. "And you'd better get into the clothes I brought along before they do see us. They've got a wee one with them who might not be used to seeing folks as they were born."

Emer smiled. "They've some real lookers, too," she remarked, reaching for the oilskin bag Kieran tossed in her direction and retrieving some dry clothing from it.

"That they do," Kieran agreed, pulling on some wool trousers and a bulky knit sweater.

Emer dressed herself in a pair of heavy tweed pants and a long wool pullover, before wrapping a bright woven shawl around her shoulders.

"Do we look like regular people now?" she asked Kieran, a smile making her liquid eyes sparkle.

Kieran shrugged. "As regular as we'll ever be, I suppose," he said. "Let's go."

The pair made their way across the rocks toward the small group that stood beneath a sheltering overhang.

"There's only five of them," Emer said suddenly. "I thought you dreamed about six strangers."

"Five, six, what's the difference," Kieran said. "They're where I said they would be, and that's that. Besides," he added, "maybe one of them fell off the boat."

"You're daft," Emer said. "Be nice to them, now," she cautioned.

"Oh, I'll do that for certain," Kieran remarked, fixing his eyes on the tall, red-haired woman who stood a little apart from the others, her head bowed as if lost in thought.

"I'm sure you will," Emer replied, her voice laced with sarcasm.

"Hallo," Kieran called out, waving his arms above his head. "Have you been waiting long?"

The sudden sound of a voice calling to them brought Leigh out of her contemplative mood. Valmont and Rasputin were pointing at a pair of figures that were approaching them from further up the shore. Tor had already positioned himself between Morgan and the strange couple, now visible through the cold, misty air as a man and a woman. The man, whose voice had announced their presence, was waving both arms above his head to attract attention to himself and his companion.

They're not wearing shoes, Leigh thought, as she watched them approach, and her faerie sight confirmed the nature of the pair. Quickly she rejoined her companions.

"They're selkies," she said.

Valmont nodded his agreement. "Theoretically, these natives should be friendly," he said. "Unless, as in Hawaii, our princely adversary has already arrived and managed to plant suspicions in their minds about our intentions."

"From what I can see, they appear to be armed to the gills," Rasputin commented, then raised his own arms and returned the strangers' hail.

When only a few feet separated the two groups, Leigh stepped forward to close the distance.

"We've come from Point Reyes," she said. "Ondine sends her greetings."

"I'm Kieran," said the brown-haired selkie, extending his hand. He gave Leigh a smile at once intimate and warm. "And this is Emer." He indicated the woman standing at his side. "Welcome to Hibernia."

As Leigh introduced herself and her oathmates, Morgan pushed past Tor and clasped hands with the selkies.

"I'm Morgan," she said. "I thought this was supposed to be Ireland."

Emer laughed gently. "That is only one of many names this island has had," she said. Then she looked more closely at the shivering group.

"I think any further conversation should wait until you are all warm and dry. Kieran and I brought a boat, but we left it up there," Emer said, pointing up the coastline. "If you think you're up for a bit of slippery travel, we can be at the boat in a few minutes. From there, we can take you to a safe place."

"Neither of you looks much the worse for wear," Valmont observed. "If you made the journey safely, I imagine we can, too."

"Oh, we didn't come from the boat by land," Kieran said, a glint of amusement in his voice. "We swam."

"I love your swimwear," Rasputin said. Morgan giggled.

"Follow us," Emer said, "and we'll try to pick out the easy route for you."

"You could let Valmont do it," Morgan said. "He's an eshu, and they always get where they're going." She thought a minute about their arrival on the island of Hawaii. "And he's only been lost once, I think," she added.

"That may be, landling," Kieran said, "but the paths of the wayfaring folk don't always account for the safety of those who travel with them."

"You never told us that," Morgan said to Valmont.

"Have I ever led you into any peril that did not threaten me as well?" Valmont asked. The childling thought for a moment, then shook her head.

"I couldn't have made a better answer myself," Rasputin said.

Tor leaned down and picked his granddaughter up, bundling his coat around her like a swaddling cloth.

"I'm ready," the troll rumbled, his voice merging with the crash of the sea on the rocky shore.

Emer turned and began walking back the way she and Kieran had come, stepping carefully between the

all kings

rocks. Kieran waited until the oathmates had filed past him before following in their wake.

Vargas awoke with an aching head. He groaned and tried to roll over, only to discover that the rest of his body felt stiff and sore. He opened his eyes and saw only darkness.

"I thought you'd never come around," Diana's voice said from somewhere nearby.

As Vargas' eyes adjusted to the lack of light, he began to make out the features of the room in which he and Diana were apparently confined. He struggled to a sitting position, biting his lip to keep from crying out as his bruised body protested being made to move. His shoeless feet brushed against something that his hands identified as heavy rope.

That explains the raw feeling in my wrists, he thought. "What happened?" he asked, his voice barely above a whisper.

Diana snorted.

"Those creatures got away again," she said, her voice filled with contempt. "I think someone drugged us when we were unconscious on the beach. I remember hearing voices and being too sleepy to open my eyes."

Vargas grunted as he, too, called up vague memories of feeling jostled and being carried away none too gently.

"So do you think they did this?" He tried to stand, but his knees gave way and he slumped back into a sitting position on what felt like a hard wooden floor.

"Either them or some confederates of theirs," Diana replied. "I've been awake for a while. I never thought I'd get you out of those ropes."

Vargas nodded his thanks, then realized that his companion was probably as blind as he was in the unlit room. "Thanks," he said. "I gather you were able to free yourself as well."

"I didn't say that," Diana said. She moved, and Vargas heard the clank of chains.

"Iron?" he asked.

"What else?" Diana answered. "They used our own manacles on me. I was afraid they would chain you up, too, but they must have thought it was unnecessary."

"Has the iron affected your memories?" Vargas asked, suddenly concerned. Diana, he knew, had rejected the delusion that she was a troll and now hunted the depraved creatures known as changelings. While on the trail of Leigh and her vile companions, Diana had been forced to resume that dark manifestation she had worked so hard to deny. Although he did not like it, Vargas had to admit Diana's knowledge of the world of the fae had its uses: it helped them meet the enemy on its own delusionary ground. Unalloyed iron—cold iron—could drive a wedge between a changeling and its madness, making the individual forget who or what he was. That had happened to their former leader, Cyprian Ryder, who had become one of the most tenacious of the Dauntain.

Now Ryder was dead, and another of their companions, a reformed eshu named Signe, had betrayed them, leaving only himself and Diana to avenge Ryder's death and bring down their quarry. Without Diana's knowledge of the ways of their enemy, they would be at a severe disadvantage in their pursuit of justice.

"I've been struggling to keep hold of the little Glamour I have left," Diana said. "After the first time I woke up down here and had to scramble to remember my name and who you were, I made myself dream." Her voice was low, as if confessing a great crime. "It was the only way I could think of to make sure I didn't forget everything that has happened since we set out on this blasted hunt."

"You mustn't hate yourself for doing what you have to do," Vargas said with a gentleness he did not feel. His seminary training had cast him in the role of father confessor to the Dauntain with whom he worked. Unlike them, he was not touched by the changeling madness, but had been recruited by Ryder into the ranks of the Dauntain as a surer way to fight spiritual corruption than any course of action the passivity of a priestly calling offered him.

"Maybe I wouldn't be so miserable if I were anything but a troll," Diana said. As a mortal, she was a statuesque, Nordic-looking blonde, athletic and muscular. When possessed by her troll form, she became a giantess, a grotesque perversion of her human self.

"Consider yourself blessed that you are not tempted by the false allure of the beautiful demons," Vargas said.

"That's easy for you to say," Diana retorted. "You don't have to look at yourself and see a walking mountain with a pair of horns on her head."

"I appreciate the suffering you have put yourself through in order to retain a grasp of our holy mission," he said. "Someday, this will all be worthwhile."

"I don't know how much longer I'll be able to stand it," Diana said. "The iron makes me sick to my stomach, and I can't use my strength as a troll to break out of the chains so long as I'm in contact with them."

"Do you have any idea where we are?" Vargas asked. "Is this some sort of warehouse or cellar? Are we still in Hawaii?"

Diana snorted. "I think we're in the hold of a ship," she said.

"Oh?" Vargas closed his eyes and listened. His ears picked up the faint hum of machinery. "Any idea where this ship is going?"

"I heard some voices just a few minutes ago, before you woke up." Diana replied. "I think I heard something about Hong Kong."

"So how did you get hooked up with Yrtalien?" Edmund asked Glynnis. They were once more aboard the black swan ship, headed for yet another destination known only to the Forsworn Prince. Yrtalien was occupied with Malacar in the stern of the ship, leaving Glynnis and Edmund to their own devices. The redcap childling and the sidhe sorceress now sat together on the ship's foredeck, enjoying a brief respite from the continual obsequiousness their prince seemed to require. "Is he your boyfriend or what?"

Glynnis blushed. "Hardly," she said drily. "Although at one time the prospect would have flattered me. Now he merely commands me, and I obey him."

"That sucks," Edmund observed. "What do you get out of it?"

Glynnis allowed herself a soft laugh. "Less than I had hoped," she said. Edmund looked up at her blankly.

"I'm not exactly a feeb," he said, "but that told me exactly nothing."

Glynnis brushed back her long black hair and sighed. "You are uncommonly persistent," she said.

Edmund gave her his widest grin, exposing his mouthful of grotesque teeth. Glynnis shuddered and looked down at her hands, now folded in her lap.

"Yrtalien was once a prince in Arcadia," she began.

"Duh," said Edmund. "He told us that himself."

"Do you want to hear this or not?" Glynnis snapped. Edmund shrugged.

"Sorry," he said. "It just came out."

"Long ago, he led a group of young sidhe—sons and daughters of the realm's rulers—in a rebellion against their parents. The rebels believed that Arcadia could no longer afford to keep itself detached from the mortal realm, that it would die without the inspiration of human creativity. Arcadia's kings and queens, however, feared that the Banality that infests the mortal world would destroy Arcadia. That, in fact, is what caused the closing of the gateways."

"I gather he lost," Edmund said.

Glynnis chuckled in spite of herself.

"That's putting it mildly," she replied. "Yrtalien and his band of rebellious wilders were overwhelmed by loyalist armies. Most of them surrendered when they saw their position was hopeless. Yrtalien, however, continued to fight on alone until he was captured."

"So they locked him up?" Edmund sounded proud of his deduction.

Glynnis nodded. "There was a trial and judgment was handed down by the High Seelie Court of Arcadia. Because he threatened to use forbidden arts to achieve his goals, Yrtalien's punishment was more severe than that of the other rebels. They were exiled to earth, their memories taken from them, and their souls placed in the bodies of unborn human babies so that they would have to come into their faerie natures on their own."

"That's not so bad," Edmund said. "Us commoners have been doing that shit for awhile."

Glynnis' face showed her displeasure at the redcap's crudeness. *He is such a flawed tool,* she thought, *but I have a limited choice in allies and he seems, on the whole, much more resourceful than Malacar. At least he doesn't cringe.*

"Instead of exile, Yrtalien was declared forsworn and placed in a prison carved from the remnants of an old faerie trod that once led from Arcadia to this world. The portal on the Arcadian side was destroyed. The other portal, which opened onto earth, could only be opened from the outside, and then only if certain rituals were performed. The knowledge of those rituals was carefully concealed, until I discovered it in the library of an Unseelie lord of my house. I had hoped that by freeing the Forsworn Prince from his captivity, I could enlist his aid in the overthrow of the Seelie rulers of Pacifica and, eventually, Concordia."

"That's a tall order," Edmund observed sagely. "But how did you know about him in the first place?"

"He found me in my dreams," Glynnis said. "He was a prisoner, but unlike the exiles, he retained his memories of his past. It was a subtle form of torture meant to impress upon him the error of his ways, without allowing him the means to make any recompense."

"Kinda dumb, huh?" Edmund said.

"Not dumb, just vindictive," Glynnis replied. "At any rate, Yrtalien was able to conserve his powers and draw Glamour from the very stuff of his prison. Eventually, he found that he could sense, although dimly, what was going on in the earthly realm near his prison. Somehow he found me and began entering my dreams, promising to aid me if I would serve him in attaining his freedom."

"Wait a minute," Edmund interrupted. "You said he was declared Forsworn. That means he was branded a liar, right?"

Glynnis nodded. "Something like that."

"So how come you believed him?"

Glynnis sighed. "It's not that simple," she said. "Even oathbreakers are capable of keeping those promises that suit their purposes. I had no reason to believe, at least not at the beginning of our communications, that our goals did not take us down the same path. It was only when I discovered the Eye of Opening, which was one of the essential components of the ritual to open the portal, that our aims began to diverge."

"Is that because he knew about Silver's Gate already?" Edmund asked.

Glynnis pursed her lips. "Silver's Gate, and the battle fought before it, is a legend known in part to many of the fae. The details of that fight and its cause, as well as the existence of the four Eyestones, are less well known. But it was clear that the Eye of Opening was a powerful artifact."

"So how did Malacar get hold of the stone? How did he get hold of two of them, for that matter?"

"I was using Malacar as my spy in the court of Duke Aeon," Glynnis said. "He was Aeon's wizard and, as such, had access to the ducal library as well as the treasury, where a number of faerie treasures had been stored. Among them were an emerald and a matching ruby. From his reports, I recognized the emerald as the Eye of Opening needed to free Yrtalien from his prison. I instructed Malacar to retrieve it for me. Instead, he appropriated both it and the ruby for himself, ensuring that they could not easily be taken from him by undertaking some rather drastic measures."

"You mean he poked out both his eyes and popped the gems in their places," Edmund said.

"I wasn't going to dwell on the details," Glynnis said. "Malacar failed to free Yrtalien, but his failure was part of Yrtalien's plan. He arranged for Malacar to surrender the gem to Leigh so that she could be the one to release him."

"So what's so special about Leigh?" Edmund wanted to know.

Glynnis looked quizzically at Edmund. "You don't know?" she asked.

"Know what?" Edmund sounded puzzled.

"She did not tell you that she and Yrtalien were once lovers and fellow rebels in Arcadia?"

Edmund's mouth opened in surprise.

"Seriously?" he asked, his voice rising with excitement. "Leigh was one of the rebels? Bitchin'!"

Glynnis held out a hand toward him, careful to keep it a safe distance from his frightening teeth.

"Hush," she cautioned sharply, looking back over her shoulder to where Yrtalien and Malacar were still engrossed in conversation. "Let us not draw undue attention to ourselves," she said.

"Oops," Edmund said, lowering his voice. "Sorry. If she ever told us that she and Yrtalien used to be a thing, I either forgot it or slept through it."

"Have I answered your original question?" Glynnis asked.

"What question?" Edmund tried to remember what had brought on the longest discussion he could remember having with the elegant sidhe noblewoman. "Oh yeah," he said after a few seconds. "I asked you what you meant about getting less than you'd hoped for."

Glynnis nodded.

"So what you've been saying is that you thought he'd help you out, but now he has plans of his own and you're just his sidekick."

"That seems to be the case," Glynnis agreed, raising an eyebrow at the appropriateness of the redcap's nomenclature.

"So why do you put up with him if he's not doing what you want?"

"I have very little choice in the matter," Glynnis murmured.

"You could leave him," Edmund suggested. "You don't have to put up with what he does to you. He can be a real shit when he wants to be." The redcap considered his words. "Actually, that seems to be most of the time."

"Do you think there's a halfway house somewhere for abused sorceresses?" Glynnis asked. "And even if there were, he would never rest until he found me. He can't afford to lose me."

"Why, 'cause you might turn him in?" Edmund's question sounded genuine.

Glynnis answered him with a harsh laugh.

"I don't know if I could throw myself on the mercy of any of the current rulers of Concordia, and they would be the only ones with any hope of giving me enough protection from him."

"Is he really that powerful?" Edmund asked.

"I thought you claimed that you weren't dumb," Glynnis retorted. "Our prince currently possesses three of the Eyestones and controls the possessor of the fourth. How much renewable Glamour do you think those gems contain and how effective are they at enhancing the prince's own magic as well as lending him their own special abilities?"

Edmund looked abashed. "Forget I said anything," he mumbled.

"I'm surprised at your concern for my well being," Glynnis said.

"Why, 'cause I'm a redcap?" Edmund looked offended. "I spent some time in juvie jail when I was younger," he said, "cause I was a chronic runaway, among other things. I saw a lot of kids whose parents beat them up, like Yrtalien does to you and Malacar. I was glad my parents just hated me."

Glynnis held her breath and risked giving Edmund's rumpled dreadlocks a cautious stroke. He raised his head quickly and grinned when she jerked her hand back.

"Don't worry," he said. "I'm not really all that fond of ladyfingers. That's a joke."

Glynnis smiled weakly. "He hasn't really hurt you yet, has he?" she asked.

Edmund shook his head. "Nah, so far I've just gotten to watch. I don't think I'd like to find out first-hand what it's like, though."

"No, you wouldn't," replied Glynnis. At first she had rationalized Yrtalien's cruelties as merely his way of demonstrating his authority and commanding obedience, much as she had used pain to compel Malacar and her other minions to do her will or to punish them for their failure. Recently, she had begun to realize that the prince enjoyed seeing others suffer and seemed to draw power from watching their pain, almost as if it were a source of Glamour for him. She shuddered at the possibility that such might be the case.

"I guess he was lying when he said he'd make me a knight and give me a horse," Edmund mumbled.

Kieran kept up a constant commentary as he guided the boat along the coast, now and then pointing toward the massive wall of sea cliffs which towered above the shoreline in breathtaking splendor. Emer sat in the rear, occasionally casting a wistful glance toward the water.

"That's Slieve League, Europe's highest cliff face," he said, a tinge of pride in his voice. "On a drier day, it makes for a nice climb. There's nothing quite like standing up there looking out over the sea and knowing that it's nearly two thousand feet to the water below."

Morgan shuddered, remembering the climb up a much smaller mass of rock that led to Ondine's freehold. She buried her face in Tor's chest.

"I hope we don't have to climb it," she whispered.

Tor patted her on the back.

"I think that's why we're in a boat," he said.

"The birds circling overhead are jackdaws and gulls," Kieran went on. "At sunset the rocks put on a spectacular show of colors. People come from all over just to stand in the right place at the right time and feast their eyes on the display."

"Where are you taking us?" Leigh asked. "And how did you know where to meet us?"

"Kieran's a true dreamer," Emer replied. "We've known for some time now that we'd be having visitors from across the sea. Only in his dream, there were six of you."

"There were six of us up until a few days ago," Valmont said, his voice carefully neutral.

"We're going to the north side of the peninsula," Kieran said. "There's a town called Glencolumbkille in a valley, but we'll not be heading for that. Between there and Slieve League is another village you won't find on any map. That's where we're going."

"Why isn't it on a map?" asked Morgan. "Is it too small or something?"

Emer laughed.

"Smaller places than Glenlea make their way onto maps," she said. "But the mapmakers can't see this place except as a huddle of ruined cottages and overgrown fields. It's a faerie town, and the Kithain who live there have been awaiting your arrival."

He wandered alone through the forest, inhaling the fragrant scent of oak and fir. A large red deer stepped across his path, and he nodded, acknowledging its presence. *Once this land was covered with trees*, he thought sadly. *Now I walk amid the remnants of the dreams of the forest.* He came to the end of the path, where the trees formed a thin border against the rolling fields beyond. *This far, and no farther*, he mused, looking outward at a world but dimly perceived. A cold wind blew toward him and he shivered, not from the chill, but from the hint of Banality carried on the breeze. Within the forest he was safe from its corruption. A step beyond and the weight of the world would crush him into nothingness. *My sanctum and my prison.*

Something had woken him from his near-perpetual slumber. Something had changed in the world outside his faerie glen. His dreams had been restless, filled with scenes of battle, of a great clash between light and dark, as if the two halves of the year had decided to go to war. He had wakened with an inescapable feeling of gloom and sadness, but with it as well had come a glimmer of hope.

The days were long gone when he could sit in his throne room in his grand palace and call forth the services of bard and scholar to interpret his forebodings. They were all gone, bard and scholar, wizard and jester, lords and ladies. The cold winds of the Sundering had taken them away, to Arcadia or—for some—to the lands of the dead. He, alone, had stayed behind, unable to leave the land to which he was bound.

He felt a warm breath on his cheek and he turned his face to see the red stag poised behind him. "You feel it, too," he murmured aloud, his low voice barely discernible above the soughing of the wind. The stag regarded him with deep, liquid eyes that were full of wisdom and abandoned nobility.

The cry of a merlin high in the air pierced the stillness of the morning. He listened intently as again it shrieked. And then he knew what had woken him.

"The stones," he said to his antlered companion. "The stones are coming home."

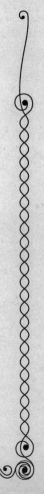

87

all kings

chapter

four

90   The black swan ship glided softly into the sheltered cove and Yrtalien led his company onto the shore.

"Where are we?" Edmund asked, looking around him at the green fields that stretched outward from the shore.

"Somewhere in Ireland," Glynnis replied, looking to Yrtalien for confirmation. The raven-haired sidhe lord nodded his head.

"Our goat-footed savant claims that here is where Silver's Gate and the Court of All Kings are to be found."

"I thought the gate was on an island that sank," Edmund said, staring back toward the ocean. "At least that's what the selkies told us."

"Your selkies don't know everything," Malacar said.

"They're not my selkies," Edmund retorted. "I thought they were kinda dumb. But they did tell us all about the two brothers whose eyes got frozen into gems, and they told us that Silver's Gate sank under the water. They didn't say jack about any Court of Kings."

"All Kings," Malacar corrected him. "That is the name of the island freehold which once held Silver's Gate. It is my belief that the Court itself survived the fall of Silver's Gate and that it relocated somewhere on this island."

"You mean Ireland?" Edmund asked.

Malacar nodded. "If that is true, then there may be a passage leading from the Court to Silver's Gate."

"So do we search the whole place or what?" Edmund asked.

"Hardly," Yrtalien responded, silencing Malacar's intended reply with a swift glance. "The ship brought us here for a reason, and it is my thought that nearby we shall find someone or something that will direct us where we need to go."

The sidhe lord retrieved the sapphire Waystone from the pouch at his neck and cupped it in his palm, closing his eyes in concentration. After a minute, he opened them again and gestured with the hand holding the gem.

"That is the way we need to go," he said. He turned and began walking in the indicated direction, away from the shore. Glynnis took Edmund by the hand and followed Yrtalien, leaving Malacar to limp along at the rear of the group.

"Where are we going?" Edmund called up to Yrtalien. "Did you ask the stone to take us somewhere?"

"We're going to the nearest town," Yrtalien said. "The grand search can wait a few minutes. I fancy a drink."

Behind the prince's back, Edmund rolled his eyes and looked up at Glynnis. She shrugged and tightened her grip on the redcap's hand. As they left the shore, Edmund turned his head to look back at where they had left the ship.

"This had better be the right place," he said to no one in particular. "Because our boat's gone."

Before long, they came to a road and Yrtalien turned to follow it. Ahead of them they could see a somber collection of buildings rise up on either side of them.

Glynnis looked carefully at the signs posted in English and Gaelic as they turned away from the thoroughfare onto a quiet back street.

"This must be Sligo," she said. Yrtalien nodded, dropping back to walk with Glynnis and Edmund.

"That was the name that came to me," he said knowingly.

all kings

"What's so special about Sligo?" Edmund asked.

"Have you ever heard of a poet called Yeats?" Glynnis responded. Edmund looked at her blankly. Glynnis sighed. "He was born here," she said. "His grave is not far from here, in the Drumcliffe churchyard."

"There's another grave here that's more important," Malacar said, hobbling up to join the rest of the group.

"Oh?" Yrtalien sneered. "And whose might that be?"

"It's said that the remains of Queen Maeve lie somewhere nearby," Malacar answered. "That ancient lady is also known to some as Mab, the queen of the faeries."

"That may be," Yrtalien said, "but for now, we're going in here." He stopped in front of a dilapidated building wedged in between a pair of small shops.

Edmund's faerie sight penetrated the structure's dusty facade and saw a modestly inviting tavern with a sign proclaiming it to be The Broken Harp.

"It's a freehold," he exclaimed. "Just like the Toybox! Cool! I want a beer."

Yrtalien opened the door and stepped inside. After a moment's hesitation, Glynnis led the others into the building.

Leigh awoke with a feeling of anticipation. Despite the strangeness of their surroundings, she and her companions had been overcome with weariness upon reaching the shelter and warmth of the faerie town. Kieran and Emer had led them directly to a small cottage near the edge of the town and pointed them in the direction of two small bedrooms at the back of the building. Leigh and Morgan took one of the rooms, while Valmont, Rasputin and Tor settled in the other. A few minutes later, after the companions had stripped off their wet clothing and donned dry garments from their packs, Emer appeared with mugs of steaming hot tea and small sandwiches.

"You've had a long journey, though your bodies may not know it yet. Drink and eat and then get yourselves into bed. Tomorrow, we'll show you around."

Her suggestion had been impossible to resist, and the companions were only too glad to comply.

"Are you awake?" Leigh called across the room to Morgan, who still lay bundled in her blankets. The childling mumbled something indecipherable and sat up, rubbing her eyes and blinking at the sunlight that pooled from the window into the center of the room.

"I'm hungry," Morgan said, throwing off the covers and standing up. Suddenly she darted out of the room. Leigh could hear her knocking on the door of the other bedroom and calling for Tor. *Poor thing,* she thought, remembering Morgan's panic after discovering in Hilo that Tor had disappeared during the night. *I wonder how long it will be before she gets over her fear of losing him again.*

She rose from her bed and straightened her clothing, a little rumpled from being slept in. Combing her fingers through her hair, she looked around for a mirror and found a tiny one on the wall between the two beds.

The face of an elegant sidhe noblewoman met her gaze from the silvered glass and she smiled involuntarily. *So this is how it is in a faerie thorpe,* she thought. Now that she was awake and aware, she could feel the Glamour that seemed to surround her. *Everything here is saturated with the stuff of dreams,* she told herself, borrowing some of the ambient magic

all kings

to alter her clothing to something more appropriate to her surroundings.

"You look great!" Morgan's voice surprised her from the doorway. Leigh stared down at her close-fitting silvery leggings, high leather boots and red velvet tunic blazoned with the silver lion of House Fiona. After a moment's thought, she armed herself with the chimeric sword given her at her knighting. *Not that I'll need it here*, she thought. Following her lead, Morgan dressed herself in chimeric clothing, choosing a long, graceful gown in the midnight blue of House Eiluned.

"Do you think this is too fancy?" she asked, standing on tiptoe to see herself in the mirror. Her black curls framed her face and barely concealed the tips of her pointed ears.

Leigh laughed. "Not at all, Baroness Morgania," she said, suddenly filled with a wild joy that she had not felt in a long time.

"I see we're all dressed in our shabbiest togs," Rasputin said, coming into the room. The pooka wore a rust-colored tunic with dark green trousers and soft boots that laced to his knees. "You should see how modestly Valmont and Tor are turned out. This whole village is too dull for words."

Morgan gathered her skirts and skipped off to the front of the house, while Leigh and Rasputin followed behind her at a walk.

Kieran and Emer were waiting with Tor and Valmont just outside the cottage. Morgan gasped in admiration as she saw Valmont swathed in crimson and dark blue robes with a gold turban on his head. His chimeric scimitar hung at his side. Tor had settled for a warrior's armor, its polished leather and shining studs making him look both formidable and proud.

"Welcome to Glenlea," Kieran said, holding his hands out for Morgan and Leigh. The handsome selkie wore a gray-blue belted tunic over loose sea-green leggings. Emer, in a filmy gown in which all the colors of water and sky shimmered with her movements, stepped forward and linked arms with Valmont and Rasputin.

"We thought we'd be giving you a tour of our freehold, poor wee thing that it is," she said. "Then we'll have our breakfast down by the shore."

"This looks like a place out of a fairy tale," Morgan said, her eyes gleaming with excitement. "Do people live in all the cottages? Kithain like us, I mean?" she asked.

The small group began a leisurely stroll down the main street of the village, a broad cobbled stone avenue lined with thatched cottages and dotted with trees and flowering shrubs.

"The whole place is enchanted," Emer said, "and all the people in it. There are some mortals who live among us, but they are gifted with the sight and are here because of their ties to the freehold's residents." She nodded a greeting to a wizened little woman hurrying past them, a covered basket crooked in her arm.

"That's Mother Cobbins," Emer said. "She bakes a powerful soda bread. I've asked her to make some up special for you."

"It smells like heaven," Leigh remarked, inhaling the aroma that lingered in the air with the woman's passing.

"Is this a selkie town?" Morgan asked, staring unabashedly at the other villagers who lingered in doorways to watch the companions pass.

Kieran laughed and shook his head. "Nah," he said. "There are some selkies here—me and Emer, for example—because the town is so near the shore. But most of the Kithain of Glenlea are boggans and pookas

all kings

and maybe a troll or two with a few nockers and redcaps thrown in to keep things hopping."

"Are there no other sidhe?" Leigh asked.

"Not on a regular basis," Kieran said. Leigh thought she detected a guarded tone to his voice. "Sometimes one or another will come for a visit, but most of them find our thorpe a bit too plain for their tastes."

"I think it's perfect," Morgan pronounced.

"We can't think of much in it we'd change," Emer admitted, her voice filled with pride.

"Well, I can, and that's the fact that you're hogging our visitors," a brash female voice announced from behind the group. A freckle-faced young woman with tawny hair and a pert, foxlike face inserted herself in between Emer and Rasputin. "You may call me anything you like, but more often than not, I answer to Brit," she said, smiling up at the startled pooka.

"Um, don't call me Rasputin," the pooka muttered.

"Suit yourself," Brit replied. "Or is that your way of introducing yourself?"

"He always says what he doesn't mean," Morgan said, trying to be helpful.

"And I always say more or less than I mean, except when I'm sleeping. Then, you'll hear the straight truth," Brit answered. "You're one of the rabbit folk, aren't you?" she asked Rasputin, fixing her clear amber-colored eyes on his face.

"Not really," he said. "And I'd never guess what you are." He attempted to move a step away from her, but found that she had linked elbows with him.

"Don't worry," she said. "There are plenty of ways for a fox pooka to hunt down a hare, and not all of them are bad for the hare. Just most."

Rasputin gave Valmont and Tor a panicked look as Brit started to stroll off with him in the direction of the seashore. Valmont turned his head toward Emer and raised an eyebrow questioningly.

"She's all right," Emer said, "if a little forward, but then most vixens are, I suppose. Brit has lived here since she was a kit. She sings in the tavern down by the end of the road." Emer pointed to a large stone and wood building with a shingled sign depicting a foaming mug.

"That's the Flowing Cup," Kieran said. "We'll go there tonight and listen to the music, if you like."

"I'd like that," Leigh said.

"Is that a metalsmith's shop?" Tor asked suddenly, pointing to a small building set a little apart from the others, down a narrow unpaved side lane.

"It is," Kieran said, "and you might be interested in meeting our village smith. He works in bronze and copper and silver, don't you know."

The sounds of metal on metal grew louder as they approached the smithy. Inside the dimly lit building, a hulking troll clad in breeches and a leather apron stood behind a large stone slab, hammering a length of yellowish metal into a broad, wedge-shaped blade. He stopped his work briefly at the arrival of visitors and nodded at the group.

"Be with you when I can," he grumbled. "Name's Hogan," he said.

Tor moved up closer to watch.

"Tor," he said.

Hogan nodded. He pounded the metal a few more times before holding it up for inspection. "That'll do for now," he muttered, laying the blade aside and putting down his hammer. He wiped his palms on his apron before extending a hand for Tor to clasp. The two trolls shook hands.

"Battle-axe," Hogan said, "double-bladed steel, am I right or no?"

Tor unsnapped his leather sheath and drew out his treasure for Hogan to view. The smith eyed the weapon and nodded, a little smugly.

"I could tell from your grip," he said. "That's a
beauty."

Tor grunted his thanks and returned the axe to its sheath. Hogan removed his apron and hung it on a peg by the wall. He grabbed a soft leather vest from another peg and donned it.

"Is it time for the morning feast you've been promising us all?" he asked Kieran as he started for the door of the shop.

"I think so," Kieran replied. He turned to the oathmates. "We decided to make a party out of breakfast in your honor," he said. "I think the food should be ready by now."

"Good," Morgan said. "I'm starving."

Using the key once given her in a moment of trust, Signe Henderson let herself in to the darkened apartment that had belonged to her fellow Dauntain, Cyprian Ryder. The graceful eshu slipped inside and closed the door behind her, then stood for a moment with her back against the door, collecting her thoughts.

He will never be coming back here. The words pounded in her head as she allowed her eyes to accustom themselves to the unlit room. *I'm not even sure why I have come, except that there is no one else that I know of who can see what was left of his earthly existence.* The pale light that shone in faintly from the single window in the small living room outlined a few pieces of furniture, including a shelf of books and a writing desk.

Signe located the light switch just inside the door and flipped it, flooding the room with a harsh glare. *Reality*, she thought, as the room took on color and tangible form. *No shadows, no uncertain shapes, nothing but solid, material substance. There is nothing in this room that even hints of something beyond the world of reason and logic.*

The walls of the room were bare of pictures; the small table that sat to one side of the armchair held only a reading lamp. A paperweight made of dark green malachite rested on the desk.

Quietly, Signe crossed over to the desk and sat down in the straight-backed chair in front of it. She tested the single drawer and found that it opened easily. Inside lay a neat stack of heavy bond stationery, along with a few envelopes, and a dark gray fountain pen. She sat for a moment, fingering the pen, calling up in her mind the image of Ryder seated in her place. *To whom would he write and about what?* she wondered. She had probably known him better than anyone else, except, possibly, Vargas, and she knew so little about his actual life.

This is why I am here, she realized. *To find out, if I can, just who this man was for whom I sacrificed my faerie self, and who died because he found it too painful to live.* She and the eshu Valmont had been occupied in their own confrontation when Ryder met his death in the sluggish stream of lava that flowed down the side of Kilauea volcano. Diana maintained that the troll warrior—Tor—who faced Ryder in single combat was responsible for the Dauntain's murder, but Signe had heard a different story. After she and Diana and Vargas had captured and subdued the five Kithain Yrtalien had promised them, she had elected to ride with the captives in the back of Vargas' hired van, to make certain that they did not try to escape.

Somehow they had gotten to her, appealing to the last vestige of her fae self. It had been the pooka's utter desolation at the thought of being sundered from his changeling spirit that had led her to question the wisdom of her role as a Dauntain. The others, too, had seemed so committed to what she had learned to call their delusion, that finally she had relented and had assisted them in making their escape. While Vargas and Diana rode in the closed front of the van heading to a safe house where they had intended to forcibly sever their prisoners from their faerie selves, she had learned the actual circumstances of Ryder's death.

The real fault lies with the bastard who betrayed all of us, she thought. *The Forsworn Prince is rightly named.* Ryder had told her about the blue gem embedded in his palm. Its power enabled him to locate creatures and objects that radiated Glamour. With it, it was simple for him to track down changelings. Because its innate Glamour was so abhorrent to Ryder, however, the stone's presence caused him pain most of the time. Yrtalien had managed to control the intensity of the pain, and had thus gained power over Ryder, using him as a pawn in his own ploy to acquire its companion gem from the sidhe female who possessed it.

According to Tor, Ryder had broken off their battle suddenly, overcome by the pain in his hand. He had appealed to the troll, who responded by severing Ryder's hand from his wrist. Finally free of his burden, Ryder had thrown himself into the lava flow. The tale, coming as it did in the troll's slow, halting speech, had the ring of truth. *He wanted this death,* Signe told herself. *He wanted to be free of his demons once and for all.*

Signe rose from the desk and walked across the spartan room to Ryder's bookshelf. It was filled with a selection of titles on psychology, natural history, and science. One book looked a little out of place. Signe removed it from the shelf and realized that it was the slender volume she had written and published privately, a fairly technical analysis of the changeling phenomenon. She smiled ruefully as she flipped through its pages. *This goes back a long time*, she thought. *It was my proof to Ryder that he had succeeded in rescuing me from my madness.*

A sheet of paper, folded in quarters, as if it had once been stowed inside a wallet, was tucked in the back of the book. Signe removed the page, laying the book down on the seat of the armchair. Unfolding it, she discovered a brief letter addressed *"To whom it may concern"* from a Dr. Adrienne Walters, a psychologist in San Francisco. It contained a request for help in dealing with a child client who manifested severe delusions of a fantasy world in which she was a faerie princess. *This was Morgan's doctor*, she realized. This was what impelled Ryder to make his first, disastrous trip to San Francisco to track down the local changelings. He had been discovered and his memories were altered so that he forgot his reason for being in San Francisco. When his memories finally returned, he had called Signe and assembled a group to continue the hunt. They had followed their quarry to Hawaii, only to fail again. This time, however, Ryder had lost more than his memories.

Signe folded up the letter and placed it in the pocket of her jacket. Picking up the book, she headed for Ryder's bedroom. Like the rest of the apartment, this, too, was barren of any kind of frivolous adornment, containing only a narrow bed, a bare dressing table, and a small chest of drawers. She began opening the drawers, finding only neatly folded clothing in most of them.

In the bottom of the lowest drawer, beneath a stack of spare sheets for the bed, she felt something hard and cold. A sick feeling flooded her as her hands touched what could only be cold iron. Quickly opening up the top drawer and removing from it a linen handkerchief, she wrapped the cloth around her hand and retrieved a pair of iron cuffs.

I wore these, she recalled, *when Ryder kidnapped me on the pretext of spending a weekend with him in the Berkshires. He told me they would come off only when I surrendered to reality or when he killed me to save me from my delusions.* At first, her body had rebelled at being in such constant contact with the cold iron bracelets. She had begged him to remove them, but he had not swerved in his determination to cure her of her sickness. Finally, her will broken by his harsh barrage of words and his unflinchingly severe punishments of her every attempt to retain some small hold on her eshu self, she had given in. He had removed the cuffs, pronounced her restored to her right mind, and promised her that she would never have to wear them again so long as she remained true to her mortal self.

In the wake of her forced rehabilitation, in what she had later come to recognize as an example of the hostage syndrome, she had not only forsworn her faerie nature, but had also joined Ryder in his hunt for other changelings. *No more,* she thought bitterly. Ryder's death and her contact with Rasputin, Valmont and their companions had restored to her the missing part of herself. *I am an eshu, and nothing will ever make me forget that again.*

She retrieved another handkerchief and carefully wrapped the iron cuffs in it, then placed the bundle in her oversized purse. Even then, she could still feel the slight unease caused by the closeness of the iron. *I'll have to find a better container for them,* she thought. She considered leaving them, but reasoned that when someone—probably the building's landlord—

eventually realized that Ryder wasn't coming back, they would be discovered. *Let them find nothing to tell them what kind of man lived in this place*, she thought. *I owe him that.* She walked over to his bed and sat down.

Finally, at long last, she allowed the tears to flow. She remembered the rare times that Ryder had slipped his vigilance and had allowed her to see something of the person behind the Dauntain mask. When he, along with herself and Diana, had resumed his faerie self in order to infiltrate Yrtalien's freehold in Hilo, she had seen Ryder transform himself into Chevalier, a lord of the sidhe. His grandeur had nearly overwhelmed her. *What would he have been like if he had not denied what he was?* She had come very close to falling in love with him several times during the years they worked together. *But it was always the failed sidhe I loved*, she realized. *It was Chevalier, not Ryder, who touched my heart.*

She rose from her seat and wiped her tear-streaked face with her hands. She had come to Ryder's apartment to salvage what she could of the man she had feared and hated and trusted and almost loved. Her book, the letter, and the iron cuffs were all that was left of him. Unlike other changelings, whose spirits enjoyed a continual rebirth, the sidhe live only once unless they consent to have a wake held to commemorate their deaths. Such a memorial would ensure the rebirth of their souls as one of the commoner kith. *There will be no wake for you*, she thought, *no returning as a commoner to an existence that would only prolong your torment. You will live on in the memory of those who knew you.* That would have to be enough.

As quietly as she had entered, Signe let herself out of Ryder's apartment, her duty to him discharged and her farewells washed away by her tears. *There is still something I have to do*, she thought as she left the building and joined the throng of people on the street. She felt a tugging inside her that, coupled with her eshu knack for traveling to where she needed to be, told her that her association with Rasputin and his friends was not yet over.

First thing in the morning, she decided, she would inquire into flights to San Francisco.

Inside, The Broken Harp smelled like strong beer and heavy smoke. Edmund's eyes watered as he tried to look through the haze that hung in the stagnant air. The tavern consisted of a large, shabby room that held an unadorned bar at the far end and a few mismatched tables and chairs in the center and rear. A foot railing ran in front of the bar. Along one side wall, several booths provided space for more intimate conversation, while a low bench ran along the other side. To the rear, a partially opened doorway revealed a back hallway. A dart board, its surface pocked with puncture marks, hung near the back door.

"Don't these guys ever open a window?" he asked.

Yrtalien ignored him and led the group across the room to an empty table in the back. Taking the corner seat, he tipped back his chair, resting his head against the wall. Languidly, he motioned for Glynnis and Malacar to seat themselves on either side of him. Edmund started to pull up a chair across from the prince, nervous at the thought of having his back to the door, but Yrtalien stopped him with a look.

"Go up to the bar," he said, "and inform the bartender that we want some service."

Several sharp replies ran through the redcap's mind before he decided against any of them. Instead, he contented himself with a shrug of assent and headed for the bar. Dragging a chair up to the bar and shoving it between the only other customers standing against the railing, a pair of long-haired toughs in leather jackets and torn jeans, he stood upon its seat and pounded his hand on the counter to get the bartender's attention.

He broke out in a broad, toothy grin when the bartender turned around to greet him, flashing a practiced smile that was every bit as broad and menacing as Edmund's.

"Are you wanting anything, boy?" the redcap bartender said, his voice a low, rasping sound devoid of pleasantries. A pungent cigar, the source of the copious cloud of smoke that filled the room, was clenched between his teeth.

"Yeah," Edmund began. "Um, my friends and I want something to drink," he said, trying to drop his own voice so that he sounded older. "Have you got any beer?"

The figure on Edmund's left choked back a snort of laughter. "Yer not from around here, are you boyo?" he sneered, turning his face toward the childling. His dark blond hair hung halfway down his back, while in front, an unruly mass of untrimmed bangs obscured his eyes. A hand-rolled cigarette hung from his lower lip. Edmund saw that the tips of his pointed ears were pierced with silver rings.

"I'm a tourist," Edmund retorted. "Make something of it, punk." He pivoted on the chair seat to face the wilder sidhe, his hands already balled into fists. Before he could make a move, a pair of hands gripped him from behind.

"Easy, there," a mild voice half-whispered in his ear. "No need to make a big thing of a friendly remark." Edmund twisted his head around and saw a mirror image of the first tough.

"Are you guys twins?" he asked, his irritability forgotten in his amazement. The sidhe holding him laughed without malice and nodded.

"Born at the same time to the same mother," he said. "I suppose that makes us twins. I'm Donal and that's my brother Dougal." He released his hold on Edmund. "And who might you be?"

"Edmund." He looked across at the bartender. "Were you just gonna stand and watch?" he asked.

"Oh, not at all," the old redcap said. "I'd a helped them beat the piss out of you and then eaten you for tea. You've got a hair-trigger of a temper, haven't you?"

Edmund shrugged. "I've been under a lot of pressure," he said. He jerked his head in the direction of Yrtalien and the others. "It's traveling with a prince that gets on my nerves."

At the sound of the word "prince," the sidhe twins and the redcap bartender stiffened. Without moving their heads, all three managed to glance in the direction of the back table.

"Is that yer man over with his head against the wall?" Dougal asked softly.

Edmund ducked his chin once in assent. "That's him," he said.

"Prince, you say," the bartender repeated.

Edmund nodded. "Don't worry, though, he's not here to bust you guys or anything. He's as Unseelie as a tire iron."

"And what makes you think we're not the Seelie Court of Sligo?" the bartender said, his voice crackling with amusement.

"Right," Edmund said. "And I'm the High King of the Faeries. By the way, have you got a name or should I just call you Bartender?"

"The moniker's Lurgan," the redcap said. "But you can call me sir."

"So can you send someone over to take our drink order?" Edmund said, remembering why Yrtalien had sent him to the bar in the first place. "He'll get upset if he doesn't get what he wants."

"Will he, now?" Lurgan remarked. "And why can't he be bothering to move his own feet up here like the rest of my customers and ask for what he wants himself?" He pitched his voice so that it would carry across the room to Yrtalien's ears.

"Bad move," muttered Edmund. "You really don't want to piss him off."

"This is my bar and my freehold," Lurgan said. "I'll do what I want here."

Edmund heard a scraping sound as Yrtalien let his chair fall to the floor and pushed the table away from him as he stood up, allowing the local trio to see his black-clad figure looming like an angel of death in the corner of the room. A crackle of energy filled the hazy air and an eerie violet glow surrounded the prince's form as he seemed to grow in stature and presence until it was impossible not to look at him and tremble.

"I expect both service and hospitality when I enter a strange freehold," he said, barely raising his voice yet filling the room with sound. "Oblige me, if you will."

Lurgan seemed to shrink as Yrtalien spoke, his face twisted in undisguised awe. The sidhe brothers straightened their slouches, their own faces reflecting some of the prince's arrogant display. Donal uttered a low, tuneless whistle.

"That's power," he whispered. Dougal nodded numbly, his cigarette falling from his mouth onto the floor.

"How about a round on the house?" Lurgan's voice was a hoarse croak as he managed to find his speech.

"So long as you're quick about it," Yrtalien said. Behind him, Malacar righted the prince's fallen chair and held it while Yrtalien resumed his seat. The violet glow receded, and the sidhe lord once again leaned back against the wall as if nothing had happened.

Lurgan drew three glasses of dark stout and set them on a tray, then quickly carried them over to Yrtalien's table and set them out in front of the trio, making sure that the prince received the first glass. He bobbed his head and scurried back behind the bar, where he filled four more glasses with the thick-headed brew and placed drinks in front of Dougal, Donal and Edmund. He kept the last one for himself.

"Wow!" Edmund said, staring in wonder at the drink in front of him. "Cool!"

As inconspicuously as possible, he watched Donal take a sip of his drink, then tried to mimic the wilder.

The bitter liquid caught in the back of his throat and he coughed, spraying the bar in front of him.

"That's harsh!" he said. "I think it's gone bad."

The brothers on either side of him started laughing. Dougal clapped him on the back.

"You're used to the watered down American stuff, I can tell," he said, winking over Edmund's head at his brother.

"No doubt," replied Donal, taking another swig from his glass. "But a seasoned drinker like you should adjust to a real drink in no time."

Edmund felt his cheeks grow red. *My first drink, and I blew it,* he thought miserably to himself. *I'm just glad Morgan isn't here to see me with foam on my chin.*

"Try it again, lad, only go slow," Lurgan advised. "Taste it before you swallow it."

Edmund followed the bartender's instructions and discovered that the second swallow wasn't as bad as the first.

"I think one of us at least should pay our respects," Dougal muttered, sliding off the stool. With a backward glance at his brother, who nodded and turned in his seat to watch, Dougal crossed the room to Yrtalien's table. He stood opposite the sidhe lord and nodded his head in greeting.

"I hear you're a prince of the Unseelie Court," he said, ignoring both Glynnis and Malacar and staring at Yrtalien.

"I am Yrtalien ap Ailil," the prince said. Next to him, Glynnis held her breath at Yrtalien's casual mention of his House. Few members of that Unseelie House existed this side of the Dreaming and fewer still admitted their affiliation with it.

Dougal's hard face took on an expression of excitement as he pulled a chair from a nearby table and sat down across from Yrtalien.

"Then it seems we have something in common," he said. "I'm Dougal ap Ailil and that's my brother Donal."

"I was hoping I had judged the lay of the land correctly," Yrtalien replied. "I have need of your assistance and your knowledge of the area." The prince leaned forward in his chair and fixed his dark eyes on Dougal. "Are you my man or not?"

Glynnis could feel the workings of a strong Glamour as Yrtalien spoke, his voice rich and cajoling. *This is the voice that won me to him*, she thought bitterly. *He will make slaves of us all before he's done.*

"My brother and I are at your service," Dougal said.

"Then I have a few questions I wish to ask," Yrtalien replied. Yrtalien gestured with his hand toward Malacar, acknowledging the satyr's presence for the first time since entering The Broken Harp. "My scholar has come upon certain references to an ancient court that may have survived the separation from the

Dreaming. We wish to confirm its existence and find it, if it can be found."

Dougal laughed. "I take it you're not acting on behalf of the current powers in the land?" He slouched back in his chair and shook his unruly mane of hair out of his face in a gesture of studied indifference.

Yrtalien's answering laugh held a trace of contempt. "Hardly," he said. His dark eyes narrowed as he attempted to size up the indolent wilder in front of him. "If your rulers are as I think they are, they would not be pleased with my attempts to recover the power that has been denied those of us who do not ally ourselves with the Seelie Court."

"Well, if it's rebellion you're looking for, you've come to the right land for that, for certain," Dougal said. "Should I be calling my brother over to join us?" he asked.

Yrtalien shrugged. "Do as you like," he said. "I wish to command your loyalty, not dictate your every action."

Dougal turned his head and shouted toward the bar for his brother. Without turning around, Donal nodded. Stopping only long enough to refill his glass, Dougal's twin rose from his seat and came to join the table of conspirators.

Edmund drained the last of his stout and burped loudly. "That wasn't bad," he said to Lurgan. The redcap bartender took the glass and winked at Edmund.

"Another round?" he asked. "It seems we've been abandoned by the high folk, you and me," Lurgan added. Edmund looked over his shoulder at the table where Yrtalien presided. The childling shrugged. "Let them talk all they want," he said, his tongue suddenly thick in his mouth as his young body struggled with the unexpected infusion of potent brew. "I just provide the muscle." The last word came out as "mushel."

Lurgan stared at the childling's drooping face and slowly put the glass aside. He reached underneath the bar and pulled out an earthenware mug, into which he poured some dark steaming liquid from a metal pot on a burner in back of him.

"Drink this down," he said, placing the mug between Edmund's hands and guiding it to his lips.

Edmund swallowed reflexively, then grimaced.

"Yuck," he croaked. "This tastes like vomit!"

Lurgan guffawed. "Just toss it down yer throat," he advised. "It'll bring the sparkle back to your eyes in no time."

Edmund closed his eyes and forced himself to swallow the rest of the liquid.

"What was that?" he asked.

"A real man's drink," the bartender informed him. "Black tea and salt."

"Bitchin'," Edmund said, already feeling less sluggish than he had a few minutes ago. "So is this really your freehold? Or do you just run it for someone?"

"It's all mine," Lurgan said. "I run this bar for myself and my friends and for no one else. I was a bit surprised when yer lot came through the door. You shouldn't have been able to find us."

Edmund's wizened young face took on a secretive look. "We can find anything we want," he said. *At least that's what His Self-Importance seems to think.*

"Can you now?" Lurgan asked. "And what were you looking for when you waltzed in here as if you'd been coming here all your lives?"

"The prince said he wanted a drink," Edmund said, then leaned over the bar until his face was only a few inches from Lurgan's. "But I think he really wants to find some people to do his dirty work for him."

Lurgan looked over Edmund's shoulder toward Yrtalien's table. "Isn't that the way of it?" he said. "The sidhe have grand plans and schemes, all of 'em, even the brothers Donal and Dougal, though they'd never be caught owning up to it. But do they ever do anything about it themselves?"

Edmund started to answer, but Lurgan cut him off.

"They do not," he said, slapping a hand on the bar to punctuate his answer. "They send others to fight their battles for them." Lurgan fell silent, impressed by his own vehemence. Edmund felt a sudden pang of hunger and looked around him for something to eat.

"Do you have any food here?" he asked. "Or should I just chew on the bar?"

Lurgan snickered. "I've got a pot of stew on the fire back in the kitchen," he said. "How about a bowl and some soda bread?"

Edmund nodded. He fidgeted in his seat while Lurgan disappeared into the room behind the bar. A few minutes later, the bartender emerged carrying a large bowl and a round loaf of light brown bread. He placed the food in front of Edmund and handed the childling a spoon and a knife. Edmund attacked the bread and stew, emptying the bowl in a few gulps and shoving huge chunks of the warm, raisiny bread into his mouth. He wiped his mouth with the back of his hand.

"Another drink?" Lurgan asked with a straight face.

Edmund nodded. "Yeah," he said. "Only do you think I can have a Coke?"

"Will ginger beer do?" Lurgan asked, reaching for a dark bottle on the shelf behind him.

The childling nodded. Lurgan uncapped the bottle and set it in front of Edmund, who picked it up and sniffed its pungent aroma.

"It's warm," he said. "Got any ice?"

The bartender shook his head. "You don't want to be pollutin' your drink with frozen water," he said. "That way you can't taste anything but cold."

"Whatever," Edmund replied, tipping the bottle up and taking a generous swig of the spicy drink. He swished the liquid around in his mouth a few times, tipping his head back to make gargling noises before he finally swallowed.

"So who else comes here besides the Hardy Boys?" Edmund asked, his stomach finally satisfied.

Lurgan cackled at the childling's reference to the wilder twins. "There's a few more of us," he said, indicating himself and Edmund.

"Redcaps?" Edmund asked.

Lurgan nodded. "And the odd pooka or two come by for a drink and some gab. They usually wait until evening, though, when they've nothing better to do."

"Is this the only freehold in town?"

"I should hope not," Lurgan said. "Nor is it the only one of Unseelie persuasion in these parts."

"What parts? Ireland?" Edmund asked.

Lurgan shook his head. "The mortals call it Ireland," he said. "We call it Hibernia or the Four Kingdoms. This is County Sligo, on the northwestern side of the island."

"So who's in charge, here? Over Hibernia, I mean," Edmund asked. "Do you have a High King?"

"We have too many kings and queens," Lurgan said, "if you're asking me, and you are. There's a king over Dublin way, and one down near Tipperary who calls herself the Queen of Munster. There's a few others besides scattered throughout the countryside who claim to be monarch of this or that, and a few of them even have followers and courts and such. Here, now, in Sligo, the closest we have to anyone who might be considered kings are those two ruffians over

all kings

there," Lurgan bobbed his head in the direction of the twins, now deep in conversation with Yrtalien.

"Them?" Edmund sounded astonished.

Lurgan nodded. "Yer man got lucky when he came here while Donal and Dougal were here." He stopped, looking thoughtful. "But then, again, maybe it wasn't just a lucky bit of timing—"

"Bingo!" Edmund said.

"Edmund!" Yrtalien called, rising abruptly to his feet.

"What?" Edmund replied. "I mean, what, sir?"

Lurgan snorted, then quickly busied himself with removing the empty dishes from the bar and carrying them back to the kitchen. The others at the table rose when Yrtalien did and now began filing toward the door of the tavern.

Yrtalien motioned with his hand for Edmund to join the group.

"Dougal and Donal have agreed to give us lodging and hospitality for the night, and to take us tomorrow to see the grave of Queen Maeve. Malacar seems to think that it might be helpful in our quest."

"You mean Silver's Gate is in a graveyard?" Edmund said.

"Not Silver's Gate," Malacar said. "The Court of All Kings."

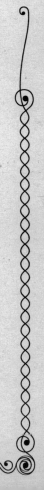

all kings

chapter

five

It was almost midnight, and The Flowing Cup was filled to bursting as the entire faerie town of Glenlea turned out to greet the newcomers from across the sea. After the sumptuous late morning meal in which the villagers met and introduced themselves to their visitors, they now hailed the oathmates as if they were long lost friends.

Leigh and her companions had arrived in the pub after spending the day wandering through the streets of the village and poking their heads into the shops where the local Kithain kept alive the old crafts. Morgan had become fascinated with watching an old boggan demonstrate his skill at glassblowing. Leigh had admired and been gifted with a fine woven shawl, which she now wore draped around her shoulders against the chilly evening.

The oathmates had started the evening as a group, enlarged by the presence of the selkies, Kieran and Emer, as well as the fox pooka Brit, who had latched onto Rasputin with a feral sense of appropriation. A large table had been cleared for them in the center of the pub and tavern. Nora, the boggan innkeeper, a fidgety wilder female on the verge of becoming a grump, had presented them with a seemingly unending procession of hot and cold foods, all grown or raised within the confines of the freehold or else harvested from the nearby ocean.

The rest of the villagers had crowded into the tavern to share in the feasting, filling every available table. When the eating was done, the tables were pushed to the sides of the room and the music and dancing began.

"We call this a *fleadh*," Kieran had told her. "The word means festival."

"You've gone to an awful lot of trouble to make us feel at home," Leigh said.

Kieran had laughed. "No trouble at all," he demurred. "In fact, your coming here provided us with a grand excuse to do what we like best—celebrate with food and song."

Now, several hours later, Leigh sank wearily into a chair between set dances and searched the crowded room for her oathmates. Valmont's tall, elegant figure was immediately apparent, since the dark-skinned eshu's height in faerie form placed him head and shoulders above the other dancers. The music started up once again, and Leigh admired Valmont's graceful movements as she watched him squire Emer through a series of intricate dance steps. *You'd never know he only learned those steps a few hours ago*, Leigh thought. *No wonder he's flirted with the Shadow Court. They, at least, recognize his inherent nobility. I'm tired of defending my kith's belief in its right to rule*, she realized suddenly. *Valmont is right. Nobility is not gained through birth, but by merit, and he, if anyone, deserves to be recognized for his honor and devotion.*

A cheer arose in the far corner of the tavern, and Leigh stood up and peered beyond the dancers to where a small crowd of older Kithain had gathered around a table. Through a break in the press of bodies, she could just see Tor and Hogan seated opposite each other, their arms locked in a contest of strength. The two trolls seemed nearly evenly matched, and the onlookers were cheering each fraction gained or lost by their favorite. The infusion of Glamour gained from prolonged contact with the enchanted thorpe had acted like a tonic for the aging troll. Leigh smiled to herself as she turned away and searched the room for Rasputin and Morgan.

She finally found Morgan among a group of childlings gathered near the front of the tavern watching the antics of a dapper young man whose kith she could not readily determine. That he was Kithain, she could ascertain. He had the delicately pointed ears and fine, sculpted features of one of the sidhe, but he stood only a little over five feet and his body tended toward chunkiness, rather than the slender elegance of the fae nobility. He was demonstrating his skill at sleight-of-hand, pulling coins and candies from the ears and noses of his rapt audience. Morgan's face radiated pleasure and excitement as she clapped and laughed at the entertainer's feats of legerdemain. *She needs this opportunity to just be a childling,* Leigh thought. *We've asked so much of her and expected so much from her since we began our quest.*

A tortured yelp in a voice she recognized as Rasputin's caught her attention just as the pooka emerged from the dance floor, limping noticeably. Brit, her face a picture of concern and embarrassment, followed close behind him. Leigh waved to Rasputin and pointed to an empty chair near her own. Rasputin sat down and, removing his left shoe, began massaging his ankle. Brit knelt down on the floor and began rubbing the injured foot as well.

"I honestly didn't know your foot would be there," she said. "I've over fifty world class championships in set dancing to vouch for my sure-footedness on the dance floor and I've never in my life stepped on the foot of any Kithain, though I've deliberately trampled one ugly mortal who bothered me." Her words burst from her in a flood.

"I think it's broken," Rasputin said mournfully, looking at Leigh as he spoke and giving her a tiny wink. "I can feel the bones moving against each other in ways they were never meant to move."

Leigh smiled in amusement. "Why don't you see if you can't find a cup of hot tea for our wounded warrior of the dance?" Leigh said, touching Brit on the shoulder as she spoke. "It would at least help him relax."

The fox pooka's face brightened at Leigh's suggestion.

"I could do that, I suppose," she said. She stood up and smiled at Rasputin. "I'll be right back," she promised and skittered away toward the rear of the tavern, leaving Leigh and Rasputin sitting on the sidelines.

"It's not really broken, is it?" she asked the pooka.

Rasputin wiggled his toes and gave Leigh a lopsided grin. "Completely and utterly crushed," he said happily. "It's a shame, too. I was enjoying her constant company."

"She does seem to have taken a fancy to you," Leigh observed wryly.

"I think she hates me," the pooka moaned.

"Does it bother you so much that she's attracted to you?" Leigh asked. For as long as she had known Rasputin, the pooka had always been a loner, even among his friends. *It's as if he's afraid to let anyone get too close to him*, she thought.

"It doesn't bother me in the slightest," Rasputin said. "I'm used to this happening all the time. Women find me irresistible, and I have to admit that the feeling is mutual."

Leigh patted Rasputin's knee sympathetically. "I guess you'll just have to grin and bear it," she said.

Rasputin gave her a reproachful look. A few minutes later, Brit reappeared in front of them carrying a tray filled with three mugs of steaming tea.

"It's chamomile," she said. "I brewed it with my own hands and nearly got trampled trying to get it here." She looked around her for a chair. Leigh spotted an empty chair on the other side of her, away from Rasputin. She pulled it closer to her and motioned for Brit to take a seat. She complied, passing the tray across Leigh for Rasputin to take a mug before handing one to Leigh and taking the last for herself. She slipped the empty tray underneath her chair and settled back to sip her drink and watch the crowd.

When the dance ended, Leigh heard Kieran's voice shouting for everyone's attention. The villagers pushed back along the walls. Those who failed to find chairs either sat atop the tables or else stood against the sides of the room. Soon Kieran was left alone in the center of the tavern.

"Friends of my heart and of the Dreaming," he said, "tonight marks a very special occasion. In the world outside this village, mortals are preparing to celebrate the last day of the old year. For us, it's just another day, since we look to the spring solstice as the beginning of our passage through the seasons. But two fortuitous events have occurred which have given us cause to celebrate, not that we need one."

The selkie paused to allow for the titter of amusement that greeted his last remark.

"We've been blessed with visitors from the far Kingdom of Pacifica, on the other side of the commodious western land of Concordia across the sea. By now you've probably met the newcomers, so I won't single them out again for you."

Leigh blushed, seeing heads turn toward her and Rasputin. *I suppose Morgan and Tor and Valmont are getting their share of attention*, she thought.

Kieran clapped his hands together and brought the focus of the crowd back to himself.

"Just after sundown," he said, "another visitor wandered into Glenlea. He's not exactly a stranger, since he's been here a time or two before, but his coming is always a joy and a pleasure. Now that we've eaten and danced and filled the air with our own voices, it's time to listen to the voice of a true bard of the fae." The selkie motioned to a figure pushing his way through the crowd toward the center of the room.

"Is that enough blarney for you, Liam?" he asked.

A delighted cheer went up from the crowd as the strange Kithain who had earlier been regaling the childlings with his tricks and capers joined Kieran. He had changed clothes since Leigh saw him, and now wore a green velvet tunic over dark green leggings and high, black suede boots. He carried a finely made guitar, secured by an embroidered strap across his shoulder.

Kieran faded back into the crowd as Liam ran a hand through his mop of curly hair before bowing to his audience. He adjusted the tuning pegs on his guitar and strummed the strings once, softly. Then, without any more ceremony, he began to sing.

Within seconds, Leigh sensed that she was in the presence of a gifted performer. Liam's voice was a rich tenor, and its warm, full texture filled the room without any apparent strain on his part. He was well into the song when Leigh realized that she could make no sense of the words and that, furthermore, he had chosen to perform his first number without musical accompaniment.

Her face must have betrayed her puzzlement, because Brit leaned over and whispered in Leigh's ear.

"That's Gaelic," she said. "And the style is called *sean-nos*, using just the voice with no instrumental backing."

Leigh nodded, lost in the sheer beauty of the singer's voice.

all kings

"It's a love song," Brit continued, this time speaking across Leigh to Rasputin. "It tells of a woman's longing for her absent lover who's been gone for seven years."

As Rasputin bobbed his head to signify that he had heard Brit's comment, Leigh thought she heard him mutter "lucky man." Then she ignored the two pookas and surrendered herself to the music.

The bard's second song was in English, and this time he demonstrated his skill with his instrument as well as his voice. Leigh recognized it as an old Irish rebel song her father had sometimes sung for her family. A sharp pang of homesickness made her throat tighten as she realized just how far away from her mortal family she was, a distance that was measured in more than physical miles. *You are farther from them than you think*, a voice inside her—not her own—seemed to say. She brought her attention back to the song and noticed, to her dismay, that Liam seemed to be staring directly at her, a knowing look on his face.

He can't be reading my thoughts, she told herself firmly, but she deliberately blanked her mind just to make certain. The bard finished "Follow Me Up to Carlow" and launched into a rousing drinking song, leading his audience in its sing-along chorus. Despite her usual aversion to sing-alongs, Leigh found herself joining in.

Liam sang for nearly an hour, shifting easily from Gaelic to English as he ran the gamut of old ballads, bawdy tunes and patriotic anthems. Finally, he voiced a quiet "thank you" to his listeners and unstrapped his guitar. Holding it by his side, he began singing "The Parting Glass," and Leigh realized that his concert was at an end.

When he had finished, he bowed again and disappeared into the crowd without waiting for the applause that followed his performance.

"That was lovely, don't you think?" Brit asked, looking at Rasputin as she spoke.

"Absolutely hideous," the pooka agreed. He leaned over and retrieved the shoe he had removed earlier in the evening. "I'll be right back," he said, and hastily moved away from Brit toward the door of the tavern. Halfway across the room, he remembered to limp.

"Look at him, the poor brave thing," Brit said. "Such pain and making such an effort to hide it." She hurried off after him, leaving Leigh alone with her thoughts.

"And what did you think of the music?" a low voice whispered to Leigh. She looked up, startled, to find Liam standing almost directly in front of her, a quirky smile on his handsome face.

"I haven't heard anything that compelling in a long time," she said truthfully. "But why, of all these people, are you asking my opinion?"

"Because although I love the people of this village dearly, it was the presence of you and your companions that drew me here this night. I have a tale to tell and a song to sing for those who seek what was lost and must once more be found."

"You have knowledge of Silver's Gate?" Leigh asked.

"And other things besides," Liam said, sitting down in the chair vacated by Rasputin. "But it's late, and there'll be time enough later in the day for what I have to tell you."

Leigh stifled a yawn and realized that she was, in fact, exhausted from the day's activities.

"Shall I walk you to your cottage?" Liam offered.

Leigh shook her head. "Thanks, but I think I need to find my friends first."

"I'll find you before noon, then," he said. "May your sleep lead you to touch the Dreaming." With a wave of his hand, he turned and sauntered off.

Leigh spent the next few minutes gathering up her oathmates and rescuing Rasputin from Brit's solicitous care. As the companions left the tavern and made their way through the village toward their cottage, Leigh told them of Liam's words.

"He wants to meet with us sometime before noon," she said. "It's so late now that I imagine we'll sleep most of the morning."

Morgan was already asleep on Tor's shoulder when they reached the cottage. Tor carried her into the room she shared with Leigh and placed her on one of the beds, then mumbled "good-night" to Leigh and went to join Rasputin and Valmont in the other bedroom. Leigh climbed into her own bed and fell asleep, Liam's songs still running through her head.

Edmund scurried up the rocky slope, his feet slipping on the loose dirt and wet stones that seemed bent on making his travels as difficult as possible. He had left the others far behind this morning, their voices an indistinct babble further down the hill. At the top of the mountain there was supposed to be a large stone cairn which some said was the grave of Queen Maeve. The twins had said that there were those who maintained that it was actually the home of Mab, queen of the ancient faeries who once lived in Ireland before the Sundering. They had spoken of an old custom that required everyone who visited the grave to add a stone to the cairn, as a way of making sure that whoever was there would stay there. The others had laughed, but had picked up stones from the bottom of the mountain anyway, making a ceremony out of selecting just the right size rock to add to the pile.

Edmund had used the opportunity to get a head start, since he already had a stone to contribute. Among the many trinkets in his bulging pockets was a small piece of volcanic rock taken from the side of Kilauea when he was in Hawaii. The volcano was sacred to Pele, and despite the threat of bad luck to anyone who took a rock from that place, Edmund had helped himself to a souvenir. He stuck his hand in his pocket, just to make certain it was still there. It was, but it seemed somehow larger than he remembered it. He shrugged and kept on walking.

The climb was supposed to take an hour, the twins said, but Edmund felt as if he had been trudging up the slippery slope all day. He looked behind him to see how far he had come and how much distance he had put between him and the grownups. A thick mist seemed to cling to the bottom of the mountain, obscuring his companions.

He realized, then, that he could no longer hear their voices. As he paused, he felt the sun beating down on him. His skin was slick with sweat. He took in a few deep breaths of hot, moist air and turned back to continue his climb. The rock in his pocket seemed to have gained even more weight, pulling at his jeans and slowing his progress. Still, he managed to take a few more steps before he stopped, face to face with a massive pile of dark, blackened rock.

Then he realized that the heat he felt came, not from the sun, but from the steaming stones, and that the fog was not the all-pervasive Irish mist he had heard about, but a thick, sulfurous vapor. The ground shuddered beneath his feat. Below him now came the sounds of battle and he could hear Leigh's voice shouting commands, though the sidhe knight herself remained engulfed in the smoky haze.

"The rock!" he thought in panic. "I have to get rid of the rock. I have to give it back!" He struggled frantically to remove the stone, now more like a boulder, from his pocket, but it would not budge. The rock cairn, now plainly visible as a crater from which spumes of reddish smoke and gouts of flame were erupting, began to glow as the black rocks turned red with the intense heat contained within.

"I'm trying to give it back, you old hag!" Edmund cried, as the weight of the rock and the shaking of the ground underneath him threatened to throw him off balance. "It was a mistake to come here," he screamed, feeling the earth split beneath him, sending him plummeting down into the bowels of the molten earth.

"I'm sorry, I'm sorry, I'm sorry!" he screamed as he fell—

"Edmund!" Glynnis' sharp voice jolted the redcap into wakefulness. He stared at the crumpled pillow he had managed somehow to shove against his side, where his pocket would be had he been wearing his jeans.

"—sorry," he muttered, his voice thick with the taste of something foul and dark on his tongue and his head pounding as if iron spikes had been driven into his brain while he slept.

"Get up," Glynnis said, her voice softer now but still loud enough to send a fresh jolt of pain through the childling's tender head. "The others have been ready for some time now."

Edmund doubled over into a sitting position and sat on the edge of the lumpy bed, his head nearly resting on his knees.

"I feel like shit," he said.

"I'm not surprised," Glynnis said, coming to sit beside him and placing her hands on either side of his head, massaging his temples with a touch that coaxed the pain away from him until he was left with only a dull throb. "How did you like your first taste of stout?" she sounded amused.

"I only had one," Edmund said. "And then I had that cup of poison that Lurgan said would cure me."

"And then you had a bellyful of food. Didn't anyone tell you that you should eat before you drink, not after?"

"Yeah," said Edmund, irked by the sidhe's condescending tone. "You. Just now."

Glynnis stood up abruptly. "Get dressed," she said. "Yrtalien is not pleased at having to wait for you to wake up, but he wouldn't leave without you."

"Where are we going?" Edmund asked, a sinking feeling in the pit of his stomach.

"To a place called Knocknarea Mountain," Glynnis said. "To pay our respects to the grave of Queen Maeve—or Mab."

"I thought going there was Malacar's idea," Edmund said. "Let him go. I want to go back to bed."

"We're all going," Glynnis said. "Including you. The best part of the morning is gone, and we not only have to travel to the base of the mountain but we must—"

"Yeah, I know," Edmund interrupted. "We have to choose a stone to take up there to make sure the old sow stays buried. What'd she do, anyway?"

Glynnis looked at the childling in amazement.

"How did you know about that?" she said. "You were already in bed and dead to the world when Donal told us about that particular bit of quaintness."

"Been there, done that," Edmund said with a nonchalance he didn't feel. "Now, will you leave me alone for a few minutes so I can get dressed?"

 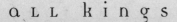

"You have five minutes," Glynnis said imperiously. "That is, unless you want our prince to come in and induce you to get ready." She turned and stalked out of the room, leaving Edmund to his own devices.

"Yeah, like you have a watch," he muttered after she had gone. Then he scrambled to his feet and began pulling on his clothes, checking his pockets as he pulled on his jeans and feeling the familiar—and still small—piece of basalt that had accompanied him all the way from the slopes of Mount Kilauea.

"And you'll stay in my pocket for awhile, yet," he said, taking a deep breath and heading for the door.

From across the street, Signe stared at the entrance to the Toybox Coffee Shop, its gingerbread and icing exterior visible to her faerie sight. She watched as several groups of people, intent on some last minute business on this last day of the year, hurried by the building without noticing anything remarkable about it. To mortal eyes, it appeared to be an empty storefront, one of many enterprises that came and went on a regular basis in San Francisco's Haight Ashbury district. Only those like her, gifted by their own fae natures with the ability to see beyond the mortal facade that protected the freehold from mortal intrusion, could sense that the "empty" shop was more than it seemed.

Signe started to cross the street, then hesitated, as she had done several times in the last hour. *Why am I doing this?* she thought. The last time she had gone inside the coffee shop, she had been with Ryder and, like him, she had hoped to uncover and purge the madness that lay within. Ryder's cursed stone had led them to the site, and from the intensity of the pain caused by the gem, they had been able to determine that the building served as a prime source of the unholy energy changelings referred to as Glamour. They had found more than they bargained for. A powerful faerie treasure within the coffee shop had driven Ryder to his knees, rendering him incapable of action and alerting the changelings within to the presence of intruders. They had been lucky to escape with only a warning.

Convinced she had made a mistake in coming to San Francisco and returning to the site of Ryder's humiliation, Signe turned and headed away from the Toybox. Something stopped her in her tracks. *This is where my fate has drawn me.* The feeling that had brought her here could not be denied. As an eshu, Signe possessed a sense of place that, almost without fail, directed her where she needed to be. Before she had met Ryder, when she was part of Boston's changeling community, an older eshu had once tried to explain the purpose for their kith's particular birthright.

"Each of our lives is a pathway through the Dreaming," he had said. "When an eshu awakens to herself, her feet are set upon a road that she must walk. At the end of her life, when her spirit prepares to rejoin the dream-world for a short time before seeking flesh once more, she is able to look back over her lifepath and trace the distance she has come, charting the course of her life from beginning to end as easily as tracing the path from one place to another on a road map. Not every stopping place is a pleasant one, but all are necessary to make the journey whole."

For a long time, under Ryder's influence, Signe had forgotten her old mentor's words. Now, as she felt the wrongness of her attempt to walk away from her chosen path, she remembered them as if he had spoken them only a few minutes before.

You are eshu, she told herself. *Act like it*. Drawing herself to her full height, Signe fixed her eyes on the coffee shop across from her and let her feet choose their own direction.

The profusion of Glamour within the Toybox took her breath away. The last time she had come here, with Ryder, she had tried to shield herself from what she believed was an aura of collective madness. This time, she surrendered to it, allowing her mortal guise to fall from her like a shed cloak. Finding her own dormant power responding to the pull from the freehold's ambient store of faerie magic, she clothed herself in finery drawn from the hot deserts of the Bedouin and the steamy delta of the Nile.

A few of the Kithain within looked up as she made her stately progress past the tables that filled the center of the room. As she passed the ornate toy chest that rested along one of the side walls of the coffee shop, she hesitated for a moment, sensing the vast amounts of Glamour contained within it. *This is what drew Ryder here*, she thought, glancing sideways at the fancifully carved 19th century steamer trunk that lent its name to the shop. Its potent magic had caused the gem in Ryder's hand to react so forcefully that the Dauntain leader had collapsed in agony in the center of the room. Signe, too, had felt the strong emanations, but had fought them as Ryder had taught her to defend against the seductive pull of Glamour.

Now she let its presence wash over her, bathing in its caress as she proceeded to the bar, where a wrinkled old boggan regarded her curiously.

"Haven't you been here before?" he asked, a guarded challenge in his raspy voice. His round, owlish eyes stared fixedly at her. She could almost see the boggan's mind at work, trying to reconcile her appearance with an image from his memory.

"I am here as a friend," she said, "and as one of the Kithain."

The proprietor's expression changed from curiosity to dawning recognition as she spoke.

"I remember you now," he said. "And the last time you were here, you did not come as a friend. Where's the other one?"

"He will trouble you no more," she replied.

"So what do you want?" There was no mistaking the challenge this time.

Signe placed both hands, palms down and fingers extended, in front of her on the polished mahogany surface of the bar, hoping that the gesture would convey to him that she had nothing to hide.

"I am eshu," she said. "My steps have brought me here to this place and to you." As she spoke, her voice took on the formal cadence of an older time, when words were more than merely sounds that signalled intent. "I come as a supplicant and as one who is willing to lend assistance to those I once pursued."

"Those are fine words," the boggan said, "but fine words are no indication of the heart of the one speaking them. What proof can you give me that you have not come here to harm those under my protection?"

"I have only my word," Signe admitted, "but that I will give you in solemn oath if you will have it so."

"Is this lady bothering you, Fizzlewig?" a husky female voice, low and bordering on menace, sounded from behind Signe. Without moving her head, the eshu glanced sideways and caught sight of a weathered nocker dressed in second-hand chic and sporting a well-worn bomber jacket. A long, white flyer's scarf was wound around her neck and her spiky, multi-colored hair protruded from the sides of her faded cabbie's hat.

Fizzlewig seemed to relax slightly at the presence of reinforcements.

"I think she's all right, Georgia," he said. "I'm just about to find that out."

Signe turned to face the nocker. "My name is Signe," she said. "Among the eshu I am called Shiminege." I haven't used that name in a long time, she thought. "It means one who sees the future."

"I'm Georgia," the nocker informed her. "Just Georgia. It's the name of a state."

Signe nodded gravely, ignoring Georgia's mocking words.

"Will you stand as witness to the oath I am about to take?" She looked at Fizzlewig for affirmation. The boggan's head bobbed up and down.

"We should have a second witness," he began, peering past Signe and Georgia as he spoke, trying to sight a likely candidate from among the Kithain in the coffee shop.

"Hang on," Georgia said and retreated toward the booths that lined one side of the coffee shop. She returned a minute later with a mousy-looking sluagh female in tow. "This is Ellen." Georgia looked at Fizzlewig. "Will she do?"

The boggan's stern features softened as he smiled at the thin-faced sluagh. "Did Georgia explain to you what's going on?" he asked, his voice a loud whisper.

Ellen nodded. "You need two witnesses for an oath of binding," she said, her soft voice barely audible above the background conversation in the coffee shop.

"Shall we do this publicly or in private?" Fizzlewig asked, attempting to sound casual.

Signe bowed her head in deference to the boggan. "I shall do whatever is necessary to demonstrate the truth of my words and the intent of my heart," she said.

"Hmph," Fizzlewig grunted. "I guess we'll take it upstairs, then," he muttered. "No sense in making a public spectacle of a serious matter." He turned away from the three women, opened a door behind him, and disappeared inside what seemed to be the kitchen. After a few minutes, he returned, followed by a boggan youth wearing a white cook's apron.

"Barklie'll watch the store while we're occupied," he said. "Won't you?"

The wilder nodded nervously. Fizzlewig slapped him encouragingly on the back. "Don't worry," he said. "We won't be long and the customers won't bite—at least I don't see any redcaps in here tonight."

Barklie's face registered a look of wild panic until he realized that the older boggan was joking. He ducked his head, a red flush creeping up to the tips of his pointed ears.

Fizzlewig removed his own apron and brushed his clothing smooth as he led the trio of Kithain to another door at the rear of the bar and up a flight of stairs to his private apartment. Inside, the boggan indicated that his guests should assemble in the central area of the large upstairs space, where a few finely crafted chairs arranged around a low table served as his living room.

"Mind your head," he cautioned Signe, tilting his head upward and drawing her attention to the low, sloped ceiling.

"Thankfully, I am not as tall as some of my kith," she murmured. Despite her relative height, she still had a few inches' clearance, stooping slightly nonetheless as she walked carefully toward the center of the room. Georgia sank casually into a heavy, highbacked chair, while Ellen perched on the edge of a smaller lady's chair. Signe settled herself in a chair that matched the one Georgia had chosen, leaving the last chair, a graceful yet sturdy bentwood rocker, for their host.

"I'll be right back," Fizzlewig said abruptly and darted back through the door and down the stairs.

Signe could feel the tension in the room as the three of them waited nervously, casting surreptitious glances at each other, until the boggan returned. In one hand he held a lit candle in a silver candleholder, his other hand cupping its flame carefully. He walked over to the table and placed the candle in its center. Drawing a slender silver dagger from a sheath at his belt, he laid it alongside the candle.

Signe recognized the glow of balefire coming from the candle's flame, its chimeric radiance filled with Glamour. Balefire served as the powering force within a freehold, both the symbol of faerie magic and the literal generator of the enchantments and protections that concealed the havens of changeling society from the ken of mortals.

"In a fancy freehold, we'd do this swearing around the balefire itself," Fizzlewig said, "but that would crowd us up against the kitchen here, so this candle-sized version'll have to do."

Signe nodded.

"Are we ready, then?" Fizzlewig asked.

"I am," Signe said.

"What do we have to do?" Georgia asked the boggan.

"Just listen, and then, when I ask you a question or two at the end, answer as truthfully as you can."

"Sounds simple enough to me," the nocker replied. Ellen dipped her head once in acknowledgment of her readiness.

Fizzlewig turned to Signe and motioned for her to stand and face him across the table. Picking up the candle, he held it in between them.

"Since this is an official oathtaking," he said, "I'd better give you my official name. I am Sir Charles Fizzlewig, holder of the fief known as the Toybox in fealty to House Fiona and the duchy of Pacifica."

Georgia gave out with a low whistle. "That's a fancy mouthful," she whispered to Ellen. The sluagh frowned and placed a finger on her lips in a gesture of silence. Georgia winked and made a zipping motion across her own mouth.

Fizzlewig paid no attention to the nocker's comments, but focused his attention on Signe.

"I charge you on your honor as a child of the Dreaming to subject yourself to the judgment of truth. By the balefire's sacred flame, by the blood that flows within your veins, and by the power of your faerie name, make an oath before all present that you come to us as a friend and that you mean no harm or malice to any Kithain, absent or present, under my protection. Swear that you speak truly, lest the balefire burn, the blood boil, and your name be lost in the mists of forgetfulness."

His speech done, Fizzlewig picked up the dagger with his other hand and held it out to the eshu.

Signe took the dagger from the boggan, holding it in her right hand so that its keen edge glistened in the flickering light of the balefire. Without removing her eyes from Fizzlewig's face, she ran her left palm along the dagger's length, feeling a sharp pain as it opened a shallow cut across the center of her hand. A red line of blood welled up from the wound. *Crossing life, heart and love lines,* she thought. She handed the dagger back to Fizzlewig, who returned it to its place on the table.

"Place your hand in the flame and state your oath," he said, his voice stern and full of authority.

Signe thrust her hand, palm down, into the chimeric flame.

"This is the oath of Shiminege," she said, speaking once more her eshu name. "I swear by my name, my faerie blood, and by the sacred fire that brings the light of magic to a cold and darkened world, that I have come to offer my help to those whom I once hunted and that I will answer truthfully any questions you may put to me to determine the sincerity of my intent. My heart is open to you, my hands are at your service, and my mouth is sworn to speak only the truth to you."

As she crafted the terms of the oath that would bind her, Signe felt the balefire's Glamour as a warm, liquid heat that surged from her hand and coursed throughout her body. *If I did not mean my words,* she realized, *this heat would consume me, burning all my Glamour from me and taking away even the small sense of what I am that Ryder left me. I have fixed my course this day along a path from which there is no returning.*

Fizzlewig waited until he was sure that Signe had finished speaking before he turned to Georgia and Ellen.

"Are you both satisfied that what you've heard is a true oath, freely given?"

"Sounds good to me," Georgia said.

"I am satisfied," Ellen whispered, her voice straining to attain an audible pitch.

"So am I," Fizzlewig said and signalled to Signe that she could remove her hand from the flame and return to her seat. The boggan seated himself in the rocker and folded his hands across his paunch.

"Now," he said in a voice that was almost friendly, "what brings you here?"

"There is a pooka named Rasputin, who, with his friends, started me on the path that brought me to this place. I feel that I am not finished with him or with the others, but there are some things I must know before I begin to search for him."

"Can't you just find him?" Georgia asked. "I mean, aren't you eshu good at that sort of thing?"

"We are," Signe replied. "And coming here was the first step along the path that leads to him. I believe that speaking with you—and demonstrating my good faith—is the second."

"I know who can tell you where he's gone," Ellen said, her voice cracking painfully with effort.

"Why don't you tell us what you know and how you came to meet Rasputin, and then we'll see what we can do for you—and for each other."

Signe started to speak, but the boggan raised a hand.

"Wait," he said, getting up and starting for the door. "Let me go downstairs and tell Barklie that we may be longer than I thought."

"Food might be nice," added Georgia.

Fizzlewig sniffed. "I had already thought of that, thank you," he said.

As Signe waited with Georgia and Ellen in companionable silence for Fizzlewig's return, she began to relax for the first time since coming to San Francisco. Even when she had assumed her faerie self at Ryder's instructions to better infiltrate Kithain society in Hilo, she had still felt out of place. Now, as she exchanged tentative smiles with her sister changelings, the aging nocker cabbie and the shy sluagh, she sensed only the comfort of being wrapped in the warm embrace of the freehold's ambient Glamour.

A few minutes ago, I was a stranger in a city that was not my own, among people who had no reason to trust or love me, she thought. *Now I am among friends again. I have come home.*

"This is it?" Edmund asked, incredulous, as he stared up at the enormous pile of stones that rested atop the summit of Knocknarea Mountain. "It's big, all right, but it's just a huge heap of rocks." In his dream, the stone cairn had seemed larger and more sinister. Under the gray sky of this winter's afternoon, it merely looked old.

Dougal smacked the redcap smartly on the top of his head.

"That 'heap,' boy-oh, is over 200 meters at the base and stands more than 10 meters," the sidhe wilder said.

"That's about 650 feet around and 35 feet high, the way you measure things across the sea," his brother added. "And it weighs 40,000 tons."

"Yeah, but it's just a bunch of rocks. Where's the headstone? I thought this was a grave!"

Yrtalien and Malacar stood off to one side of the mound of stones, their heads bent close in whispered conversation. The satyr seemed to be urging the sidhe lord to some course of action, gesturing toward the prince's neck, then miming the act of holding a small object in front of him at arm's length. Yrtalien shook his head.

Glynnis walked up to the cairn. Finding a space between two larger rocks in the cairn's side, she wedged the rock that she had carried up the mountainside carefully into place. That done, she stepped back and regarded the stone mound, a look of deep concentration on her face.

"There may have been something here once, long ago," she said finally. "But it's gone now."

The brothers added their stones to the cairn and then glared at Edmund. "Oh, yeah," the redcap said and reached in his back pocket for the small, lumpy rock he had selected before the group had begun their ascent. At the same time, he felt with his other hand for the volcanic rock he had taken from Kilauea. *I wouldn't want to get the two mixed up*, he thought, still shuddering at the memory of his nightmare.

"Aren't you gonna dump your rocks?" he called over his shoulder to Malacar and Yrtalien. The prince shot Edmund a withering look. Edmund glanced upward at Donal and Dougal. "He gets put out when you don't address him with proper respect," he said, pitching his voice so that only the twins could hear.

"We noticed," Donal said, a faint smile on his face. "Didn't we?"

Dougal nodded. "Several times, we noticed."

Yrtalien waved his hand dismissively at Malacar, brushing aside the satyr's insistent arguments, and strode toward the group at the base of the cairn. Like the others, the prince deposited his stone amid the other rocks. Malacar limped after him, still wheezing from the exertion of the climb, which had taken its toll on his bad legs and aging body. Almost grudgingly, he added his rock to the cairn.

"I take it this is not the Court of Kings you were telling us about, then," Dougal said.

"All Kings," Malacar corrected him. "And I don't know whether it is or not." He glared accusingly at Yrtalien as he spoke. "I won't know unless you test it with your precious stones," the satyr continued, his voice at once wheedling and accusatory. The prince sighed in exasperation.

"Look, you aging sniveler," Yrtalien said scathingly, "if this overgrown heap of geological rubbish contained even a fraction of the amount of Glamour such a place as your mythical court would have to possess, I would have been able to sense it through the Eyestones long before we reached the top of this mountain. Use your eyes—your eye, if you will. There is nothing here but rocks brought up the hill by every tourist who has ever visited this place."

"You haven't even tried," Malacar muttered. "So large a cairn must contain something important." His seamed face took on a look of sudden inspiration, his single eye seeming to glow with a canniness that had nothing to do with the ruby in its socket. "How do you know that the custom of adding rocks to increase its bulk didn't originate with those who desire to seal away forever the secrets it contains?"

"Hey, goat-face," Edmund said, feeling nervous at the thought of spending any more time near the mound of stones. "If the prince says there's nothing here, there's nothing here, so get over it. You were wrong." He turned to Yrtalien, hoping that the prince would appreciate his show of support. "Can we go now?"

"Edmund is right," Glynnis said, her voice soothing, as she came to stand beside Yrtalien. "We're accomplishing nothing by standing around gawking at a monument to ages past."

"There are those who believe that the cairn is some sort of passage grave," Donal said offhandedly, "although, as you can see, it's never been excavated."

Yrtalien turned toward him, a look of renewed interest on his face.

Oh, great, Edmund thought. *The twins are gonna start something.* "Let's just leave," he mumbled, even though he realized that no one was paying him any attention.

"Or, they may be talking about one of the other tomb sites nearby," added Dougal in a laconic tone that matched his twin's. "There's one on the mountain's eastern spur that has some passing interest to the experts—historians and archaeologists and such."

"We could probably spend the rest of the day just visiting all the stone tombs in the area," Donal said. "Maybe one of them is the place you're so keen on finding."

"Why didn't you tell us of these other places earlier?" Yrtalien asked, sounding peeved.

"This one," Donal said, pointing upward at the pyramidal cairn, "was the only one you seemed to be interested in, and it is supposed to guard the remains of Maeve of Connaught."

"Or Queen Mab herself, if you listen to some folk," Dougal said.

"Look, who is this Maeve or Mab or whoever?" Edmund walked a few steps away from the others and sat on the ground, crossing his legs and propping his chin on his elbows. "If we're gonna just stand here and talk, at least fill me in on what she's got to do with this stupid court Malacar's so hot on finding."

Glynnis walked over to Edmund and sat down beside him. "Yes, Malacar," she said, her voice laced with false sweetness. "Why don't you explain, so that a childling can understand, just why you insisted on dragging all of us up here?"

She's jealous of Malacar! Edmund realized suddenly. *The old fart's got Yrtalien's ear and she feels left out of things—just like I do.* The thought comforted him slightly.

Malacar looked questioningly at Yrtalien. While the others had been talking, the prince had taken up a position leaning against the stones, his face a study in affected boredom. One hand toyed with the neck pouch containing the Eyestones.

"Go ahead, Malacar," Yrtalien said. "Repeat for Edmund's benefit, since he missed the discussion last night, the story our hosts told us about your vaunted Maeve of Connaught. If you acquit yourself well enough, I might reconsider my decision to test the cairn with the Eye of Opening."

"I wouldn't mind seeing that myself," Donal said softly, looking at his brother and arching an eyebrow.

That's what's going on, Edmund thought, seeing the exchange between the twins. *Those sons of bitches just want to see Yrtalien use the gems. They don't really care if there's anything there.*

Malacar cleared his throat, a harsh sound that reminded Edmund of a toilet flushing. "According to legend, or ancient history, Maeve was the queen of Connaught, one of the four great provinces of early Ireland."

"That was about 5,000 years ago," Donal said. "It was very early Ireland."

"Let the scholar speak," Dougal admonished his brother.

"She coveted a fabulous bull owned by the neighboring chief of Cooley, in Ulster, and when he refused to lend it to her, she invaded his lands to steal it."

"The queen was a cattle rustler?" Edmund asked. Dougal snorted in amusement.

"Cattle was a sign of wealth in those days," he said. "Not to mention virility. Those who had the best bulls had the mightiest herds." He looked at his brother and winked.

"Am I missing something?" Edmund asked, glancing back and forth from Donal to Dougal, trying to puzzle out the unspoken messages that darted between them.

"Never mind," Yrtalien interrupted. "Go on with your fascinating tale, Malacar."

The satyr nodded, failing to conceal his annoyance. "The warriors of Ulster had been cursed by the goddess Macha so that whenever they were roused to battle, they would be incapacitated by pain, as if they were women in the throes of labor. Maeve, knowing this, thought it would be a simple matter to help herself to the prize. What she didn't reckon on was the hero Cuchulainn, who was unaffected by the curse. He fought Maeve's forces single-handedly, holding them off for three days until he died from his wounds. The armies of Connor Mac Nessa, the king of Ulster, arrived and drove off the attackers."

"What about the bull?" Edmund asked.

"While the fighting was going on," Malacar continued, "some of the queen's raiders sneaked into Cooley and stole it."

"Huh," said Edmund. "So this great hero died for nothing."

"Most heroes die for nothing," Dougal said. "That's why Donal and I stay as far away from them as possible."

"The bull escaped," Donal said, "and made his way home, where he promptly dropped dead."

"What a wimp," Edmund said. "So why is this queen such a big deal?"

"It's believed that Maeve was strong with the blood of the Tuatha de Danaan," Malacar said.

"The wha—?"

"The oldest of the fae," Glynnis interjected. "It is from them that all other faeries are derived, or so we have been told. They taught mortals how to dream and, when those dreams became dark and violent, they departed this world in sorrow and bitterness."

"They were pretty violent themselves," Dougal said. "The old stories are rife with wars and bickerings to rival the Olympians."

"Huh?" Edmund looked confused. "I thought they were Greek."

Malacar sighed heavily. "The Olympians themselves—including the satyrs—may have been even older faeries," he began, but Yrtalien cut him off.

"Don't start with that tired old theory of yours," he said. "Finish your tale."

"Some even hint that Maeve was, herself, one of those oldest of the fae and that she elected to remain behind after the others had fled." Malacar said, trying to recoup the ground lost by the unexpected digression.

"Why would she do that?" Edmund wanted to know.

"Maybe she wanted to be a big fish in a small pond," Dougal said. "No competition."

"I gather that you subscribe to the theory that she remained behind, then," Glynnis prompted.

Malacar nodded vigorously. "Not only Maeve, but others as well. They may still hold the memory of where to find the Court of All Kings and Silver's Gate—"

"Wait a minute," Edmund said. Glynnis put a hand on his knee to quell a further interruption, but the redcap brushed her hand aside. "I told you what the selkies said about the island that sank. Silver's Gate was there, not on some stupid hilltop!"

"And Maeve is buried here," Malacar snapped, "or entombed here waiting for deliverance."

"You think she's still alive, after all this time?" Glynnis asked. "Under 40,000 tons of stone steeped in the world's accumulated Banality?"

"I think the path to Silver's Gate—wherever it lies—is here, and I suspect that the way to the Court of All Kings may be in this place as well." Malacar's voice rang with defiance.

"You mean you think there may be a faerie road hidden inside the cairn which leads to Silver's Gate? A gateway to a gateway?" Donal looked thoughtful for the first time since the pair had guided their guests up the mountain. He turned his gaze to Yrtalien.

"If that's the case, my lord prince," he said with a sardonic emphasis on the world prince, "then maybe it's worth seeing it stand up to your stones."

"No way," Edmund protested, fearing what was coming. "You were wrong the last time you tried to find a gate," he reminded Malacar. His voice shook with suppressed anxiety.

"There's one way to settle this," Yrtalien announced.

He's gonna do it, Edmund thought, feeling his stomach grow suddenly queasy.

"Don't do it!" the redcap yelled, jumping to his feet to stand in front of the cairn. He saw, however, that Yrtalien had already removed the emerald from his pouch and was holding it in front of him as he began pacing slowly toward the mound of rocks.

"Move aside, Edmund," he commanded, giving the childling a perversely mocking smile. Edmund dove to one side as he saw the Eye of Opening begin to glow, first faintly, then growing in intensity.

"It's gonna blow!" he screamed and threw himself onto the ground, squeezing his eyes shut and covering his head with his hands.

The ground underneath the group gave a single, violent shudder. Edmund screamed as the visions of his nightmare crowded into his mind. Glynnis gasped, and one of the brothers cursed softly. Then everything was quiet. Edmund opened his eyes slowly. He sniffed, half expecting to smell smoke, but breathed in only the chill winter air.

"Get up," Yrtalien said. "The show's over."

Edmund scrambled to his feet. The others stood approximately where he had last seen them, except that Dougal was bent over, rubbing his foot where a stone from the cairn had dislodged itself and fallen onto it. Donal picked up the rock and replaced it in the space where it had been, patting it firmly into place.

"So much for your grand opening," he said, looking at Malacar. Yrtalien, too, gave the satyr a reproachful look and tucked the emerald carefully back into its pouch.

"What happened?" Edmund asked.

"You felt the quake," said Glynnis, her face slightly pale but otherwise expressionless. "That was it. The stone rocked the cairn and one of the rocks fell to the ground."

"There's a wee smidgeon of dust still in the air," Donal said, pointing to a faint wispy trail of what looked like fine smoke in the sky above the cairn. The breeze quickly carried it away.

"Maybe we should check the other places you mentioned," Malacar said.

"No." Yrtalien's barked response carried the sound of finality. "This was a fool's chase spurred by a fool's arrogance," he said, glaring at the satyr. The prince turned to the sidhe brothers and gave them a polished smile.

"Thank you for your indulgence of the whims of an aging grump," Yrtalien said, indicating Malacar as he spoke. "Let us go back down the mountain and decide how best to get on with our real quest."

As they retraced their path down Knocknarea Mountain, Edmund had a thought.

"Whatever happened to Queen Maeve?" he asked. "I mean why do they call that her grave?"

"She died, of course," Dougal said. "King Connor killed her while she was taking a bath."

"That was harsh," Edmund replied.

Freed at last from its stony imprisonment, the thing that had for countless centuries railed at its captivity took to the air in agony and exultation. What she was or who she might have been mattered less to her than the desperate need that propelled her onward. She hungered for Glamour, and the taste of it that she had managed to siphon from the glittering stone that had unlocked her prison only whetted her desire. The bright green source of her deliverance had rebuffed her attempts to sate herself and the dark, opalescent presence of another font of Glamour—curiously tainted with the essence of Banality—had prevented her from lingering near the faerie beings whose natures might have fed her further.

Incorporeal, an immortal longing kept alive by will alone, she traveled on the winds in search of someone who would respond to her fathomless sorrow. She sought another tortured soul to whom she could cry out her millennia of unheard pain. She was swift, she was desperate, and once, long ago, she was one of the fae. Now she was only the remnant of her fading memories. She was the Bean Sidhe.

It was nearly noontime when the oathmates were awakened by Emer pounding on the door of their cottage, carrying large covered plates loaded with brown bread, eggs, sausages, fresh tomatoes and a pot of hot tea.

"I told Brit not to come around until later this afternoon," she said as she hovered over the companions while they made short work of their late morning meal. "I said you had business to attend to that didn't include the likes of her."

"That's too bad," Rasputin said, his eyes twinkling. "I was hoping she'd spend a lot more time with us."

"How's your foot?" Emer asked, a mischievous smile on her face.

Rasputin bit into a slice of warm soda bread and mumbled something incoherent.

"I hope there's still a bit of tea in the pot!" Liam's voice sounded from the doorway. The wilder minstrel wore a heavy woolen tunic over comfortable trousers and carried his guitar slung across his back. His shoulder-length, tawny-colored hair was pulled back at the neck and tied with a green cord.

"Please come in," Leigh said. "We've been expecting you."

Liam entered the cottage and seated himself at the table, laying his guitar carefully on the floor beside him. Emer found a clean mug and poured him a cup of tea.

Leigh began the introductions, but Liam interrupted her, waving aside her attempts at formality.

"I believe I know all of you," he said, "so it only falls for me to introduce myself to those who've not yet met me."

"I met you first," said Morgan. "You pulled a coin out of my ear."

"I did, didn't I?" Liam said. "And do you still have it?"

"Of course I do," Morgan said, reaching for the pouch she wore tied at her waist. "I put it in my pouch last night—it's gone!" Her face registered a look of amazement and consternation.

Liam laughed. "Have you never heard of faerie gold, child?" he asked. "Real as rain until you need it, then— poof!—gone like the mist on a sunny morning."

Morgan's lower lip extended in a pout. "Where did it go?" she asked, curious in spite of her disappointment.

The minstrel shook his head. "Now that would be giving my secrets away," he said. "Why don't you ask him?" He indicated Valmont, who was watching the exchange with studied indifference. Morgan looked up at the eshu.

Valmont shook his head. "Sorry," he said. "There are some mysteries that must forever remain unsolved." Inclining his head to Liam, he nodded a silent greeting. "I hope you are not one of those mysteries," he said.

"I was just getting around to that," Liam said, standing up and bowing with a flourish to the group around the table. "I am Liam—another name for William—O'Keegan, minstrel of the four green fields, singer of songs, teller of tales, a nomad among nomads, and procurer of shiny baubles from the ears of fair young colleens." His last comment was addressed to Morgan and accompanied by a broad wink.

"Not to mention a man of few words," Rasputin said blandly.

"Clurichaun, actually," corrected Liam. "Although you may be more familiar with our other name, bandied about and degraded as it has been."

"What's that?" Morgan asked.

"Why, leprechaun, of course," Liam said. He saw a look of skepticism cross Leigh's face and beamed at her. "I see you're not certain I'm telling the truth."

"We hang around with a pooka," Tor grumbled, helping himself to the last sausage. Rasputin sniffed loudly.

"I protest," the pooka said. "I always tell the truth. It's not my fault if I'm misunderstood."

Leigh still looked dubious. "I always thought lepre—clurichauns, I mean—were supposed to be—" she paused, flustered.

"Shorter?" Liam asked, his eyes wide with innocence. Leigh blushed.

"We are," the clurichaun admitted, "though not so short as the press has made us out to be. I prefer to think of myself as compact—short enough to stand beneath my hat, when I'm wearing one, but tall enough so that my feet reach all the way to the ground when I'm standing on them."

Morgan giggled.

"Do you have a pot of gold?" she asked.

Liam nodded gravely. "Filled to the brim with the very sort of gold that I pulled from your ear last night."

"In other words, you don't have one," Morgan said.

"It's a bit more complicated than just having or not having," the clurichaun responded. "Long ago, when the sidhe departed the world, those of us who stayed behind had not only to take on the appearance of mortals, but we also had to adapt ourselves to a land filled with people who thought of us as demons and devils and other assorted nasties. Some, like the pookas, hid in the form of animals, while others—like the boggans, or brownies as they've come to be called, made themselves indispensable as housekeepers and fix-it-alls. We developed our own mechanism of survival—by making folks think we were wee harmless creatures who rewarded with piles of gold those mortals canny enough to outwit us."

"So mortals who see you really do see you as tiny," Leigh remarked.

"No," the clurichaun said. "They remember that they saw us as tiny. There's a difference."

"Aren't you going to tell them about the drink?" Emer said, a small smile tweaking the corners of her mouth.

"I wasn't," Liam muttered, "but now I suppose I must." He reached for the pot of tea and helped himself to another cup before he spoke. "We have a slight weakness for strong spirits," he said.

Leigh nodded. "My father—my mortal father—sometimes uses the phrase 'drunk as a leprechaun.'" Tor nodded, as if the words were familiar to him as well.

Liam flinched visibly. "Too much liquor makes us either maudlin or mean. The latter afflicts those of us who happen to be feeling Unseelie at the time. It's not something we're especially proud of, but there it is."

"This isn't why you sought us out, though, is it?" Valmont asked.

Liam shook his head. "No, it's not," he said. "Your coming here is something I've been awaiting for quite a few years, now."

"Our coming?" Leigh asked.

The clurichaun nodded. "Yours and that of the stones."

"But we don't have the stones!" Morgan said, her childish voice rising in distress.

"Not now," Liam said. "Or I would have felt their presence, that's for certain. But you did have them and perhaps may again, if you're inclined to follow a bit of advice from a world traveler and a former bearer of one of the Eyestones."

Valmont arched an eyebrow in surprise at the clurichaun's statement. "You had one of the stones?"

"I did," Liam replied. "I gather you know something of the story of how the stones came to be made and how Silver's Gate came to be lost—"

Several heads nodded at once.

"A selkie named Ondine told us the tale," Leigh said. With help from Valmont, she recounted the story of the ancient battle in front of Silver's Gate, one of the last portals to Arcadia to close at the time of the Shattering. "Because the brothers' hatred and pride condemned the selkies to remain trapped in the mortal world, the queen of the selkies cursed them. They turned to stone before the gate and their eyes became the Eyestones."

"Then the queen's anger caused the island to sink under the ocean," Morgan said. "Just like Atlantis."

"That's close enough for a jig," Liam said. "Did she tell you, too, about how the stones were carried away to safety and hidden among the remaining Kithain and their cousins?"

"We know the selkies entrusted the Shadowstone to the menehune of Hawaii," Valmont said. "The Eye of Opening—or the Keystone—showed up in San Francisco in the possession of a satyr. We believe he still possesses another of the gems, the ruby."

"The Changestone," Liam offered. "The satyrs were chosen as guardians of the ruby, the nockers were given the emerald, and we clurichauns were gifted with the sapphire—the Waystone."

"So how come it ended up in the hands of the Dauntain?" Tor asked, his voice a low rumble.

Liam's face grew somber as he looked around him.

"I could lie and say it was stolen from me," he began, "and I could probably convince you that I was telling the truth. But it wasn't that way. Or, I could blame it on the power of the Waystone and maintain that I had no choice in the matter. But it wasn't that way, either."

"Just how was it?" Valmont asked.

Liam shrugged.

"The Waystone had been passed down from generation to generation of clurichauns since it was first given to us, and in its own time it came to me to be the one to carry it. It's the nature of the gem itself to be taken about from place to place, for it is the pathfinder, and it does no good to hide it in one spot. When it was given to me by my predecessor, I guarded it faithfully, letting it take me from place to place—sometimes far from Hibernia. Every place I came to by dint of the Waystone, I learned something new or made new friends—and once or twice an enemy. One night, a few years ago, I found myself in your land, in one of your magnificently huge cities—New York, I think it was—and, as has always been my custom, I gravitated to a little bar in a part of the town heavily populated with people whose ancestors came from Ireland. They had no need of my music, there was already some band of punks making raucous thrashing sounds that hurt my ears, so I turned to the bar—and I turned to the drink."

"I should've known," Tor said. "You got drunk and gave it away." The troll sounded bitter. Valmont placed a hand on Tor's shoulder and murmured a few words to calm him down.

"Well, yes and no," Liam said, his face pained. "There was this man next to me at the bar. I could tell just by looking at him that he was Kithain, one of the sidhe as a matter of fact, but he was so wrapped up in Banality that he almost froze the hairs on my—head." He glanced quickly at Morgan, then looked away. "I'd had somewhat to drink, for certain, but I was nowhere near what you'd call over the wall with it. I struck up a conversation with the man, trying to figure out if he was even aware of what he was. I thought maybe he'd had one too many run-ins with cold iron or colder thoughts and that perhaps I could jog his memory."

"Did you realize that he was one of the Dauntain?" Leigh asked.

Liam nodded. "About the same time as he realized that I was one of the fae," he replied. "That was when it happened."

"When what happened?" Morgan interjected.

Liam stared at the childling for a long moment before speaking. "You are one of the true dreamers, aren't you?" he asked, his voice gentle and sad.

"I have dreams sometimes," Morgan answered.

"And they sometimes come true—though they're not always exactly the way I dreamed them."

Liam nodded. "The same with me," he said. "I realized as I was talking to the man that I had dreamed about him earlier, dreamed and then forgotten it until that moment. As soon as the memory came back to me, the stone began to burn a hole in my pocket, like it was telling me that my time for carrying it was over and it was ready to be passed on to another. It was that simple—and that complicated. I pressed the sapphire into his palm and said something about destiny—I can't recall the exact words—and then left."

The clurichaun fell silent, lowering his head as he finished his tale.

"He's dead," Tor said. "I killed him. That's how the stone came to us."

"You did not!" Morgan said. "You told us he threw himself into the lava after you cut off his hand to stop the pain!"

Liam's head jerked up, a look of surprise on his face. "Lava?" he asked.

"A story for a story," Valmont replied. "And, like yours, this one isn't the most pleasant of tales. It seems our own track record is far from perfect." The eshu recounted the companions' misadventures in Hawaii. As he spoke, Morgan got up from her seat and joined her grandfather, climbing onto Tor's lap and leaning her head against the troll's chest, her eyes blinking back tears.

The eshu paused and glanced at Tor. "Shall I describe what happened on the volcano?" he asked.

Tor shook his head. "I'll tell it," he muttered.

Morgan felt her grandfather tense as he took a deep breath before beginning to speak.

"Dauntain or not, he was a good, solid fighter," Tor said, "and I'm not as young as I used to be. I outmatched Ryder in strength, but he was quicker and might have outlasted me in the long run. We were almost up against the lava stream, trading blows back and forth, when all of a sudden he doubled over and dropped to his knees, clutching his left hand like he was trying to rip it off."

Tor spoke haltingly, his voice sounding strained. Morgan could hear his heart pounding inside his chest. *It wasn't your fault, Grandpa,* she said over and over to herself, hoping that her thoughts would find their way to him and give him comfort.

"He looked up at me and held out his arm. His whole hand was glowing. That's when I realized what he was asking me to do—so I did it. He looked relieved, but I knew that as soon as his brain caught on to what had just happened, he'd be in a lot of pain. Before I could do anything about it, he stood up and just leaned back into the lava. I reached for him, but—"

His voice broke with a harsh sound.

Valmont finished his narrative with their return to the selkies at Point Reyes and their journey to the Irish coast. "That is as much as we know of the fate of the Waystone," he said, looking steadily at Liam.

The clurichaun bowed his head. When, a few moments later, he raised his eyes again, his face was soft with sorrow.

"I had hoped that the Waystone would bring him back to himself," he said quietly. "I thought that its ability to locate sources of Glamour would open his eyes again and make him see the truth he'd been denying for so long."

"It seems to me that you should have known that he would twist the stone's power to his own ends," Rasputin said. "I know I would have been able to foresee the workings of destiny."

"Rasputin's right," Leigh said. "You've no more reason to blame yourself for doing what seemed necessary than we have for making decisions that may not have been the wisest."

"Like asking Edmund to come on the quest?" Morgan said. "I wish I'd never invited him along."

"So that's why there are only five of you," Emer said. "Kieran saw six of you in his dream."

"As did I," Liam said.

"Does everyone around here dream true?" Morgan asked suddenly.

Liam laughed. "Not everyone, but it does seem that this country has an overabundance of people—mortals and Kithain alike—who are gifted with the second sight."

"If you dreamed years ago that we'd come here," Morgan said, "does that mean that we've just been acting out your dream?"

The clurichaun frowned and shook his head. "Not at all," he said. "Time works a bit differently in true dreams, I think. It doesn't take into account things like past, present and future or cause and effect. Your actions up to now determined my dreams, not the other way around."

"Oh," Morgan said, sounding unconvinced.

"So you came here because you dreamed about us," Valmont said.

"I knew that the ones who would return the gems to their place of origin would be coming to Glenlea and that they would need to know more about the nature of the treasures they possessed."

"But we don't have them," Leigh said. "Not

anymore. I'm surprised you weren't drawn to Yrtalien instead of to us."

"He may have them," Liam responded, "but that's not to say that he'll be the one to take them where they need to be. Remember what I said about dreams and time."

"We really have no desire to hear about what the gems do," Rasputin said. "Don't bother to tell us any more than we know already."

Liam chuckled. "I intend to do just that," he said. He reached down and retrieved his guitar, moving his chair back to give himself room to hold his instrument.

"The original rhyme was in Gaelic, or at least the version of it that came to me," the clurichaun said as his fingers began picking out a tune on the guitar. "I've put it into English and given it a bit of a tune to make it easier to remember. Listen."

The path is blue but the door is green;
Black are the shadows that lurk unseen;
Red brings the changes that lie in wait
Over the threshold of Silver's Gate.

One sees the road, one holds the key;
One drains the chill of mortality;
One shapes the fortunes of those who wait;
Four cross the threshold of Silver's Gate.

"Wait!" Morgan cried as Liam started to put his guitar down. The childling climbed down from Tor's lap and ran into her bedroom. A few minutes later, she returned clutching her diary and pen. Reclaiming her seat on her grandfather's knee, she opened the small journal and laid it in front of her on the table. "I want

all kings

to write the words down," she said.

Liam repeated the song more slowly, while Morgan transcribed his words into her diary.

"There!" she said triumphantly when he had finished. "Now we'll have them when we need them." She looked over what she had written. "It's awfully short though. I thought you said you'd tell us all about what the stones did."

"And I will," Liam responded, "at least as much as I know about them. The verse is just a tickler, a quick way of keeping the gems straight in your mind."

"We already know that the Keystone opens things," Valmont said. "Is that the extent of its power?"

Liam shook his head. "That's just the beginning. It not only opens things that are locked, like doors or portals, it can also act as a doorway to the heart or to the mind. The Waystone is a pathfinder, both in the mortal world and along the faerie trods. More than that, it will lead its wearer along the path of his or her chosen dream. The Shadowstone has the power to absorb and transform Banality. In some ways it's the most powerful and the most dangerous of the stones. The Changestone confers the power to change your appearance in the mortal world, but its real magic lies in its ability to transform you into your true self, to restore you to your faerie nature."

"That would be disastrous if it happened in the wrong place," said Valmont.

Liam nodded his agreement. "It's not a power meant to be used this side of the Dreaming," he said. "Have you thought about the consequences of your finding Silver's Gate?" The look in his eyes belied the innocence in his voice.

"Of course we have," Rasputin said quickly. "Everything we've done so far, in fact, has been according to a carefully calculated plan of action.

That's why we're currently without the stones."

"Stop rubbing it in," Tor grumbled. Rasputin ducked his head and tried to look embarrassed.

"Our charge was to find and open Silver's Gate," said Leigh.

"Then what?" Liam asked. "Were you just going to leave it open and walk away from it without even poking your heads inside?"

Leigh felt her face grow hot. "I suppose we thought that when the time came, if it came, we'd know what to do."

Rasputin started to open his mouth, but saw Tor's face and snapped his jaws shut.

"The stones are meant to find the gate, open it, cleanse those who hold them of the taint of Banality and give them suitable forms to wear when they cross over into Arcadia along the silver path."

Of course, Leigh thought, with a certainty that had no relation to her conscious mind. *I've known all along that this would be a one-way journey.*

"That never even crossed our minds," Rasputin said.

"Well, it's crossing them now," Liam responded. "So take a good look at the thought while you have the chance."

"What's the point?" Morgan asked. "We don't have the stones anymore. Even if we knew where to go to find Silver's Gate, without the Eyestones, we can't do anything about it."

"Ah, but that's where I come in," Liam said. "Haven't you been listening to a word I've said?"

"You said you would tell us about the stones," Leigh said, exasperation beginning to show in her voice. "And you've done that admirably. But that still doesn't account for the fact that we are here and the stones are somewhere else—with the Forsworn Prince."

"And with Edmund," Morgan said bitterly.

all kings

"No, it doesn't," Liam admitted. "And that's the other reason I was drawn to Glenlea. The stones aren't the only way to find Silver's Gate, you know. They're just the simplest."

"And what is the other way?" Valmont said. The clurichaun's haphazard manner of imparting information was beginning to tell on the eshu, and his weariness was evident in both his face and his voice.

"I don't suppose you've heard of the Hidden King," Liam said.

"Oh, everyone's heard of him," Rasputin mumbled. "I was thinking about him just the other day."

"No, we haven't," Leigh replied. "We only just got here, remember?"

"And I'm trying your patience," Liam said. "I apologize for that."

"Is this a test or something?" Morgan asked, sounding hopeful.

Liam rewarded her with a soft smile. "In a manner of speaking," he answered. "For the Hidden King will not be found by those who give up easily or who get discouraged when answers don't come to them immediately."

"Tell us about this king," Valmont said. "We would be grateful for any direction you could give us."

The clurichaun's eyes narrowed as he stared at the waiting faces around him. He nodded once, briskly.

"It's been said that if you knock on the door of any freehold in Ireland, you'll find a king or queen in residence there. That's an exaggeration, but it also holds a germ of truth. There are many Kithain who claim the title of king, and some, in truth, are generally recognized as such. But there is no High King in Ireland such as your King David in Concordia. The closest we have to an overall ruler of the fae is the one we call the Hidden King."

"Why is he hidden?" Morgan asked. "Is he running from something?"

"He is," Liam said. "From Banality."

"We're all running from that," Tor said.

"But you have some protection through your mortal bodies," Liam replied. "The Hidden King has no such covering of flesh and bone. He exists solely within his enchanted glen, safe within a pocket of the Dreaming he has trapped this side of Arcadia."

"Are you saying that he is one of the true fae?" Leigh asked, incredulous.

"That's precisely what I'm saying," Liam responded. "There are still a few of them left from the old days, before the Sundering. For one reason or another—either because they got stranded when the gates to Arcadia closed or because they had some compelling reason that kept them from leaving— they remained behind, surrounding themselves with high enchantments so that the world outside could not touch them. They've become prisoners of their own dreams, you might say."

"That doesn't sound at all like what happened to Yrtalien, does it?" Rasputin mused.

"I suspect the principle is the same," Valmont said, "but, unlike him, they seem to have chosen their imprisonment."

"So who is this Hidden King? And what's he got to do with us?" Tor asked.

"Some say he was the last High King of Hibernia, and that he refused to leave the land he had ruled, believing that his going would bring a sadness to the land from which it would never recover."

"Does he have a name?" Morgan wanted to know.

"I'm sure he does," Liam said, "but it's not known to me."

"Where is he, then?"

all kings

"If I knew where he was, then he wouldn't be 'hidden' now, would he?" The clurichaun's eyes sparkled as he bantered with the childling.

He's enjoying this far too much, Leigh thought.

"Well, if you don't know who he is or where he's hiding, then what good is he?" Morgan sat back, impressed with her own logic.

"It is said that he still keeps a court of sorts, and that there are some sidhe who consider him their liege, bringing their problems to him and letting him know what is going on in the world outside his glen."

"How?" Leigh asked.

"He speaks through their dreams," Liam said. "His lords and ladies travel to the edges of his glen and camp there for the night. When he has need, he sends them dreams. I suppose it works in reverse as well."

Yrtalien spoke in dreams before his release, Leigh realized. *That's how he managed to arrange for us to find his prison.* Suddenly, the clurichaun's words carried more meaning than they had before. Liam stared intently at Leigh.

"You know the truth of my words," he said. Leigh could only nod. Once again, she felt as though the minstrel could read her thoughts.

"He spoke to you, didn't he?" Valmont asked in a voice that intimated that he already knew the answer.

"I've said that I'm a true dreamer," Liam responded.

"Then you've been to his glen," Leigh said.

"I didn't say that," Liam countered. "I've been to a forest near the Derryveagh Mountains where I spent the night and dreamed a dream, but I can't say for certain that I visited his glen. I will say that I was near enough for his sending to reach me."

"Is that the dream that brought you to us?" Valmont asked.

Liam nodded. "The very one," he said.

Rasputin sighed with apparent relief. "I thought I was the straightforward one around here," he said. "That was an incredibly direct way of telling us that this Hidden King sent you here to find us."

"I'm glad you appreciate my subtlety," Liam said. "Your kith doesn't have a lock on circuitousness, after all."

"Then it seems that we need to go spend a night in the woods," Leigh murmured.

"Something like that," Liam agreed.

"Will you take us there?" Morgan asked.

"I was thinking of offering to act as your guide," the clurichaun responded. "Unless you'd rather someone else do the job. I'm certain Brit would be more than happy to steer you around the countryside, though it's doubtful she could find the spot where the king's glen lies."

Rasputin paled. "What a marvelous idea!" he exclaimed in a panicky voice.

Leigh looked questioningly at Emer, who had been listening quietly to the lengthy discussion.

"What about you or Kieran?" she asked. "Will you come with us?"

The selkie shook her head. "Neither of us likes to get that far from the sea," she replied. "You're better off with one of the landfolk." She waved a hand in Liam's direction. "I think you could do far worse than have Liam for a guide."

"I'm inclined to agree," Valmont said. "After all, he was sent to us."

Liam watched the discussion with an amused look on his face. "If I didn't know better," he said, "I'd believe that you were making me dance to my own tune."

Morgan stood up from her seat and walked over to Liam. The childling curtsied formally before him.

"Liam O'Keegan," she said, "we'd be honored if you would act as our guide to where we can find the Hidden King."

"I thought you'd never ask," the clurichaun replied.

"How soon should we be on our way?" Leigh asked.

"I think that in the morning will be soon enough," Liam said. "One more night in Glenlea, especially the night that marks the passing of the old year in the mortal world, can't hurt anyone."

Below her, as she traveled through the night, driven by hunger and longing, she sensed a source of what she needed most, a gathering of Glamour that beckoned her as a beacon draws a ship to safe harbor. Her formless spirit circled high above the small collection of cottages that nestled in a valley amid low rolling hills. Her faerie sight, all the keener for her lack of mortal eyes, recognized the village for what it was—a place that had no location for those blind to the Dreaming. She drifted lower, unable to resist the intoxicating profusion of concentrated faerie magic.

Silently, like the wind upon which she traveled, the Bean Sidhe glided through the quiet streets, past darkened houses and shuttered shops. She tasted the dregs of the festivities that had only just ended, savoring the ghostly echoes of harps, fiddles, and raucous laughter that had faded from the range of corporeal hearing. The ambient enchantment washed over her and, though she was unable to grasp the power that sustained the freehold itself, she followed its pull toward a source from which she could derive the Glamour she needed.

Deep within her, something dark awoke, emerging from dormancy to surround her with a malignant craving. Part of her, yet apart from her, it permeated her being with its own warped presence, bearing about it the stench of the

166

death that should have been hers but which had somehow been denied her. Caught between life and death, existing in a nightmarish dream of eternal dying, the Bean Sidhe felt her torment rise up within her, rising as an anguished scream of desolation.

She sought a victim from among the beings whose Glamour she sensed all around her. Her attention focused on a cottage at the end of the street, where a fellow sufferer groaned inside his troubled dreams.

Rasputin stood atop the highest point of Slieve League, his back to the sea that crashed nearly 2,000 feet below him. Trapped by the pair of Dauntain who had followed him halfway across the world, the pooka held his ground while his companions fled to safety. "It's me you want!" he shouted at the female troll and her human ally.

He reached within him, trying to tap his store of faerie magic before their attacks could overwhelm him, but found only an emptiness inside. He looked down, and saw that he was standing on a dark-stained rock from which a sickening cold radiated, permeating his body and eating away at his faerie essence. Iron, he realized, just before his attackers struck with their iron-tipped clubs. He collapsed, losing consciousness.

He woke in a small bare room. Although his eyes were closed, he knew that he was not alone. He was lying on what felt like a concrete floor, and his body felt bruised from the blows he had taken. Cautiously, he opened his eyes and found himself staring at a pair of worn work boots.

"No," he whispered to himself as he recognized the figure who loomed over him clutching a heavy belt in one hand, a look of vindication on his hardened, weathered face.

"Rafael," his father said coldly, raising his arm to strike the helpless pooka. "You have run away from me for the last time."

Rasputin tried to roll away from the blow but the wall trapped him. Covering his head with his arms he opened his mouth to scream—

The mournful howling cut through the dreams of everyone in the cottage, jolting them into wakefulness.

Morgan threw off her covers and launched herself across the room toward Leigh, who now sat bolt upright, her hand groping for something she could use as a weapon.

"What was that?" Leigh's question hung unanswered in the air.

Morgan wrapped her arms around Leigh's neck and buried her face in her companion's shoulder. Leigh put one arm around the shivering childling and held her close, trying to provide a comfort she did not feel.

In the other bedroom, Valmont wrestled with a screaming Rasputin, trying to waken the pooka from his nightmare. Tor hurled his bulk from his bed and grabbed for his axe.

"Get the others," Valmont snapped. "I can't wake him."

Tor rushed from the room, crossing the distance between the two bedrooms in a few broad strides and shoving the door to his granddaughter's room open with his shoulder. He took in the sight of Morgan huddled protectively against Leigh and nodded brusquely.

"It's Rasputin," the troll said. "He—"

Leigh rose from the bed, transferring Morgan into her grandfather's arms. Then the sidhe knight hastened to Rasputin's side. Valmont looked up at

Leigh's arrival, his dark face full of concern. Rasputin continued to scream hoarsely, his eyes fixed on something visible only to himself.

"I've tried shaking him and slapping him," the eshu said. "Nothing seems to work."

Leigh laid her sword down and knelt by the pooka's side. Tor, with Morgan in his arms, stopped just inside the doorway.

"Rasputin," she called softly, hoping that her voice would penetrate whatever dread imagining held him in its grasp. The pooka failed to respond.

"He's starting to fade!" Morgan cried. "Do something!" Tor let his granddaughter slide to the floor and followed as she approached Rasputin and the others.

The room around Morgan grew hazy and indistinct as she neared the pooka's bedside. Morgan caught a slight movement out of the corner of her eye and turned to focus on the source, gasping at what she saw.

A majestic faerie woman with hair like golden flames and a look of untellable sorrow on her noble face shimmered into view beside the tormented pooka. Morgan's eyes grew wide as she watched the figure gently stroke Rasputin's hair. Glamour seemed to pour from the pooka into the lady's fingertips, coursing through her body and setting it aglow with magic.

"You're hurting him!" Morgan said, knowing as she formed the words that they were not audible to her companions.

"I hunger," the woman whispered, her voice filled with tears and longing. "He feeds me."

"Please stop," Morgan begged. "Please leave him alone."

The woman turned to the childling and Morgan could see a sick shadow surrounding her like an aura of hatefulness. "Make that leave him alone," she said, pointing, not at the woman, but at the shroudlike emanation that clung to her. The golden-haired woman stared at Morgan, her eyes searching the childling's face as if trying to read her soul. She drew back from Rasputin and seemed to struggle with herself, her face exhibiting warring emotions as Morgan watched, fascinated despite her worry.

"Who are you?" the childling asked.

The woman shook her head. "I had a name," she responded, "but it went from me. I was a queen, but that, too, is gone. I am nothing but my pain."

"You've taken too much from him," Morgan said. "It's time for you to go."

The faerie woman extended her arms and seemed to grasp the darkness that surrounded her, pulling it closer to her and forcing it into herself. Shaking her head so that her long golden hair swirled about her like a cape, she gave a bittersweet laugh and stepped backwards into the corner of the room.

"You have seen me as I am," she said, "and you do not shrink from me. For your kindness, I will depart."

"You're very beautiful," Morgan said, "except for that icky thing that hurt Rasputin." She thought she saw the woman's eyes crinkle in a half-smile as the figure began to grow transparent, fading into a wisp of smoke that drifted upward and out of the room through the thatched roof.

Morgan blinked and became aware of her companions.

Rasputin moaned once and stopped thrashing. His eyes regained their focus and filled immediately with tears.

"I feel ecstatic," he whispered, slumping against Valmont, who gathered the weary pooka into his arms and clutched him fiercely. Morgan joined them, hugging Rasputin from behind. Leigh looked up at Tor, a puzzled expression on her face. The troll, equally at a loss to explain Rasputin's sudden recovery, shrugged.

"What just happened?" Leigh asked.

"She's gone," Morgan said.

The companions heard a commotion outside the room. Tor turned around and saw Liam hurrying into the house.

"You're too late," Tor muttered. "It's all over."

Liam squeezed past the troll and entered the bedroom.

"Is everyone all right?" the clurichaun asked, his face lined with worry.

"Rasputin had a nightmare," Leigh said. "It took some time to wake him up. Did you hear his screams?"

Liam shook his head. "It wasn't his screams we heard," he said gently. "It was the cry of a Bean Sidhe. The whole village is awake and wondering who her victim was."

Leigh felt her face grow pale. She had grown up in a household steeped in Irish legends and had heard stories of pookas and faeries long before her discovery that she, herself, was one of those magical creatures. Her father's tale of the banshee, the wailing spirit that heralded an approaching death, had frightened her when she was young.

"What does it mean?" she asked the clurichaun, unwilling to voice the superstition that her father had attached to the dreaded creature.

"The Bean Sidhe's wail can cause a body to sicken and die," Liam said bluntly, "and it can drive the Glamour right out of one of the fae, which is just as bad, if not worse." He stared at Rasputin. "He's looking a little fuzzy," he pronounced.

The pooka extricated himself from his companions' embrace and shrugged. "I'm fine," he said. "Just let me get back to sleep."

"Not yet," Liam said. "You've lost something that needs replacing." The clurichaun reached inside his vest and withdrew a silver penny whistle.

"A little music may help restore what's been taken from you," he said. Putting the whistle to his lips, he began to play a delicately lilting melody that filled the room with its joyous sounds. As the song progressed into more and more complex rhythms, Rasputin seemed to grow stronger and his pooka nature solidified around him once more.

We almost lost him, Leigh thought. Without missing a note, the clurichaun nodded solemnly at her, as if he heard her unspoken words.

Morgan settled herself on the bed, sitting between Rasputin and Valmont, who had once more resumed his air of cool detachment. Tor and Leigh sat on the large cot that served as the troll's bed. The companions listened as Liam's music worked its soft, soothing magic, driving away the earlier terror and replacing it with a warm, melancholy joy.

"She was very sad," Morgan whispered to no one in particular, but she thought she saw Liam give her a knowing wink.

all kings

part

chapter

two

six

Sorcha urged her mount deeper into the oak woods, certain that she had left the others far behind. The dun-colored mare responded to the faerie knight's skilled hands on the reins, weaving in and out of the trees with a sureness born of years of trust between horse and rider.

This time, they'll not find me, Sorcha thought grimly. It was against the rules of the hunt to use fae magic to conceal herself, but even so, the young sidhe noble was tempted by the thought of how easily she could shift the appearance of the trees just enough to confuse her pursuers. She shook her head, pushing the thought from her mind. The last time she had tried to trick her fellow Riders, she had suffered for it. For a week, none of the others would speak to her or otherwise acknowledge her presence.

As the youngest and newest of the Silver Court's Riders, Sorcha too often found herself selected as the target for the diversionary games that occupied much of the courtiers' time between more formal gatherings. Today's "hunt" was the idea of Lord Tiernach, the ranking knight and acknowledged leader of the elite group of noble changelings. He'd remarked that even though the last redcap had been driven from the vicinity of their liege's resting place, the broad expanse of forest that spread, in the mortal world, over much of the Derryveagh Mountains and which grew even deeper and more vast within the circumference of its enchantments, the Riders needed to keep their hunting skills sharp.

"Your 'cap' looks red enough to me, half-blood," he'd remarked to Sorcha, staring pointedly at the dark red curls that framed her face. She had tried to protest that it was already the third time in as many weeks that she had been given the least enviable role to play in the Riders' sport, but the others had backed Tiernach, leaving her with the choice of acceding to their decision or breaking the unwritten code of obedience.

Until she performed some feat that sufficiently impressed her fellow knights, she would remain the least among the best. *And with Tiernach and Rowena to impress, that day will be a long time coming*, she thought. Lady Rowena had sponsored her to the Riders, but the steely-eyed Fiona knight seemed determined to show no favoritism toward her ward. In fact, she was often a harder taskmaster than the other knights, reminding Sorcha frequently that in order to "overcome the disadvantage of her birth," she would have to prove herself more than equal to the "true nobility" to earn her place among them. Only Sir Odhran consistently showed her the courtesy due a fellow knight, but his patronage was suspect since he, too, labored under the stigma of being born into the wrong house. *At least they don't claim that he's less than a true sidhe. Members of House Liam may be labeled as oathbreakers, deserving of the title or not, but all agree that they are full-blooded fae.*

Sorcha felt a small knot of anger form in her chest as Lord Tiernach's epithet rang once again in her ears. When, centuries ago, the other noble Houses fled for the safety of Arcadia, the sidhe of House Scathach refused to abandon the world of mortals. Like the commoners who remained behind, they had chosen to harbor their faerie natures in human flesh, intermingling with mortal bloodlines and strengthening their ability to withstand the onslaught of Banality. They welcomed the return from Arcadia of the other noble Houses, whose hidden places they had managed to preserve and defend with some degree of success throughout the lonely centuries in which they kept alive the memories of the sidhe in the minds of mortals. But their reunion with their kithmates had been less than happy. The newly arrived fae of Houses Gwydion, Fiona, Eiluned, Dougal and Liam had looked with scorn upon their "tainted" cousins, making it clear that they considered all the descendants of Scathach to be half-breeds, barely higher than the commoners.

Privately, Lady Rowena counseled patience, a virtue the headstrong Sorcha found difficult to cultivate.

"How many times must I prove myself?" she once asked her mentor.

Lady Rowena's answer seemed to sum up all Sorcha's frustrations and bitterness.

"As often as is necessary," the elegant sidhe noblewoman had replied. "And every time it is necessary. One failure is one too many."

And so Sorcha, from the day of her introduction to the Rider's august company, had tried to ignore the guarded—and not so guarded—insults, the oblique references to her "curious" heritage, and the constant testing of her mettle, hoping that one day she would be accorded the full honor of her noble calling.

At least they cannot deny me the right of Dreaming in the Glen of the Hidden King, she thought as she moved a few steps deeper into the woods. The trees around her now were very old, older than their counterparts in the mortal world. Oak and ash, yew and birch, their primeval splendor existed only in the king's protected realm. Once the island held vast stands of trees. Now only a few protected woodlands remained in all of Ireland. The forest in which

178

Sorcha and her companions took their sport lay encapsulated in one of those preserves, but only those with faerie sight could find the hidden trails that led beyond the boundaries of the physical world. And only those who found favor with the king whose Glamour warded this ancient remnant of forest could penetrate beyond the fringes of the forest freehold.

In the distance, Sorcha heard the sharp crack of a snapped twig break the stillness of the forest. The others had picked up her trail and would be coming after her if she did not take steps to elude them. The terms of the hunt required her to evade her pursuers from dawn to sunset, still a little more than an hour away. Already, she had gone deeper into the forest than customary. She dared not go deeper still lest she betray the pact that existed between the Riders and the king they served. As one of the few true sons of the Dreaming, the king could not bear close contact with the mortal world. His faerie nature, unprotected by human form, condemned him to remain apart from those he ruled, appearing to them only in dreams.

Entering the glen's outer circle was a privilege granted the Riders. On certain nights, they would go still deeper into the woods, to a small clearing where they would make camp and spend the early evening feasting and dancing, as their ancestors once did in the time before the Sundering. Then they would sleep, and in their dreams the king would come to them to hear and give counsel. Despite the claims of royalty made by others of the sidhe, the Riders of the Silver Court knew who truly held the lands of Hibernia in trust.

But that is neither here nor there, Sorcha thought as now the winds brought the sounds of voices and the careful plod of horses hooves. *This time the "fox" will win in this game of fox and hounds*, she told herself. She slipped to the ground, slapping the rump of her mare as she landed. "Go," she whispered to the animal, sending it away from her toward the outer boundary of the forest. Finding a tree with a sturdy lower branch jutting out above her head, she leaped, catching it with her hands and pulling herself up.

The warriors of House Scathach fight with more than weapons, she thought grimly, settling herself into a comfortable position among the leafy branches. In this part of the forest, a perpetual summer ignored the passing seasons of the world outside. Deeper within the freehold, it was rumored, existed spring glades and autumn bowers. Only winter's bare and lifeless shroud was barred from the king's domain.

From her perch, Sorcha listened as the sounds of horses and hunters moved farther away, following the trail of her unburdened mare. She smiled to herself. For once she would not have to bear the humiliating taunts of her fellow knights for allowing herself to be caught.

She caught sight of a figure moving on foot carefully through the trees. Fearful that one of the Riders had discovered her ruse and decided to backtrack, Sorcha held her breath as the shape of a young man became visible below her. *Not man*, she corrected herself, seeing the elongated ears that draped the sides of the figure's expressive face. Pooka.

She watched as the strange pooka stopped for a moment, leaning against a slender white birch and looking around him anxiously. *No doubt he's lost*, she thought. *But he shouldn't be here at all.* She started to climb down from her hiding place to deliver notice to him that he was trespassing, when a large red deer burst into sight, bolting across the path of the startled pooka and disappearing further into the forest.

Almost immediately, the strange Kithain hurried after the beast.

"No!" Sorcha cried out. Quickly she scrambled down from the tree, dropping the last few feet to land silently on the soft, moist earthen floor of the forest. The deer—and the pooka who followed it—were headed straight for the forest's center, into the forbidden heart of the Hidden King's dwelling. The Scathach knight's face hardened as she turned from hunted to hunter in the space between heartbeats.

Fortunately, neither deer nor pooka took any thought for covering their trail. Though they were out of sight, Sorcha could see the marks of their passing. Soundlessly she moved through the trees, her keen eyes sighting the cloven-hoofed depressions made by the deer and the clumsy shoe prints of the pooka.

She felt the change as she crossed from outer circle into inner forest. Her hair crackled with the upsurge of Glamour that seemed to emanate from the trees themselves, and she felt the last vestige of her mortal form begin to fade from her. At the same time, she noticed that the footprints had changed, too. The king's magic protects him well, she thought, as she noted and followed what had become the small paw prints of a hare.

Lord Tiernach was the first to notice the subtle change in the nature of the forest, a slight ripple in the air that signaled a breach in the enchantments that warded the king's freehold. He turned in his saddle to catch the attention of Lady Caitrin, his hunt partner.

"Someone has entered the forest," he said. Caitrin reined in her mount, quieting the animal with a hand on its neck, and listened. After a moment, she nodded.

"You're right," she said. "This has not happened in some time."

Tiernach thought of the clurichaun they had recently surprised in the Dreamers' Glen, then eliminated the possibility that the fellow might be making a return visit. The forest itself had taken no notice of his presence and it was only luck that brought the Riders to his campsite and then only after he had already spent the night undisturbed in the clearing. For whatever reason, the enchantments had accepted his presence, so it was unlikely that a return visit would cause the almost tangible sensation that now prickled the hairs on Tiernach's neck. This was something else entirely.

"Shall I tell the others?" Caitrin asked. She was already turning her horse as she spoke. Tiernach nodded, grimly. If there were strangers in the forest, it was the Riders' responsibility to investigate lest someone trespass who might endanger the king. This was the event for which all their mock hunts prepared them.

"Tell them to spread out and cover the whole of the outer circle," he said. "Bring any strangers you find to the Outer Court."

"And Sorcha?" Caitrin's voice carried a faint hint of distaste, born partly of her Eiluned snobbery and, Tiernach knew, partly from jealousy that already Sorcha was more skilled than she in stealth and weaponry.

"Don't worry about our erstwhile 'fox,'" Tiernach said. "This time, our quarry is real."

Liam had warned them when they arrived at the outer edge of the forest that it was no ordinary wood.

It had not taken them long to travel from Glenlea to the Derryveagh Mountains, tucked away in the northwest corner of Ireland. The clurichaun had provided them with two cars and they were able to drive for most of the distance. For the last hour, however, they had been traveling by foot through the low mountains.

"These are not like your Rockies," Liam said, when Morgan remarked that the highlands looked more like hills than mountains. "But what they lack in height, they make up for in age. They are some of the oldest mountains in the world—as old as your Appalachians. In fact, they're part of the same chain, only separated by a couple of thousand miles of ocean." The clurichaun pointed out Errigal mountain to them, its conical top rising two thousand feet above them.

"If you climb to the top, you'll find that there's not much room there, unless you're a goat or some other creature with good balance. But the view is magnificent."

Following their guide, the companions found themselves approaching a forested area filled with oak trees. "This is actually part of the National Park," Liam told them as he led them through the woods. "We've just come in by a less well-known route. I didn't think you'd want to bother meeting with a lot of tourists and official folk."

As they moved farther into the forest, the light shifted, growing darker and greener as the heavy growth of trees filtered the sunlight through the leafy canopy.

"Keep close to one another," Liam warned. "When I came here, I had no one else but myself to keep track of, but the twists and turns of the path can be confusing."

"What path?" Tor grumbled as he attempted to sidestep a fall of deadwood. Beside him, Morgan giggled and leaped nimbly over the obstacle.

"Oh, there's a trail," Liam assured him. "But it's not made for just anyone to find." The clurichaun looked up at Valmont, who walked next to him, and smiled. "Your sort should be familiar with the winding road of circumstance."

Valmont nodded, too intent on trying to sense a pattern to the clurichaun's movements to answer. Liam chuckled.

"There's no rhyme or reason to finding the way," he said. "It's more a matter of feeling where the Glamour's strongest and letting yourself be led."

"Since when did it suddenly become summer?" Leigh asked, stopping abruptly as she realized that the trees around her were in full foliage. "It's January and these are oak trees. Their leaves should be—"

"—on the ground?" Liam finished her thought.

"We've obviously been traveling through here far longer than we suspected," Rasputin offered. "Maybe we should think about eating something." The pooka ducked his head to avoid a low-hanging branch.

"It's not been that long," their guide responded, his eyes sparkling with amusement. "But we have left the sight of mortal eyes, if any were here to see us. This is a sure way of knowing that we've entered the king's territory."

"Unless, of course, it happens to be summer when you come here," Valmont said.

"The change is obvious in any season," Liam assured him. "Look at yourself. Look at the others, for that matter." The clurichaun halted his progress and turned around to face the oathmates.

"He's right!" Morgan exclaimed. "We don't look like ourselves anymore. I mean, we look like we should look—only more so!"

Leigh stared at her companions and saw that Morgan's outcry was, if anything, an understatement. Even in Glenlea, where they were surrounded by a profusion of Glamour, their mortal forms still clung to them like a shadow that was barely perceptible but visible nevertheless. Here, it was as if the flesh that encased their faerie natures no longer existed.

She looked at Valmont and her heart seemed to stop as she realized that she had never fully seen an eshu until now. *He is as dark as a moonless sky*, she thought, unable to tear her gaze away from his tall, muscular form. Clad in flowing robes of crimson and gold, his scimitar gleaming from its place at his sash, he embodied the spirit of a kith whose culture was ancient and full of mysteries. Valmont caught her eye and inclined his head, a small smile on his angular, sharp-boned face. *He sees me as I am as well*, she thought. No, she corrected herself. *He sees me as I was before my exile from Arcadia.*

Quickly, she turned her head away from Valmont and found herself staring in amazement at Rasputin. The pooka's rabbit features were plainly evident in his long velvety ears and wide-spaced, liquid eyes. Dressed in a russet and dark green tunic with slashed sleeves, he seemed ready to take center stage in some lavish entertainment. He was the duke's jester, she remembered. He leaned casually against a tree, but Leigh could see his powerful haunches—and they were haunches, not thighs—tensed as if ready to spring away at the slightest sign of danger. *Not your average bunny*, she thought.

Morgan's delighted laughter caught her attention next. The childling captured the essence of the term 'fairy princess' as she pirouetted in front of Tor. Her delicately pointed ears and ethereal features could never be mistaken for those of a mortal child.

In Tor, the change was most apparent. The troll loomed over his companions like a mountain come to life, his craggy face crowned by a pair of ridged horns, the hallmark of his kith. Leigh's throat grew tight as she remembered how near they had come to losing him.

"Don't gawk so," Liam spoke, touching Leigh's shoulder lightly from behind her. "You're a sight to behold, yourself."

She whirled around to see that the clurichaun was in the middle of performing a deep, courtly bow. He raised his head and winked at her. His own features were sharper than she remembered, and he moved with a suppleness that made her believe that he could, perhaps, disappear in the blink of an eye.

"He speaks truly, Dame Eleighanara," Valmont said, his voice formal, as if he were addressing her in front of the duke's court. "The beauty of the sidhe is no exaggeration, if you are an example."

Leigh blushed at the eshu's compliment.

"We are all beautiful," she said, feeling suddenly self-conscious. She looked down at herself and saw that she was clad in her knight's armor, its chimerical substance shimmering in the forest's dappled light.

"Just don't be turning on your natural charm," the clurichaun warned her jokingly, "or we'll spend the rest of the day basking in your glory."

"Stop it," Leigh said, lowering her head. "We came here for a reason and I think we need to get on with it."

Liam nodded. "Remember what I said about staying close to one another," he cautioned. "This," he said with a gesture that encompassed the group, "is just a small part of the power of this place. It gets even more intense the farther we go into the forest."

Once more he began leading them through the woods.

Morgan reached for Tor's hand as the group turned to follow the clurichaun. Valmont dropped back and let them pass, then held out his hand for Leigh to take. "We might as well not take any more chances than we need to," he said.

Leigh regarded his outstretched hand for a moment before clasping it firmly.

"No excuses," she said, surprising herself. "This is the way it should be."

Valmont's impassive face softened. Behind them Rasputin sniffed loudly. Laughing, Leigh extended her other hand to the pooka.

They grew silent as they picked their way through the dense forest, contenting themselves with listening to the rustle of small creatures hidden in the underbrush and the occasional chitter of squirrels high in the branches overhead. A few minutes later, Rasputin stumbled as his foot found a soft spot in the forest floor, letting go of Leigh's hand to regain his balance without pulling her down.

Leigh and Valmont took a few more steps before they stopped to let Rasputin catch up with them, but when they turned around, they saw only the endless depth of the forest behind them.

"Wait!" Leigh called ahead to the others. "Rasputin's gone!"

"I don't think they can hear you," Valmont said to her. "They're no longer in sight either."

"So Ireland has no High King or Queen," Yrtalien remarked, watching from the passenger's seat of Dougal's mini-van as the countryside unfolded around

all kings

him. Intent on the winding road ahead, Dougal nodded absently.

"The position is what you might call open," Donal answered. "Are you interested in applying for the job?" The sidhe wilder sat between Glynnis and Malacar in the back seat. Consigned to the very back of the van, Edmund twisted around to kneel on the seat so that he could stare out the rear window.

"Aren't there any cities in this country?" he called out, bored by the procession of rolling hills and small cottages that marked their passing.

Donal snorted. "You've just been in Sligo," he answered. "If you want a big city, we'll have to go all the way to Belfast or Dublin or else down to Cork, but I don't think that what your prince is looking for will be found in any of those places."

"So we're stuck driving around looking for rocks, huh?" Edmund said. "How come you're so sure Silver's Gate isn't in the middle of a city?" he asked. "We found a gate in the middle of San Francisco."

"I know because of the stones," Yrtalien said, the testiness in his voice quelling further argument on Edmund's part.

He's lying, Glynnis realized. *The gems aren't telling him anything. If they were, we wouldn't have to rely on an escort to shepherd us about from place to place in search of Silver's Gate.* The sudden insight made her smile. It was strangely comforting to know that the Forsworn Prince's powers had some limits. He had claimed that once the stones were all together, they would prove an unerring guide to the lost Arcadian gateway, but so far, he had only used them to assess the amount of Glamour in any given area.

After their return from the abortive visit to Maeve's cairn, Yrtalien had spent the evening at the brothers' house poring over maps of the island. When she had dared to ask his purpose, he had told her he was familiarizing himself with the lay of the land. Now, Glynnis felt certain that the prince had been searching for likely places for the gate's location. If and when they found Silver's Gate, he would undoubtedly claim that he had been led by the stones.

Involuntarily, she glanced at Malacar, seated on Donal's other side, his face turned, like Yrtalien's, toward the window. Does he suspect as well? she thought. She almost pitied the satyr, caught as he was in his private dream that there once existed a court in which all faerie races were represented equally by their own kings. The egalitarian nature of the modern world fostered such notions in the minds of commoners. Like the others who arrived in the mortal world, part of the great return of the sidhe in 1969, she had been shocked at the changes that had taken place since the Sundering. She had spent the first few years of her enforced exile studying the tides of history and following the growth of the popularistic ideal. Thus, although she sided with the nobles in the Accordance War which established the right of the sidhe to rule over the changeling fae, she understood the grievances of the commoners who had survived for centuries without overlords. Where she parted company with her Seelie cousins, however, was in the matter of which sidhe should comprise that rulership.

She had hoped that Yrtalien's coming would result in the restoration of the balance of power between Seelie and Unseelie courts and end the monopoly of the Seelie rulers. Instead, she discovered that the Forsworn Prince had plans that went beyond her own dreams of sharing power. *He means to force Arcadia back into the world, and Silver's Gate is the portal which will give him the means to do so, if he can find it.*

She had yet to tell Yrtalien her own theory about the court Malacar sought. From Edmund's unskilled recital of the selkie's tale, Glynnis was convinced that the sunken island was the resting place not only of Silver's Gate but of the Court of All Kings—where Seelie and Unseelie had once shared power and where, with any luck at all, both courts might do so again.

"The marina is just ahead," Dougal announced, slowing the van to a stop. Roused from her thoughts, Glynnis saw that they had arrived at Castle Archdale Country Park, on the shores of Lower Lough Erne. "Donal and I used to come here to fish when we were younger, before we figured out that we had better things to do with ourselves. We can take a roundabout path down to the boats and from there get over to White Island. They don't run the ferries in the middle of winter, but I don't think we'll have a problem in conning a boat ride from someone."

The six Kithain got out of the van and began making their way across the Park grounds.

"So what's so special about this island, anyway?" Edmund asked. "I thought we were looking for a sunken island. This one still floats."

"There's an old church on the island that has some curious bits of statuary on it that your prince is interested in seeing. Legends say that they are pagan statues that were once part of an older temple," Donal replied.

"Or a court," Malacar added. Yrtalien sniffed disdainfully.

"I doubt that your precious court can be found in such an obvious place," the prince said. "But I want to see these carvings for myself. Maybe the stones will shed some light on what they really mean."

"Like a secret decoder ring?" Edmund asked. "Cool!"

Once again, Glynnis detected an underlying falseness to Yrtalien's explanation. *There is some scheme at work here,* she thought, *and it involves paying a visit to the island's prehistoric sites and exposing them to the power of the gemstones.*

"Aren't you afraid that they'll run out of juice before we find Silver's Gate?" Edmund continued.

Yrtalien touched his hand to the pouch at his neck, a gesture that had become almost a habit since acquiring the stones.

"Hardly," the prince said. "These are singularly powerful treasures. They are meant to contain a vast amount of Glamour. Besides," he added cryptically, "I know how best to take care that they don't exhaust their supply."

Glynnis stumbled as Yrtalien's words thundered in her head. *Of course,* she thought. *He's visiting the ancient places not because they might lead him to Silver's Gate. He's systematically draining any Glamour they might hold. I wonder if the brothers know that their new friend is Ravaging the Glamour of their country's past.*

Morgan thought she heard Leigh's voice calling out behind her. Still holding Tor's hand, the childling looked over her shoulder where her companions should have been and saw only an unbroken stretch of trees.

"I don't see the others, Grandpa!" she cried. Tor glanced behind him to confirm Morgan's statement, swearing softly as he realized that the others had disappeared. He heard Morgan's quick intake of breath and turned his head forward again. Liam was nowhere to be seen.

Instinctively, he reached down and scooped Morgan up into his arms, transferring her slight weight to his left side to leave his weapon hand free.

"What are we going to do?" Morgan asked. Her initial surprise at finding herself alone with her grandfather in an unfamiliar and unmistakably enchanted forest had ebbed, giving way to a resolve not to give in to the beginnings of panic.

"Keep going in the direction we were headed," Tor said. "Sooner or later we're bound to run into something—or someone." He took a step forward, then paused, uncertain of his orientation.

Morgan pointed ahead of them. "That way," she said, indicating a barely discernable path between the trees ahead of them. "Liam turned left just before he reached that silver tree."

Tor blinked, making sure that what he saw was not a trick of the odd sunlight that illuminated the forest. The tree Morgan indicated was, indeed, silver—not the stark white of a silver birch, but sword-bright silver.

"And there's a gold one just beyond it!" Morgan's face radiated her delight. "It's just like the story of the dancing princesses! Mother drew pictures for that one," she said, then paused, her voice suddenly catching. Wordlessly she locked her arms around Tor's neck and hugged him, hiding her face in his neck. He gave her a careful squeeze in return.

"They're just fine," he said gruffly. "You'll see them again soon."

Morgan sighed and raised her head again.

"I'm all right, Grandpa," she said. "It's just that sometimes I wish Mother and Dad could be here, too."

Tor considered his granddaughter's words. His daughter Alicia, Morgan's mother, was a talented artist, and her fairy tale illustrations for children's books exhibited an otherworldly streak that might have suited her for wandering around in a magical wood, but the troll shuddered at the thought of his son-in-law Gordon's attempts to make sense of a reality that defied his image of the world. Both Morgan's parents now knew about and accepted their daughter's faerie nature and, under her enchantment, had been able to see for themselves that the childling's "imaginary" world was anything but that. Nevertheless, Gordon still tried to find ways to make his new knowledge "fit" into his previous conceptions.

As if she could read Tor's thoughts, Morgan shook her head and laughed softly.

"I guess I don't really wish that," she said. "But I do miss them."

Tor nodded. "I know," he replied, trying to sound reassuring. He started walking again, heading for the stretch of silver and gold trees that beckoned to him.

All around him strange plants writhed in the jungle's steamy heat. He ducked under ropy vines and caught his rucksack on a rotting branch. The steady drone of tiny, stinging insects cluttered his mind, keeping him from concentrating on anything but the next few steps. Ahead and behind him, his platoon mates were strung out in a line. On either side, the thick vegetation crowded against him. Anything could be in there, he thought, his ears straining to hear the telltale sounds that might signify the presence of a sniper. This is the perfect spot for an ambush—

—the anguished warrior led his wounded lady into the shelter of the redwood forest, far from the sounds of the battle that raged beyond them. Satisfied that they had eluded the enemies that pursued them, he eased her to the ground at the base of a large tree.

"You'll be safe here," he said, torn between his desire to stay with her and his oath, in danger of being broken,

to protect her.

"I am dying," she said, a bitter laugh escaping her pale lips. "The ultimate safety." Her elegant features hardened into a mask that only partly concealed her pain.

"My faithful protector," she said, reaching up to place a hand on the warrior's broad, craggy cheek. "I release you from your oath to me, for there is no point in it any longer."

"My oath was made to you and to all that bear your blood, until the last star loses its light forever." He dropped to his knees and cradled her in his arms. She leaned her head against his chest. With a gesture that seemed to take all her remaining strength, she lifted one hand to her throat and removed a small silver locket from around her neck. She pressed it into the warrior's hand.

"This is for the child who will one day come under your protection," she whispered. "She will be of my blood, and a small part of me will look at you from behind her eyes."

She fell silent, exhausted by the effort of speech. For a long time he held her, listening to her soft breathing. He closed his eyes and counted the seconds between each labored breath. When she was silent for far too long, he dared to open his eyes and look at her still, lifeless face. He clenched his fist around the locket—

"Stand your ground, intruders!" a sharp voice called out from one side. Tor snapped to attention, his hand reaching for his axe. "Go no farther into this wood."

"Leave the weapon alone!" another voice behind him commanded.

"Who are you?" Morgan called out, her small voice carrying clearly through the crisp air of the forest.

Tor scanned the surrounding area, trying to pinpoint the locations from which the voices had come. Then, as if his vision had suddenly come into sharp focus, he saw them—four riders on graceful horses that moved as silently as smoke carried on the breeze. The chimeric armor of the riders glimmered in the waning light, their iridescent colors blending with the silvery and golden trees that had concealed their presence.

One of the riders urged his mount forward until he was nearly upon Tor and Morgan. Tor stepped back involuntarily, bringing his free hand up to shield his granddaughter.

"I am Sir Odhran," he replied in a voice that seemed less harsh than those of his fellows. "And you are trespassing on lands claimed by one who does not suffer intruders lightly. Leave here at once or submit to our judgment."

"Are you talking about the Hidden King?" Morgan asked.

The sidhe knight's face underwent a subtle change, from stern implacability to guarded suspicion.

"What do you know about that?" he asked.

"Only that we came here to find him and ask for his help," Morgan replied. "And you may address me as Baroness Morgania," she added. "And this is my protector and knight-at-arms." She indicated Tor. "You may address him as sir."

Tor thought he heard one of the riders snicker softly and mutter something indistinct to his nearest companion. *So, they aren't as unified as they would have us think*, he told himself.

"I'm afraid we can't leave the way we came," Tor said. "We're not sure which way that is."

"What does submitting to your judgment mean?" Morgan asked. "Are you going to test us?" She turned around in Tor's arms, her face shining with excitement. "Remember the sea monster who guarded the sea trod to Hawaii?" she breathed.

all kings

The knight who had been addressing them nodded to Morgan, in acknowledgment of her rank, then gave a smaller bow of the head to Tor. The troll returned his gesture defiantly.

"Baroness and sir," he said, his voice cool and uninflected, "if you will not leave here of your own accord, I must insist that you accompany us to a place where we may determine the consequences of your intrusion." He extended his arms toward Morgan. Tor took another step away from the knight and found himself pressed against the side of a horse that had come up behind him soundlessly.

"She stays with me," he growled. Morgan straightened herself in Tor's arms. The troll caught a flash of silver around her neck as she shook her dark curls back from her face. *The locket*, he thought. *I gave it to her on the day of her Chrysalis.* A memory came to him then with a certainty that left no room for questions. *Her name was also Morgania.* "I assure you both that I will harm neither of you and that I only have the lady's comfort in mind."

Morgan looked at Tor, her eyes wide with anticipation. "I've never ridden a knight's horse," she said wistfully. "I think it will be all right, Grandpa." At her obvious reference to Tor, Sir Odhran's brows knit in a puzzled frown. He looked from Morgan to the troll as if expecting some explanation. Oblivious to the knight's reaction, Morgan stretched out a hand shyly toward the dark chestnut steed, just touching its velvety nose. The horse stood patiently under her caress.

Tor sighed and allowed Sir Odhran to lift Morgan onto the saddle in front of him. "Had I a mount that could bear your weight and height," the knight said, his voice polite but distantly formal, "I would offer you

the option of riding as well." Tor nodded brusquely. "I'd
prefer to walk beside my granddaughter," he said. Again,
Sir Odhran frowned, but said nothing.

The other knights formed up around Tor and
Morgan and, turning away from the clearing of silver
and gold trees, led the pair through the woods.

"Do you think Liam knew this would happen?"
Morgan said to Tor as they traveled through a stand
of oak and rowan trees, following the course of a small
brook. From her seat atop the horse, Morgan's face
was nearly level with Tor's and she was able to whisper
without drawing Sir Odhran's attention.

Tor shrugged. "I wouldn't put it past the measly
leprechaun," he grumbled. At the sound of the troll's
deep rumble, Sir Odhran turned and looked
questioningly at Tor.

"Leprechaun?" he asked.

"He means clurichaun," Morgan said.

The knight's face took on a look of sudden
realization, but he held his tongue. What would
happen to the strange Kithain who had violated his
liege's domain was not for him to decide.

Even though she knew it was useless, Leigh called out
the names of her missing companions. Valmont
watched her, his face impassive, until she finally grew
silent. He gave her a sympathetic shrug.

"If they were able to hear you, I'm certain they
would have answered," he offered by way of
consolation.

Leigh grimaced. "I had to try," she said. She started
to pull her hand from Valmont's grasp, but he
tightened his hold and shook his head.

"Not unless you want to find yourself separated

from me as well," he cautioned. "Rasputin let go of your hand for no more than a few seconds."

"Where do you think he is?" Leigh asked.

"Perhaps he's with Morgan and Tor." Valmont sounded doubtful. "Or maybe he and Liam are together."

Leigh smiled faintly. "The thought of those two together—"

"This is the land of the pooka and the clurichaun," Valmont observed.

"And the sidhe," Leigh added.

Valmont nodded. "Of course, the sidhe."

Leigh's eyes narrowed. "I didn't mean anything in particular by that," she said, her voice rising in defense.

Valmont took a step forward, pulling Leigh along by the hand. After a second's resistance, she allowed him to lead her a few more steps into the woods. Neither one spoke as they stepped carefully through the springy undergrowth, making their way from tree to tree. The forest seemed to undergo a subtle change with each step. The air became crisper and tangier, full of pungent earth smells and animal odors. *This is the way forests used to be,* Leigh thought. *This is the forest all trees dream about.*

"Perhaps this wasn't accidental," Valmont said, breaking the silence.

"What do you mean?" Leigh asked. "Liam warned us to stay together."

"And you notice how well we heeded his words," the eshu replied. "He could have insisted that we all link hands."

"What are you leading up to?" Leigh sounded wary.

"Morgan and Tor are undoubtedly together," Valmont said. "At least, I can't imagine them getting separated again."

Leigh nodded. "And Rasputin is by himself," she said. "You don't think this has something to do with the Bean Sidhe's visit last night, do you?" Her face reflected her concern.

Valmont shook his head. "I don't know," he said. "Morgan seemed to think, at least from what she told us about her communion with the creature, that the Bean Side would leave Rasputin—and all of us—alone. At least, for a time," he amended.

Leigh still looked worried. "I still worry about Rasputin. He always seems to be alone, even around others. That seems so sad, somehow."

"In case you haven't noticed, Rasputin is far from carefree most of the time, and as sociable as he seems to be, he has few real friends—except for us."

"Brit certainly took an interest in him," Leigh said, smiling to herself at the thought of the fox pooka's determined pursuit of Rasputin on their arrival in Glenlea.

"You saw how actively he encouraged that," Valmont responded. "He deliberately discourages anyone who tries to get close to him."

"Unlike you," Leigh said, the words slipping from her before she had a chance to stop them. Her face reddened.

Valmont laughed. "I have to admit that I enjoy the company of others," he said cryptically.

"You certainly enjoyed our stay with the selkies," Leigh recalled.

"Ondine and I are both storytellers at heart," Valmont said a little too quickly.

"And Kanani?" Leigh tried to keep her voice light.

Valmont turned his head away from Leigh and stared at something off to one side of their route.

"She gave her trust and her love to me so easily, I could not refuse her," Valmont said, his voice filled with an aching softness.

"You have a reason for everything," Leigh said. This time she could not keep the tartness from coloring her words.

"Everything but you." Valmont's words echoed like a snapped branch in the forest.

Leigh stopped, jerking the eshu slightly off balance with the suddenness of her action.

"No," she said, shaking her head. "I don't think I want to continue this conversation."

Valmont took a step away from Leigh.

"Let go of my hand," he said coldly. "Then you won't have to." He relaxed his hold until their hands were linked by only the slightest contact.

Leigh stared at him angrily. "You know I won't let go," she said.

"Leave me, Eleighanara," Yrtalien ordered. "You can expect the mercy of your House if you surrender to them now. Our rebellion has failed."

"You intend to fight on," she said, her voice accusing. "If you can put yourself at risk, so can I."

The dark-haired wilder prince threw back his head and laughed, his voice as wild and reckless as his nature. When his laughter died, he leaned down and kissed Eleighanara's hand.

"I risk nothing," he replied, "because I have nothing. Already am I branded forsworn and no atonement in this realm will rid me of that shame." His mouth curled upward in a sneering smile. "Perhaps I will make it my badge of honor," he said. "The Forsworn Prince has a certain ring, does it not?"

Eleighanara's heart broke within her.

"They will send their armies against you."

Yrtalien nodded. "I expect no less."

"You cannot stand alone against them."

"I will do what I must, regardless of the cost. Arcadia

must change or else it will die from stagnation."

"It cannot change," Eleighanara said. "This place has sealed itself away from all possibility of change."

"Then the seals must be broken," the prince replied. "Winter must come in order to renew spring."

Eleighanara's face grew white as she realized the import of his words. "You mean to bring Banality to this place!"

"What else will act as a catalyst for the kind of change that will keep Arcadia alive?"

"There must be another way." She sounded desperate.

"All other ways have been closed to us," Yrtalien said. "Your family—all our families—have seen to that. It is the only way they can perpetuate the old order and prevent the change in rulership that must come with the passing of the seasons."

"I swore an oath to you," Eleighanara said. "I will not break it."

Yrtalien shook his head ruefully. "I will not brand you forsworn if you do," he said. "I understand expediency, as many here do not."

"If honor were expedient, then it would not be so highly prized," Eleighanara retorted.

The Unseelie prince shrugged. "You are everything that I am not," he replied. "Stay, then, if you must. Perhaps there will be another chance for you to save yourself."

He turned away from her and strode toward the other oathmates, all of them rebellious scions of the noble houses of Arcadia. Eleighanara watched him for a few minutes before she, too, went to join the others.

"I will not let you go," she whispered.

"Do I?" Valmont's question brought Leigh back to the present. She stared blankly at the handsome eshu, trying to remember the statement that prompted his reply. When she did she burst into tears, angry at herself for doing so but unable to prevent the flood of feelings from overwhelming her.

Valmont pulled her toward him and put his arms around her.

"You were somewhere else, weren't you?" he asked, his voice a whisper against her ear. Leigh nodded, forcing back the sobs and willing herself to return to some semblance of her usual composure.

"Another blast from the past?" the eshu asked, his voice deliberately cheerful. Leigh felt the muscles in his arms relax and knew that if she wanted to she could easily extricate herself from Valmont's embrace. She remained where she was, drawing comfort from the steady beat of his heart. She rested her head against his chest and closed her eyes.

"Forgetfulness is the curse of the sidhe," she murmured. "But sometimes, I can remember bits and pieces of my life before I came here—before my exile from Arcadia."

"Your past with Yrtalien?" Valmont asked. Leigh had shared a portion of her memories with her companions, enough so that they knew that she and Yrtalien had once been oathmates and that they had rebelled against the rulers of Arcadia. Her exile had been her punishment. Yrtalien's crime, more serious because of his lack of remorse, had resulted in his imprisonment.

"I did let him go," she said. "He would have destroyed Arcadia to fulfill his ambitions."

Valmont lifted an arm and stroked Leigh's hair.

"You had no choice," he said. "You are not an oathbreaker."

"I broke my oath to him," she said.

Valmont pushed Leigh away from him gently, holding her at arm's length and staring at her until she met his gaze.

"Listen to my words, Eleighanara, knight of House Fiona and oathmate of Valmont Iyapo," he intoned.

"Sometimes one must appear to break the letter of an oath to remain true to its spirit. That is why you are not and never can be an oathbreaker. Believe me." His voice reverberated through the woods.

Leigh felt as if she were suddenly released from a prison of invisible bars.

"Thank you," she said, simply. She stepped away from Valmont and held out her hand. He clasped it firmly.

"Iyapo?" she asked.

Valmont nodded, smiling. "It means 'many trails.' It is an old eshu name."

Leigh returned his smile.

"Not 'many lovers'?" This time, the bantering tone was genuine.

"Only one at a time," Valmont said. They began once more to thread their way through the trees, this time in a companionable silence. Around them, the trees grew even stranger, until they found themselves walking through a stand of tall oaks that seemed to glimmer with an inner light, their leaves sparkling with the glint of golden acorns.

"I remember a forest like this in Arcadia," Leigh said suddenly.

Valmont nodded. "Perhaps we are not so far from that place in this enchanted wood," he said, his voice reverent. He reached out to touch the bark of a nearby tree and seemed to feel a quiver in his fingertips from the enchantment that permeated its essence.

"I am glad we have made some sort of peace with one another," he remarked. "We have been at odds too often in the past."

Leigh nodded. "My parents called me willful and argumentative," she said. *Both sets—mortal and fae*, she added to herself.

"And I am deceptive and calculating," Valmont replied. "At least so I have been told."

"It's hard to argue with someone whose hand you're holding," Leigh commented. "Maybe we should make this a habit, if we can put up with each other."

"I would enjoy the challenge," Valmont said. "And I do have a reason for you now."

"Oh?" Leigh asked, still trying to accustom herself to the transformation that had taken place.

Valmont nodded. "You are everything that I am not, and that draws me to you."

"Don't say that," Leigh remarked. "It reminds me of something I'd rather forget just now." They continued walking, stopping now and again to point out some detail of the thickening wood that caught their attention—here a slender sapling whose bark shimmered like burnished copper, there a massive oak with leaves of silver and gold—all evidence that the places where they walked closely mirrored the lost realms of the Dreaming.

"Do you know where you're going?" Leigh asked when Valmont hesitated for a minute, then steered them both at an angle from their previous course. The eshu looked at her and arched an eyebrow.

"I am not certain of our destination," he replied, "but there is something about certain paths that seem more 'right' than others." He shrugged. "I find it difficult to explain it more precisely—"

His words were cut off by a whistling sound in the air above them coupled with a solid 'thock' as a slender arrow landed in the ground just in front of their intended path.

Valmont's instinct was to dive for cover, pulling Leigh along with him into the shelter of the nearby trees, but the Fiona knight had already taken steps of her own, pulling her chimeric sword from its sheath and planting herself firmly in front of her oathmate.

"Heed our warning and transgress no further!" a woman's voice, sharp and clear, called out from behind the pair. Leigh strained to see the person who had issued the command.

"Who are you and by what right do you challenge our presence here?" she called out. From his place just behind her, Valmont felt a glow of pride at the bravado in his companion's voice. *She will not let herself be threatened*, he thought. He eased his sword hand toward his scimitar, tucked into his belt sash, ready to draw at need.

A group of sidhe riders mounted on steeds whose hooves seemed to glide over the ground emerged from the woods, as if from the trees themselves. Led by one who was obviously a sidhe noblewoman as well as a knight, they moved to surround Leigh and Valmont, keeping well out of sword reach. Leigh noticed that one of them held a bow in his hands, an arrow nocked and ready to fire.

The woman, obviously their leader, angled her head toward Leigh in a mocking show of disdainful greeting.

"By the right of guardianship and by our solemn oath to keep this sacred place free of those whose presence would contaminate it, I issue fair warning that you are here without invitation and without our leave." As an afterthought, she added, "I am Lady Rowena of House Fiona, Knight of the Riders of the Silver Court and duly appointed guardian of this wood."

"And I am Dame Eleighanara of House Fiona, Knight of Goldengate fief. This is my sworn companion Valmont Iyapo." Leigh's voice rang with defiance.

"At least she knows the niceties, for all that she consorts with common folk," a laconic voice commented from among the knights that watched them from their vantage point of safety.

Leigh flushed and turned angrily toward the speaker, but Valmont placed a restraining hand on her shoulder.

"It is nothing I have not heard before," he said quietly. "Leave it for more important considerations."

Leigh forced herself to ignore the slur, returning her attention to the haughty Fiona knight before her.

"We have come to ask an audience from the lord of this glen," she said, trying to keep her voice from betraying her indignation.

"And we have come to refuse you that audience," Lady Rowena replied. "Our lord sees no one except those sworn to him. And he does not suffer the presence of commoner Kithain at all."

"That's two," Leigh murmured in a voice intended only for Valmont's ears. Behind her, the eshu nodded grimly, keeping his grip on Leigh's shoulder. *He's holding himself back as much as he's trying to keep me from saying something I'll regret*, Leigh realized. In a louder voice, she addressed Lady Rowena.

"Our need is urgent," she said. "We have heard that this is a place for wise counsel and it is that advice and guidance we seek." The courtly speech came to her lips with an ease that she had not known before. "Perhaps if you could speak to your lord on our behalf, he would consent to meet with us."

"Impossible," Lady Rowena replied flatly. "We have our orders to conduct you to a place where you—and your other companions—will be judged according to the severity of your trespass."

Leigh shook her head, incredulous. "We have done no wrong!" she insisted. "We are here to fulfill a quest—"

"That will be determined when the full company of Riders has met in judgment on all who have this

court of

day intruded upon our domain," Lady Rowena pronounced. "Sheathe your weapon and come with us."

Leigh looked over her shoulder at Valmont, who could read the bitter acknowledgement of personal defeat in her eyes. He smiled at her encouragingly.

"The final cards have yet to make their appearance on the table," he said softly. "Besides, this may be the only way we can find the others." Leigh nodded glumly and sheathed her sword.

"We will go with you," she said, her voice firm and unwavering, "but only so that we may have a further chance to advance our cause before someone with the authority to grant our request." *There*, she thought, staring at Lady Rowena. *As Edmund would say if he were here, "Sit on that, your Ladyship."* The thought of the missing redcap brought an involuntary smile to her face, one which immediately disappeared when she remembered why the childling was no longer with them. Linking hands once more with Valmont in a blatant show of solidarity, Leigh approached the riders.

Surrounded, they allowed themselves to be led away from their path.

Rasputin looked up from where he had stumbled and found that he was alone in the forest. *No, not alone*, he realized, as he saw a large red deer standing directly in front of him regarding him with an alert and fearless curiosity. The pooka brushed himself off and nodded a greeting to the animal.

"Who are you? Bambi's father?" he asked. He thought he heard a politely disdainful sniff from the beast as the stag turned away from him and slowly began stepping through the forest. After a few steps, it paused and looked over its shoulder at Rasputin.

"If you think I'm going to follow you, you're greatly mistaken, Sir Red Rump," the pooka mumbled as he moved after the deer. *Red Flank*, he seemed to hear in his head.

"Flank, then," he said. "I certainly hope that you've come to get me even more lost than I seem to have gotten myself." The deer's stubby tail twitched as if in response. Rasputin shrugged. As he trailed the animal deeper into the forest, the pooka began to notice the profusion of animal life that lurked on the fringes of his progress. A red fox and her kits scurried across the path almost under his feet and he had to stop abruptly to avoid them. Overhead, he heard the raucous call of something that sounded like a raven. Soon he began to notice other things, as the trees around him changed color, becoming silver and golden sentinels whose leaves shimmered in the gilded light as he passed.

Just an ordinary stroll through the woods, he told himself. *I hope the others are as thoroughly confused as I am.* Suddenly, he saw a lean gray shape bound into sight just behind the stag. Like a bolt shot from an arrow, the red deer leaped away from the snarling form and disappeared into a heavy stand of trees and bushes. The other beast continued on its trajectory, heading away from the deer and vanishing into the underbrush. Rasputin shook his head. *That couldn't have been a wolf*, he thought. *St. Patrick or some such drove them all out centuries ago.*

He stopped, trying to get his bearings now that his only other companion had deserted him. Leaning against a silver birch whose bark seemed to invite him to rest against it, he wiped the moisture caused by his recent exertion from his face and looked around.

Suddenly, the deer burst from the foliage almost on top of him, leaping across his path and continuing into the wood. Without thinking, Rasputin ran after the animal, trying without much success to match his pace to that of the fleet-footed deer. As he ran, the trail grew more and more difficult for him to follow. Thorny bushes seemed to grasp at his clothing and stones appeared to place themselves deliberately in his path. Always, the deer was just on the edge of his vision, threatening to vanish if the pooka slowed his frantic pace or stopped to take a breath.

In the back of his mind, Rasputin felt the beginnings of an idea take hold. As he continued his pursuit, the idea grew into a compulsion. Rasputin felt his limbs begin to contort without his conscious direction and around him the air began to shimmer with the telltale mark of Glamour. *Of course*, he thought. *This is the most unnatural way I can think of to keep up with old Red Flank.* With an inner sigh of relief, Rasputin slipped into rabbit form and, as a slim brown hare, made his way easily over a forest floor that seemed tailored for his powerful haunches and agile paws.

Enjoying a freedom he had not felt in a long time, the pooka bounded along the trail, gaining on the loping stag. His keen nose picked up many scents unnoticeable to his human form, among them the faint aroma of fox and the unmistakable odor of a wolf somewhere in the wood. *Maybe it wasn't St. Patrick after all*, he thought briefly as he gathered himself for a prodigious leap over a small tufted hillock that provided him with a convenient excuse to exercise his animal agility.

He had no warning of the net until it fell atop him, its weighted ends trapping him low to the ground. Panicking, he tried first to shift back into his human shape, but found that it was impossible.

Failing that, he began to thrash around inside the prison of the net, succeeding only in getting one of his hind legs caught between the mesh so that he could not pull it back through. *This is the dream I had on the way to Hawaii,* he thought as he tried to quiet the thunderous pounding of his rabbit-sized heart. He heard someone approach and smelled a distinct leathery aroma coupled with the tang of excitement exuding from his captor. Sinking into a deep stillness born of despair and an overwhelming sense of fatality, Rasputin closed his eyes and waited, wondering briefly if it would be an arrow or a knife that would be the instrument of his doom.

He felt himself snatched up into the air as someone grabbed the net and hauled it upward, forming a basketlike cage. Startled by the sudden upward motion, Rasputin opened his eyes and saw that he was being held suspended by a young sidhe knight dressed in light armor and riding leathers, her face aglow with triumph and self-congratulation.

"Hah!" she said, more to herself than to her captive. "We'll see what Lord Tiernach and the others think of this." Rasputin managed a feeble struggle of protest, but his captor only laughed.

"None of that, now," she snapped, still too pleased with herself to sound more than playfully chiding. "I know what you are and I'm not giving you the slightest opportunity to grow into yourself until I can make sure that you won't slip away from me."

"That was the furthest thing from my thoughts," Rasputin tried to reassure her, but found, to his chagrin, that all he could manage in his present state of agitation was a shrill, almost soundless squeak.

"Save your breath," the sidhe said. "You'll need it later to explain your presence here, if a pooka's words can ever be believed."

Securing her grasp on the net, the young huntress swung the net containing her catch over her shoulder and strode off into the forest, away from the path the deer had taken. Rasputin took one look at the ground beneath him and closed his eyes again, resigning himself to the jostling ignominy.

Edmund was supposed to be sleeping. At least he had told the others that he was tired after the day's trek to White Island and that he wanted to go to bed. He closed the door to the small upstairs room that served as his bedroom and walked over to the small shuttered window next to the bed. He opened the shutters and stood looking out at the sky. The house that Dougal and Donal shared along with a few of their mates, including the bartender Lurgan and a crusty boggan housekeeper named Hettie, lay a few miles outside Sligo. *We might as well be in the middle of nowhere*, the childling thought as he stared out over a darkened landscape lit only by a few lights from houses here and there. *This whole country is in the middle of nowhere.*

Below him, he could hear faint voices and knew that Yrtalien and the others were busily planning where they would go tomorrow. On their way back from the island, someone had mentioned the Giant's Causeway, and although Donal had protested that so many tourists visited the place that it was unlikely that they would find anything of interest there, the prince and Malacar both seemed intent on making the trip. Edmund didn't feel up to listening to the endless round of discussions the adults seemed so fond of, so he begged off, claiming sleepiness. *They were probably glad to get rid of me,* he thought.

With a sigh, he closed the shutters and sat on the bed.

"Here goes nothing," he muttered as he withdrew a small pouch from his pocket and opened it to remove the tiny, painted clown figurine it contained. Setting the miniature beside him on the bed, he focused on the Glamour within him, softly whistling his own version of a circus march to direct his faerie magic toward the clown.

The figure began glowing, enlarging until it reached its full chimeric size and became his familiar companion, the three-foot tall, white-faced clown he had christened Mr. Dumpy. The clown saluted Edmund cheerfully and scooted upward on the bed to sit on the pillow.

"Hello yourself," Edmund said, remembering to keep his voice low. "I bet you thought I'd forgotten you."

Mr. Dumpy shook his head. Edmund grinned.

"I'm glad you understand I can't have you around all the time," he said apologetically. "I would if I could, but I'm afraid Mr. Glamour Hog would wanna suck you dry or stick you in the pouch where he keeps the stones."

The clown shrugged.

"In case you didn't know it, we're in Ireland." Edmund was never sure just how aware of his surroundings Mr. Dumpy was when he was reduced to his inanimate form. The fact that Mr. Dumpy, along with the other chimerae from the toy chest, possessed a physical counterpart—unlike most chimeric creatures—led the childling to hope that the clown could sense what was going on even when his magic was dormant. At least Mr. Dumpy never seemed to need elaborate explanations to bring him up to date on what transpired between activations.

Mr. Dumpy nodded.

Edmund removed his worn baseball cap and ran his hands through his spiky dreadlocks, then replaced the hat, mashing his hair down carefully.

"I thought when we found Malacar and got the last stone that we'd go right to Silver's Gate and open that sucker up," he said. Mr. Dumpy bobbed his head up and down in agreement.

"Well, guess what?" Edmund asked. The clown gave Edmund an inquisitive look and shrugged his shoulders.

"Right," said Edmund. "No gate." He leaned closer to his friend and whispered, "I don't think Prince Irritation knows how to use them."

The clown looked shocked.

"We're just bumming around the countryside looking at old graves and weird statues. It wouldn't be so bad except that the whole place's full of these things and it looks like we're going to visit every last one of 'em." He sighed. Mr. Dumpy sighed with him.

"Do you know what it's like being stuck with a bunch of self-important fart-faces?" he asked. Mr. Dumpy looked as if he were considering the question, then nodded emphatically.

"Oh, yeah," Edmund said, remembering. "You were locked up for years inside the toy chest with all those soldiers, weren't you? I bet that was hell!

"The Bobsey twins would be all right," he said, thinking of Donal and Dougal, "if they weren't trying to get the prince to run for king of Ireland or something." On their way back from White Island, the brothers had continued the conversation they had begun during the trip to the historical site. According to them, the country had four rulers, one for each of the four provinces that once made up Ireland, as well as numerous other petty kings and queens, but they lacked an overall monarch like Concordia's King David. "I don't know why they think *he'd* make such a hot king, except he's as Unseelie as they are and he claims to be from Arcadia. I bet they don't know that he was a criminal there," he confided in the clown.

"No, wait," he said. "He did tell them he was the leader of some great rebellion against the rulers of Arcadia and that they imprisoned him for causing trouble. That seemed to make him some kind of hero to them."

Mr. Dumpy's look mirrored Edmund's perplexed scowl.

"To me, that just makes him a loser," the redcap said. "Go figure."

Mr. Dumpy patted the childling's shoulder sympathetically.

"I wondered what he's promised *them*," Edmund said. "I got some cool armor from him," he added as he thought of the black chimeric mail the prince had fashioned for him in Hawaii, "but he also said he'd give me a horse and make me a knight. Now he claims I have to earn it."

He and Mr. Dumpy regarded each other in silence for a few minutes. Then Edmund slumped forward on the edge of the bed, propping his head in his hands, his elbows resting on his knees.

"I never thought I'd miss ol' Moron," he said. "She's got her nose stuck up her rear most of the time, but now and then she's okay for a girl. I wonder what she's doing now. If the Dauntain have her, she's probably a goner. They'll have her singing Barney songs and watching soap operas 'til she turns green." He chortled at the thought of Morgan with sickly green skin, but sobered almost immediately when he saw the look on Mr. Dumpy's face.

"Hey," he said, feeling suddenly distressed. "I'd never do something like that to you. I swear."

The clown continued to stare at him. Edmund felt his face redden. "Yeah, I know," he admitted, his voice barely audible even to himself. "I swore an oath to them, too. You don't hate me, do you?" He tried to keep his lower lip from trembling as he waited for the clown to reply.

Mr. Dumpy looked at him thoughtfully, then slowly shook his head. Edmund gave a sigh of relief. "Do you still like me?"

The clown nodded, this time with less hesitation.

"You're just about the only one who does," Edmund said. "The others put up with me. Sometimes, they don't even do that. I thought for awhile, on the boat, that Glynnis sort of liked me, but now she's into something she won't even talk to Yrtalien about. And the brothers are too busy sucking up to Mr. Big Head to notice me most of the time. I'm tired of just hanging out with the big guys."

Mr. Dumpy held up one hand and used the other to tick off four fingers. He held the thumb up to Edmund and looked expectant.

"Oh, yeah," Edmund said. "I forgot Malacar." He cupped a hand over one eye and snarled in imitation of the satyr's perpetual frown. "I wish I could forget the old bag. I'd rather have the guy with the stone in his hand around than old Red Eye. At least he had some decent armor. Malacar smells like mothballs."

Mr. Dumpy held his nose between his thumb and forefinger.

"Exacto!" Edmund said. The clown patted the pillow next to him. Edmund yawned.

"I guess I am sorta sleepy," he said, flopping down to lie on his back, his hands locked behind his head. He turned his face sideways to look up at the clown perched on the other pillow.

"Did you ever wish you could go back in time and do something differently?" He asked.

Mr. Dumpy thought about it, then shook his head.

"I guess not, seeing as how you just sort of do what you do." Edmund stared at the ceiling. "I wish—"

The creak of footsteps on the stairs outside his door cut him off before he could finish voicing his thoughts.

"Quick," he whispered, panicking. "Get small again. Someone's coming!"

The clown obediently began to shrink in size, the chimeric glow that surrounded him dwindling in intensity until it vanished altogether, leaving a painted miniature clown on Edmund's pillow.

Edmund scrambled out of the bed and threw back the covers. He kicked off his shoes, trying to be as quiet about it as possible, and climbed back into the bed, pulling the covers up to his chin. Snatching up the figurine, he stuffed it back into its pouch. He shoved the pouch into the pocket of his jeans. *Let 'em think I was so tired I fell asleep with my clothes on*, he thought as he squeezed his eyes shut and turned on his side so that his back was toward the door.

He heard a scrape as the door to his room eased open. *Glynnis*, he thought, feeling relieved that it wasn't the prince. *She's the only one who wears perfume.* He lay as still as possible while Glynnis walked softly into the room and turned off the light by his bed.

"Poor little fool," she whispered. "At least you can get away by claiming sleepiness. Some of us aren't so lucky." Then she left the room as quietly as she had entered, closing the door behind her.

Edmund lay awake after she had gone wondering what her words had meant. Finally, after giving up on trying to understand the most enigmatic of his new companions, he drifted off to sleep.

The sun had set, and although the forest was in darkness, a ring of chimeric lights illuminated the open space within the forest to which the companions were led. A small pavilion had been erected in the center of the clearing the Riders of the Silver Court referred to as the Outer Circle. Leigh and Valmont, still holding hands, joined Tor and Morgan, standing just outside the pavilion. Their sidhe escort dismounted, leaving their horses to gather near the edge of the clearing.

Leigh looked around, counting heads.

"Where's Rasputin?" she asked.

"If that's the name of your pooka lackey, he's right here, bagged up where he belongs!" A young sidhe dressed in riding leathers entered the clearing. Suspended from one hand was a large, tawny hare in a heavy rope net.

Leigh bowed her head.

The newcomer walked up to the aloof knight who had introduced himself as Sir Tiernach and who was obviously the ranking member of the group.

"I see you've been hunting rabbits, Lady Sorcha," Sir Tiernach remarked dryly as she presented him with her catch. "The rest of us have rounded up more dangerous prey."

The young knight stood her ground, jutting her chin out defiantly. "This is no ordinary beast, sir," she responded, her voice quavering on the edge of civility. "Before he entered the Inner Forest, he had two legs like the rest of us." She cut off her speech abruptly as if suddenly regretting her choice of words. Lord Tiernach's eyebrow rose in disapproval.

"He got as far as the Inner Forest?" he asked, his voice somber.

Sorcha blushed. "He was following the deer," she began.

The knight who Leigh recognized as Lady Rowena laughed scornfully. "Do you expect us to believe that the king's deer deliberately led an intruder past the outer ring of the forest?"

"I expect you to believe the truth of my words," Sorcha replied hotly. "Perhaps that is too much to ask."

"You overstep your bounds, girl," Lord Tiernach snapped. "You are but recently joined to this company. You have not yet proven yourself worthy to remain within it. Such hot-tempered language does nothing to advance your cause before those who doubt the suitability of your House for true service to the king."

Leigh and Valmont exchanged puzzled looks. "Dissent in the ranks," Leigh murmured to the eshu.

Valmont squeezed her hand. "I was noticing the profound difference between their cooperative natures and our own group's harmonious relations."

Leigh gave Valmont a faint smile. "Nobody's perfect," she said. "I suppose even the Knights of the Round Table had their bad days."

Valmont nodded. "Have you noticed the conspicuous absence of one of our number—if, in fact, that poor rabbit is Rasputin?"

"Liam!" Leigh said. Valmont's look was answer enough.

One of the knights looked pointedly at the pair of whispering Kithain and cleared his throat. Valmont inclined his head. "I think we are being politely told to shut up," he said.

Leigh shrugged in response. She turned her attention back to the confrontation between Sorcha and Lord Tiernach. The young knight looked subdued, evidence that she had decided not to pursue her line of defense.

Lord Tiernach gestured toward the sack containing Rasputin.

"Pookas need privacy in order to resume their human forms," he said. "Take that sack into the pavilion and close the flap. If the animal is really what you claim, that should provide him with enough seclusion to effect his change. We will give him a thirty-count to do so. At the end of that time, I shall declare open season on hare."

Sorcha bowed to her lord and walked toward the pavilion. She placed the net inside and closed the flap. At Lord Tiernach's signal, one of the other knights began a slow, measured count.

The tent flap opened on "twenty-five" and Rasputin emerged from within, his face pale but smiling.

"Sorry to keep you all waiting," he said, his voice a little shaky. "I had to take the time to pull myself together and straighten my ears."

"This is no joking matter, pooka," Lord Tiernach said, motioning for Rasputin to join the others.

"His name is Rasputin," Morgan said from her place beside Tor.

"I would expect him to answer for himself," Lord Tiernach said, his voice assuming a patronizingly kind tone as he responded to the sidhe childling.

"Yes, sir," Morgan replied, "but you might not understand his answers."

"Now that you are all together," Lord Tiernach began, but another knight—the one Morgan knew as Sir Odhran—interrupted.

"Your pardon, Sir Tiernach," he said, "but there may still be one missing."

"Oh?" Tiernach's voice was skeptical.

"The young lady made mention of a clurichaun—"

"Damn!" Tiernach said softly. "Him again?" The sidhe knight quickly pointed to a pair of his subordinates. "Take your horses and find that meddlesome pest," he barked.

"That won't be necessary, your Lordship," Liam's voice sounded from the edge of the trees. "I'm right here under your very eyes." The clurichaun sauntered into the center of the clearing and took his place with the oathmates. "Now we're all together and you may continue." He winked at Morgan, who smiled in return.

"Step forward," Lord Tiernach ordered. The six Kithain walked forward into the center of the clearing. The sidhe knights formed a circle around them. Leigh counted fourteen, including their leader.

Lord Tiernach stepped into the circle.

"It is the judgment of this fellowship," he said, "that you depart from this place and return no more to disturb its peace."

"No!" Morgan said, her childish voice resonant with indignation. "You haven't even heard what we have to say!"

"You have nothing to say that can sway this court's decision," Lord Tiernach said.

"I believe you are mistaken," Valmont replied.

"Silence!" Lord Tiernach ordered. "This is no place for a commoner's voice."

"If he's a commoner, then I'm a pooka," Rasputin said. His comment drew befuddled looks from both his companions and the knights who surrounded them. The pooka shrugged.

"Rasputin's right," Leigh said. *I think.* "Valmont Iyapo has demonstrated more nobility and trueness of heart than many who bear both title and rank. I am Dame Eleighanara of House Fiona, ambassador from Duke Aeon of Goldengate and I hereby acknowledge my oathmate Valmont as my equal in nobility and in rank." She glared at Lord Tiernach.

Liam leaned down and whispered something in Morgan's ear. She looked up at him and nodded eagerly, allowing the clurichaun to push her gently forward.

"My oathmate's words are true," Morgan said. She closed her eyes and tried to remember the courtly phrases she had heard so often from Lady Alyssa and the other courtiers at Duke Aeon's palace back in San Francisco. Opening her eyes, she approached Valmont. "Kneel," she said, her voice ringing with an unexpected authority. Her small form began to glow as the Glamour surrounded her like a brilliant aura. Leigh's eyes shone with approval as she nodded to Valmont, urging him to comply with Morgan's request. Unable to tear his gaze away from the radiant noblewoman Morgan had suddenly become, Valmont dropped to one knee in front of her. Morgan touched him gently on the shoulder.

"By my right as baroness to ennoble any whom I deem fit to bear the title, I hereby proclaim you a knight and raise you to the rank of the nobility." She looked questioningly at Leigh. Without hesitation, Leigh came to stand beside Morgan. With a flourish that defied their speechless guards, she drew her chimeric sword and placed it in Morgan's hands, retaining her own grip to enable the childling to support the weight of the blade. Morgan touched the sword to Valmont's shoulders in the formal ritual of investiture.

"Rise, Sir Valmont," she said, returning the sword to Leigh, who sheathed it quickly and returned to her place. As the newly knighted eshu rose, Morgan turned to Sir Tiernach, an ingenuous look on her face.

"Now may he speak?" she asked. Then she looked at Liam. "Should I make you, Grandpa, and Rasputin knights as well?"

"Don't you dare," Tor grumbled. "That's the last thing I want." Rasputin opened his mouth as if to reply to Morgan's question, but Tiernach's voice cut him off.

"This has gone far enough!" the knight said, his voice hot with outrage. "Leave this clearing at once or prepare to defend your right to stay."

"We are prepared to do just that," Leigh said, her own voice matching Tiernach's in intensity. "I invoke the ancient rite of Fior and demand that our cause be decided through trial by combat." She drew her blade and presented it in salute to the assembly.

For a few moments, only the sighing of the wind could be heard within the clearing. Even Leigh seemed shocked by her own words.

"Well, at least we have proof of her House," Lady Rowena remarked wryly to the knights on either side of her.

Sir Odhran moved to stand beside Lord Tiernach. "She has the right," he whispered in the knight's ear. Tiernach nodded glumly. He cleared his throat.

"The challenge to trial-by-combat has been duly given. Who among us will accept the challenge and act as champion to enforce our judgment?"

"I will," a woman's voice answered immediately. Sorcha advanced from the circle of knights, her young face determined and her hand poised to draw her sword. A few other voices echoed her response, but no one else stepped forward. Sorcha knelt before Lord Tiernach and bowed her head.

"I beg leave to use this opportunity to prove my worthiness to stand among you," she said. She raised her head and regarded the older knight with an impassioned gaze. "It is not chance that brought this circumstance to pass," she added. "You know my skill makes me the equal of most."

"And your recklessness too often undoes your vaunted prowess," Lord Tiernach responded.

"Let her words stand as spoken," Lady Rowena said abruptly. "As her sponsor, I admit I have had my doubts about bringing her into our company, but no one can deny the virtue of her intent."

Lord Tiernach pondered his companion's words. Finally he nodded.

"So be it," he proclaimed. "The hour is late, however," he added, "and such a matter of import is best decided in the light of day, when eyes are at their keenest." He gestured for Sorcha to rise, a thin smile on his face.

"Lady Sorcha has demonstrated her desire to act as our champion," he said. "We shall spend the night in this clearing so that both combatants may rest and prepare themselves for the ordeal that lies ahead."

On Lord Tiernach's orders, Lady Rowena led Leigh and Sorcha inside the pavilion, a roomy structure that reminded Leigh of the elaborate tents that decorated the sites of modern medieval pageants. A filmy curtain, strung along a silken rope that ran through the middle of the tent, hung near the rear of the pavilion. Lady Rowena pulled the curtain partway across the interior.

"Each of you will have one half of this space," she said. "You may have as much or as little contact with each other as you wish. There are those who believe that it is good to know one's adversary before meeting on the field of combat, and there are others who prefer to remain ignorant of those they will face in battle. The decision is yours."

all kings

Sorcha and Leigh both nodded to indicate that they understood Lady Rowena's words.

"What about my friends?" Leigh asked. "Will they be able to visit me?"

"They may," Lady Rowena replied, "but this is not a night for frivolous communication." Her voice sounded prim, reminding Leigh of Lady Alyssa, whose strict adherence to courtly custom and formal protocol maintained decorum in Duke Aeon's household. "You will notice that when the curtain is entirely drawn across the interior, it divides the entrance in half. Your friends will enter your half of the tent, and any who elect to visit Sorcha will use the other side."

"Not that I'll be expecting a steady stream of well-wishers," Sorcha said. Lady Rowena shot her a glance so full of unspoken meaning that Leigh decided to forego any attempt at interpretation.

"As the champion of the Riders of the Silver Court, you will be in all our thoughts this night." Lady Rowena's voice was heavy with rebuke.

She didn't say any of them would visit her, Leigh noticed.

"Is there anything special we're supposed to do?" she asked.

Lady Rowena's smile was almost too kind. "Besides contemplating the seriousness of your role as champion for your side and taking whatever measures are necessary to render you fit to present a fair accounting of yourself on the morrow?" she asked mildly. "No, there is no special 'thing' that you must do. I would, perhaps, advise sleep at some point in the evening."

I've just been put in my place, Leigh realized. She stole a glance at Sorcha, who was listening intently to the exchange, and saw a hint of relief on her counterpart's face.

"Thank you, Lady Rowena," Leigh said. "I think that answers my question sufficiently."

Lady Rowena nodded. When both Leigh and Sorcha refrained from speaking, she nodded once more and left the pavilion, closing the flap behind her and leaving them alone.

Leigh turned to Sorcha. "I guess you can't accuse her of favoritism," she commented wryly.

Sorcha's only reply was to finish drawing the curtain, closing off the space between them. Leigh shrugged at the rebuff.

"You know where to find me if you want to talk," she said to the vague figure visible on the other side of the semi-opaque curtain. Left to her own devices, she proceeded to examine the space in which she was to spend the evening. The pavilion was sparsely furnished, containing what appeared to be a couchlike bed, a small cushioned chair and a low table. *This might be the tent of an officer on a battlefield out of the pages of history*, she thought, noting the archaically eclectic style of the furnishings. *But whose history?*

Leigh felt her thoughts begin to race as the impact of her hasty challenge began to set in, becoming mixed up with her newly acknowledged feelings toward Valmont. With an effort, she emptied her mind and put her body through a rigorous series of martial exercises. After awhile, she entered a state of awareness that encompassed only motion and stillness.

The oathmates, along with Liam, set up camp on one side of the clearing. Opposite them, the sidhe knights formed their own encampment, complete with a chimerical campfire. The heatless flame, created from the Glamour that permeated the forest, formed a focus for the Riders who gathered about it like moths drawn to its inviting glow. Within the clearing, the winter chill failed to penetrate, and neither group seemed concerned with the prospect of spending a night without shelter.

"Are we going to have a fire, too?" Morgan asked, eyeing the activity in the other camp wistfully.

"I suppose we could conjure one up to match theirs," Valmont replied. "I would be more interested in coming up with something for us to eat."

"That won't be necessary." Sir Odhran, accompanied by one of the younger knights bearing a tray laden with food, approached the four companions. "For this night, we are your hosts, and it falls to us to see that you have meat and drink to sustain you until morning." He directed the knight to set the tray down on the ground in the center of the group, then dismissed him to join the other Riders.

"Will you join us?" Morgan asked, remembering her manners.

Sir Odhran hesitated.

"Maybe he doesn't want to be seen hanging out with commoners," Tor muttered.

The knight drew himself up and bowed stiffly to Morgan, ignoring the troll's comment.

"I would be happy to share your company for a time," he said. As he spoke he glanced around him at the group, finally giving Tor a long, hard look. Tor grunted something that might have been an apology had it had intelligible form.

The oathmates, along with Liam and Sir Odhran, seated themselves upon the ground around the tray of food.

"Fresh strawberries!" Morgan cried, helping herself to a handful. Rasputin eyed the assortment of cheeses and breads, while Liam began passing around pieces of fresh bread and cold meats. Sir Odhran allowed the clurichaun to give him a small helping of food.

Valmont eyed the pavilion in the clearing's center. "Are the combatants being fed?" he asked.

Sir Odhran nodded vigorously. "Each has been taken a tray not unlike your own, Sir Valmont." He seemed to stumble over Valmont's new title. "You need not be concerned that your lady is being neglected."

At the sidhe knight's reference to Leigh, Valmont gave a faint smile.

"Oh, she's not just his lady," Rasputin said around a mouthful of bread and cheese.

"Of course," Sir Odhran agreed. He studied the group for a few minutes, then took a deep breath, releasing it in a determined sigh.

"If I might be so bold as to ask about a matter that was brought to my attention earlier—" he began, only to stop, his voice floundering.

"We are your guests," Valmont said. "You may ask what you like and we shall answer as truthfully as we can."

"Some of us," Morgan said, carefully not looking at Rasputin as she spoke.

The sidhe knight focused his attention on Morgan.

"Baroness?" he said.

Morgan nodded. "Morgania, of House Eiluned," she finished. "Most people just call me Morgan, though. We're not as formal where I come from as you are. At least, not outside court."

Sir Odhran nodded. "You referred to your stalwart protector as your grandfather," he said, indicating Tor with a barely perceptible movement of his head.

"Yes," Morgan replied. "He is my grandfather."

"I see," Sir Odhran said in a voice that belied his words.

αll kings

"I was about to say that," voiced Rasputin.

"Morgan's mother is my daughter," Tor said.

"Such a mixture of Kithain in one family is—um—highly unusual, at least here," the knight said, his tone noncommittal.

"Is there something wrong with it?" Morgan asked, frowning in her attempt to understand her host's interest in her relationship to Tor.

"If, as is believed by some, the placement of a sidhe's spirit in a human form is not accomplished by whimsy," Liam said, "what better way to acquire a sworn protector than to be born into a mortal family that already boasts a troll guardian?" The clurichaun looked pleased with his answer.

Sir Odhran considered the explanation for a moment, then nodded as if satisfied.

"I suppose," he said.

Morgan produced a silver locket from beneath her clothes and showed it to the knight. "Grandpa gave me this on the night of my Chrysalis," she said. "It belonged to another sidhe he protected a long time ago."

Sir Odhran leaned down to take a close look at the small faerie treasure that was Morgan's dearest possession and a strange look came over his face. He sat up again suddenly and regarded Tor with a newfound respect.

Valmont noticed the change in the knight's demeanor.

"Is something the matter?" he asked, his voice low.

Sir Odhran seemed on the verge of replying, then simply shook his head.

"It is a most interesting keepsake," he said. "Now, if you'll forgive me, I shall join my own companions."

"Wait," Tor said. Sir Odhran halted and looked at the troll.

Tor gestured with his head toward the pavilion. "Can we go see her tonight, or is that place off limits to visitors?"

Sir Odhran looked relieved. "Of course you may visit her," he said. "In fact, she will probably welcome your good wishes for her performance tomorrow. I suggest that you make your visits short, however, for she will need her rest." He bowed formally to the group and marched back across the clearing to his own camp.

"Maybe we can all go together," Morgan said.

"Oh, I think it would be better if you went in one at a time," Liam responded quickly, flashing a glance at Valmont. "That way, you can each say something to her that will be just between the two of you."

As they sat around the fire discussing who would be the first to visit Leigh, Valmont drew the clurichaun aside.

"You're very good at finding explanations for things," he commented.

Liam smiled broadly and gave the eshu a wink. "It's what I do best—except for singing."

Leigh sat on the couch and picked at the food on the tray that rested on the table in her half of the pavilion. Her initial hunger had faded after a few mouthfuls of bread and meat, giving way to a restlessness that made her stomach queasy. Under normal circumstances, the act of eating or preparing fine food—and the meal in front of her, despite its simplicity, deserved at least four stars—served as one of her chief sources of replenishing her faerie magic.

"You'll not last more than a sword-pass or two if you don't eat more," a voice called out from within the tent. Leigh looked up to see Sorcha, one hand holding the curtain which she had pulled aside a few feet, standing near the doorway.

Leigh grimaced. "You sound like my mother," she remarked.

Sorcha stiffened, and her face grew suddenly hard. "What's that supposed to mean?" she snapped.

Leigh regarded the young sidhe with surprise. "It means exactly what I said. When I lived with my family, my mother was always trying to make me eat, as if food solved all the world's problems—or mine, at any rate."

"Your mortal mother," Sorcha said, still sounding belligerent. The word "mortal" hung in the air between them.

"Yes," Leigh replied, drawing out the word to give herself time to decipher the coded message that lay in Sorcha's tone and attitude. *Valmont would pick this up right away*, she thought, calling to mind the eshu's fluency in the language of gesture and nuance. "What did you think I meant?"

The young knight thrust her chin upward in the same gesture she had used earlier in her confrontation with Lord Tiernach. "I'm every bit the sidhe that you are," she said.

Leigh's face mirrored her sudden comprehension. "You think I insulted you," she said.

"Didn't you?"

Leigh shook her head slowly. "The comment your leader made about your House, what did he mean?"

Sorcha laughed bitterly. "Maybe you meant no insult after all," she said.

Leigh gestured toward the empty chair. "Why don't you come in and explain what I said to make you angry."

Sorcha shrugged, dropping the curtain and entering Leigh's half of the tent. She sat uneasily in the small cushioned chair, her hands gripping the arms so that her knuckles turned pale.

"Have you heard of House Scathach?" Sorcha asked.

Leigh's eyes widened. "No," she said. "From the others' comments, I thought you might be House Liam."

"Hardly," Sorcha said, a cold half-smile pulling at her lips. "They, at least, are accounted true sidhe even if their honor is put to the question more often than not."

"And your House isn't?" Leigh asked.

"Not according to some," Sorcha replied. She crossed one leg over the other and leaned forward in her seat. "We never left for Arcadia when the others did," she said. "All the cold centuries while your kind basked in the warmth of the Dreaming, House Scathach stayed behind and nurtured what little it could of human hopes and dreams. In order to do this, we married into mortal families—so that our essences would be perpetuated through our descendants."

"Like the commoners," Leigh said, then bit her lip as she saw Sorcha's reaction to her comment.

"Exactly." The young knight's voice cut like steel.

Leigh sighed.

"I was born into a mortal family," she said carefully. "I was kicked out of Arcadia sometime after the mass return."

"In other words, you took over the body of an unborn child," Sorcha said, her tone accusatory. "With us, it's not like that. Our blood is so mixed with that of our mortal kin that when we're born, we displace no one. For that, we're called half-breeds."

"I guess I don't understand what the problem is," Leigh said. "But then, I associate with commoners, myself." She smiled as Valmont's image rose in her mind along with flashes of her many arguments with the eshu on the unfairness of the sidhe's exclusive claim to noble blood. She had defended, with an arrogance born of unconscious assumptions, the right of the sidhe to rule. Now, with a new awareness born from trust in her oathmates—all of them commoners, except for Morgan—she had begun to revise her convictions. *Then there's Yrtalien*, she thought, *a vivid reminder that nobility does not always equal virtue.*

"I noticed," Sorcha said. For the first time since entering Leigh's half of the tent, the tension in her face disappeared, giving way to a real smile. "We're a fine pair of champions."

Leigh grinned.

"I wish this situation didn't have to come to blows," she said. "We didn't come here to fight our cousins. We just want a chance to fulfill our quest, but no one seemed interested in even hearing our side of the story."

Sorcha leaned back in her seat, relaxing her death-grip on the chair arms.

"It was probably the only thing that would get their attention," she said. "They love dramatic gestures, in case you haven't noticed."

"How did you come to be one of the Riders?" Leigh asked.

"You noticed, then, the great love they all have for me," Sorcha commented.

Rasputin couldn't have said it better, Leigh thought.

"More or less," she answered.

"Lady Rowena sponsored me for membership," Sorcha said.

Leigh looked surprised. "She didn't exactly leap to your defense when Lord Tiernach insulted you," she observed.

Sorcha shrugged. "That's her way, I suppose," she

replied. "Anyway, Lady Rowena noticed my swordsmanship during a local tournament—we're both from the Kerry region—and approached me about joining the Riders. She'd already told me too much about them to back down when she found out that I belonged to a tainted House."

"So the Riders are a secret society, then?" Leigh asked.

Her guest nodded. "Very. It's made up of warriors from all over Ireland who have sworn themselves to protect the lord of this forest against any who might mean harm to him or who want to use his power for their own personal ends."

"The Hidden King?"

"Where did you hear that term?" Sorcha asked, her voice suddenly suspicious.

"A little clurichaun told us about him," Leigh said. "He's been here before."

Sorcha smiled cryptically. "I know," she said. "It drove Lord Tiernach daft trying to figure out how he slipped by our notice. The forest usually responds to the entrance of anyone not attuned to it." She cut off her speech abruptly, as if she hadn't meant to say so much.

"That's all right," Leigh interjected quickly. "We have no reason to want to betray any of your secrets."

"After tomorrow," Sorcha replied, "you won't have the opportunity to."

Leigh nodded. "After tomorrow, I hope your comrades will be more disposed to listen to us." Absently, she reached for some strawberries and cheese. "Why is he called the Hidden King?"

"That should be obvious," Sorcha said. "Only the Riders know of his existence, and we intend to keep it that way. He's one of the old fae, ancient even at the time of the Sundering. Some say he's full Tuatha de Danann."

"They were the legendary heroes, weren't they?"
Leigh asked.

Sorcha nodded. "You've heard of them?"

"My father brought me up on all the Irish myths,"
Leigh said. "His family came to America before he was
born, but they raised him on legends and ballads from
what they called the old country."

"Oh?" Sorcha looked interested. "What part of
Ireland?"

Leigh shook her head, feeling a little embarrassed
at her ignorance. "I'm not sure," she replied. "Bally-
something, I think."

Sorcha laughed. "That's like saying you have
relatives in New Something in America," she said.

"Are you and your family close still?" Leigh asked.
"Your mortal family?"

"What other family is there?" Sorcha said. "Yes,
we're fairly close. Our House has never been quite as
hush-hush about our faerie blood with our mortal kin
as some other Houses I could mention."

"Like all of them," Leigh said.

"Just about," Sorcha said. "My brothers—I have
four—all know I'm one of the fair folk. My parents
are dead, these five years now."

Leigh gave a sympathetic nod. "How do your
brothers feel about what you are?" *My parents would
lock me up if I tried to tell them, just like Morgan's tried
to do with her,* she thought.

"They're proud of it, though they don't go around
broadcasting the knowledge to all and sundry," Sorcha
said. "They're pleased that maybe one of their sons or
daughters will prove to be like me."

"You said something a few minutes ago that puzzles
me," Leigh said, changing the subject as a thought
suddenly crossed her mind. "When I assured you that
the knowledge of the Riders' existence was safe with

us, you said that after tomorrow we wouldn't have the opportunity to betray you."

Sorcha nodded grimly. "Assuming I win, of course," she said in a voice that almost sounded confident, "you'll be sent from the forest, but not until your memories of having been here have been taken from you."

Leigh felt her face grow pale. "You can't do that!" she exclaimed.

"I'm afraid we'll have to," Sorcha replied.

"You don't understand," Leigh said. "This king of yours can tell us how we can finish our quest. If you keep us from him, then someone else will find and open Silver's Gate and what havoc he will cause when he does will be on the heads of all of you who stood in our way."

Sorcha stood up, her face once again the face of a cold-blooded warrior of the sidhe. "We never asked you to come here," she said. "Whatever happens is no fault of ours. If you can't finish your quest on your own, then you're not very good at such things, are you?"

Before Leigh could answer her charge, Sorcha turned and crossed into her half of the room, drawing the curtain closed behind her.

"Good luck to you, too," Leigh muttered. *She's right, though,* Leigh thought bitterly as she slumped on the bed. *We've done this to ourselves.* She sighed and tried to recover the composure she had attained before her opponent's visit. *It's too bad there are no dry runs for quests.*

"May I come in?" Leigh looked up at the sound of Morgan's voice. The childling was standing in the doorway, holding an armful of summer flowers. The sight of her small oathmate brought a smile to Leigh's face and she beckoned Morgan into the room.

"These were growing near the edge of the

clearing," the childling said as she handed the flowers to Leigh and kissed her on the cheek. "Sir Odhran said I could pick them for you."

Leigh thanked Morgan and laid the blossoms on the pillow. Their heady scent filled the air around them.

"Are the others coming to see me, too?" she asked, looking anxiously over Morgan's shoulder toward the entrance. Morgan nodded.

"We're taking turns," she said. "I asked if I could be first so I could give you the flowers." In spite of her worry over Sorcha's words, Leigh was amused at Morgan's logic. *I need to tell them about the Riders' plans in the event that I lose*, she thought.

Morgan chattered on about the method the companions had used to determine their visitation order. "And Valmont's name came up last," she said. "He didn't seem to mind, though."

Leigh smiled. *Neither do I*, she thought.

all kings

chapter

seven

Rasputin roused slowly from a fitful sleep. A soft veil of dew covered the ground in the clearing, though none of the early morning moisture lay near the sleeping Kithain. "Must be a natural phenomenon," the pooka mumbled, rising to his feet and stretching to loosen muscles grown stiff by a night in the open. Despite his attempts to drive away the last vestiges of sleepiness, he still felt unaccountably tired.

A soft noise caught his attention, and he looked toward the pavilion in time to see Valmont quietly closing the flap. The eshu crossed the clearing, hailing Rasputin with a silent warning not to waken the others. Rasputin arched an eyebrow and cocked his head. Valmont's only response was a smile.

"You look like you've spent the night running for your life," Valmont whispered to Rasputin. "What's wrong?"

"Nothing," the pooka said. "I slept like a babe in its mother's arms all night. I had the loveliest dreams, too," he continued. "I can recall them down to the last detail."

Valmont studied the pooka's haggard face, noticing lines and creases along his brow that had not been there the night before.

"You didn't receive another visitation, did you?" he asked.

Rasputin seemed lost in concentration, as if trying to snatch at the last wisps of his dreams. Finally, he shrugged and shook his head.

"I'm positive it had nothing to do with that," he said.

On the other side of the clearing, the Riders had

begun to stir. A pair of knights bearing trays of food and accompanied by Lady Rowena made their way to the pavilion and entered, one on either side of the divided doorway. She paused outside the pavilion for a moment before she, too, went inside.

"I suppose we'd better wake the others," Valmont said, looking down at the sleeping forms of Morgan and Tor and Liam. "If their hospitality is worth anything, they'll be bringing our breakfast before long."

By the time one of the Riders arrived with a tray of coddled eggs, warm bread, tiny sausages and bowls of honey-soaked berries, the others were awake.

Liam took one look at Rasputin and quickly brought out his guitar.

"I think maybe a little morning music is called for," he announced cheerfully. Valmont gave him a grateful smile.

"We'll save some of the food for you," the eshu said, "unless you think you can eat and play at the same time."

The clurichaun chuckled softly. "That's not one of my better skills," he admitted.

"What's going on up at the tent?" Tor asked the knight who had brought the food.

"Lady Rowena is instructing the combatants in the protocols of this morning's challenge," the young sidhe replied. "There are certain formalities that must be observed to guarantee a just outcome to the battle."

"I thought that the best fighter would win," Morgan said.

The knight gave Morgan a pitying look. "Both of the champions will be bound by the force of Glamour," she said, her voice assuming the tone of a lecturer. "The power of the forest's enchantments will ensure that whoever is in the right will gain the victory."

"Oh," Morgan replied, looking disappointed. "So why do they have to fight, if the outcome is already determined?"

"Why does the success of any of our magic depend on the performance of certain actions—some of which seem to be entirely pointless?" Valmont looked at the knight as he posed his question.

The Rider seemed relieved to be able to pass on the burden of explanation to the eshu. Excusing herself, she walked quickly to the other side of the clearing.

"You mean the entire fight is just a prop to make the magic work?" Morgan frowned.

"It's a little more complicated than that," Valmont said. "The fight symbolizes the intent of both parties. Without it, there would be no focus for the Glamour to take hold and reveal the truth."

"So Leigh will win," Morgan replied, her voice firm and clear. "Won't she?"

"If she doesn't," Tor said, "we might as well pack it in and go home."

Morgan looked anxiously from her grandfather to Valmont. "Is that true?" she asked.

The eshu nodded. "It's a distinct possibility," he replied somberly.

"Why don't we put aside what we can't control for the moment," Liam said as he began to finger a sprightly tune on the guitar. "I have a ballad or two that should get us all through breakfast and then some, if you'll just settle yourselves down and eat while I provide the entertainment." He looked pointedly at Rasputin. "You especially," he said to the pooka. "You could use a little bolstering of the spirits, if I'm not mistaken."

"You couldn't be further from the truth," Rasputin replied, settling himself down with a hunk of bread and a bowl of berries as the clurichaun began to play.

"If it weren't for all the people cluttering up the place, this would still be impressive," Dougal remarked as he stood with Yrtalien and the others atop the massive basalt formation known as the Giant's Causeway.

All around them, vertical columns of volcanic rock jutted upward from the sea, so close together that they formed a honeycomb of stepping stones off the northern coast of Antrim.

"Legend has it that the causeway was built by Finn MacCool himself as a pathway between his home and that of his sweetheart—a giantess—so that he could go and visit her on Staffa Island in Scotland."

"Who's Finn MacCool himself?" Edmund asked, staring out in unabashed amazement at the expanse of bizarre rock formations.

Donal laughed. "He's one of Ireland's most famous figures," he said. "A lot of the landmarks in Ireland are supposed to have been caused by his escapades. The Isle of Man, for instance, sprang into existence because Finn scooped up a clod of earth and hurled it out into the sea. The hole left by the missing lump of earth became Lough Neagh, the largest lake in Ireland—in all of the British Isles, in fact. I suppose he would be sort of like your Paul Bunyan."

"This place is dead," Glynnis said, her faerie vision seeing a once beautiful piece of natural artistry now devoid of inspiration. Standing beside her, the Eyestones cradled in the palm of his hand, Yrtalien nodded.

"I told you there'd be nothing here," Dougal remarked. "What magic there was has been eaten up by the National Trust. They're the ones who maintain the place and put up all the signs telling you which walks you can take and what to look at."

Malacar shivered in the cold, his bad leg aching as the bitter wind gusted in from the sea. "This would be a dismal place for a gateway," he grumbled, "or a court, for that matter."

"No one asked your opinion," Yrtalien said, an ugly scowl marring the fine lines of his handsome face. "I wanted to come here to see the place for myself. Occasionally, places that once possessed large amounts of magical energies still resonate long after those energies have faded."

"Huh?" Edmund asked.

Glynnis looked at him and shook her head. "Never mind," she said.

"Can I wander around some?" the childling asked. "Or are we gonna leave now that we've seen the place?"

Yrtalien shrugged. "Do as you like," he said. "Now that we're here, we might as well see the sights like the other tourists." He laughed mirthlessly. Seizing the opportunity, Edmund darted off, leaping from rock to rock with reckless abandon.

"There are 40,000 or so of these columns," Donal called to the redcap's back. "Try not to break any of them."

It took the childling only a few minutes to find what he was looking for. He pulled out the already tattered pamphlet he had picked up at the display center at the entrance to the causeway and glanced at it to make sure he was in the right place.

"This looks like the Middle Causeway, all right," he said to himself, comparing the diagram in the pamphlet to the evidence of his eyes. The rocks were lower and wider at this point. One formation in particular resembled a child-sized chair.

"Hey!" he called out to a passing family of sightseers. The man turned his head toward the sound, while his two children ran ahead of him.

"Is this the Wishing Chair?" Edmund asked, pointing to the rocks that seemed to match up with the pamphlet's description.

The man nodded hastily. "That's it," he said, and gave Edmund a wave before hurrying to catch up with his children.

Edmund scrunched down into the seat, taking a quick look around him to make sure that none of his companions were in sight. He fished Mr. Dumpy out of his pocket and hastily fed some of his Glamour to the chimeric clown.

"I don't have a lot of time," he told his friend, pulling the clown onto his lap and locking his arms around the figure's corpulent midsection. "Old Prince Charmless will probably want to leave soon. I need your help. I think I made a real mistake hooking up with the prince and I don't know what to do about it." Mr. Dumpy looked over his shoulder and gave Edmund a sad grin. "This may be my only chance to make things turn out the way they were supposed to." The clown's smile widened.

"Since there's not a lot of Glamour left here, I thought you might help pump the place up a little for me." Mr. Dumpy nodded, his painted eyebrows frowning in concentration. The figure seemed to fade just a little and Edmund felt a tingle in the air around him.

"Thanks," he whispered. *I have to do this right*, he thought and considered carefully what he wanted to say.

"I wish," he began, then stopped. "This is stupid, isn't it?" Mr. Dumpy shrugged and smiled.

"Yeah, you're right," Edmund replied. "It can't hurt. And who's to know if it doesn't work?" He took a deep breath and started over, this time closing his eyes.

"I wish that I could find some way to get myself out of this mess and fix any screw-ups so that they never happened and so that I was with people who didn't treat me like I wasn't there even if they yell at me sometimes and even if I think one of them is a snotty-faced pea-brain. At least they paid attention to me once in awhile."

His wish made, Edmund opened his eyes. "I feel like I should blow out a candle or something," he said. Mr. Dumpy obligingly held up his index finger. Edmund blew on the make-believe candle.

"Well, that's that," he remarked. "I guess you'd better shrink down again," he told the clown. When he had Mr. Dumpy safely ensconced in his pocket, Edmund scrambled out of the stone seat and made his way by a roundabout route back to the others.

"It's about time," Yrtalien commented as the childling rejoined the group.

"Are we ready to leave then?" Dougal asked. "If so, we can still make it to Ballycastle and Rathlin Island. The island's still got a bit of wildness left to it and there are some old ruins there you might find worth looking into."

Yrtalien took Glynnis by the arm and followed the brothers back toward the causeway entrance. "Maybe the day won't have been totally wasted," he remarked. Malacar hobbled after the prince, while Edmund dawdled at the rear of the group.

I guess all I can do is wait, he told himself, crossing his fingers for good luck as he wondered if his wish would come true.

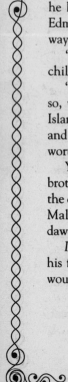

Leigh and Sorcha faced each other in the center of a ring formed by those who would witness their solemn contest. Lord Tiernach, as the senior of the Riders, stood between the two sidhe knights, ready to pronounce the oaths of binding that would invest the trial-by-combat with the force of Glamour.

Morgan tried to keep from fidgeting as she stood by Tor's side. On her other side, Valmont stared impassively at Leigh, his clenched jaw and taut neck muscles the only signs of the eshu's tension. Next to him, Rasputin looked thoughtful. Liam's Glamour-inspiring music seemed to have refreshed the pooka, but his face still bore a few lines of worry. Beside Rasputin, the clurichaun stood quietly, his attention focused on the center of the ring.

"They have real weapons!" Morgan whispered urgently to Tor. The troll nodded without looking down at his granddaughter.

"They're about to start," he answered, his low rumble drawing a warning look from the Riders standing on his far side.

Lord Tiernach held a quiet conversation with Leigh and Sorcha. From the brief nods and muttered responses, the combatants seemed to be signaling their readiness to begin.

"Let's hope our champion doesn't forget herself this day," one of the knights standing near Tor mumbled to the Rider next to him.

His companion nodded curtly.

"It would be a pity for her to fall prey to the curse of her House."

Tor's head turned at the ominous statement. He was on the verge of asking the knights what the words meant when, as if some silent signal had been given, the hushed conversations stopped abruptly. A great stillness filled the clearing.

Morgan felt a prickling sensation at the back of her neck, a sure sign of vast amounts of Glamour. Around her, the other spectators seemed to sense the change in the air as well.

Within the circle, Lord Tiernach nodded, first at Leigh and then at Sorcha. He lifted his arms and addressed the group.

"This day we invoke the solemn right of trial by combat to decide the fitness of the challenger and her companions to remain in this forest freehold." He turned to Leigh.

"Dame Eleighanara of House Fiona, you have issued the challenge. You have the right, now and at no other time, to withdraw that challenge and retreat with honor, along with your companions, from this place. Do you wish to continue your suit?"

"I do," Leigh replied, her voice strong and clear in the crackling air.

Lord Tiernach nodded. The sidhe lord's attention turned to Sorcha.

"Lady Sorcha of House Scathach," he said. "As champion of the Riders of the Silver Court, the choice of weapons has fallen to you. For the benefit of all those who are here assembled, I will ask you to state that choice so that there shall be no cause for question at a later time."

"I choose steel blades," Sorcha announced, one hand unconsciously moving to the hilt of the sword that hung at her waist.

"You will fight to first blood," Lord Tiernach proclaimed, this time speaking to both of the designated champions. "When one of you draws blood, both combatants will step away from the fight and await our judgment. Is that understood?" he looked from one to the other as each in turn signaled her acknowledgement of the terms of battle.

Morgan tugged on her grandfather's arm. Tor turned his head and looked down at the childling, his face fixed in a stern frown.

"They could really get hurt," Morgan mouthed. She bit her lip, suddenly realizing the risk her oathmate was taking.

Tor grunted softly. "This is what being a knight is all about," he said.

The Rider next to Tor hissed. Tor whipped his head around and fixed him with a stony glare, then looked back at Morgan.

She blushed and fell silent, her small face troubled.

"Draw your weapons," Lord Tiernach commanded.

In a rehearsed gesture, Leigh and Sorcha pulled their swords from their sheaths and presented them, hilt first, to Lord Tiernach. The sidhe noble grasped the hilts of both swords with his hands, linking the combatants, through him, to each other.

"Because you have chosen to appeal to the power of the Dreaming to bestow its favor upon the side whose cause is most righteous, I invoke the threefold oath of Honorable Combat. By the earth which lies ready to receive your blood, by the sky which bears witness to your struggle, and by the trees which stand as sentinels and guardians over the events of this day, I bind you both to the power that sustains us. May your will be steadfast, your blows clean and true, and your honor without blemish."

The air began to shimmer around the three knights in the center of the ring, and a soft glowing light arose from within Lord Tiernach to encircle Leigh and Sorcha. Their blades gleamed as if touched by sunlight.

Lord Tiernach released his hold on the swords and stepped back.

"The binding is complete," he announced and

all kings

began moving toward the outer edge of the circle. "Salute each other and begin when ready."

Signe's papers and baggage were in order and she had no trouble clearing Irish customs. She inquired about cab fares to Dublin, where she had made a reservation for herself in one of the city's more modest hotels. She stood for a moment in the crowded airport, listening to the conversations going on all around her. Her newly reawakened poet's soul tried to memorize the lilting cadences of Irish speech.

After hearing her oath at the Toybox, Fizzlewig and his friends had confided in her what they knew of the whereabouts of Leigh and her oathmates. Their information led her to the selkies of Point Reyes, who, in turn, had directed her to Ireland. She declined their offer of magical transport, although the idea of traveling by sea trod presented her with a strong temptation.

I must make my own way to where I need to be, she said, repeating to herself the words she had spoken to Ondine. *Retracing the steps of those I seek will only lead me further from them.*

She shouldered her single large bag and made her way to a waiting cab. Once she had given the hotel's address to the driver, she settled herself in the back seat and began flipping idly through the guide book she had picked up in the airport gift shop.

This is such an old country, she thought, scanning the section on historic landmarks—some of which dated to before recorded history. *It's almost as old as the homeland of the eshu.*

She felt no sense of urgency and decided to trust her instincts. *A few days as a tourist won't hurt,* she said to herself, reveling in her first real taste of freedom after so many years of following Ryder and his Dauntain companions. *I will know when it is time for me to begin searching in earnest.*

Leigh raised her sword in salute to her opponent. Sorcha's return salute became the prelude to her opening attack, forcing Leigh to angle her own blade to meet it. Leigh stepped backward quickly, a maneuver which unbalanced her opponent and sent Sorcha careening forward. Adjusting her grip on the unfamiliar weapon, Leigh pivoted, bringing her sword around to block Sorcha's anticipated return.

So far, so good, she thought. She had reckoned on her opponent going for the quick strike in hopes of scoring an early victory. The disappointed look on Sorcha's face confirmed Leigh's assessment of her rival's game plan. The young Scathach knight set herself for another thrust, coming in low, trying to get underneath Leigh's guard. Again, Leigh evaded her attack, this time with a sidestep.

Each fight has three critical moments—the beginning, the middle, and the end. Neglect one, and you've lost the battle. The words of Sir Cumulus, Leigh's instructor in swordsmanship at Duke Aeon's freehold, came back to her as she brought her own sword up for her first attack, trying to catch Sorcha before she could realign herself. Her blade swished cleanly through the air as Sorcha danced out of its reach.

"What's going on?" Morgan asked Tor, her face mirroring the worried tone of her voice. "Why isn't Leigh going after her?"

"Give her time," Tor replied. "She's testing the waters."

"She'd better not spend too much time sizing up Sorcha," the Rider next to Tor commented, interjecting himself into the conversation. "Our girl is bent on making that first cut."

Tor nodded, his concentration focused on his oathmate.

Sorcha cursed as her rival evaded yet another sure blow. The Fiona knight's movements were unlike any she had seen before. *It's like fighting water*, she thought. *There's no resistance where you'd expect it to be*. She caught her lower lip between her teeth to help her focus on her present situation. Physically, Leigh outmatched her. She had counted on her own quickness and natural agility to allow her to slip inside the taller, stronger knight's guard and land a telling blow.

Valmont watched Leigh's movements stoically, trying not to betray the pounding in his chest or the tightness in his throat. He resisted the impulse to compare her techniques to his own. *This is her battle*, he told himself. *I cannot fight it for her.*

"I'm so glad this is going to be a short fight," Rasputin said. The pooka shifted his balance nervously from one foot to the other, dancing in place.

"She'd better strike soon, or the Scathach curse will be her undoing," Liam observed.

"What Scathach curse?" Valmont asked, his voice sharp with sudden anxiety.

"Battle frenzy," Liam said. "They fight like sharks— or piranhas—once they get roused, and it looks to me as if she's about to do just that."

Leigh's arm shuddered with the force of Sorcha's blow. *That one was serious*, she thought, letting the shock dissipate through the rest of her body and gearing up for a counterattack. Before she could set herself, however, Sorcha was on her again and Leigh felt the edge of her rival's blade brush against her gauntleted hand. Too close.

Sorcha swore aloud at her failure to connect with the unprotected skin just above Leigh's glove. *That should have been my victory*, she thought, feeling the madness build up inside her.

Leigh retreated quickly, realizing that she had fallen into a pattern of defense that would not stand up to a fight to first blood. *The beginning's over*, she thought. *It's time to skip right to the end and finish this, if I can.* She cleared her mind of everything but the flow of energy that directed her sword arm. As she advanced, she felt a calmness in the center of her being. Without conscious direction, her blade cut through the air in front of her, setting up a barrier of flashing steel that her opponent could not penetrate.

"It's about time," Tor muttered under his breath, his voice rumbling like distant thunder.

Morgan felt the excitement in the air as Leigh made her move.

"The Glamour," she cried. "It's on our side!"

Next to her, Valmont breathed a sigh of relief. Rasputin stopped fidgeting.

Sorcha suddenly found herself on the defensive. Something snapped within her. Her face hardened into a mask of wild anger as she frantically met each blow with one of her own. All except one.

Leigh drove her blade into an opening in Sorcha's desperate parries, its edge finding the Scathach knight's unprotected forearm. A bright red line of blood welled up from the shallow wound. *Just enough for a mark*, Leigh thought. From the gasps around her and the sounds of triumph in the voices of her oathmates, she knew that the victory was hers. Out of the corner of her eye, she saw Lord Tiernach step into the circle.

"Stand down," the sidhe lord commanded. "First blood has been drawn."

Leigh lowered her sword and began to back away.

"No!" Sorcha screamed, her voice a howl of rage and defiance. "To the death!" Mindless of her wounded arm, she redoubled her attack, heedless of everything but the desire for blood.

Caught unprepared by Sorcha's refusal to accept defeat, Leigh felt a sharp pain followed by a warm wetness blossoming just under her left arm. A hot wave of nausea swept over her.

Morgan screamed, "Somebody do something!" The childling's voice was frantic.

Valmont and Tor both rushed forward, reaching for their weapons. Across the circle, Lady Rowena and Sir Odhran advanced on the battling warriors. Lord Tiernach, closest to Leigh and Sorcha, attempted to place himself between them, but a swift elbow to his stomach from the Scathach knight sent him reeling.

Clutching her left arm to her side, Leigh raised her sword once more. This time, she was fighting for her life. She could sense the others approaching, but they were still seconds away from intervening.

"Give it up," she cried out to Sorcha. "It's over!"

Sorcha ignored her plea, swinging her sword high in an attempt to slice just above Leigh's breastplate. Leigh threw her full weight into the parry. Sorcha's arm bent back and she lurched off balance.

Now! Leigh thought, stepping inside Sorcha's guard and hooking one foot behind her nearest ankle. The Scathach knight went down, her sword falling free onto the ground beside her. Leigh straddled her, pinning Sorcha's sword hand with a carefully planted foot. She pointed her sword at the young knight's neck. She felt suddenly light-headed and clenched her jaw to keep from losing consciousness.

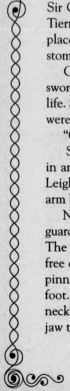

Valmont and Tor came up: Tor stood behind her to steady her, while Valmont slipped an arm around her waist and tried to move her away from the prone knight. Leigh shook her head. "Not yet," she mumbled, her voice barely audible. Lady Rowena stood at Sorcha's head, ready to assist her from the field. Sir Odhran moved to help Lord Tiernach to his feet.

"Yield me this victory," Leigh said to Sorcha, who glared up at her, her breath coming in shallow gasps. "This day's fight was fair. There is no shame in it."

Carefully extending her left arm so that she would not aggravate the wound in her side, she held a hand out for Sorcha to grasp and moved her foot to release the knight's wrist. Sorcha's gray eyes darkened to the color of iron. She reached upward as if to take hold of Leigh's proffered hand, but suddenly lunged instead for Leigh's sword arm, grasping Leigh's wrist with both hands.

"I'll die first," she hissed. "It's more than any of them would do." She jerked Leigh's wrist down so that the blade pierced her own throat just below the neckline.

Horrified, Leigh pulled back, a scream of outrage escaping her lips. Tor locked his arms around her chest and hauled her backward, while Valmont dropped to his knees and began frantically trying to stop the spurting blood that gushed from Sorcha's neck. Lady Rowena's outstretched hand stopped the eshu.

"Let her go," the Fiona noblewoman said softly. "This is her choice to make."

"I will not have her death be on my oathmate's hands," Valmont answered, his voice harsh.

"I, for one, will stand witness that Dame Eleighanara bears no blame for this knight's death," Lord Tiernach said. Beside him, Sir Odhran nodded, his face somber.

"If she can be saved—" he began, giving Lady Rowena a beseeching look.

"She would never forgive us—and we, in our turn, would never let her forget this defeat." She looked down at Sorcha and smoothed her dark red curls away from her forehead. Sorcha's eyes closed as she struggled for enough breath to speak.

"It's not the same for me," she gasped, her voice garbled as her windpipe filled with blood. "Is it, now?" Her hands clawed at the ground as a harsh rasp escaped her and her features suddenly relaxed into a waxen rictus of death.

Leigh buried her face in Tor's chest and wept. Tor held her in his arms. *It never changes*, the troll thought as he realized that this was not the first time he had comforted a young warrior after her first encounter with death.

"Is it always like this?" Leigh whispered, her voice still punctuated by long racking sobs. Tor closed his eyes and saw Ryder's face just before he cast himself into the molten river of lava, a face full of relief and weariness at a burden too long carried and willingly surrendered. He watched again with dreamlike clarity as his first Lady Morgania closed her eyes, resigned to a fate she could not avoid. Once more, he felt the heat of the jungle around him as he looked upon the surprised and puzzled face of a black-clad youth, his lungs punctured by a stab from Tor's bayonet.

"Sometimes it's worse," the troll replied, unable to give her the consolation she wanted. "Sometimes they don't want to die."

Valmont stood up and looked sadly down at Sorcha's lifeless form.

"She did not have to die," he said, feeling a cold hatred form in the pit of his stomach. *The sidhe do not reincarnate*, he thought, as the full import of

Sorcha's decision took hold of his speech. "What kind of chivalric code allows—no—encourages this kind of waste when there is such a need for courage like hers?"

"You cannot understand," Lady Rowena said, still sitting beside Sorcha's body.

A hundred angry comments rose to his lips, but the eshu pushed them all back. He shook his head slowly.

"No," he replied. "I cannot understand, but I do not believe it is due to any lack on *my* part." He turned and walked over to Leigh and Tor.

Sensing Valmont's presence behind her, Leigh stepped backward out of Tor's embrace and turned to the eshu. Her tear-streaked face was full of pain. She started to speak to him but felt her knees begin to give way beneath her.

"You're wounded," Valmont said, catching her before she fell. Picking her up in his arms, the eshu started toward the pavilion. "This is something I won't be prevented from doing," he whispered to her.

Tor hurried over to Morgan and the others. Rasputin had his arms around the childling, who had begun to cry quietly. At the sight of her grandfather, she abandoned all pretense of bravery and threw herself into the troll's arms. Tor cradled her against his shoulder.

Rasputin looked up at Tor.

"Don't say it—whatever it is," Tor grumbled. "I'm not in the mood."

The pooka lowered his head quickly. Liam placed a friendly hand on Rasputin's shoulder and steered him away from the battle scene.

"I really wasn't going to say anything," the pooka said mournfully. "There's not much you can say at a time like this."

Liam clucked sympathetically.

"I know exactly what you mean," he said. "That's why most dirges are wordless tunes."

Deep beneath the waves, the remnants of a broken dream began to resonate with old memories of a time long past. Cushioned by the weight of time and water, the light of its enchantments still glimmered faintly, a soft beacon in the endless ocean night. *Too long and long enough*, the twin pillars of stone seemed to sigh. *Near but not yet near enough*, a frozen statue whispered, her voice a soundless cry in the silence that surrounded her. *Soon*, the trio of voices spoke together. *Let it be soon.*

Leaning on Valmont for support, Leigh left the pavilion. It was nearly dark and the chimeric globes that hovered among the trees once again provided the only light for the clearing. The eshu's healing magic had begun its work on her wounded side, but she was still unsteady on her feet. From across the clearing, Morgan spotted her and ran up to greet her oathmate. The childling's eyes were puffy from crying, but her tears were no longer visible. She opened her arms to give Leigh a hug, but Valmont stopped her with a look.

"Careful," he warned her. "She's still a little sore."

Morgan looked chagrined.

Leigh leaned down and hugged Morgan gently.

"It's okay," she said. "I won't break."

"Will you be all right?" Morgan asked.

"I'm feeling better already," Leigh reassured her.

Morgan sighed with relief.

Leigh's gaze turned inadvertently toward the site of her earlier battle, now indistinguishable from any other spot in the forest glade. She frowned, puzzled.

"They've taken Sorcha away," Morgan said.

"Who? Where?" Leigh asked.

"Lady Rowena and a few of the other knights left a little while ago. They said they were taking her—her body home to her family." Morgan's eyes began to fill again with tears at the reference to Sorcha's death.

She's trying awfully hard to be a baroness instead of a child about this, Leigh thought. *I don't know if I could have done so well when I was her age.*

With Morgan and Valmont on either side of her, Leigh covered the remaining distance to the spot where they had camped the night before. Tor stood up and offered an arm to Leigh, guiding her gently to a seat on the grassy floor of the clearing. Rasputin smiled cheerfully at his oathmate and patted her knee.

"It's terrible to see you looking so ill after your mild brush with danger," he said. "I told Liam that you probably wouldn't be interested in hearing one of his maudlin songs," he added, "so he promised not to play anything for you this evening."

Leigh smiled. She found herself looking forward to hearing another of the clurichaun's ballads.

Valmont took advantage of Leigh's involvement with Rasputin to catch Tor's attention. "What's this about taking Sorcha's body home to her family?" he asked, his voice edgy with concern. "Won't there be a problem with how she died?"

"Sir Odhran gave the impression that they had it covered," the troll replied.

Overhearing the conversation, Leigh turned to them. "Sorcha told me last night that her brothers knew what she was," she said. "I suppose that means that they won't try to have me arrested on murder charges."

Morgan gasped. "Can they do that?" she asked. "Wouldn't it be self defense?"

"The point is," Valmont said, "our presence in Ireland is on legally tenuous grounds. We didn't exactly pass through customs as we entered the country."

"I thought you said we didn't have to worry about that," Morgan replied.

The eshu nodded. "Under most circumstances, that would be true. I don't know what would happen if we became the subjects of a police investigation."

"I suppose they'll congratulate us on our cleverness and give us the keys to Dublin," Rasputin quipped. The pooka's attention shifted to a point beyond his immediate companions. "Don't look now," he said. "Nobody is on his way over."

Lord Tiernach approached the group. Leigh attempted to stand in deference to the ranking member of the Riders of the Silver Court, but he motioned for them all to remain seated.

"I am relieved to see you looking so much better than when I saw you last," he said to Leigh, who nodded her thanks at his expression of concern. "I regret that your victory came about under such difficult circumstances," he continued, "but it is, nonetheless, a victory for you under the terms of the challenge." He gestured toward the edge of the clearing, where the other Riders were mounted and waiting. "We have extra horses to carry you to the Dreamers' Glen, where you will join us for the evening."

Morgan eyed the assembled Riders dubiously.

"Do you have a horse for Grandpa?" she asked.

Lord Tiernach looked vaguely embarrassed. "There is one stronger and larger than the others," he began, but Tor cut him off with a jerky shake of his head.

"Thanks," he said. "I'd be just as happy on foot."

The sidhe lord looked relieved. "It is not a lengthy journey," he said, "but it will be less strenuous for those who accept our offer of mounts."

"Do I get my own horse this time, or will Sir Odhran let me ride with him?" Morgan asked. Leigh and Valmont exchanged amused glances at the childling's deftly posed question.

Lord Tiernach bestowed a smile on the young baroness. "Sir Odhran informs me that you have the natural seat of a born rider," he said. "There is a dappled mare just for you."

Rasputin leaned over and whispered in Morgan's ear.

"Don't believe him," the pooka said. "It's probably some poor pooka like me who's been trapped in horse form for years because they won't leave her alone."

Morgan giggled. At the sound of her light-hearted laughter, some of the dreariness that had settled over the clearing began to dissipate.

"Where's Liam?" Valmont asked.

Lord Tiernach barely managed to conceal a wince.

"The minstrel is already with the others," he said blandly. "We shall leave for the Dreamers' Glen as soon as you are ready."

Valmont rose and offered his arm to Leigh as the others got to their feet. Together, they accompanied Lord Tiernach to the waiting company.

Yrtalien woke suddenly, bridging the gap between deep dreaming and full wakefulness with a single breath. Beside him, Glynnis still slept. Without disturbing her, the prince slipped from the bed and walked over to the window. Bracing himself against the expected blast of cold air, he eased the shutters open and looked out over the darkened landscape.

She is out there, he thought, remembering the dream that had jolted him from his sleep. *The Dauntain could not hold them*. He closed his eyes and grasped at the fading images that had been so vivid only moments before. Leigh and her oathmates stood in a forest of gold and silver trees. Just out of sight, another presence—one of great power and majesty—seemed to beckon. A soundless conversation took place. Without hearing the words, Yrtalien knew—in a manner made possible only in dreams—that the unseen speaker was telling Leigh where to find Silver's Gate. Leigh shook her head and held out her hands, their empty palms upraised.

Yrtalien opened his eyes, unable to recall any more but satisfied that he had retained the core of the true sending. *She knows the location of the gate, but she needs the stones to open it*, he mused. *I have the stones, but lack the knowledge of where to take them.* "I am not yet done with you, Eleighanara," he whispered, his breath turning to wisps of steam that traveled outward into the night.

"We are nearing the heart of the forest," Sir Tiernach said, stopping his horse and turning in his saddle to speak to Leigh, who rode at his side, closely followed by the rest of her companions. The procession had been traveling along a winding trail lit only by chimeric torches held by a number of the Riders. Leigh acknowledged Sir Tiernach's words as she looked back over her shoulder at the line of mounted sidhe, their armor shimmering in the faerie torchlight. For a moment, she knew how mortals must have felt on those rare occasions when they caught sight of the hosting of the sidhe.

"Do not be surprised at what you may see," the sidhe lord added. "Our liege has had centuries in which to spin his dreams, and some of his creations wander freely as far as the place to which we go."

"Will we see a unicorn?" Morgan asked, her voice wistful. Leigh risked a quick glance at Valmont and felt her face redden slightly as the eshu returned her look with a smile and a barely perceptible wink.

"I have never seen one," Lord Tiernach replied gravely, "but that does not mean that you will not."

He urged his horse onward, leading the group through a landscape that seemed to change with every step. As they passed through a stand of copper and silver trees, Leigh recognized the limits of her own earlier foray into the forest. Silver gave way to gold, and the trees seemed to come alive around them, their leaves sounding like windchimes heralding the passing of the sidhe.

"Maybe you'll see the king's deer again," Morgan said to Rasputin, who rode just behind her. Her voice carried like a tiny bell down the line of Riders.

"Let us hope not," Sir Odhran said sharply from his place near the companions.

"Why not?" Tor asked. The troll walked beside Morgan, keeping pace with the leisurely gait of the horses.

Sir Odhran looked off into the distance as he answered.

"Some believe that the creature appears only to those whose lives are in imminent danger of—sudden change." He fell silent, a troubled look on his face.

"Sorcha saw the deer, too," Morgan said, then bit her lip as she realized the import of her words.

all kings

The procession continued on in an uneasy silence until they reached a second clearing.

"Welcome to the Dreamers' Glen," Lord Tiernach said, stopping at the entrance and motioning for the others to precede him into the forest's center.

She fed on Glamour, devouring it in gulps like the famished creature she was. Once, she remembered, the land below her fairly sparkled with faerie magic—the land and the shining people that dwelt upon its surface and within its Dreaming-drenched hills and vales. Now she saw only faint shadows of what once was, many of those shadows tainted with a harsh glare or a sickly gleam that spoke of Glamour twisted into what it was never meant to be.

She drifted, crossing an intangible border into a darker version of the dark world into which she had so recently been freed. This is the land of the dead, she thought, or at least the borderlands where spirits still hover. She sensed the presence of other hungry souls, filled with longing for what they could no longer have. She fed on their longing, drinking in their unfulfilled love, hate, despair, and hope, and growing stronger. The taste of their dreams was like ashes in her mouth, and soon she was back in the world of the living, once again searching for the old magic that had filled her with life and love and lust, that had once made her the envy of kings and champions in four great kingdoms of earth and in the fifth kingdom of the Dreaming.

"It is late," Sir Tiernach cautioned as he gathered the companions together in the center of the Dreamers' Glen. "It would perhaps be better to return another night when the full evening lies ahead of you."

Leigh shook her head. "We've come this far," she said, "and I, for one, am tired enough to fall asleep the minute I lie down."

Tiernach nodded. "I only wanted to give you the benefit of a full night in the glen should you desire it."

"Will you be staying here with us?" Morgan asked.

"Yes," Tiernach replied. "Both for our own sakes, for many of us are in sore need of the refreshment of the spirit that a night in the Dreamers' Glen provides, and for the sake of our king."

"What do you mean?" Valmont asked. Ever since entering the glen, he had been feeling a stirring within him that went deeper than bones or blood. *This place is a crossroads,* he thought, *a meeting of worlds that is not quite a portal or a gate or even a faerie trod but a little of all of them.*

"You have obviously heard of the Hidden King," Tiernach answered, "or else you would not be here."

"I stumbled upon this place the first time, myself," Liam said brightly. Tiernach's frown summed up his commentary on the clurichaun's interjection.

"What you may not know, considering the source from which your knowledge has come," he continued, glancing briefly at Liam, "is that the reason for the Riders' existence is to act as a buffer against those who would harm the king."

"Who would want to do that?" Morgan asked, her eyes wide with an innocence known only to those who have not yet fully grasped the concepts of mean-spiritedness and opportunism.

Lord Tiernach's answering laugh was short and bitter.

"There are many who want power in this land— power to rule and power for their own ends—and the lord of this forest holds a great store of the last real Glamour in this realm."

"Well," Rasputin remarked, looking puzzled. "That certainly explains that. I was hoping you'd give us a definitive answer as to why you are all so secretive about your king and your forest."

"You must forgive our ignorance," Valmont said. "We have only been in this country for a few days. It is not easy to absorb the nuances of politics in such a short time."

"People have been trying to understand Irish politics for centuries," Leigh murmured.

Lord Tiernach's expression softened. "Of course," he said. "You cannot know how difficult it is for us to hold the responsibility for keeping one of Hibernia's biggest secrets from leaking to the world outside— even as far as to others of our kind. We have, perhaps, grown oversolicitous in our desire to keep this land from becoming utterly stripped of its faerie magic."

"Is that really a possibility?" Leigh asked.

He nodded sadly. "So many of our greatest faerie treasures now lie moldering in museums, bereft of the power they once had to inspire us with Glamour. The places where magic used to be are now despoiled or have become havens for sightseers. The forests are no more—except for a few pitiful remnants." He broke off abruptly.

"I believe I understand," Valmont said, his voice full of sympathy.

"What about your rulers?" asked Leigh. "Is there nothing any of them can do?"

"They try," Lord Tiernach said. "Or some of them do. But without a High King, no consensus can be reached—and thus no real actions taken. Nor do we know what actions we would take if we could."

"Why doesn't your king—the one who lives here—

just come out and declare himself High King?" Morgan tried to stifle a yawn as she asked her question.

"Were he to leave these confines, the Banality of the outside world would destroy him," Lord Tiernach said.

"So he is one of the true fae, as Liam told us," Leigh observed.

Lord Tiernach gave the clurichaun a sharp look. Liam inclined his head in a small bow to the knight.

"It wasn't hard to figure it out," he said.

"He is full of the wisdom of the Dreaming," Lord Tiernach told them. "It has long been our custom to visit this glen to meet with him in the only way that will ensure his safety yet give us the benefit of his counsel. We sleep here, and we dream."

"Perhaps, then, it is time for us all to sleep and dream," Valmont said, looking at Morgan, who leaned groggily against Tor's leg, fighting to keep her eyes from closing.

Lord Tiernach indicated the grassy floor of the glen. "Here are your beds," he said. "I and the others will take our rest along the edges of the clearing." He nodded to the companions and walked off to join the other Riders, some of whom had already staked out spots near the outer rim of trees.

"Shall I play you a song to sleep by?" Liam asked, bringing forth his guitar and seating himself cross-legged on the ground as the oathmates arranged themselves in the center of the glen.

"That would be completely unacceptable," Rasputin said. "We'd prefer not to hear any more of your hideously overblown repertoire."

The clurichaun laughed appreciatively. "I'll take that as a compliment," he said. The song he began had a soothing, almost hypnotic melody. "This is one of the parts of the threefold song, once a powerful

 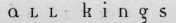

enchantment known only to the true bards of the land. It is the *suantraí*, or slumber song." The soft strains of music filled the clearing with its lulling tones. He looked around as, one by one, the oathmates settled down and closed their eyes. By the time he had finished playing, everyone in the clearing was deep in slumber. Carefully, he put his guitar down on the ground beside him, stretched out on the soft, thick grassy carpet, and let the memory of the *suantraí* carry his thoughts into the realm of the Dreaming.

Morgan was the first to awaken. She stood up and rubbed her eyes, shaking the sleep from her. She heard a rustling sound on the edge of the clearing and peered into the darkness, trying to see what had caused it. Something large and white strode forward from the trees and regarded the childling with steady gaze. Morgan's eyes grew wide and she inhaled sharply.

"A unicorn!" she breathed, not daring to do more than whisper. Without stopping to consider her actions, she began walking slowly toward it, her hand held out in what she hoped it would take as a gesture of friendship.

When she was only a few steps from it, she could see the animal in all its glory. *It's not at all like a horse*, she thought. *It's much, much finer than a horse could ever be.*

She reached out to touch its nose and felt as if she brushed thick velvet. A tingle ran through her as she felt her small body infused with more Glamour than she had ever thought possible. She pulled her hand away quickly, afraid that she would fly apart if she prolonged her contact with the magical creature. Silently, the unicorn turned and walked back into the woods, stopping to look over its shoulder at her, an invitation to follow in its large, liquid eyes.

Leigh and Valmont woke simultaneously, their hands intertwined. The eshu sat up in time to see Morgan disappear into the woods. He rose quickly, pulling Leigh after him.

"Wake Tor and Liam," he said, turning to prod Rasputin's slumbering form gently with his foot. The pooka groaned and blinked his eyes. Valmont pointed in the direction Morgan had gone.

Soon the oathmates and Liam were following the distant figure of their childling companion, moving effortlessly through trees that glistened like gemstones in the moonlight that filtered down from the night sky.

Should we be doing this? Leigh thought, remembering Lord Tiernach's warning. She almost voiced her question aloud, but something stopped her from speaking. *This doesn't feel wrong*, she realized.

The unicorn led Morgan past a forest of crystal and diamonds, each tree more splendid and graceful than the last, until finally it stepped into a place the childling could only describe to herself as Fairyland. Ahead of her was a castle with walls that reflected the light of the moon and the stars. A silver path led toward the castle, and the unicorn proceeded up the path to take its place beside the lone figure who stood halfway between the castle and the edge of the clearing.

She felt a hand on her shoulder and looked up to see Leigh and the others standing behind her.

"I'm glad you're here," she said. "That's the king, I think."

The companions saw a figure wreathed in the light of Glamour, his features impossible to distinguish through his glowing aura. Their eyes received only impressions of hair like spun gold and silver and copper, eyes that were at once as pale as morning and as dark as midnight, and a form that stood up to no description other than "beautiful."

His power was undeniable, and they bowed before it without question.

"You have come at last," a voice filled with the sadness of centuries said quietly, as if some great deed had just been accomplished. "Yet there is one of you who is not here, and another who is here because he once carried a treasure that linked him to this place."

Morgan dared to look up from her bow. "You mean Edmund," she said. "He took the stones and left us."

The figure nodded solemnly and gestured for the group to rise. When they did so, he took a step closer to them and now the companions could see that his face was both younger than they expected and far, far older than they could have imagined.

"I have seen your coming many times," he said softly, "or perhaps I have seen the same coming once and remembered it many times. But there is a sadness that shadows you, and I feel the loss of one of my Riders."

Leigh felt her face grow hot with shame.

"We fought to win our right to meet with you. Sorcha died by my blade."

"Your words are true, but they do not tell the tale as it happened," the king said. "By your blade, yes. But not through any fault of yours. This is the first sacrifice that must be made before what you desire will come to pass. Still, your guilt is almost more than I can bear."

"It is almost more than I can bear," Leigh echoed.

"You have come to find Silver's Gate," the faerie king spoke as if he had rehearsed the words a thousand times. "You are not yet ready to find it."

"What must we do to make ourselves ready?" Valmont asked.

"One of you must surrender guilt and another pride," the king said in a voice that carried the force of Glamour and the weight of his faerie power. "One must be forgiven and one must learn to forgive. One of you must remember, and another must forget. When those things are done, return again to this place and I will give you the secret of Silver's Gate. Return now to your broken slumber and waken, and remember my words."

The castle and the shining figure began to fade like morning mist as all around the companions, the sounds of birds began to grow louder and louder until they opened their eyes to find themselves once more in the Dreamers' Glen, now bright with the light of the morning sun.

chapter

eight

Sir Odhran greeted the companions when they awoke from their night in the glen. Across the clearing, the other Riders were gathered in small groups, some talking quietly, others seeing to the horses. Lord Tiernach stood apart from the rest, apparently lost in thought.

"We would be honored to have you join us for the morning meal," Sir Odhran announced.

"Will you have more strawberries?" Morgan asked, sounding hopeful.

The knight laughed. "I believe there are strawberries and cakes with morsels of butterscotch melted through them, as well as some more substantial fare," he answered.

"A butterscotch cake?" Morgan repeated, her eyes wide.

"I think cakes are actually what we call cookies," Valmont said to her.

As the oathmates crossed the clearing to join the Riders at their breakfast, Sir Odhran fell into step beside Tor.

"I would like to extend an invitation to you, and to the others as well, to join me at the court of King Bran in Leinster," he said, addressing the troll with an unexpectedly formal tone.

"Oh?" Tor responded.

Sir Odhran nodded. "I believe it will be good for you and the others to meet with some of the other Kithain of Hibernia. I would be pleased if you would consider my request and give me your answer by the time we leave the forest."

Tor nodded. "We'll talk about it over breakfast," he said.

"There are some other things we need to talk about," Leigh commented.

"You can't be referring to the dreamless sleep we all undoubtedly experienced," Rasputin said.

Leigh smiled at pooka. "I was thinking that we might compare notes."

"Did you see a unicorn?" Morgan asked, her eyes twinkling as she remembered the wonder of the great beast.

Valmont shook his head. "I'm afraid not." He looked at Leigh and grimaced, then glanced at the others questioningly. All of them except Rasputin shook their heads.

"I think you were the only one," Leigh said, smiling.

"Oh, I saw it," Rasputin said quietly, lagging a little behind the others and speaking more to himself than to them. "It looked nothing at all like a great red deer."

Yrtalien leaned against the door to Edmund's room, trapping the redcap childling inside. Outside, a hard rain was falling, turning the dirt lane that led from the house to the nearest road into a sluggish river of mud that had mired the van and threatened to delay their planned outing for the day. Edmund could hear the brothers' curses over the sound of spinning tires as they labored to free the van's wheels from the tractionless ooze.

"Is this a social call?" Edmund asked the prince, trying to conceal his nervousness at being alone with Yrtalien, a situation he had successfully avoided until now.

Yrtalien smiled beatifically at the redcap childling, who sat on the edge of his small bed, his feet dangling over the side.

"We haven't really had the opportunity to socialize," he said, his voice cool and almost friendly. "I thought I would take advantage of this enforced hiatus in our plans."

I don't like the sound of this, Edmund thought. His hand strayed toward the pocket containing Mr. Dumpy. He caught himself before actually reaching for the pouch which held the chimeric figure and instead gripped the edge of the bed.

"To do what?" Edmund asked dubiously.

Yrtalien laughed softly. "Why, Edmund," he said, his voice falsely soothing, "you look as though you are afraid of me." His dark eyes glittered with barely suppressed mirth.

"Huh," Edmund said, trying to decide whether he should admit his fear to Yrtalien or try to tough it out. *Either way could piss him off big time*, the redcap thought. *I wonder if he knows what I did up at the giant's place?* "I thought I was looking respectful," he finally admitted.

Yrtalien shook his head slowly. "Subtlety is not your strong point, Edmund," he said teasingly. "Relax, I'm just here for a friendly visit. Still, I'm glad to see that you seem to have absorbed last night's example of what I can do if I'm so inclined."

Edmund nodded, gulping audibly. The previous evening, after their return from the Giant's Causeway, Yrtalien and Glynnis had quarreled in the room that they shared. From what he overheard, Edmund guessed they were disagreeing over Malacar. Yrtalien had discovered Edmund crouched outside the door and invited the redcap in to witness yet another display of his power over the hapless Glynnis.

I'll bet there were a shitload of wingless flies around his house in Arcadia when he was a kid, the redcap thought, glancing furtively at the prince to see if

Yrtalien's face gave any evidence of being able to hear his unspoken commentary.

"I've been thinking about the story you told us of the closing of Silver's Gate," the prince began. "I want to hear it again, more slowly and with as much detail as you can remember."

"I'm not real good on details," Edmund said.

"We'll see about that," the prince replied. Yrtalien opened the pouch that hung from a slim cord around his neck and withdrew the three eyestones from it. He cupped them in his hands and uttered a soft phrase. An eerie glow began to form inside the circle of his joined palms as the stones' Glamour stirred within them.

"Come here and touch my hands," Yrtalien commanded.

"I don't feel like it," Edmund said, stricken with the sudden desire to flee. He glanced at the window, trying to calculate his chances for survival were he to throw himself through the opening it provided.

"I expect you to do as I say," Yrtalien said, all pretense of friendliness gone from his voice. "You have a choice. Either come over here willingly and put one finger on my hands or else I will invoke the stones' power at a distance and you will simply have to grin and bear it—if you can—until I see fit to release you from its grip."

Feeling like a condemned criminal, Edmund slowly slid off the bed and walked toward the prince. He eyes began to fill with tears and he shut them tightly, trying to blink back the unwelcome wetness. *I haven't cried since I was six*, he told himself. *I'm not going to start now*. Steeling himself against the inevitable, he opened his eyes again and swiftly closed the distance between himself and Yrtalien. Before he could renege on his action, he jabbed his index finger toward the prince's hands, making contact with the glow that surrounded them. *It can't be worse than sticking a finger in a candle flame,* he thought.

It was. Edmund's finger seemed to scorch and shrivel as if he had plunged it into a vat of molten metal or a river of lava. The searing sensation ran through his body, sending waves of fiery agony through every nerve. Edmund opened his mouth and tried to scream, but his lungs were an inferno so intense that he could not force himself to breathe.

His legs gave way beneath him and he stumbled to the floor, breaking contact with the prince's flesh.

As suddenly as it had come upon him, the pain was gone. Edmund knelt, doubled over, at Yrtalien's feet, his small body wracked with harsh, tearless sobs as he gasped for breath.

"Now," the prince said quietly, "suppose you go back to the bed—crawl if you have to—and tell me, from the beginning, everything you can remember about the fall of Silver's Gate. I am most interested in hearing the story of the twin brothers."

Edmund forced himself to stand. Still trying to choke back the tears that now ran unchecked down his cheeks, he lurched for the bed, his legs rebelling at every step.

In the yard below, he could still hear the muffled voices of Donal and Dougal as he haltingly began to relate the story of the ancient battle between Seelie and Unseelie brothers on the threshold of Silver's Gate.

Signe stood for a long time drinking in the stormy colors and bold brush strokes that had drawn her to the painting mysteriously titled *For the Road*. In the foreground, a steed seemingly created from smoke and mist pranced nervously at the edge of a forest path that formed a tunnellike archway. The far end of the tunnel was bathed in pale light that held only a hint of golden warmth. At the end of the path, a figure—like the horse composed of blue and gray hues—stood framed in a cold brilliance that spoke to the eshu of another world beyond the forest's dimness. The painting's title had originally attracted her attention, but the power of the artist's enigmatic vision was what held her to one spot in Dublin's National Gallery.

"Jack Yeats," a husky female voice said from just behind her. Signe turned sharply and saw a tall, heavyset blond woman dressed in a thick fisherman's sweater and tweed jacket over jeans and brogans. Her faerie sight penetrated beyond the woman's mortal guise, revealing the troll essence that lay concealed within the human form. Her pale-blue skin and white-blond hair reminded Signe of Diana, but where her former companion's features had been taut with repressed anger and resentment, the stranger's face exuded contentment.

"Who?" Signe asked, then noticed that the woman, too, was staring at the painting. "Oh, the artist, you mean," she answered for herself. She glanced around at the other paintings in the room. "The whole room is dedicated to his work," she commented.

The woman nodded. "The poet's brother," she said, this time turning to Signe to gauge her response to the words. Signe nodded.

"Yeats' father was a painter, too," the eshu said, grateful for the keen memory that allowed her to recall necessary details at appropriate times.

"My name's Bridie," the troll said. "Actually, it's Bridget, but I feel more comfortable being called something less feisty, if you know what I mean."

"I think so," Signe replied. "I'm Signe." She held out her hand for the woman to shake.

"And you're from America," Bridie said.

"From Boston, mostly."

"I couldn't help noticing something else about you," the troll added, her eyes sparkling as she, too, saw with a vision that detected more than Signe's mortal shape. Signe grinned. *A few short weeks ago, that comment would have sounded like a condemnation*, she thought. Her eyes strayed back to the painting.

"It still retains its power, even after being exposed like this," she said.

Bridie nodded. "I come here from time to time to get my inspiration, but I try not to be greedy about it. He's much more important to us than he is to the art world in general," she went on, "so there are fewer hungry gapers to drain these works of the Glamour that's left in them. Some say the whole Yeats family had a touch of the faerie blood."

"I hope I haven't infringed on anyone's territory," Signe said hesitantly. Bridie shook her head. "Only mine, and I don't mind sharing with an out-of-towner who doesn't know any better." The tone of her voice was teasing and caught the eshu by surprise. Diana had never shown any tendency toward such lighthearted banter.

"I've just spent the morning trying to give myself a tour of the city," Signe said. "Frankly, I'm tired of holding conversations with myself."

Bridie rewarded her comment with a large grin. "Then let me take over for awhile," she offered. "And why don't we start with something to eat? I'll bet you didn't know about Irish gourmet cuisine."

Signe shook her head. "Just the old joke about an Irish seven course dinner," she said.

"I don't want to hear it," Bridie replied, laughing.

"We could have hare and champ at Pier 32," she continued, "or how about oysters and Guinness at the Sandbank?"

"I think I'll leave the choice up to my tour guide," Signe said, feeling as if a burden had been lifted from her. *This is the first step—no, the second—in finding out where I need to be*, she thought as she followed her new-found friend into the streets of Dublin.

At his private residence in the northern outskirts of Dublin, Bran of House Gwydion, the Seelie King of Leinster, listened intently to the messenger who brought word from Sir Odhran. He had long ago learned not to question the mysterious comings and goings of his most trusted knight, even though there were those in his court who disapproved of Bran's reliance on a member of House Liam. *Whatever other allegiances he may have*, the king mused, *he will not let them come into conflict with his duty to me and mine*.

The boggan wilder recited her memorized speech in a single breath. "He rang me from a roadside phone, sir," she added at the end of her delivery. "He said it was urgent and he knew he could trust me not to botch the words up since I've carried messages from him to you before."

Bran nodded, barely hearing the boggan's explanation and concentrating instead on the information just imparted. He roused himself enough to express his thanks and offer payment to the expectant courier.

"Your name is Bairbre, isn't it?" he asked. He recalled seeing the wilder at court, usually in the company of Sir Odhran's entourage.

The boggan smiled shyly and dipped her head. "It is, your Highness," she said. "I'm a student at Trinity College."

"History, no doubt?" Bran asked. As the king's archivist, among his other duties, Sir Odhran cultivated a number of Kithain—and mortals as well—whose interests lay in Ireland's past.

Again, Bairbre nodded her head.

Bran removed a gold ring, one of several, from his hand and handed it to the boggan.

"This once belonged to a Frenchman who sailed with the French Armada that landed in Bantry Bay in 1796. Take it, with my thanks."

Bairbre's eyes grew wide with pleasure as she accepted the gift and the historic Glamour that made it a minor treasure. She bowed to the king and made her exit.

Once she had gone, Bran rose from his chair and paced around the room that served as his informal audience chamber away from court. Sir Odhran's message had been given in a code devised along with the king to ensure the confidential exchange of information through third parties. Although the words themselves were obscure, their meaning was explicit.

"So he has been found at last and is coming here," Bran mused aloud. His elegant brow wrinkled in dismay as he mulled over the request Sir Odhran had included along with his message. Assembling the court of Leinster on such short notice would not be a problem. The king's herald and his fleet of pages would take care of summoning all the nobles and any interested commoners in the region. Inducing the other great kings, as the rulers of Hibernia's four kingdoms were called, to convene at the Court of Leinster was another matter entirely and would have to be handled very carefully to avoid stirring up any hint that Leinster's king was overstepping his bounds.

King Fiachra of Connaught will not be a problem, the king thought, fondly dwelling for a moment on his friendship with the ruler of Ireland's western counties. *He owes me for the prize stallion I gave him to build up his stables. Queen Nuala may prove a little more difficult, as touchy as she is.* The Queen of Munster, in southwestern Ireland, ruled the largest of the four kingdoms in area, and she resented the slight edge Bran, as king of the more populous area around Dublin, had over her in the subtle hierarchy that dictated royal protocol in Hibernia. Bran sighed, trying to come up with some way to approach her that would not offend her sense of her own importance. *Perhaps simple flattery will do the trick*, he thought, then rebuked himself for his delusion. He shook his head sadly and walked over to a small cabinet and unlocked its glass door to withdraw the small harp that rested inside it. The instrument tingled with the residual Glamour of its former owner, a student of Turlough O'Carolan, Ireland's greatest harper. *This will have to do.* He consoled himself with the thought that he still possessed a finer harp, once played by the master himself. Finally, there was Ulster's King Finn. The sometimes rocky, always tenuous state of affairs between Belfast and Dublin in the mortal realm made it difficult at best and usually impossible for him to have much contact with his northern counterpart. The reports he had received from his agents in the north indicated that Finn was a genial ruler, beloved by his people and greatly concerned by the shadows that loomed over the Kithain of Ulster.

If I can somehow convince him to come as well, Bran thought, *it will be the first time in centuries that Hibernia will host a court of all kings.*

Morgan was disappointed when Sir Odhran directed the group to leave their horses with one of the other Riders at the edge of the forest.

"Unfortunately, we can't ride them all the way to Dublin," Leigh told the childling as Morgan sadly patted the nose of the animal she had been riding.

"I know," Morgan said philosophically.

"Besides, our cars are somewhere in—that direction," Liam said, pointing toward a road that could just be seen from where they stood.

"This isn't the same place we entered," Leigh observed, looking around her.

The clurichaun shook his head. "No, it isn't," he said, his voice implying that no other comment would be forthcoming. He turned and set off toward the road, the others falling into step behind him. Sir Odhran had agreed to travel with the companions so that he could conduct them to the court of Leinster.

"We'll need to make a brief stop—perhaps in Donegal—so that I can ring someone in Dublin to tell the king of our coming."

"I still don't understand why you're so eager to present us to this King Bran," Tor grumbled. "I hardly went to court back home."

"You truly do not know, then?" Sir Odhran asked. He seemed about to say more, but Valmont put a hand on the noble's arm.

"Some of my friend's memories are inaccessible to him," the eshu said quietly.

Sir Odhran fell silent. When the group reached the place where their cars awaited them, he offered to drive one of the vehicles. Valmont agreed readily and climbed into the passenger's seat of the car next to the knight. As if he could read the eshu's thoughts, Liam deftly steered Tor and Morgan into the vehicle he was driving. Leigh and Rasputin joined Valmont and Sir Odhran.

Once the two car caravan was underway, Valmont acquainted Sir Odhran with Tor's fading memories as well as the troll's reluctance to speak of a past he had trouble remembering. The knight nodded thoughtfully.

"Does our visit to court have something to do with Tor?" Leigh asked.

Sir Odhran smiled. "It does," he said, "but it seems that I am the only one who knows anything about that in the present company."

"Is your knowledge anything you would care to share with us?" Valmont's voice held just a hint of impatience at his sudden coyness.

"You were not the only ones who dreamed last night," Sir Odhran said.

"Did you share a dream with the other Riders?" Leigh asked.

"Not this time," Sir Odhran replied. "The dream that came to me directed me to do as I am doing now."

"Including letting us in on all the minute details?" Rasputin asked.

Sir Odhran seemed to consider his reply before he spoke. "I believe that, having set events in motion, it would be best for me to simply let matters take their course."

"In other words," Leigh said, "you intend to keep us in the dark."

"Only so that the light, when it comes, will shine more brightly," Sir Odhran replied. Honking his horn at Liam's car ahead of them, Sir Odhran indicated that he wished to stop at the next town.

"I'll only be a minute, if you wish to walk around while I locate a call box."

Liam took the opportunity to take the oathmates on a brief tour through the small town. "The Vikings once built a garrison here," the clurichaun informed

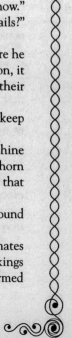

them as they passed by the ruins of Donegal Castle, which formed part of the town's center. "The castle came later, in the 15th century. It was home to the O'Donnells until the English kicked them out of Ireland."

"The Flight of the Earls," Leigh said.

Liam looked at her in surprise. "You are Irish, after all!" he said, his voice teasing.

"My father's keen on the history of his ancestors," Leigh replied. "I suppose I remember more than I realized."

"This land is good for jogging the memory," the clurichaun said. He led them into Donegal's market square and stopped before an obelisk that marked its center. "This is a monument to a quartet of Franciscan monks who penned—or quilled—a manuscript called the *Annals of the Four Masters in the 1600s*. It covers the whole of Irish history up to that time, beginning forty days before the Great Flood."

Rasputin nodded sagely. "I've heard of it," the pooka replied.

"The manuscript? Or the Flood?" Valmont asked.

"Everybody's heard of the Flood," Morgan said. She looked puzzled and a little hurt at the soft laughter that accompanied her pronouncement.

Sir Odhran found them a few minutes later. "We'll be in Dublin soon," the knight informed them before they resumed their trip.

"Will we go directly to the court?" Leigh asked.

Sir Odhran shook his head. "It may take a day for everyone to assemble. The court isn't in Dublin itself, but a little outside the city. I thought you might wish to spend the night as my guest."

"I know a few places in Dublin where you can hear some grand music," Liam said.

"Better than yours?" Leigh asked.

court of

The clurichaun gave her a broad grin. "Hardly, but close enough for dreams."

Signe and Bridie finished off their meal of fresh oysters with cups of rich Irish coffee. Bridie listened thoughtfully as Signe explained, as much as she dared, her reasons for coming to Ireland. The eshu carefully omitted any reference to her former association with the Dauntain, managing to sound as if she had simply lost track of some friends she needed to find.

"Do you know where these people might be?" the troll asked.

Signe shook her head. "I haven't a clue—other than what my instincts tell me."

"Well, they led you to me," Bridie said, "so that must mean that something I know will send you on your way. Your friends sound like they might stand out in a crowd," she observed. "I can check with some of my mates and see if they've heard of a group of Kithain from America that matches their descriptions—a troll, an eshu, a pooka and a pair of sidhe, one of them a childling, right?"

Signe nodded, smiling at the visual image conjured up by Bridie's assessment. "Just your typical congregate of tourists," she said.

"You mentioned a redcap childling, too," Bridie said. "I almost forgot him."

"He's not traveling with the others," Signe replied. "At least, not to my knowledge." She hesitated. "He's fallen in with a pair of sidhe who, I fear, will lead him down paths I would rather not see him take."

Bridie laughed sharply. "The thought of a redcap being corrupted by the noble ones strikes me as odd," she said. She grew serious when she saw that Signe was not sharing her amusement. "Sorry," she added.

Signe described Edmund, along with Yrtalien and Glynnis, to the troll. "Sounds as if they're a bit to the down side of Seelie," Bridie commented when Signe grew silent. "It could be that they've been drawn to the North," she added.

"What do you mean?" Signe asked.

"We have our fair share of both courts in most places," Bridie replied, "but the Troubles have attracted a lot of Unseelie to Ulster. Many of them seem to thrive on the potential of danger."

"I thought the Troubles were over," the eshu said.

"That remains to be seen," Bridie agreed. "But this land has been in one sort of trouble or another since its beginning. There's no reason to think that old habits will suddenly change themselves."

Bridie paid the bill for both herself and Signe, refusing to accept the eshu's attempt to split the cost of the meal. "It's my treat," she said. "Just say thank you and be done with it."

"Thank you," Signe replied obediently.

As they left the restaurant, Bridie spotted a young man, a nocker dressed in mechanic's coveralls, waving to her from across the street. "That'll be Michael," she said, motioning for the nocker to join them. "He makes a living for himself maintaining the vehicles of some of the local Kithain—including those of the nobility. He usually has a good ear for what's going on, as well."

Michael ogled Signe as Bridie made introductions. The troll cuffed him on the side of the head.

"None of that, now," she grumbled to her friend. "This is a lady, so behave yourself or you'll answer to me."

The nocker mumbled something that sounded like an apology and then cocked his head at Bridie, a crooked smile revealing a mouthful of bad teeth.

"Maybe you'd like to bring her with you to court tomorrow evening, then?" he asked. "Bran himself is convening a special gathering and the word's out that he's bringing in the other great kings."

Bridie looked at Signe. "Maybe this is the next step?" she suggested.

Signe closed her eyes and let her mind drift aimlessly around the idea of attending the Leinster court. She felt a resonance deep within her responding to the thought. She opened her eyes again and smiled.

"Maybe it is."

Yrtalien held the three eyestones in his hand, allowing himself to bask in the cascade of Glamour that roiled within them. The rain had finally cleared just before noon, and he had been able to continue his tour of the countryside, visiting the Carrowkeel Passage Tomb Cemetery where he was able to scavenge the Glamour that still lingered around some of the fourteen passage graves scattered atop a hill above Lough Arrow. The early downpour had dissuaded other visitors to the site, so Yrtalien and his companions had the cemetery to themselves.

The creativity of the neolithic peoples who had constructed the complex, corbeled stone structures, primitive though they were, was still a potent source of old magic. Dougal's speculation that some of them might be the physical remains of freeholds once belonging to the sidhe and abandoned at the time of the Sundering had led the prince to look for evidence of chimeric residue among the ruins.

So far, here at Carrowkeel, he had found nothing to support the sidhe wilder's claim. It was possible—even likely—that after so many centuries, the delicate dream-constructs that turned hovels into palaces had all disappeared, worn down by the persistence of archaeological theories that left no room for faerie castles in the middle of nowhere. The Glamour he felt radiating from the passage graves was of human origin, and represented the dreams of their long-dead builders.

He stared at the stones in his hand, then looked contemptuously toward Malacar, now rooting around near the opening to one of the smaller mounds. The ruby gem in the satyr's eye glowed faintly from its proximity to its companions, but its aura lacked the Glamour-drenched luster of the stones in the prince's possession. Yrtalien sighed. *This has gone on long enough,* he thought, feeling a perverse desire to demonstrate his power for the second time in one day.

Putting on his warmest smile, he called the satyr over to him.

Malacar hobbled across the uneven ground to stand before the prince, his haggard features almost puppylike in his eagerness to find favor with his new master.

Yrtalien gestured expansively with his free hand, taking in the whole of the hilltop cemetery and the vista beyond and below it.

"I hope you have been enjoying the splendid wildness of your surroundings," he said, his voice low and seductive.

Malacar blinked nervously, his face twitching as he tried to formulate an answer that Yrtalien would find acceptable.

"I have been spending my time trying to detect something here that might be useful to your cause, my Lord." His voice reeked with false humility.

Yrtalien frowned. "That is unfortunate," he replied. "I would have thought that, with only one eye, you would have a greater appreciation for the transience of visual beauty and would have spent your last few moments of sight storing up memories for the years of darkness ahead of you."

Malacar's face grew slack with sudden comprehension. He covered his ruby eye with one hand and fell to his knees, his body trembling uncontrollably.

"You promised," he whimpered. "You said that if I would swear my allegiance to you that you would not take my one remaining eye from me." His words degenerated into an unintelligible babble as his fear overtook his reason.

Yrtalien laughed softly and put a hand on the quivering satyr's shoulder.

"I believe I said that you would not be separated from your treasure," he said. "I did not mean to imply that it would remain forever in your head, where it does you little good except to prevent you from running into things and does me no good at all."

Malacar lurched backward in a frantic effort to distance himself from Yrtalien. The prince stopped him with a word, weaving strands of faerie magic into the grasses at Malacar's feet so that the satyr was entangled in a web of long green tendrils.

The prince held the jewels in front of the satyr.

"Will you give the Changestone to me willingly, or will you force me to wrest it from you?" he asked softly. "I assure you, the latter option will not be pleasant—at least for you. Take your hand away from your face." The last statement was a command backed by the Glamour from the stones. Malacar howled as his hand jerked downward, responding involuntarily to Yrtalien's order.

At the satyr's scream of despair, Donal looked up from his examination of one of the smaller structures near the edge of the cemetery.

"What's going down?" he asked Glynnis, who stood a few feet away with Dougal and Edmund.

Glynnis turned toward the sound. Her elegant face grew pale and she closed her eyes briefly before answering.

"I believe the prince is acquiring the last of the Eyestones," she said in a voice drained of emotion. The brothers exchanged glances and started moving toward Yrtalien.

Glynnis put out a hand and caught Dougal by the sleeve. He halted, looking over his shoulder at her. Donal stopped as well, coming to stand by his brother instead. Edmund looked away and concentrated on staring at the sun that was just beginning to dip behind the horizon.

"Shouldn't we do something?" Dougal asked.

"What did you have in mind?" Glynnis responded, her voice bitter. "Do you really think it worth intervening on Malacar's behalf, or are you perhaps intent on lending your support to the prince?"

Dougal's expression hardened. "We may be harder than our Seelie cousins," he said, "but that doesn't mean we enjoy seeing an old man tortured."

"Oh?" Glynnis drew herself up to her full height and brought her own small resources of faerie Glamour to bear so that the beauty that she normally kept dimmed in deference to Yrtalien now overpowered the brothers.

"And do you likewise object to the tormenting of children?" She angled her proud chin toward Edmund, who had been uncharacteristically silent and withdrawn all afternoon. "Or women?" The last words were spoken so softly that the brothers had to concentrate on reading her lips to make them out. "He has taken pains to treat you gently because so far you have given him what he wants. Beware his wrath if your will comes into conflict with his whim."

Yrtalien watched as Malacar struggled feebly against his living bonds. "This is beginning to bore me," he said, remembering that he had used the same methods once before to render the satyr helpless. "Give me the stone and be done with it," he commanded. Holding the stones in one hand above the satyr's balding head, Yrtalien used his other hand to mime the actions of a puppeteer manipulating the invisible strings that controlled the actions of a marionette.

Malacar's face froze in horror as his arms stiffened, no longer under his control. With quick, jerky movements, his elbows bent, bringing his hands, clawlike, toward his face.

"No!" he screamed, tears streaming from the eyesocket where the ruby began to glow with an infernal light. "We swore an oath! You promised you would leave me my eye!"

Yrtalien laughed as he watched Malacar's hands rip and tear at his face, gouging the ruby from its socket, leaving a bloody hole in its place. Plucking the ruby from the satyr's fingers, Yrtalien released his control over Malacar's body. Sick with pain, the satyr collapsed, clutching his ravaged face in an attempt to stop the flow of blood.

"You forget," he whispered coldly, certain that Malacar could hear him despite his preoccupation, "I am called forsworn for a reason." The prince leaned down so that he could wipe Malacar's blood from the ruby onto the grass at his feet before placing the ruby alongside its companion gems. The electric shock that traveled from his palm through the rest of his body at the union of the four gems filled the prince with a heady rush of power. He looked around him for a way to dissipate some of it, certain that if he did not do so, either he or the gems would explode in a cataclysmic outpouring from the overload of faerie energies. He saw Glynnis and the others huddled conspiratorially further down the hill.

Glynnis felt a tug at her sleeve and looked down to find Edmund's hand clutching her near the elbow. Mutely, the redcap pointed toward Yrtalien's approach. Behind him, on the hilltop, Malacar lay crumpled in the grass.

Glynnis took one look at the prince's face and at what lay in his outstretched palm and dropped to her knees, trying to hide the sudden panic building up inside her. Donal and Dougal remained standing, but eyed each other warily. Edmund folded himself into a fetal position, frantically trying to make himself as inconspicuous as possible.

"What have we here?" the prince said, his voice deceptively pleasant. "Are we discussing rebellion in the ranks?"

Dougal glared at him defiantly. "We were just having a little talk about tactics," he answered. Beside him, Donal nodded. Glynnis started to speak in her own defense, but realized that anything she said would be useless to dissuade Yrtalien from the course of action he intended to take. Instead, she extended one hand protectively over Edmund.

"It's not fair," the childling muttered. "Not twice in the same day."

"Edmund!" Yrtalien's voice made the redcap's head jerk upward convulsively. He smiled at the childling. "You wanted a chance to wield the power of the stones," he said, his tone beguilingly warm. "Come stand by me and I will show you one of my favorite tricks—from the other side, this time."

Edmund started to rise, but felt a small gouge in his hip coming from inside the pocket where he kept the pouch that contained Mr. Dumpy. *What do I do?*

he thought frantically to his chimeric friend, not sure whether the miniature clown retained any sentience in his inanimate form. The pain he had already felt once, this morning, would be nothing compared to what was coming. Of that he was certain. Part of him wanted to plaster himself to the prince's side. It was his chance to prove that he deserved the power Yrtalien was offering him. *This is a test*, a tiny voice said inside his head. Edmund wasn't sure if the thought came from him or from a suddenly responsive Mr. Dumpy, but a calm came over him in the midst of his fear and panic. *I hate tests*, he groaned inwardly. He shut his eyes as tightly as he could and tried desperately to visualize himself once again sitting with Mr. Dumpy in the Wishing Chair on the Giant's Causeway.

"I don't want the stupid stones," he said. Kneeling next to him, Glynnis grabbed one of his hands and squeezed it.

"So be it," Yrtalien replied. "Let us get the lines of command absolutely straight," he announced, invoking the power of the stones and unleashing their raw Glamour to engulf the four Kithain in front of him in an inferno of chimeric flames.

Stepping backward to lean against the side of one of the stone mounds, Yrtalien settled back to enjoy the symphony of screams that filled the darkening sky with the agony of inspiration.

chapter

nine

298 Sir Odhran's spacious residence, an abandoned house on the outskirts of Dublin, west of Phoenix Park, reflected the dual nature of most changeling freeholds, its dilapidated facade a disguise for the elegant chimeric structure it concealed. Unlike many of the returning sidhe, who elected to resurrect the elaborate palaces of their fading memories atop their freeholds' physical counterparts, Sir Odhran opted for the more modern, though still historic Palladian look of the 18th century Anglo-Irish Ascendancy.

Upon their arrival the evening before, Sir Odhran personally conducted his guests to an upper wing where he allowed them to choose their accommodations for the night. The other members of the household, a boggan wilder named Bairbre and a satyr youth just past his childling stage who gave his name as Ewan, showed the companions where they could find linens and towels.

"A hot bath would be lovely," Leigh murmured.

"The house is officially listed as vacant," Sir Odhran murmured, "but somehow no one has ever bothered to disconnect the utilities."

"Selective memory is a useful tool under certain circumstances," Valmont replied, referring to the faerie talent for confusing the minds of mortals so that they remembered only what was convenient for the agent of their befuddlement.

After a dinner of roast lamb, several styles of potatoes, crisp greens and tiny onions in the spacious downstairs dining room, Liam led the refreshed companions on a pub-crawling tour of the city's more prominent music spots. Sir Odhran remained behind, claiming weariness. When his guests had gone, he rang the king's residence and received confirmation that a full court would be held the following evening. Satisfied, the knight retired to his library and spent the rest of the evening poring through his collections of chronicles relating to the Accordance War.

By the time the companions returned, weary but exhilarated from their evening's exposure to traditional music of all varieties, Sir Odhran was already asleep.

After breakfast the next morning, the knight led his houseguests on a brief tour of the house's several wings, each of them filled with works of art and other mementos of Irish history. Leigh blinked in amazement at the profusion of artifacts displayed in cabinets, perched atop mantlepieces, hanging on the walls or standing in corners. Sir Odhran noticed her reaction and gave a small chuckling laugh.

"Some of these are chimeric replicas," he admitted. "As a historian, I admit to having a weakness for surrounding myself with reminders of this land's past."

"Forgive me if I sound rude," Valmont began, but Sir Odhran cut him off smoothly.

"One of the rules of my household is that no guest ever sounds rude. Please, feel free to speak your mind within my hearing."

Valmont acknowledged the knight's gracious comment with a small bow of his head.

"I had not thought the sidhe to be so interested in a past that occurred while they were apart from the mortal world," the eshu said. "One of the differences between your kith and the ones you refer to as commoners is that we cannot ignore the effects the centuries have had on our outlooks toward both the physical world and the Dreaming. What you fled, we had to bear."

"I thought you sounded like you were as old as the hills," Rasputin said dryly. "Now I know."

Liam snorted softly.

Valmont felt his face grow hot and cold in the same instant. He turned toward the pooka and the clurichaun, a sharp reply on his lips, but Leigh touched him on the shoulder.

"We know what you meant," she said.

Valmont bit back his hasty retort. "Forgive me for worrying at a sore spot in my ego. I suppose I did sound a little pretentious," he admitted.

"No more so than many—no, most—of the sidhe," Sir Odhran said. "As a recently recognized noble, you have the right to sound officious." The knight's ironic smile gentled his polite rebuke. "Actually, your comment is fairly accurate," he added. "Most of the sidhe would like to make the gap between our departure and our return vanish and pretend that the intervening centuries held nothing of significance for them or anyone else. I differ with them in that respect. That is, perhaps, why King Bran has honored me with the position of court archivist. I act as his memory, when necessary."

"Where are Tor and Morgan?" Leigh asked suddenly, realizing that the childling and her grandfather were not with the group.

Liam pointed down the long upper hallway which ran between the east and west wings of the mansion. "There they are," he said.

Tor stood with Morgan near the top of the broad stairway. The troll was staring in open admiration at a pair of crossed broadswords that hung on the wall at the head of the stairs.

Sir Odhran's face underwent a subtle change, his dark eyes growing intense with an inner fire. He walked quickly over to Tor and Morgan.

"Feel free to take them down and examine them," he said. "They are real blades, enchanted like your own battleaxe. One of them, the plainer of the two, is my own weapon. The other, with the silver lion on the hilt, belonged to a friend of mine." His voice faltered for a moment. "He fell during the Accordance War. I brought his sword here, to rest alongside mine."

A soft chime downstairs signaled the arrival of someone at the front door. Sir Odhran looked puzzled but started downstairs, pausing as he heard Bairbre's voice calling up to him.

"I've got it," the boggan said. Sir Odhran turned once again to Tor and Morgan.

Tor was about to reach for the Fiona blade when Bairbre coughed loudly from the bottom of the stairs.

"Pardon me for interruptin'," she said, "but there's a man here who wants to see the visitors." Her voice sounded anxious.

Sir Odhran gave the oathmates an inquisitive look.

"Are you expecting anyone?" he asked, sounding mystified.

One by one, Leigh and the others shook their heads. Sir Odhran led the way downstairs.

"Please show him into the drawing room," he told Bairbre. "Tell him we'll be along in a moment." It was clear from his words that the knight intended to confront the stranger alongside his guests.

Bairbre cleared her throat again, hesitating at carrying out Sir Odhran's request.

"Um, there's one thing," she said, looking furtively toward the door, which she had apparently closed in the visitor's face.

"Yes?" Sir Odhran asked mildly.

"He's a regular mortal, sir," she said. "How could he know what this place is or how to find it?"

"Maybe our mysterious caller has the sight," Liam murmured from the back of the group.

"Ask him in, please, Bairbre," Sir Odhran repeated. He glanced over his shoulder at the others trailing down the stairs after him.

"If he has been able to penetrate the enchantments that protect this house from most mortals, perhaps we can withstand any Banality he might bring to it for a short time." Still, Leigh noted, his voice sounded worried.

Bairbre opened the door a few inches and held a muffled conversation with the person outside. Then she pulled the heavy oak door wide to admit a tall, rangy looking young man in his early twenties, his dark red hair and gray eyes reminding Leigh of someone, though the resemblance remained tantalizingly outside her full kenning.

The boggan gestured toward the drawing room to one side of the entryway, and watched as the visitor entered, joined by Sir Odhran and his guests.

The knight gestured for the young man to seat himself, but he remained standing, hands tucked into the pockets of his heavy, sheep-skin jacket.

"I'll not be more than a few minutes, sir," he said, addressing Sir Odhran but turning so that his pale gray eyes focused on Leigh. *There is so little Banality attached to him that he might as well be Kithain*, Leigh found herself thinking as he spoke again. "My name is Connor McSkeath," he said, "or Connor mac Scathach, as my sister, may she dream forever, insisted. You must be Dame Eleighanara." There was a controlled hardness to his voice as he spoke Leigh's faerie name.

I have four brothers. Leigh recalled Sorcha's words to her the night before their battle. She found herself nodding numbly, her mind furiously at work trying to formulate some adequate response to the brother of the knight who had died at her sword.

"Lady Rowena brought her back to us," he said, his voice just kept from breaking by the clenched lines of his jaw. "She also gave me directions on how to find you. We'll be having a small gathering in her honor—a wake—tomorrow evening, and my brothers and I want to have you come down since you were there when she—when it happened."

Leigh opened her mouth, but found that words had deserted her.

"She was very brave," Morgan said, her small voice filling the gap left by her oathmate's flustered silence. "We would be honored to pay our respects if you think she would have wanted us to."

"Is the Lady Rowena in town?" Sir Odhran asked. The knight seemed relaxed in Connor's presence, as if he, too, had realized the stranger posed no threat to the Glamour of the household.

Connor nodded. "She rode with me to town but said she had to go make herself presentable. There's some formal function later. She'll be coming to the wake and said that she'd meet you there if you decide to attend. You, too, sir," he added as an afterthought.

"I appreciate your kind invitation," the knight replied. "My acceptance will hinge on whether or not my duties allow me to absent myself from home so soon after having returned."

"Thank you," Leigh said, finally finding her voice. "Is there anything we should bring? Food?" She remembered her grandmother's wake several years ago. Her parents' kitchen table was full of casseroles and cold cuts that had seemed to last forever, all presents from Gramma's friends and neighbors.

"It's not necessary," Connor said, "though nothing given freely and in the memory of one that's departed for a better place is ever refused by my brothers or me."

Leigh nodded, mentally reviewing her repertoire of culinary specialties in an attempt to come up with something portable and relatively easy to prepare in unfamiliar surroundings.

A few more polite words passed between Sorcha's brother and the oathmates before he took his hands from his pocket and solemnly shook hands all around. Without any other farewell, he stepped from the room and let himself out of the house.

"A most unusual young man," Sir Odhran replied, the beginnings of a smile on his lips. "Not unlike his sister," he added.

"We seem to have a full schedule for the next two days, at least," Valmont observed.

Leigh looked up at Valmont's words. "Sir Odhran," she asked, "would it be possible for me to use your kitchen this afternoon?"

Her host nodded. "I'll find Bairbre and get her to show you where things are before she leaves for her afternoon classes at the college."

"Can I help?" asked Morgan. Leigh smiled at the childling and nodded. "I can use a good assistant chef," she said.

The drive from Dublin to Newgrange took the oathmates past the Hill of Tara. "Long ago the sidhe held their High Court beneath the hill," Sir Odhran said, gesturing to the left from his seat beside Liam, who acted as driver for the court-bound Kithain.

"I thought the Irish chieftains met there," Leigh said. "There was something about a stone—"

"*The Lia Fail*," Liam said, "the stone of destiny. Until the 11th century, Tara was the seat of the High

Kings of Ireland. They got the idea from us, you know—as well as the stone."

"I take it the site is no longer used by your king," Valmont said as the clurichaun drove past the landmark without slowing his speed.

"Like most of the places we once held, it has been worn out by hosts of well-meaning tourists and diggers—archaeologists," the clurichaun said. Sir Odhran nodded. The sun had set and the sky was quickly growing dark. By the time they reached the turn-off for Newgrange, along what Liam called the "scenic route," there was little to see outside the windows of the car except the starry night sky.

"This is the Boyne Valley," Liam said. "It's called the cradle of Irish civilization. Some of the tombs and mounds here are older than the pyramids." He caught Valmont's eye in the rear-view mirror and gave the eshu a wink.

"It is said that the dreams of my people were old before the pyramids were conceived," Valmont said, the barest smile visible on his otherwise expressionless face.

Rasputin sniffed superciliously. "If I weren't sworn to secrecy, I could tell you some things about the ancient culture of the pookas that would make all of you feel like historic upstarts," he said, sweeping his long ears back in a theatrical gesture. Beside him, on Tor's lap, Morgan stifled a giggle.

"It's not funny," Rasputin said.

Liam parked the car just off the road, at a spot seemingly chosen at random.

"Here's where we take the rest of the journey by foot. Am I right?" the clurichaun asked Sir Odhran, who was already getting out of the car and opening the door to assist Leigh from the vehicle.

"If you'll get the torches out of the boot," the knight advised Liam, "we'll get ready for the walk to court."

"A torchlight procession," Leigh murmured.

"Like the one through the forest!" Morgan said. "Only we had horses, then," she added wistfully.

"Isn't someone going to see us traipsing across the countryside carrying lit torches and wonder?" Tor asked. The troll was plainly uneasy.

Sir Odhran shook his head. "This," he said as he adjusted an elaborate gold brooch on the shoulder of his cloak, "should obscure us from the sight of anyone who might question our presence." Liam removed an armful of torches from the trunk of the car and passed them out to the waiting Kithain.

"There's a small copse of trees just ahead," Sir Odhran said, pointing further off the road. "We'll make our preparations there."

In the brothers' house near Sligo, Yrtalien held court before a subdued group of Kithain. The prince occupied the largest chair in the parlor, a comfortable high-backed armchair by the fireplace. His hands, each of them cradling two of the Eyestones, rested in his lap. Glynnis, her delicate face now haggard and worn from pain and from the exertion of her magic to heal Malacar's bloody eye-socket, sat on a low stool at Yrtalien's feet. The blinded satyr huddled miserably in a corner of the room, one hand clutching Edmund's shoulder. Donal and Dougal, both visibly shaken by their recent ordeal, stood uneasily near the parlor door. Hettie and Lurgan had left for the Broken Harp before the others had returned from Carrowkeel and would not be back until well past midnight.

Making sure that he had the attention of everyone in the room, Yrtalien turned a beatific smile on his audience.

"I trust you have all taken this afternoon's demonstration to heart," he said quietly, looking at each person in turn and receiving a sign of acknowledgement. When the prince turned his head toward Malacar, Edmund poked the satyr sharply with his elbow.

"Nod your head, dumb-ox," he mumbled. Cowed, Malacar did as he was told. The prince laughed.

"See?" he said, watching Malacar cringe at the sound of the now useless word. "You don't need eyes to respond to your surroundings. All you need is a trained guide-dog, and you have that in young Edmund."

Edmund felt his face grow hot. Yrtalien had informed him on the way back to the house that Malacar was his responsibility from now on. The childling chafed at being drafted into leading the satyr around, but saw no easy way out of his predicament.

"Now that you have felt the power I command," the prince continued, "I believe it is time for me to make my intentions clear." He paused, listening to the silence that attended him.

From her place at Yrtalien's feet, Glynnis dared a furtive glance at her lord. *I wonder why I did not see it before*, she thought numbly. *He has been locked away in a dream-pocket between the worlds and now he has been almost continually exposed to more Glamour than most of us experience in a lifetime. He has fallen into Bedlam and we are trapped in a nightmare from which there is no escape.* Just as the world's Banality could erode a changeling's faerie nature, too much Glamour could drive Kithain into a state of madness called Bedlam, in which the victim found it impossible to distinguish between the physical world and the chimeric world born of his own deluded perversions of the Dreaming. In its final stage, the demented Kithain disappeared fully into dreams, vanishing from the physical world as if he never existed. *He has not yet gone that far into madness. If he did, it would be a blessing for us all.*

"I have considered matters carefully, and it seems to me that this land suffers from a certain lack—that of a High King. I believe it my duty to address that need, although the other rulers of Hibernia do not yet know it. You here are privileged witnesses to my declaration of intent to rule this land as High King in the name of House Ailil."

The prince stood abruptly, holding his cupped hands level with his waist, the Eyestones glimmering in his palms.

"I shall now hear your oaths of undying fealty," he said. Looking down at Glynnis, who was nearest him, he smiled at her. "Beginning with you." His handsome features hardened as he commanded Glynnis to kneel and place her hands over his own, encircling the four gems.

In a growing state of panic, Edmund listened as first Glynnis, then the brothers knelt before Yrtalien and spoke the words that bound them in obedience to him. Even across the room, the childling could feel the Glamour imbue the oaths with the force of compulsion, binding the speakers' will to that of Yrtalien.

"What's going on?" Malacar hissed in the redcap's ear.

"The prince is swearing 'em in," Edmund muttered harshly to the satyr. "Now shut up until it's your turn." *What am I going to do when he calls on me?* Edmund thought, his mind racing. *I thought one test would be enough! If I take the oath, I'll never be able to get away and my wish will never come true, unless I go back on my word and then I'll be forsworn just like him.* The idea gave him hope.

Yrtalien signaled for Edmund to bring Malacar to him. Whimpering under his breath, the satyr placed his hands on Edmund's shoulders and shuffled uncertainly behind the redcap until the prince's voice commanded him to kneel.

Edmund ducked away from Malacar's grip as the satyr groaned his way into a kneeling position.

This is it, the childling thought, feeling time running out before he had a chance to figure a way around his dilemma. *If I were Rasputin, I could just lie my way through it. But then, no one would believe me, and I'd have to make some disclaimer like Rasputin did when we became oathmates. If Valmont were here, he'd know what to do, as sneaky as he is.*

All too soon, Yrtalien had dismissed Malacar, shoving the satyr to one side with his foot. The prince turned his attention to Edmund.

"I have held your oath for last, Edmund, because I am not certain that you are fit to swear allegiance to me as the others have done. You have already broken one oath, and that makes you forsworn."

Edmund's knees buckled underneath him as a wave of relief washed over him. *I'm off the hook!* he thought. His momentary feeling of rescue vanished as he saw Yrtalien's eyes narrow. *Maybe not*, he corrected himself.

"Instead," the prince continued, "I will take something from you to keep as hostage for your good behavior. Give me the pouch you have in your pocket," Yrtalien commanded.

Edmund felt his eyes fill with tears. Already on his knees, he looked up at the prince beseechingly.

"Don't take him from me," he pleaded, his voice trembling.

Yrtalien shook his head. "I'm afraid you have brought yourself to this," he said, a false sadness coloring his voice. "I've known about your chimeric friend for some time now," he added, compounding Edmund's misery with humiliation. "Give it to me!" This time, the prince's voice seemed to explode with power and Edmund reached into his pocket and drew out the pouch that contained Mr. Dumpy. His hand shook as he carefully laid the pouch in Yrtalien's hands, atop the Eyestones. *Please don't come out of there*, Edmund thought fiercely to the chimeric clown. Through rising tears, he looked at his prized possession, now part of the prince's growing cache of treasures. *I'm sorry!*

Yrtalien dismissed Edmund with a curt nod. "That's done, then," he said. "I trust that my guardianship of your little toy will keep you honest?"

Edmund bit his lip as hard as he could to keep from bursting into tears as he nodded disconsolately to the prince.

"I want to hear your promise," Yrtalien snapped.

Edmund tasted blood in his mouth as he forced himself to look into the prince's eyes, blinking the tears back and holding his eyes open as wide as possible so that he would not cry in front of everyone.

"I promise," he said, clasping his hands behind him. The prince arched an eyebrow expectantly, as if waiting to hear more. Out of the corner of his eye, the redcap could see Glynnis' lips moving silently. "I promise, my Lord," he said.

Only after he had led Malacar back to the corner and sat glumly with the others as Yrtalien proceeded to explain his plans to raise an army for an assault on Silver's Gate did Edmund allow himself to uncross his fingers. *A promise isn't an oath*, he told himself fiercely. This time, he had the distinct feeling that he had passed the test. *I hope this was the last one.*

Sir Odhran led his guests through the stone entryway to Newgrange, their lit torches casting a soft, chimeric illumination along the dark corridor that stretched ahead into the center of the mound.

Once inside, Liam pointed upward to an opening above them. "On the day of the winter solstice," the clurichaun said, "the sunlight strikes through here and lights the place up. Legends say that this was once the home of the Tuatha de Danann themselves—or else their front door into the mortal world. This is also where the High Kings of Ireland—the mortal ones, anyway—were supposedly buried."

"Is this where the court meets?" Morgan asked, looking around her at the long expanse of standing stones that lined the passage before them. Like the others, she had dressed herself in her best court clothes, Glamour-spun finery that demonstrated both house and rank among the nobles of faerie society. Her silvery gown and black and silver cloak reflected glints of torchlight, transforming her into a creature of exquisite beauty, a sorceress of House Eiluned, the sidhe house of magic. In contrast, Leigh's crimson gown and silver cloak seemed to blaze with the fiery passion of her Fiona heritage. Sir Odhran, dignified in the green and gold uniform of a knight sworn to House Gwydion, his king's house, shook his head.

"This place has been stripped of its power by excavators and sightseers," he said. "Since the return, it has become merely the path to the actual court. Follow me, and I will show you."

The knight held his torch aloft and began walking farther into the mound. Valmont, dressed in an exotic display of finery that borrowed elements of both Egyptian and Nigerian royalty, offered an arm to Leigh. Together, they followed Sir Odhran down the corridor. Tor, clad in a long black and silver tabard that covered his gleaming battle armor, clasped Morgan's hand and fell into step behind Leigh and Valmont. Liam, wearing bardic array boasting iridescent threadwork against black velvet, took his place alongside Rasputin, whose dark russet and green silks seemed almost understated in the presence of his more flamboyant companions. The pooka winked at Liam as the pair brought up the rear of the small procession.

"Least, but not last," he quipped.

Sir Odhran's voice counted out the paces as he stepped his way down the passage. Halfway down, he stopped and executed a half-turn until he was directly in front of one of the pillars. He ran his hand along its spiral carvings, tracing the design. The pillar began to glow, becoming translucent with an inner radiance before shimmering into nothingness.

Morgan gasped. "It's a door!" she said.

"It is the way to the court of Leinster," Sir Odhran said, stepping through the doorway and beckoning for the others to follow.

"Why isn't anyone else here?" Morgan asked. "Does everyone use this way to get to the court?"

"Most of them do," Sir Odhran replied. "The others have gone on ahead."

"So we're fashionably late, then?" Liam asked.

Sir Odhran gave the clurichaun a smile that hinted at something known only to himself. "No, we should arrive precisely on time," he answered.

"Where is this court?" Leigh asked.

"Beneath another passage tomb—or so it's called by those who are unaware of its true origin—about

court of

two miles from here at Dowth."

Morgan's eyes grew wide and she started to say something, but Sir Odhran held up a hand to her.

"I should have said two miles by normal measure. This is the king's trod, something of a short cut."

As their eyes adjusted to the dimness of their surroundings, the companions could make out a thin silver line that stretched ahead of them.

"This is the path of dreams," Sir Odhran said softly. "Do not lose sight of it."

The 19th-century plunderers of the mound at Dowth failed to penetrate its heart, leaving much of its interior unexplored. Within the ancient site, in a realm apart from the world of archaeologists and spectators, the faerie King of Leinster, Bran of the House of Gwydion, held court. The large circular chamber, protected and enhanced by faerie magic, shone with the light from a thousand chimeric stars that glimmered from a midnight ceiling far overhead, bathing nobles and commoners alike in a silvery radiance. A ring of massive oaks, their branches wound with mistletoe, formed the outer walls, creating a forest clearing deep beneath the earth.

Four arched entryways of freestanding stone led into the chamber, one for each of the four provinces of Hibernia. In its center, an elevated platform of stone, carved with spirals and whorls, supported four silver thrones. Upon the thrones, the four faerie rulers of Hibernia sat in splendor, their eyes as often on one another as on the assembly.

On a throne topped by the gold falcon against a green field of his house, King Bran seemed to bask in his achievement, the bringing together of all four

Hibernian monarchs. His auburn hair, held back from his forehead by a thin gold fillet, framed a face both ageless and wise. Dressed in royal robes of green and gold, he rested at ease among his peers, his gray eyes half closed in quiet contemplation. On Bran's right, King Fiachra of Connaught sat quietly below the blazon of House Dougal, three golden gears against a red background over a black arm-and-hammer on a field of gold. The contrast between Fiachra's dark brown eyes and golden hair gave him an air of brooding intensity that belied his gentle, inquisitive nature. His black court dress, accented in red and gold, added to his dramatic appearance. On Bran's left, her throne surmounted by House Eiluned's blazon, twin silver crescents on black atop a black pentacle on silver, Queen Nuala held herself with rigid poise. Dressed in silver overlaid with black lacework, her long black hair worn high upon her head to expose the graceful curve of her neck, the Queen of Munster watched the parade of courtiers with predatory green eyes, bestowing an occasional smile. To Nuala's left, beneath House Fiona's silver lion backed with crimson, King Finn of Ulster wore his elaborate crimson and silver with casual grace. Blond-haired and amber-eyed, with a beauty that singled him out even among a kith known for its attractiveness, he lounged in his throne with the ease of a lion overlooking his pride.

"Usually, there's only the one throne in the center," Bridie informed Signe as they stood along the outer edge of the gathering, watching the intricate interplay of the seasoned courtiers as they busied themselves with the arcane subtleties of fae politics. "The king must have dreamed fast and hard to come up with three others just like his own for this occasion."

"You said that this was a special meeting of the court," Signe said. "Do you know its purpose?"

Earlier in the evening, after the ceremonies which opened the court, Bridie had presented Signe to the king, a brief formality which lasted only a few seconds. Afterward, they had been free to mingle, mostly with other commoner Kithain. Although most of the attendees were King Bran's subjects, the other rulers had brought retinues of their own, and Signe had spent most of her time listening to the diverse accents that colored the melodious voices of the Irish Kithain. Many of the conversations she overheard were in Gaelic, or perhaps some older tongue preserved by the fae of Hibernia.

"From what I've been able to gather," Bridie informed her, "they're expecting the arrival of some long lost hero of the return—of your Accordance War, if I'm not mistaken."

"That seems odd," Signe replied, "that you would do honor to a veteran of a foreign war."

Bridie laughed, but quickly grew serious again. "You might say it's the way of the Irish to glorify warriors, whatever battle they might have fought. This is a land that loves war, in case you haven't noticed."

Signe nodded thoughtfully. "It doesn't seem so different from any other country," she said. "Generals receive more laurels than poets everywhere."

"I'll not deny that," Bridie agreed. "This particular hero, though, has connections to some of the nobles here. It happens that many of them originally fought in the Accordance War and, after it was done, came here where they felt they belonged."

"A reverse emigration, then?" Signe asked, smiling at the irony of the statement.

Bridie nodded. "When the sidhe returned to Ireland, they more or less stepped in and took over. At least, so they claim. And who are we poor commoners to gainsay them?" Her words, though bitter, were delivered in a tone that implied a past forgiven if not forgotten.

A single horn sounded inside the chamber, and a sudden hush fell over the gathered crowd. King Bran lifted his hands in signal to his fellow rulers, and the four monarchs rose in an unprecedented gesture to greet the latest arrivals to the court beneath the hill.

"There is one more thing you should know about the place where King Bran's court meets," Sir Odhran said, pausing for a moment to make certain that everyone was still with him.

"Before the Sundering, there was both a Seelie and an Unseelie court for each of the sidhe kingdoms. In Leinster, from Beltaine to Samhain, the Seelie court met at Newgrange. During the winter half of the year, from Samhain to Beltaine, the court—now become Unseelie—moved to Dowth. A story connects it with an ancient druid curse that placed upon it the name Dubad, or darkness. Upon our return to this world, we found Newgrange nearly drained of its magic, while deep within Dowth mound there was still a large area of protected enchantment. Despite its Unseelie past, it has become our year-round court hall. There is no way to gain entrance to the court from the mound itself, so it seems relatively safe from even continued excavations of the site. The public is not yet allowed access to it, either, and if we have anything to do with it, that will remain the situation." He smiled a little, looking somewhat abashed at his long-windedness.

"At any rate, this is the reason for our circuitous journey this evening."

"That was a most uninteresting dissertation," Rasputin said from the back of the group. "I'm sure none of us needed to know any of that."

"Rasputin says thank you," supplied Morgan helpfully.

They traveled onward a few more steps when Sir Odhran stopped once more, this time to point out a faint light ahead of them.

"There is the entry to the court," he said.

"It looks like a forest," Leigh murmured. Sir Odhran nodded. "The court is held under the stars," he said, "but not the stars of the earthly sky. Those of us who helped reinforce the enchantments of this place attempted to reconstruct here our memories of Arcadian skies. One need only look up, it is said, to remember something of what was lost when we returned from the Dreaming."

At the end of the passage, a pair of huge oaks formed an archway. Just beyond it, the companions could see a starlit hall filled with shining people. The air around them tasted and smelled and felt of Glamour.

Sir Odhran led the way into the court, followed by Leigh and Valmont, Tor and Morgan, and, finally, Rasputin and Liam. Once the entire group had entered, before they could make any response to the silent, standing host of the Irish fae that regarded them, Sir Odhran raised his voice.

"Your Majesties, Lords and Ladies of the Court, and Kithain all, I have the honor to present to you Sir Torvald Lord's Son, the Protector of House Eiluned, savior of the Fiona Banner, hero of the Battle of the Redwoods—and with him his companions from the fief of Goldengate in the Kingdom of Pacifica." He continued to name the others, but his words were drowned out by the thunderous applause that greeted his opening announcement.

Morgan looked up at her grandfather, her mouth open in a distinctly undignified expression of amazement.

Leigh felt a sudden rush of moisture fill her eyes and turned to Valmont just in time to see the eshu's jaws tighten in an attempt to keep his own tears from spilling onto his cheeks. Rasputin's face broke out in an unabashed grin, while Liam stared at his feet, a tiny smile tugging at the corners of his mouth.

Tor heard the words, and only when they were done did he realize that Sir Odhran was referring to him. Confused, he looked up to the ceiling, and his eyes were filled with an array of brilliant stars. And he remembered.

The return of the sidhe to earth had reawakened in Tor the oath that had for centuries lain dormant in his line of trolls. Rather than join with the other commoners to make war against a kith they considered to be invaders and usurpers, Tor had sought out Lady Morgania of House Eiluned, who—with Lord Groton, the Fiona lover whose house she now considered her own—commanded the forces of the sidhe in the lands that would come to be known as Pacifica. There he pledged himself to her protection, reaffirming an oath spoken long before the Sundering. As the battles of the Accordance War spread west, Tor fought alongside his lady, his axe carving a pathway to victory for Morgania and her army time and time again—until the final battle that clinched the supremacy of the sidhe along the western coast at the cost of Morgania's life. Tor had brought her safely through a host of the enemy to secure the banner of House Fiona and allow her and Groton to combine their skills with sword and magic to overwhelm the commoner throng.

When the sheer numbers of their foe managed to break through their lines, Tor placed himself as a living shield before his lady, blocking a hail of blows from weapons of steel and iron that would have struck home without his skill. Still, he could not stop the arrow that would cost Morgania her life.

With Lord Groton's blessings, Tor carried Morgania away from the battle, finding shelter for her. It had not been enough, and she had died in his arms, bequeathing him her silver locket and, through it, passing his duty to protect her to a future generation of her blood—his granddaughter Morgan.

Someone spoke his name, and Tor became aware of his present surroundings. A sidhe lady, dressed in silver and black, her raven hair and bright green eyes striking a familiar chord in Tor's flood of memories, was speaking to him, her hands held out in welcome.

"I spent some years looking for the troll knight who served my sister Morgania," she said, her voice a husky reminder of a voice Tor had not thought to hear again in his life. "She would have wanted no finer witness to her death, for because of your actions, many of us survived those bloody days to find safe haven here in Hibernia. On behalf of all of us, you have our thanks." She smiled, and her smile brought a lump to Tor's throat.

Tor muttered something he hoped sounded like thanks, too overcome to be certain of his exact words. As she moved away from him, to give way to the next in a long line of courtiers waiting to greet the newfound hero, Sir Odhran sidled up to Tor.

"That is Queen Nuala of the kingdom of Munster," he whispered, clearly impressed by what he had just witnessed.

Turning to Morgan, Nuala laid a hand on the childling's head, caressing the black curls that matched her own.

"You are of my blood and of my house," she said softly, "and my sister's namesake as well, I understand."

Morgan curtsied deeply. "I hope I can live up to both, your Highness," she said solemnly. Then she smiled. "I also hope that when I grow up I will be as beautiful as you are."

A born diplomat, Leigh thought, hearing Morgan's reply to the elegant queen. She sensed someone standing near her and looked away from her companions into the amber eyes of a sidhe lord, who gifted her with a brilliant smile that radiated warmth and an almost irresistible charm.

"Dame Eleighanara," the sidhe noble said, "if it were not already apparent to me that you are of my house, I would make it so by decree. Welcome to our gathering."

Leigh bowed formally, her knight's training superseding a more ladylike curtsey. "I am honored to be here, your—" she said, pausing as she realized she did not know how to address the speaker.

A soft laugh filled in the gap created by her ignorance.

"Finn will do," he replied, "for outside my own kingdom of Ulster, I am merely a noble among other nobles." The words were spoken with modesty, but Leigh detected that they were not quite as genuine as they sounded. Reaching for Valmont, she took the eshu's arm and brought him forward to present him to the King of Ulster.

"Your Highness," she began, "may I present Sir Valmont Iyapo, knight of Goldengate and my sworn companion."

King Finn's eyes narrowed as he acknowledged Valmont with a brief nod.

Leigh felt Valmont's arm grow taut beneath her hand. *Please don't say anything hasty*, she thought.

"My Lady is most kind to grant me the status of noble," Valmont said. *There have been kings among my kith for thousands of years. She was only recognizing my right to stand as her equal.* Valmont watched the King of Ulster's face closely, seeing in it an unconscious arrogance the eshu had come to associate with the sidhe. *He really does believe his kind were born to rule.* The urge to make known his long-held grievance against the commoner-noble dichotomy that built barriers between Kithain who should be united in the war against the disappearance of the Dreaming found its way to Valmont's tongue. Then, as he glanced toward Tor and saw the looks of genuine respect and admiration coming from the nobles who surrounded the troll, Valmont felt his anger dissipate. *I have done little but posture and complain about the respect I have not truly earned,* he realized. Swallowing his bitter comment, he bowed his head to Ulster's king.

"In the presence of such genuine nobility as that of my oathmate, Sir Torvald, I can only feel it is an honor I have yet to earn," he added.

Valmont's comment took Leigh by surprise. Ready to defend whatever hasty words her oathmate and, recently, her lover might give voice to, she instead found that there was no cause for anything other than a sense of fierce pride in Valmont's genuine humility. *I never thought he had it in him.*

Finn's face relaxed at Valmont's words. Smiling once again, he extended a hand to the eshu. "Your lady's faith in you seems to be well placed, Sir Valmont," he said.

When Finn had gone on to pay his own respects to Tor, Leigh looked up at Valmont, her eyes still bright with unshed tears, though the reason for them had changed.

"Thank you," she said simply.

Valmont arched an eyebrow. "I only spoke what was in my heart," he said. "Nobility does not rest in titles, but in deeds, and I have done nothing to compare with Tor's actions."

One of you must surrender his pride. The words of the Hidden King crystallized in Leigh's mind. Without thinking, she spoke them aloud. Valmont stared at her, then exhaled slowly, his breath coming in a soft hiss as he recognized the moment that had just passed.

"He also said that one of us must remember, and I believe that has now happened as well," Valmont observed. "I suppose the other conditions will be met soon enough."

Leigh nodded wordlessly.

Rasputin stood with Liam on the edge of the crowd, watching with interest as his oathmates were swallowed up by courtiers eager to say a few words to one or the other of them.

"Why don't you put yourself forward?" Liam said. "You deserve as much attention as the others are getting."

Rasputin's face grew thoughtful, as if he were, in fact, considering the clurichaun's advice.

"You're probably right," he said, making no move to join the milling crowd. "I can think of nothing I'd like more than to kiss knuckles and shake hands."

Liam shrugged. "I know how you feel," he said. "I understand you do a bit of performing yourself."

"Never," Rasputin admitted.

"I thought as much," Liam said. "I find that most of us who are used to taking center stage by ourselves do less well when we're plunked down on the stage of life itself—or court, as is the case this evening."

"Rasputin?"

At the sound of the woman's voice, the pooka turned and found himself staring at a female eshu. It took him a minute before he recognized Signe, but a Signe unlike the somber-faced Dauntain he had encountered in Hawaii.

"I've been looking all over for you," he said, his voice wary.

Signe laughed. "That should be my line," she said. She turned to the female troll who stood just behind her.

"Bridie, this is one of the people I've been looking for," she said. Rasputin hardly heard the more formal introduction that followed in his relief that the troll was not Diana. "He and his friends were responsible for returning me to myself." She returned her attention to Rasputin. "I just wanted to say thank you," she said.

Rasputin shrugged. "It was nothing, really," he said. "It wasn't as if it was a matter of life or death."

"I suppose you caught up with this rascal in much the same way I did," Liam said, stepping forward to introduce himself to the two women.

"Oh?" Signe looked amused at the dapper clurichaun.

Liam nodded. "By following your nose," he said. "They fairly reek of import, don't you think?"

"I let my dreams take me where I needed to be," Signe replied. "They brought me here."

"Actually," Bridie interjected, "your dreams brought you to me and I brought you to court."

"And do you know where they'll take you next?" Liam asked. "Your dreams, I mean?"

Signe shook her head. "I thought when I saw Rasputin and the others come in, I would know that my path lay with them. Now I'm no longer certain."

Liam nodded wisely. "Things of the fae are never certain," he said. "That's for sure."

Across the hall, Valmont spied Signe talking with Rasputin and nudged Leigh. As they were about to join the pooka, a slim figure interposed himself between them and their target. The oathmates bowed before the sidhe lord they recognized from earlier conversations as Fiachra, King of Connaught.

"I have been comparing notes with my neighbor," the king said, nodding in the direction of King Finn, who was once more seated on his throne, idly watching the byplay of the court. "Both of us have heard rumors of a new prince of the sidhe who has lately come here from the west. We have only the barest of details as to his movements or intentions, but I hear from one of my trusted agents that you and this strange prince may be connected."

Leigh followed the king's gaze and thought she saw him looking in the direction of a knight wearing the colors of House Dougal who she remembered as one of the Riders of the Silver Court. The morning after their vision in the Dreamers' Glen, Leigh and her oathmates had explained to the Riders the reason for their journey to the Hidden King's domain. *I wonder how much of that information has made its way back to this land's rulers through their "trusted agents,"* she thought.

She glanced at Valmont, who gave her a small nod. She took a deep breath.

"Your Majesty," she said, "if this prince is who I fear he is, I do know him well enough to know that he is not to be trusted."

Fiachra looked at her shrewdly. "So I surmised from what I have heard."

"What have you heard?" Valmont asked abruptly.

Connaught's king smiled ruefully. "Less than I would wish and more than I would like to hear," he answered. "He and an entourage which includes a one-eyed satyr, a redcap childling, a lady of the sidhe, and a pair of Unseelie wild cards have been visiting ancient sites throughout the north and northwest. Wherever they go, they leave less Glamour, as if they possessed some capacity for draining the magic from the very stones of our past."

Leigh felt her stomach grow cold.

"We are here for the same purpose," she said, "but our intentions are very different. If you have any idea where he might be found, we would appreciate anything you could tell us. Part of our reason for being here is to find something that has been lost for a very long time, but the other part is to stop him from finding it first."

Fiachra nodded. "I have heard that he is based in Sligo, but that he has been as far north as the Giant's Causeway. So far he has not yet made himself known to my court, but I fear that is only a matter of time. I'm afraid that is the sum of what I know."

"I am sorry for any trouble we may have brought in our wake," Leigh began, but the king cut her off with a gentle laugh.

"Trouble does not need an excuse to come here," he said. "It migrates to this land of its own accord." He stepped out of their way and motioned for the pair to continue in the direction they had been going before he stopped them. "I do not wish to detain you any further with dour speculation," he said, turning from them with a smile of farewell.

"We knew that we would have to cross paths with him eventually," Valmont said when the king had left.

"I was hoping it could be avoided somehow," Leigh confessed. "I suppose I wanted to wake up one morning with the stones resting on my pillow."

Valmont shook his head. "That would be far too easy," he said. "We are responsible for his being here in the first place. Have you considered what we might have to do to stop him?" he asked suddenly.

Leigh closed her eyes. "I have avoided that particular problem," she said. "I guess it's caught up with us at last."

By the time they joined Rasputin and Liam, Signe was nowhere to be seen. The pooka greeted his oathmates with a cheery smile that contrasted with the worry in his eyes.

"Just in time," he said. In his characteristically roundabout manner, Rasputin repeated Signe's conversation to Valmont and Leigh. "I suppose we won't be seeing her again," he finished.

"I am glad to see that we have had some part in returning her to the Dreaming," Valmont said quietly. Leigh nodded. "I wonder what happened to the other two?" she mused aloud.

Valmont looked up at the chimeric stars in the sky. "I don't think they will be a problem for awhile," he said cryptically.

The rest of the evening passed in a blur of casual conversations with new acquaintances, culminating in a command performance by Liam, whose reputation as a bard seemed to extend throughout much of Hibernia judging from the warm response that greeted his music. When he had finished, the court began to wind down. Sir Odhran appeared with Tor, who carried a sleeping Morgan on his shoulder, to convey the oathmates back to his home.

"It will be morning in a few hours," the knight said, "and you have an appointment in Kerry later in the day."

"Sorcha's wake," Leigh said guiltily. "I almost forgot." She looked at Valmont. "After that, we begin our hunt."

The eshu nodded grimly.

Signe watched the oathmates take their leave and touched Bridie on the arm. "Should we be going? Or are we going to stay until the party's completely over?"

The troll looked at her friend and grinned. "Do you feel the urge to go with them?" she asked, indicating the departing companions.

"Not this time," Signe said. "I will know when the time comes for me to take to the road again."

Bridie nodded. "Good," she said. "There's still a lot of Dublin you haven't seen."

Edmund felt a gentle tug on his ear and came awake instantly.

"Mr. Dumpy!" he exclaimed, then covered his mouth and listened to see if his shout had wakened anyone else in the house. Across the room from him, on the makeshift cot that had been moved into his room this evening, Malacar snored fitfully, unaware of the chimeric clown that stood beside Edmund's bed, his bright red fringe of hair and white painted crown barely clearing the top of the mattress.

Edmund scrambled out from underneath the covers and bent down to throw his arms around the chubby clown, hoisting him up to sit beside him on the edge of the bed.

"I knew you'd find a way to come back to me," he whispered, his voice filled with wonder in spite of his confident statement. Then he frowned. "How did you manage to get away?" he asked.

The clown shrugged and grinned, his sadly smiling face gleaming in the moonlight that came through the window.

"Trade secret, huh," Edmund said. "That's okay, you don't have to tell me. What are you doing here?

Won't his Mightiness be pissed if he finds out you're gone?"

Mr. Dumpy held out a white-gloved fist to the childling. Covering his mouth with his other hand as if to suppress a giggle, the clown uncurled his fingers to display a glowing blue stone resting in its palm.

Edmund's eyes opened wide.

"That's the Waystone!" he said, nearly forgetting the need to whisper. "What are you doing with it?"

The clown rolled the gem toward his fingertips, catching it between his thumb and forefinger and offering it to Edmund.

"You want me to take it?" the childling asked. Mr. Dumpy nodded vigorously. Edmund could almost hear the clown say, "Well, duh," as he shoved the gem toward Edmund. The redcap took it gingerly in his own hand.

"It won't melt into my palm, will it?" he asked.

Mr. Dumpy shook his head. The clown pointed to Edmund and then to the open window. Edmund felt his heart pound as he realized the implications of what he had in his hand.

"You want me to take this and use it to find the others!" he said.

Mr. Dumpy sighed in relief. Edmund eased himself from the bed and began to gather his things into his backpack as quietly as he could. A few minutes later he had shouldered the pack and held out his hand to the clown. Mr. Dumpy held up a cautionary hand and began fishing around with his other hand in a back pocket Edmund had never noticed. When he found what he was looking for, Mr. Dumpy held out a handful of paper.

Edmund looked at the crisp rectangles that rested on his palm. "This is money!" he said. "Real Irish money, like the twins have."

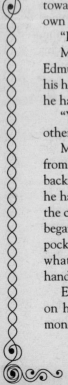

Mr. Dumpy looked up at the ceiling and pursed his lips in a silent whistle.

"Cool!" Edmund said admiringly. "Let's go, then!"

Mr. Dumpy shook his head and pointed to Malacar's sleeping form.

Edmund looked puzzled. The clown looked exasperated and mimed waking the satyr and tugging him by the arm.

"You can't be serious!" Edmund said. "You don't want me to take the old sockethead. Do you?"

Mr. Dumpy nodded slowly.

"You are serious! But how am I going to explain you to him?" As soon as he spoke, Edmund slapped himself in the face. "Never mind," he said. "It's not as if he can see you or anything," he said, feeling foolish. "Do I have to?" he asked plaintively.

Mr. Dumpy just stared at him and tapped his foot.

Edmund sighed. "Fine," he said. "We'll take the old goat along, but he'd better not get us into trouble. How'm I gonna get him out the window without breaking his neck?"

Mr. Dumpy cocked his head at Edmund and this time pointed to the door.

"Won't the others wake up when they hear us traipsing through the house?"

The clown shook his head.

"Okay—" Edmund sounded dubious, but decided that questioning the clown's plan was no longer an option. "Give me a minute to get him up and ready," he said.

Malacar woke more quietly than Edmund expected, but the redcap shoved both hands across the satyr's mouth just for good measure.

"Don't say a word, blind man," he whispered in as threatening a voice as he could manage without volume. "We're getting out of here, understand? We—

I—have the Waystone." *Oh, shit*, Edmund thought once the words were out of his mouth. *He's sworn himself to the prince. He'll tell!* "Before you think of ratting on me," he said, this time putting his mouth against Malacar's ear so that he could inject a tone of menace to his voice without risking being heard by the others in the house, "think about this. If I split without you, you'll be all alone. Do you think Glynnis or the Deadly Duo will take over being your sight hound?"

The satyr shook his head.

"I don't think so either," Edmund said. "I know you're bound to Mr. Bigshot, but just pretend that you're spying on me. That way you won't have to break your oath, if that means anything to you. Or let's say I'm kidnapping you. Whatever works, okay?"

Malacar nodded, his hands groping for Edmund's wrists. Edmund closed his teeth lightly on the satyr's ear. Immediately, Malacar grew still.

"'Isten," the redcap mumbled. "I'n 'oing 'oo 'ake 'y 'ands a'ay. 'On't 'ell."

Malacar gave a single, cautious nod and Edmund eased his hands away from the satyr's lips. At the same time, he released Malacar's ear lobe. He grabbed the satyr's wrists and helped him sit up.

"Where are you going?" Malacar whispered harshly. Edmund gave him points for not yelling and began to relax. He looked over his shoulder at Mr. Dumpy, who was standing in the open doorway giving Edmund a thumbs up sign. Edmund had a sudden inspiration.

"I'm going to take us to Leigh and the others," he whispered. "That's what the prince said we needed to do anyway," he said, remembering the conversation Yrtalien had with them earlier in the evening, after the ritual oathtaking. The prince had outlined his plans for locating the oathmates and using the stones to force them to open Silver's Gate. He had also assigned Donal and Dougal the task of assembling as many Unseelie Kithain as they could to form an assault team to back up his takeover of the gateway to Arcadia. "We're just getting a head start," he added. "Besides," he said, still marshaling his arguments to ensure the satyr's cooperation, "you really don't want to stay here, do you?" For good measure, he backed up his suggestion with his own Glamour, patting the satyr on the knee as he spoke to focus his magic.

Malacar seemed to consider Edmund's words. "You're not as dumb as I thought," he grumbled. Edmund decided to ignore the verbal slap in the light of his apparent success.

"Stay put while I get your clothes," Edmund whispered. As quickly as he could he helped Malacar dress, then took the satyr's hand and assisted him to his feet. Mr. Dumpy led the pair out of Edmund's room and down the stairs to the back door of the house. Edmund noticed that they seemed to walk in a vacuum, making no sound even though Malacar's limp usually resulted in a shuffling gait that was anything but quiet. At the door, Mr. Dumpy stood aside to let Edmund and Malacar pass, waving at Edmund with a sad smile.

"Aren't you coming?" Edmund asked.

The clown shook his head.

"He'll kill you if you stay!" the redcap said. "Or drain you or whatever. He'll destroy you."

Mr. Dumpy shook his head and gave Edmund a knowing look.

Trust me, Edmund seemed to hear in his mind.

"Who are you talking to?" Malacar asked out loud.

"Shut up," Edmund hissed. "No one you need to know about," he said. He looked at Mr. Dumpy again. "Are you sure you know what you're doing?" he asked.

The clown nodded, reaching out to pat Edmund on the shoulder and then holding out a hand for the redcap to shake.

"This isn't goodbye forever, is it?" he muttered disconsolately as he solemnly clasped hands with his chimeric friend.

Mr. Dumpy shook his head from side to side. He stepped back into the house and waved once more to Edmund, then silently shut the door.

"What was that all about?" Malacar mumbled.

"Never mind," Edmund said. "Let's get out of here while we can. Can you drive?" he asked, eyeing the twins' van parked in the rear of house. "What am I saying? We'll have to hoof it. I hope you don't mind walking."

Securing his grip on Malacar, Edmund held the Waystone out in front of him, using a small bit of faerie magic to activate the stone as he had seen Yrtalien do countless times. "Take me—I mean, us—where we need to go," he commanded. The stone began to glow bright blue and Edmund felt a tug in the direction of the road that led from the brothers' house to Sligo.

"We're off," he whispered to Malacar and jerked the satyr forward, following the pull of the Waystone.

From his window upstairs, Yrtalien watched quietly as Edmund and Malacar slipped away into the darkness, their forms limned by the sapphire glow of the Waystone. A small sound at the door alerted the prince. He smiled at the chimeric clown poised in the doorway.

"Nicely done," he said to Mr. Dumpy. "Now, back in your pouch."

The clown's faerie magic faded as he reverted to

his miniature inanimate form. Yrtalien picked up the small figurine and placed it in his neckpouch, along with the three remaining Eyestones.

Such a gullible fool, the prince thought. *Now that the stones have all been brought together, they are attuned to one another once more. The three I have will seek out the fourth.* "You cannot escape me so easily," he said, though it was Leigh's face, rather than Edmund's that appeared in his mind. Satisfied, he crossed the room and settled himself into bed for a well-deserved sleep.

Rasputin tossed fitfully in his sleep, his mind full of restless dreams involving red deer and Signe and a seductive sidhe queen with honey blond hair who smiled at him and clasped him gently to her breast, like a mother comforting a lost child. She seemed sorrowful when at last she released him. *I shall return when you need me most*, she promised him as her form began to fade into an insubstantial, ghostlike creature. Blackness engulfed her like a shroud and from that formless form a harsh, despairing wail arose.

Rasputin woke with it, screaming. Almost immediately, Liam was at the pooka's side, his pennywhistle already primed to play.

"She's back," he whispered darkly to the others as, one by one, they gathered around the sobbing pooka to give him what comfort and Glamour they could. The clurichaun's music restored much of Rasputin's ravaged magic, but it was the end of sleep that evening for the oathmates and the household of Sir Odhran.

chapter

ten

Lady Rowena rode with the companions as they traveled southwest from Dublin toward County Kerry's Dingle peninsula, a journey that took them on a diagonal course from the eastern coast of Ireland to her western edge in less than 250 miles.

The Fiona noblewoman directed them along a roundabout route that circled the perimeter of the peninsula, adding a few more miles to their trip but allowing the oathmates to view some of the land's most awe-inspiring seascapes. Leaving the main road at Tralee for R559, the tour road that ran along the outer rim of the peninsula, they drove past the fishing port town of Dingle, once a haven for smugglers, but now mainly a tourist attraction. Beyond Dingle, the road carried them along the coast past the ruins of Dunbeg Fort and along the Slea Head promontory, where the now-deserted Blasket Islands' rocky outlines could be seen across the Blasket sound. Swinging northward, they drove past Clogher Head where the road turned away from the coast and headed northeast toward their destination, the McSkeath homestead, a large farmhouse with several smaller buildings, nestled in a valley south of the village of Ballyferriter.

The late afternoon sun was setting as they drove up to the house and parked their car alongside several other vehicles.

Leigh, who had been silent and introspective for most of the journey, was the first out of the car, cradling the cloth-wrapped loaf of nut and raisin bread which she had baked the day before to bring to Sorcha's family. Without waiting for the others, she began walking slowly toward the house.

"Are you all right?" Valmont asked, falling quickly into step beside her and trying to slow her down until the rest of the group caught up with them.

Leigh started to nod, then changed her gesture into a weary shake of her head.

"Not really," she said. "I feel like a murderer coming to visit the home of her victim."

Valmont stepped in front of Leigh and seized her by the shoulders.

"Listen," he said, his voice all the more intense for its softness, "you did not kill her. It was her own doing."

"I was the cause of her death," Leigh whispered. "It's the same, whichever way you look at it."

Behind the pair, the rest of the group gathered, waiting for some sign that they should continue on to the farmhouse.

"Someone's coming," Tor said, catching sight of a figure coming out of the front door and walking toward them. The troll recognized Connor, the McSkeath brother who had traveled to Dublin the day before to invite the oathmates to his sister's wake.

"Welcome and come in," he said, nodding first at Leigh and Valmont and then at the others. Wordlessly, Leigh handed him the loaf of bread. Then she and the others followed him into the house. Liam lagged a little behind the others, carrying his guitar slung on his back.

The small, comfortably proportioned living room was filled with people, both mortal and Kithain. At the far end, surrounded by a ring of lit candles in tall bronze stands, Sorcha's coffin rested. Three men of varying ages, all resembling Connor, stood nearest the coffin. They looked up at the new arrivals, and one of them, by looks the oldest, came forward to greet Lady Rowena with a formal embrace. He looked at the oathmates and his face, already serious, grew even more somber.

"Are these the ones?" he asked Lady Rowena. She started to nod, but Leigh stepped forward.

"I am Eleighanara," she said, "and these are my friends."

Sorcha's brother nodded, his steel-gray eyes expressionless. "I am Peadar, and these are my brothers Gannon and Fearghus." He angled his head in the direction of the two men still standing beside the coffin, as he spoke. "You've already met Connor."

Leigh started to speak, but the one introduced as Fearghus cut her off, coming away from the coffin to stand so close to Leigh that she could feel his breath in her face.

"I for one am glad that you've come," he said in a voice that was anything but friendly. "I wanted to lay eyes on the one who ended my sister's life before her time."

At his outburst, the conversations that had been going on quietly in the background ceased abruptly.

"She is blameless in your sister's death," Valmont said, interposing himself between Leigh and Fearghus. The eshu's nostrils flared with anger and his eyes glittered with a dangerous gleam.

"Stand down, Valmont," Leigh ordered, her voice sharp with command. She closed her eyes to calm herself, then spoke more gently to her oathmate. "Please, this is not your fight." She forced herself to look directly into Fearghus' eyes.

"I cannot deny some portion of blame for your sister's death," she said. "But her blade was as sharp as mine. She lost her footing and moved into my sword. There was nothing I could do to stop it." *It's not quite the truth*, Leigh thought, *but I will not tell them, if they don't already know it, that Sorcha brought about her death by her own hand.*

"She gives a fair report of what happened," Lady Rowena said, placing a hand on Fearghus' shoulder. He shrugged it off and pulled away from her and Leigh, but he seemed a little less angry than before. "I was a witness, and I saw Eleighanara try to pull back on her sword to keep from wounding your sister."

Gannon walked up behind his brother and steered Fearghus away from Leigh toward a door that led further into the house.

"Maybe we should leave," Leigh murmured, nearly colliding with Rasputin, standing mutely behind her, in her blind attempt to retreat.

"She looks so peaceful," Morgan said, clutching her grandfather's hand tightly as she stood at the edge of the coffin and peered at Sorcha's still features, fixed in icy repose.

"The embalmers in town did a lovely job, didn't they?" an older woman, dressed in black and wearing a heavy shawl over her shoulders, remarked from her seat to one side of coffin.

Morgan nodded, unable to take her eyes away from her first sight of death's aftermath. The old woman's face suddenly seemed to crumple into a look of pain. She pulled her shawl over her head and, shutting her eyes, began a high-pitched wail of grief, rocking back and forth to the rhythm of her voiced sorrow. Morgan shrank back into her grandfather's side. Rasputin stiffened at the sound, his large eyes growing even larger.

"Stay," Peadar said to Leigh's back, looking into Valmont's eyes with a determination that suggested his own authority within the household. Still holding Leigh's arm, Valmont slowly turned her away from the door.

"Mrs. Goherty doesn't object to your being here," the eldest of Sorcha's brothers said, motioning with

all kings

his head toward the swaying figure, whose cries were building up to a grand crescendo. "She only keens when she feels comfortable with those around her," he added. "She and some of the other neighbor women have been here since we brought Sorcha back from the funeral people in town." He looked around at the empty seats immediately surrounding the old woman. "I guess the others have taken a break," he said, a rueful smile passing quickly across his face.

"I didn't come here to cause any more pain," Leigh said, her voice soft and subdued. Peadar nodded.

"I know that," he said, "and Connor knows that. I think, perhaps, that Gannon knows it as well and will soon make that clear to Fearghus. The pain is here already, and you belong here with it."

Rasputin felt a light touch on his back and turned around to find Liam standing behind him.

"Why don't we go outside and around the back?" the clurichaun said. "We can pay our respects when things are a little quieter."

Rasputin gave Liam a grateful look. "I was just beginning to enjoy the melody," the pooka mumbled as he allowed the clurichaun to lead him out of the house.

"Mrs. Goherty?" Morgan asked, finally looking away from the body and staring at the old woman. "That's my babysitter's name!"

The old woman broke off her keen and opened her eyes as she pulled the shawl back down across her shoulders. She sized up the childling before her with interest.

"That wouldn't be Martha Goherty, would it?" she asked.

Morgan blinked. "I don't know," she said. "I always just called her Mrs. Goherty. I didn't think about whether she had another name."

The old woman clucked and shook her head. "My late husband's first cousin was a Goherty who moved his family to America after the Great War," she said. "Their daughter Martha was a great friend of mine. I heard they moved out to California or Nevada or one of those places."

Morgan nodded politely. "They might be the same person," she said, sensing that the woman would be satisfied with nothing less. Tor, sensing his grand-daughter's lack of expertise at the niceties of mourning talk, steered Morgan away from the potential second cousin of her former babysitter with a gruff nod to the woman. "We're blocking traffic," he told Morgan as he guided her to the other end of the room. A young woman appeared from the back of the house carrying a cup of hot tea and handed it to Mrs. Goherty, who accepted it with a smile. "Keening's hard work," she said as she brought the cup to her lips.

Despite Malacar's growing complaints of hunger as night turned into morning, Edmund pushed on as the Waystone led him through Sligo and along the scenic road that ran northeast from the brothers' house. Finally, the redcap shoved his hand into his back pocket and retrieved a half-eaten granola bar, a veteran of his trip from Point Reyes to Hawaii the month before.

"Here," he said, shoving it into the satyr's hand without breaking his steady stride. "A little of this goes a long way, believe me." Malacar grumbled plaintively but began chewing on the stale morsel. "We'll get some real food later on," the redcap promised him. *Just as soon as we're far enough away so that we can stop for a couple of hours*, he thought.

all kings

Edmund's legs were beginning to tire just after sunrise and he considered finding a place off the road to rest. As he rounded a curve in the road, he spotted a tour bus parked by the roadside, apparently so that its passengers could step outside and take photographs of their surroundings.

"Yes!" he exclaimed and jerked Malacar forward to join the group of tourists.

"Where are we?" the satyr asked, hearing and sensing the presence of strangers milling around nearby. "What are we doing?"

"Button your hole," Edmund hissed. "Try to look like my grandfather or something," he said. The redcap started whistling tunelessly to awaken his faerie Glamour as he insinuated himself and Malacar into the line that was beginning to form near the door of the bus.

"We just showed you our passes," he said to the bored-looking tour guide that stood near the head of the vehicle. "You told us we could sit up front near the driver," he added for good measure. "I get bus-sick, remember?" He saw from the glazed expression that came over the face of the guide that his magic had taken effect and he led Malacar to the choice seats on the bus. He helped the satyr fiddle with his seat belt before he buckled himself in and waited for the rest of the bus to fill. He noted with satisfaction that there were still a number of empty seats as the bus pulled back onto the road and continued on its way. In his hand, the gemstone seemed to hum, as if it were content with the vehicle's direction.

"Get some sleep, Grandpops," Edmund advised Malacar. "It'll be awhile before we get to—where are we going?" he asked, raising his voice and sticking his head into the aisle to look back at the other passengers.

"Donegal," a man called out with a drawl that sounded vaguely Texan to Edmund. "We'll be there in less than an hour unless this piece of junk breaks down."

Edmund settled back in his seat and let the rumbling of the bus' engine lull him to sleep. An idea began to form in his mind as he let himself relax for the first time since leaving Sligo. *There's gotta be a post office in Donegal*, he told himself before he tumbled into an exhausted slumber.

Behind the main farmhouse, a group had assembled in a smaller, shedlike building that held a few tools and a broken plow. A pair of oil lanterns on the floor of the shed illumined the faces of nearly a dozen people, most of whom looked up as Liam guided Rasputin inside.

The pooka's faerie sight registered the fact that he was among Kithain. His face brightened and he sank to the floor gratefully next to a rangy figure with a houndlike face and a shock of shaggy hair covering his eyes.

"The name's Wolfe," the dog-pooka said, grinning at Rasputin. "Named after Wolfe Tone," he added, referring to one of Ireland's most famous patriots.

"Naturally," Rasputin said.

Liam shoved in on the other side of Rasputin and made a general introduction to the crowd, naming both himself and the pooka, although it seemed as if most of the gathering already knew the clurichaun.

A slender arm reached across Wolfe and slapped the pooka's knee. "How's the foot? Still broken?" a familiar female voice asked Rasputin. The pooka glanced behind the dog-pooka and caught sight of the speaker.

"Brit!" he said. "I thought you might be here." His voice sounded anything but enthusiastic. Across the room, Emer waved at the pooka. Kieran sat next to her, resining up the bow of a fiddle.

"We were hoping we'd run into you again," the selkie maiden said, her bright eyes shining in the smoky lantern-light. "Are you surprised to see us?"

"Of course not," Rasputin said, and this time he sounded almost cheerful. Next to him, Liam had unslung his guitar and was adjusting its tuning, holding his ear close to the sound box. The pooka noticed that a few others, including Wolfe, had brought out an assortment of instruments.

"Some of these musical folk came down all the way from Doolin just for the occasion," Liam said. When Rasputin gave him a puzzled look, the clurichaun smiled. "It's not often that a wake is held for one of the sidhe, even a half-sidhe as some people allege."

The clurichaun stopped his tuning to take a clear jar from a dark-haired, catlike woman sitting next to him. He took an appreciative sip and passed it on to Rasputin.

"Try this," he said. "Best medicine for discomfort and bad memories in the world."

Rasputin sniffed the jar suspiciously before tasting its contents. His eyes watered as he rushed the potent liquid down his throat.

"That's heavenly," he sputtered.

"No, it's *poitín*—or poteen, as some call it," Liam advised. "Feels like someone ran a lit candle down your throat, doesn't it?"

Rasputin shook his head, still unable to speak.

"Take another sip," Wolfe said, giving the pooka a toothy grin. "It'll ease the blow of the first."

Before he realized who had spoken, Rasputin did as he was told. Several people in the room broke out in friendly laughter as the pooka discovered that the candle in his stomach had become a bonfire. Wolfe relieved him of the jar and slugged down a hefty mouthful before passing it on to Brit.

Someone sitting near Emer began a lively tune on a wood flute and the drone of a pair of Uillean pipes soon picked up the strain followed by the driving thump of the bodhran, a goat-skin hand-held round drum played by Kieran with studious intensity.

Next to Rasputin, Liam began fingering a complex rhythm on his guitar, texturing the music as a background to the fiddle that took over the melody from the flute. Rasputin felt the fire in his gut begin to die down to a steady warmth as he listened to the strands of music weave themselves into a series of variations on a single pattern. He barely noticed when Brit switched places with Wolfe and leaned her head on Rasputin's shoulder.

"This is for Sorcha," the flute player called. "May she come back as the queen of the pookas!"

In Donegal, the bus stopped for a walking tour of the town. Malacar continued to snore heavily, so Edmund checked with the tour guide to make sure he could safely leave his sleeping "grandfather" on the bus.

"He's blind and won't go anywhere," he told the guide, this time using a small portion of the stone's Glamour to enhance his logic. *This is great*, he thought. *It's like having that stupid pink drum-beating rabbit in the palm of my hand.*

As soon as he could break away from the tour group, he began asking around until he found the post office. Catching the attention of a harried-looking postal clerk, he pulled the small volcanic rock from his pocket.

"How much does it cost to send this back to Hawaii?" he asked the clerk.

Connor walked up with Leigh and Valmont to stand by Sorcha's coffin.

"It's hard to believe she's gone," he said quietly. "She was like a torch that wouldn't stop burning." He looked up at Leigh, his eyes moist with tears.

"I'm so sorry," Leigh whispered, feeling the inadequacy of her words yet not knowing any that were more meaningful.

"Lady Rowena has told most folks that it was an accident," Connor said cautiously, looking carefully at Leigh and Valmont to gauge their reaction. Valmont's expression remained unchanged except for a slight rise of his brows.

"She wanted so much to be one of them," Connor continued, gesturing with one hand to the corner of the room where Lady Rowena stood talking quietly with Peadar. "She was so proud when her ladyship agreed to sponsor her in the Riders, though there were times when she couldn't understand why her patron was so hard on her." He shook his head. "I have to admit, it sometimes puzzled me as well."

So much for a secret society, Leigh thought.

"How much do you know about—the Riders?" she asked.

Connor gave her a tight-lipped smile. "Who do you think protected the freehold of the old king before the return of the high sidhe?" he responded. "Scathach warriors formed the original Silver Riders after the other houses left."

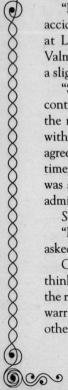

"What happened?" Valmont asked, his interest piqued.

Connor shrugged. "From what I heard, and mind you, I'm not exactly in the loop, the returnees had better swords and shinier armor. It took a few years, but gradually they replaced the original Riders with their own lords and ladies. Sorcha thought she'd be the first in a new generation of our blood to reclaim what she felt to be her hereditary post."

Leigh looked down at Sorcha's face, locked in the unnatural calm of death. "Valmont tried to save her," she said, suddenly remembering Sorcha's last moments. "They wouldn't let him." Her voice grew hard as the flash of insight brought a burst of anger to the surface.

"Is that true?" From behind them, Fearghus' voice cut through the background murmur. Valmont turned to the young man and nodded. "They said she had made her choice," the eshu replied, careful in his choice of words, "and that it was not our place to overrule her." Despite his caution, he could not help sounding bitter.

"I had a talk with Fearghus in the kitchen," Gannon said to Connor, coming up to stand beside his brother at the coffin. "He's a bit calmer, now." Connor's face relaxed slightly.

Fearghus touched Leigh lightly on the shoulder to get her attention. When she turned to him, he lowered his head, unable to meet her eyes.

"I owe you an apology," he said. "I believe you had no intention of harming her."

This time Leigh did not try to stop the tears that rose to her eyes. Something broke within her and the tightness that had been building in her chest and back eased as she let out a deep, sobbing breath.

"Thank you," she said, finally feeling released from the burden of guilt she had carried with her into the house.

all kings

"Will you be staying for the funeral tomorrow?" Connor asked.

Leigh looked at Valmont first, and then at Tor, who sat uncomfortably on a chair that was too small for him, while Morgan, perched on his knee, chatted with a flame-haired girl a year or two older than herself. The childling kept stealing looks at the coffin, despite her apparent interest in her new friend's conversation.

"I don't think so," Leigh said. "We hadn't planned to stay overnight."

Connor nodded. "Don't feel obliged to," Connor assured her. "We plan on a small service—just the family and a keener or two, if we can't avoid them. We have a family plot not far from here, where we've buried our dead for centuries." He looked at Leigh and smiled. "Her body to the earth, her heart to the Dreaming, her spirit to the cycle that will bring her back to us someday."

"Where's Rasputin?" Valmont asked, belatedly aware of the pooka's absence.

"I expect he's out back with your clurichaun friend," Connor said. "There's more than one way to honor the departed. Listen."

Leigh concentrated, and thought she could hear the strains of music coming from somewhere outside the house.

"No, the pookas were here first," Wolfe maintained, his voice carrying above the sound of the music, now a lilting hornpipe carried by flute and penny whistle. "Animals have been around much longer than humans. Every time a dog twitches his leg, a pooka is born somewhere."

"Who do you think taught the Egyptians to worship cats?" the dark-haired pooka, predictably named Caitrín, purred. "It certainly wasn't the eshu."

"Bless you," Rasputin mumbled, and giggled at his own joke. "Does that mean that satyrs are actually pookas?" he asked, slurring his words slightly as he took another small sip from the nearly empty jar and passed it to Wolfe.

"Are you kidding?" Brit said, looking up at Rasputin. She had stretched out in the middle of the floor so that her head rested in Rasputin's lap. He looked resigned to his fate. "They tried to join the pookas, claiming to be half-goat, but we told them to butt out."

"There's some truth behind all those stories of gods taking the form of animals and mixing with mortals," Kieran said, taking a rest from his drumming. "Some say the selkies are descended from Manannan Mac Lir's penchant for taking seal form to go courting." Liam looked at him quizzically. Kieran shrugged. "I don't know if it's true," he offered with a smile, "but the children of Lir were transformed into swans, that's in all the legends. They were pookas, if no one else was."

Heads nodded all around at the selkie's pronouncement.

Rasputin leaned back against the wall and let the talk flow around him, for once content merely to listen without the need to say more than he already had. Brit's head was warm in his lap and he felt himself begin to nod off. He jerked his head to rouse himself, but Wolfe pushed him gently back against the wall.

Liam put down his penny whistle and turned to Rasputin. "Take your ease," he said softly. "You're among friends and well-wishers here. No one'll hurt you while you sleep."

"No one has ever hurt me," Rasputin mumbled. "I've only hurt myself by not forgetting."

"At least part of that is true," Liam answered. He looked at Rasputin, his voice so soft that only the pooka could hear his next words. "She's drawn to your pain as well as to the Glamour that surrounds the lot of you," he whispered. "Tell your past goodbye and she'll seek out someone else."

Rasputin sighed and closed his eyes. *Remembering is so hard,* he thought, as the image of the young, battered boy he had been formed and faded in his mind. *Forgetting should be easier than it is.* Picturing a shiny playground in his mind, Rasputin planted a smiling image of his younger self atop a tall slide surrounded by a host of laughing playmates. *Stay there forever,* he told himself, and surrendered to the implacable pull of sleep. His dreams, when they began, took him to a vast court of pooka kings and queens. One king, though not a pooka, sat astride a red deer. He looked at Rasputin with a beatific smile. *One of you must forget,* he seemed to say. Rasputin looked at him and felt a small jolt of happiness. *Never,* he agreed, feeling his past tumble away from him like a rock falling from a great height into the sea. The ancient king nodded, satisfied.

"What did you say?" Brit asked, hearing Rasputin mumble something in his sleep.

Liam looked down at the fox pooka and smiled. "I think his words were 'I am the Rabbit King' or something to that effect," the clurichaun said.

It was late afternoon when the last in a succession of tour buses and friendly rides deposited Edmund and Malacar at the side of the road.

"Are you sure you want to be traipsing around this country so near evening?" the driver of the van asked solicitously. "Glenveagh Castle isn't even open this time of year."

"Don't worry about it," Edmund said to the recently enchanted mortal. "We know where we're going." He waved cheerfully as the vehicle drove away.

Malacar sniffed the air. "We're out in the open!" he said in a half-snarl, half-whine. Edmund looked up at the satyr. "Huh," he said, "your nose must be getting smarter cause you can't see." There was a tinge of admiration in his voice. He checked the stone he held and nodded to himself. "This way." He grabbed Malacar's sleeve and began to tug him off the road.

Malacar balked. "This has gone far enough!" he cried, twisting his hand around so that he had hold of Edmund's wrist, his gnarled fingers surprising the redcap with the ferocity of their grip. "I am not a piece of baggage to be lugged around at your whim without any thought to my own comfort or peace of mind. If you had any sense, you'd let me have the Waystone so that I could use it to see by and take us somewhere other than the middle of nowhere."

Edmund jerked away, using all his strength to escape the satyr's grip. His hand tightened on the stone.

"Look, slimepit," he snapped, "I didn't have to bring you in the first place. I could've just snuck out of the house without waking you up and you never would have known it until the prince fried your brains for letting me get away. You should be glad I didn't just dump you somewhere or leave you on a bus to Ballyhooly or someplace like that!" He turned away from the satyr and began stomping away from him, trying to make as much noise as possible.

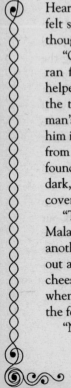

"Wait!" Malacar cried, feeling around in his perpetual darkness and finding nothing to latch onto for support. "You can't leave me here!"

Edmund stopped and whirled around. "You got one chance," he snarled, pitching his voice as low as he could and trying to sound sinister. "If you can crawl to me by the time I count to ten, I just might reconsider and take you with me. One—" The redcap watched smugly as Malacar stumbled forward to the ground, catching himself on his hands.

"Two—" Gropingly, the satyr began trying to crawl toward the sound of Edmund's voice. *He's doing it!* Edmund chortled to himself. *I can't believe I'm making the old fart grovel!*

"Three—you'd better step on it!" he chided. Hearing the unbridled glee in his own voice, Edmund felt suddenly ashamed. *I sound just like the prince*, he thought. *This is really sick.*

"Oh, forget it," he said, disgusted with himself. He ran forward and caught Malacar by one arm and helped him to his feet. "Let's just go," he mumbled to the trembling satyr, brushing the dirt from the old man's cloak. He took the satyr by the hand and led him in the direction indicated by the Waystone, away from the road to Glenveagh Castle. After awhile, he found himself tramping through a forest. Just before dark, he located a small open space with a few moss-covered stones large enough to sit on.

"This is where we stop," he announced, guiding Malacar to one of the stones and taking a seat atop another one. He reached in his backpack and pulled out a tin of sardines, a few winter apples, a wedge of cheese and a round loaf of bread that had been fresh when he bought it earlier in the day. He divided up the food between him and Malacar.

"Now what?" Malacar asked after they had eaten.

Edmund drained the last of the oil from the sardine tin.

"Now we wait," he said. He stared at the empty metal can for a few seconds before his popped it into his mouth. "Hey, y'know what?" he asked, chewing thoughtfully on the oily metal container. "If there were more redcaps in the world, litter wouldn't be such a big problem."

chapter

eleven

The oathmates spent the night with Lady Rowena, who owned a small freehold just outside Tralee.

"Are you certain it is time for you to return to the glen?" the sidhe noblewoman asked her guests over breakfast.

Leigh nodded. "We talked about it last night after we left the McSkeath place," she said, looking to her oathmates for confirmation. "The king set the conditions for our return, and we've met most of them—or we seem to have."

"Then there are still some things that have not yet been done," Lady Rowena said.

Morgan set down her glass of milk and nodded at her host. "I think the king meant for me to forgive Edmund," she said. "Only I can't do that until I see him."

"The final condition refers to Edmund," Leigh said. "And we can't do anything about that until we find him. Valmont thinks that our best means of doing that is to start for the king's glen, and he's our expert on travel."

Valmont smiled, but made no other comment. *Something has definitely changed since we dreamed the king's dream*, he thought as he looked around the table at his oathmates. Tor sat quietly working his way through an enormous plate of fried eggs and potato cakes. *He looks younger, as if his recovered past has given him back some of the years he has lost.* Rasputin, still looking groggy from the previous evening's back-of-the-house festivities, played with his food, swirling honey into his oatmeal in fanciful patterns. *Even his face has lost its haunted look*, the eshu observed. The changes that had come over himself and Leigh were not as visible, but both of them were quicker to smile and slower to take offense at imagined or even real slights. *We have somehow been purified.*

At the foot of the table, Liam drained the last of his morning tea with a loud slurp, winking at the companions as he watched Lady Rowena try to conceal her disapproval of his manners. "I hope you don't mind my accompanying you," he said.

Leigh shook her head. "You brought us to the forest," she replied. "I assumed that both you and Lady Rowena would go back there with us." She glanced at the older sidhe, who nodded calmly.

"The Riders are in the habit of comparing dreams after a night in the glen," Lady Rowena said. "It seems that only Sir Odhran and I were directed to return with you. If you are set on going there today, then I need to ring him and arrange for him to meet us there."

"What about the other Riders?" Valmont asked.

Lady Rowena allowed herself a small smile. "They have their own instructions," she replied mysteriously as she excused herself from the table and left to make her call to Sir Odhran.

Yrtalien listened as Donal and Dougal reported on their previous day's activities. The brothers had managed to enlist the aid of more than a dozen of their Unseelie acquaintances, an assortment of redcaps, trolls, nockers and other Kithain who were lured by the promise of future power or the prospect of a good fight.

"I don't think they know what they're getting themselves into," Dougal observed. Donal nodded in support of his brother's observation.

Yrtalien smiled. "Of course they don't," he said amiably. "That's what footsoldiers are for." Since swearing allegiance to him, the twins had ceased to banter with one another, buckling down to the tasks assigned to them with grim determination. The prince leaned back in his chair and patted the pouch containing his treasures.

"We all know our instructions, then?" he asked, looking around at the brothers and Glynnis.

Donal shrugged. "We're to gather the troops and follow you, my Lord," he said, his voice slurring over the honorific. "Where are you going, if I may ask?"

"I'll be following the stones," Yrtalien replied. "Three of them led me to the fourth one before. I expect they shall do so again. Make certain that you're not seen by our quarry until I call for you," he cautioned.

"Whatever you say, m'Lord," Donal said.

"And you?" Yrtalien turned to Glynnis. "Do you know what you are to do?" His low voice was a malicious purr.

Glynnis stared expressionlessly at Yrtalien. "My duty is to be at your service," she responded dully.

"I'm glad we finally have that straight," the prince snapped. He rose suddenly from his seat. "Let's be on our way."

The oathmates, along with Lady Rowena and Liam, joined Sir Odhran at the edge of the forest within Glenveagh National Park and began the trek through the woods that would take them to the faerie glen at its heart. They were beginning to feel the first stirrings of Glamour that signaled the beginning of the king's domain when Morgan spotted a pair of figures in a small clearing ahead of them.

"Edmund!" she cried, breaking away from her oathmates before they could stop her and running forward.

The redcap childling had no warning of Morgan's approach until she burst through the trees, launching herself at him and hugging him with all her small strength.

"Yuck!" he said, pushing himself away from her. "What's that awful smell?" he asked, trying to hide the unmistakable relief he felt at seeing his nemesis again.

Morgan frowned. "It's the rose perfume you gave me at Yuletime, remember?" she said.

"Oh," Edmund replied. "It smelled better in the bottle." He fell silent, scuffing his feet in the underbrush.

Morgan stared at her former oathmate. *Someone's hurt him,* she thought. *He's not the same as he was before he ran away from us.* She had made up her mind earlier that she would put Edmund's betrayal behind her so that she could meet her part of the king's conditions. It had been a conscious decision that had taken a lot of effort. Now, as she looked at the forlorn childling standing uncertainly in front of her, she realized that no effort was involved in what she felt.

"I'm sorry I was mean to you," she said. "Will you forgive me?"

Edmund's head jerked up at Morgan's words. "Huh?" he asked, taken aback.

Morgan, too, looked surprised at her own words.

"I thought I came here to forgive you," she said in a voice full of wonder. "But it's not you who's supposed to be forgiven. It's me."

Edmund blinked.

Valmont and Leigh stood with the others at the edge of the clearing, watching the two childlings. Tor started to push forward, but Rasputin put a hand out to stop him.

"Let them have their trivial discussion," he whispered. Tor halted, remaining poised to intervene if necessary.

"Will you do it?" Morgan asked again. *He's got to*, she told herself, feeling a sense of urgency.

"But I'm the one who broke the oath," Edmund said. "You've been Miss Perfect all along. I'm just the Forsworn Redcap."

Morgan looked embarrassed. "I don't know if you can unbreak an oath," she said, "but maybe since you're here, you didn't really break it to begin with. Maybe you just found a weird way to keep it."

Edmund stared at Morgan, astonished. Then he grinned as a sudden feeling of elation spread over him.

"Will you?" Morgan persisted, her voice tight with desperation.

"Will I what?" Edmund asked, still reveling in his newfound liberation from the onus of being an oathbreaker.

"Forgive me!" Morgan said, sighing heavily.

"Oh, that!" Edmund said. "Sure, why not?" Seeing Morgan's face, he backed away suddenly. "Just don't hug me again, okay?"

Morgan put her arms back down by her side. "Okay," she said. She looked over her shoulder and caught sight of her companions waiting just outside the clearing.

"You can come out now," she said. "It's done—both parts of it, I think."

"Who's this?" Sir Odhran asked, spotting Malacar huddled on the far edge of the clearing, a befuddled look on his ruined face.

"Oh, that's just Malacar," Edmund said. "He used to have two of the stones in his head, but he doesn't anymore so now he's blind as a bat. I had to bring him with me."

"What's going on?" Malacar said. "Whose voice is that? I thought you said your friends were going to be here!"

"Hello, Edmund," Leigh said, coming up to the redcap. Impulsively, she leaned down and hugged him briefly. Seeing his obvious discomfort at her display of affection, she released him. "Welcome back."

Liam walked over to the sightless satyr and touched him on the shoulder.

"I don't suppose you play the harp?" he asked, his voice crisp with amusement. Before Malacar could respond, he continued. "I'm called Liam. Some call me a clurichaun and others call me things I'd rather not repeat in mixed company. Did you know that the greatest harper in all Ireland was a blind man?" he asked, grasping Malacar's elbow and helping the satyr to his feet. He motioned for the others to go on with their reunion.

"Well, I suppose we won't have to worry about him for awhile," Valmont observed. He nodded a greeting to Edmund.

"I think we need to get started again," he said. "We can talk while we're walking. We all have a lot of catching up to do."

"Perhaps Lady Rowena and I should lead from here since we know the quickest way to the Dreamers' Glen," Sir Odhran said, offering his arm to his fellow Rider.

The companions fell into step behind the two nobles. In response to a question from Leigh, Edmund began to relate his experiences since parting company with his oathmates. Halfway through his account, he paused.

"What's this Dreamers' Glen?" he asked.

all kings

Morgan giggled. "Finish your story," she said. "Then we'll tell you ours."

"It's time," Signe said to Bridie as the two Kithain cleared the dishes from their morning meal.

The troll nodded philosophically. "Do you want me to come with you?" she asked.

Signe smiled. "That's up to you," she said. "An eshu's path is not necessarily best for those who walk it with her, but I won't deny that I prefer not to walk alone."

"Give me a few minutes to get my things," Bridie said. "Do you know where we're going?"

Signe shook her head. "Not yet," she replied. "But I will."

Night had fallen by the time the group reached the Dreamers' Glen.

"It seems different from the last time we were here," Valmont observed, looking around at the clearing filled with emerald grasses strewn with wildflowers that sparkled like gemstones.

"Oh, I'm sure that path was there before," Rasputin said. The pooka pointed to an archway of silver birches on the far side of the clearing. A tunnel of smoky blue trees stretched past the arch.

Lady Rowena and Sir Odhran exchanged quizzical glances with one another at the oathmates' conversation.

"I believe that your dream has already begun," Sir Odhran said quietly. Leigh turned to look at him, but had to strain to see him behind the glittering mist that seemed to separate the oathmates from the others.

"Liam?" Leigh called out to the clurichaun on the far side of the foggy barrier.

"Don't worry about us!" Liam answered, his voice coming as if from a great distance. "Take the high road—we'll join you when it's time."

"Is this where you saw the unicorn?" Edmund asked Morgan. The childling nodded emphatically.

"I wish you could have been here to see it," she said.

"I thought we had to go to sleep first," Tor said, his face mirroring his puzzlement.

"I believe we have only to dream," Valmont replied. "And that does not always imply slumber. Shall we?" he asked, leading the way across the clearing toward the shining archway.

Her need drove her far to the west, leaving the land behind her and heading out toward the sea where, far below her, she felt a great stirring underneath the waves. He is coming, she thought, and what he brings with him will feed me for a thousand thousand years. Her faded memory retained a few images that were still sharp and clear—a laughing king and a shining host of faerie knights, a bright gateway through which she used to pass freely between two worlds, and above and through it all, the unbearably beautiful music of the Dreaming. She had only to watch and wait above the patch of roiling waters.

The Hidden King was waiting for them, as before, in front of his castle, but this time they could see his face and form clearly outlined in the starlight that bathed his realm in its soft radiance. His features were as finely etched as if carved from crystal yet there was nothing frail in the strong line of his jaw or the firm set of his mouth. He wore armor that seemed made from the light of the stars beneath a midnight-colored cloak made of something richer than velvet. He smiled and held out both his hands as the oathmates approached him. One by one, they approached him and knelt, placing their hands between his according to the ancient tradition of fealty. No words passed between them and no oaths were made, but the king's Glamour surrounded them as they received his blessing. Edmund was the last in line to kneel before the king.

This is it, the redcap childling thought. *If I've screwed up, he'll blow me apart, I know it!* He glanced upward anxiously at the king's face as he shoved his hands out for the ancient sidhe to clasp and thought he saw the barest smile on the lordly face above him. *Your oath is renewed, as if it had never been tarnished*, he heard inside his head as the king's hands closed over his. His knees were shaking as he rose to stand with his oathmates.

The king gestured toward a circle of stones to one side of the path that led to his castle. Within the center of the ring, a fire burned steadily with the cold, pure light of Balefire.

"This is the path that will take you to Silver's Gate," he said. "By coming here you have come to your journey's end, and to its beginning as well. This is the time for questions, if you have them, for later there will only be time for actions, and in your deeds you must not falter if you are once more to open the way to the Dreaming that has so long been lost." He walked over to the stone ring and sat down on one of the smaller stones, beckoning for the others to join him. When they were all seated, he looked around at them, his eyes gleaming with mirth.

"Surely one of you has a voice!" he chided, as no one spoke.

Finally Edmund took a deep breath. "Yeah, your Greatness," he said, his voice husky with an unfamiliar tone of reverence. "The others told me about you, but do you have an actual name or are you just called the Hidden King?"

The air around them filled with the sound of a hundred bells at the king's laughter.

"I have had many names since my beginning," he said. "Mac Lir and Ailill among them. For now, if you need a name, let it be Meilseoir. It means king." He pronounced it mell-shy-er, but Leigh heard Valmont mouth the word "Melchior."

Edmund nodded. "I'm Edmund," he said.

The king smiled. "Your name means Protector."

Edmund considered the king's statement. "Oh," he replied.

"Leigh's name means Light," Morgan said, finding her voice at last. "The menehune told us that when we were in Hawaii."

"And you are Morgan, the Child of the Sea," the king said. He turned to Tor and nodded. "Son of Thunder," he named the troll. "Traveler along many Roads," he said, looking at Valmont. Finally his gaze rested on Rasputin.

"Mad monk," Edmund whispered to Morgan. She rolled her eyes upward and bit her lip to keep herself from giggling.

"One who has been made Whole," the king said softly. Rasputin returned the king's look without flinching.

"That's what Rasputin means?" Edmund asked aloud.

"No," replied the king. "That is what Rafael means."

all kings

"This circle is a gate to a faerie trod, is it not?" Valmont asked, bringing the conversation back to their immediate concern. King Meilseoir inclined his head in affirmation.

"Where in the mortal realm does it lead?"

"To the westernmost edge of what is now, I believe, called Achill Island," the king replied.

"We still don't have the stones," Leigh said. "How will we open the gate without them?"

"You have one," Edmund said, pulling the Waystone from his pocket. He stood up and started to walk toward Valmont to hand the blue stone to the eshu. "You're the traveler," he said. "I don't need it anymore."

"He is not the one to hold the Waystone," the king said. "There are two Seelie and two Unseelie gems. The Keystone and the Waystone are for the Spring Warrior and the Summer Queen. The Shadowstone and the Changestone are for the Autumn Lad and the King of Winter."

"But there are six of us," Morgan pointed out. "Does that mean that two of us don't need to use the stones?"

Meilseoir gave her a sad smile, but did not reply.

"Keep it until later," Leigh told Edmund. "What about the other Eyestones?" she asked the king.

"They are on their way to where you will soon be," he replied.

"That means that Yrtalien will be there," she murmured.

"Did you not realize that when some doors open, others must close?" The king asked softly. Meilseoir stood up and crossed the ring to stand before Leigh, placing his hands on either side of her shoulders and raising her to face him.

"Eleighanara, daughter of the House of Fiona, I have spent centuries locked within my dreams, and in some of them I have seen your past and glimpses of your future. You came to this world in exile and under Geasa, a compulsion that has until now been concealed from you in order that it might come to pass without interference. Look into my eyes and remember."

Leigh raised her eyes to meet those of the king and the ground dropped out from under her.

She stood before the bright gate that opened up before her, her heart still filled with the pain of her imminent crossing into the world of mortal flesh and cold iron nightmares. Her father laid a hand on her forehead, his stern face as unyielding as the stone pillars that marked the gate.

"By the stars that shine eternal, by the threads of the Dreaming, by the stones that will stand until time itself is no more, I bind you to the words I am about to speak. The wound between the world of mortals and the world of dreams must one day be healed. It is your fate to begin that healing. I send you unwilling from the Dreaming for this purpose—that you may find within you the wisdom you now lack, that you use that wisdom to lift a curse that was never meant to be and restore to a loyal kith its ancient guardianship, and that you return to us bringing with you ambassadors from the world we left so long ago in order that you and they discover the means of joining together that which once was sundered. Let nothing and no one come between you and your quest. Find your true heart in the other world and keep your false heart from profaning the Dreaming. Finally, let no other Geasa bind you until your purpose is done. As the words are spoken, so let them come to pass in their fated time."

The force of the Geasa blinded her so that she staggered backward through the portal and fell for an endless time.

Leigh felt the world around her become solid once more as the king released his hold on her. *So that is why I could swear an oath of fealty to my duke and loyalty to my oathmates but could not be bound by the duke's Geasa*, she thought. She watched as the king turned from her and returned to his stone seat.

"Yrtalien will try to stop us from going through," she said to her oathmates.

"Or he will try to go through first, so that the connection will be reforged from his base ambitions and dark Glamour," the king said. "But he cannot open the gate without you. Nor can it be opened without all four of the stones. You will be in danger from him, but not before the gate is open. Until then, he will not harm you."

"So are we gonna go now, or what?" Edmund asked.

"That's a question I hoped I'd never hear again," Rasputin said, smiling at the redcap's impatience.

The king nodded. "It is time," he said. "When we get to Achill Island, it will be morning."

"What about the others?" Tor asked.

"They are sleeping," the king replied. "When they awaken, they will know what to do. Time passes differently in this place, and outside it, some are already well along on their journey toward the place where dreams will rise from the waters to embrace the air and sky once more. Many are the dreamers this night, and I am in all of their dreams."

He gestured for the companions to rise and join him around the Balefire. As he approached the flame, it grew to form a fiery door.

"Follow me," he said.

"You can't go through!" Morgan exclaimed. "You'll die if you step outside your freehold. That's what Liam said."

"What general or what king, for that matter, will send his armies where he himself will not go?" Meilseoir asked in response to the childling's protest.

"I have the Glamour of six heroes to shelter me for the time it will take to do what I must do, for I am part of this event as much as are all of you."

Holding out his hand for Morgan to take, the Hidden King stepped into the door of flames and out into the world of cold and iron.

all kings

chapter

twelve

372 Twenty miles from the western coast of Ireland, at the edge of County Mayo in the province of Connaught, sits Achill Island, a fractured piece of the mainland broken off eons ago during some great upheaval of the land. The island's eastern side is separated from the rest of Ireland by twenty feet. A bridge stretches across the gap, connecting Achill to the rest of the country. Like much of Ireland's west, Achill Island has seen the grinding poverty of the Famine, the haunting loss of its people through emigration, and, now, the onslaught of the tourist trade, bringing some prosperity but destroying much of its wild beauty in the process.

Facing west, towering cliffs line the island's seaward side, and a ridge-back trail runs to Achill Head, at the westernmost tip. From time to time, near Keem Bay, sharks ply the waters.

The morning sun was a pale white circle of cold light in the gray sky as the air around Achill Head shimmered and parted like a shining curtain drawn aside to reveal a heretofore unseen doorway.

King Meilseoir stepped through onto the ground and gasped as the chill of the mortal world insinuated itself within his immortal faerie spirit. Still holding his hand, Morgan felt the shock as if it were her own. "Quick, Edmund!" she called back over her shoulder. "Hand me the stone!"

Standing halfway between the worlds, Morgan saw Edmund shoving his way from the back of the group. Letting go of Tor, she reached for the redcap's outstretched hand and pulled Edmund and the Waystone through. Morgan took the stone from her

oathmate and pushed it into the king's hand, where
it began to glow with a brilliant blue light.

By the time the others had joined them atop Achill
Head, the Glamour from the sapphire had begun to
counter the effect of the king's sudden entry into the
physical world.

"Are you all right?" Morgan asked anxiously,
looking up at the king's face, now lined with the marks
of his inner pain.

Meilseoir nodded.

"Thanks," Morgan said to Edmund. The redcap
shrugged. "Easy come, easy go," he replied.

The oathmates and the Hidden King stood atop a
narrow ridge barely wide enough to hold them all. Half
a mile away to the west, the ridge continued, growing
even more narrow until it ended at the edge of a steep
cliff. Morgan looked down and quickly looked away.
Cautiously she stepped backward until she was
pressing against her grandfather's comforting bulk.

"When Yrtalien came through, there was a human
body waiting for him," Leigh recalled as the image of
the prince's release from his chimeric prison replayed
itself in her head. "He took it over so that he would
be able to exist in the world." She looked around her
as if expecting to see a convenient mortal for the king
to inhabit, then shook her head as she put the thought
from her.

Valmont touched her shoulder and pointed to a
figure approaching them from the landward end of the
ridge. Leigh's face grew pale as she recognized Yrtalien.

"I hope you're not afraid of heights," Signe said as she
and Bridie began the walk that would take them along
the cliff tops from Moyteoge Head to the tip of Achill

all kings

Head. The troll grinned and shook her head, patting her ample form.

"If I fall off, I'll just bounce right back up," she said.

The early morning walk afforded the two Kithain a spectacular view of the sea and they reveled in the sight. Halfway to their destination, Bridie stopped suddenly and caught Signe's attention.

"What's that?" Bridie said, pointing out a group of people who were hidden in a valley on the landward side of the ridge.

Signe peered downward.

"Offhand, I'd say it was an army of Kithain, though a small one," she replied, detecting the glint of real and chimeric weapons in the hands of the rough-looking crowd. Near the head of the group she recognized an elegant sidhe female, standing a little apart from the others and appearing ill-at-ease in their company. Lady Glynnis, Signe thought, recalling the name of Yrtalien's companion at the prince's Hawaiian freehold. She also saw a pair of sidhe, alike enough to be twin brothers, among the assembled Kithain.

"I don't think they're here to help our friends," she commented.

Bridie sighed. "Should we do something?" she asked.

Signe continued to watch the group for a few minutes, then shook her head.

"Not now," she said quietly, "and not here. Let's continue on and hope we haven't been seen. Maybe there will be a chance for us to take some action later on."

Glynnis held the shard of a mirror in front of her and peered steadily into it, feeling her faerie magic pour from her to transform the looking-glass into a window overlooking the spot where Yrtalien now made his overture to the oathmates.

He was right in assuming that they would come without reinforcements, she thought, seeing the familiar faces of Leigh and her companions clustered atop the narrow ridge. They seemed to be staring directly at her, and she realized that she was seeing them through the eyes of the Forsworn Prince. *He is still in love with her*, Glynnis realized as her vision focused almost exclusively on Leigh, passing briefly over the others as if merely counting heads. *He will try again to win her, and if he succeeds, she will learn what it is to fall under the spell of his madness*. Her oath to the prince bound her actions, not her thoughts, and Glynnis felt a wave of pity for the young Fiona knight.

"When do we move out?" Donal asked, coming up behind Glynnis so quietly that she started, nearly losing her tenuous connection with the distant prince. She shook her head.

"I will give the signal when it is time," she said harshly. On the edge of her vision, partly concealed by Tor's bulk, Glynnis detected a face that did not belong to any of the oathmates. Her expression froze as centuries seemed to vanish and she was standing once more outside a crumbling freehold, frantically trying to push her way through a gateway to the Dreaming that was collapsing under the weight of the mortal world's rampant disbelief. *I thought he died long ago*. The face passed out of her line of sight, but she felt a small glimmer of hope rise up within her.

Donal shrugged and walked over to his brother. Dougal turned away from a troll who had been complaining about the enforced idleness when a battle had been promised, and greeted his brother with a hard smile. Although they had done their best to carry out Yrtalien's plans to the letter, neither of them found any joy in their work. The night just past had been a sleepless one as the brothers had tried to find some way out of their predicament. They had gone over Edmund's tale of Silver's Gate and had come to an inescapable conclusion. The prince needed all four stones to open the gate, but he only needed a pair of brothers to ensure that the portal remained open.

As they waited now for the orders to climb the ridge and launch their assault, no words passed between the twins, but they clasped arms solemnly, as if some tacit agreement had been reaffirmed.

"Surely you are not surprised to see me, Eleighanara," Yrtalien said as he stopped a few feet away from the companions. He held out a hand toward her, palm facing upward just out of her reach. The three stones glimmered in the pale morning light. "After all, I have something you need."

Leigh stared at the stones, not daring to look at the face of the prince she once loved.

"You have nothing I need," she said. "The Eyestones do not belong to you."

Yrtalien laughed.

"Do you actually think they are yours, then?" he asked. He plucked the emerald Keystone from his palm and held it out to her. "You already have the Waystone in your possession, do you not?" he asked. "This is its companion, meant for one whose heart belongs to the Seelie half of the cycle of seasons. The other two are Unseelie gems and mine by default," he said. "Take the emerald and we will open the gate together." He smiled at Leigh, his dark eyes glittering with a feverish intensity.

"She does not have the Waystone." King Meilseoir stepped forward to stand beside Leigh, his ageless face radiant in the sapphire glow that surrounded him. "I do."

Yrtalien's expression betrayed his surprise at the sight of the king.

"I thought you were long dead," he whispered.

"Your father, my sister's husband, wanted it," the king said without rancor, "and he made certain that I could not follow the rest of his household into the Dreaming." It was Meilseoir's turn to smile, although it was a smile of sadness. "He never realized that I intended to stay here, where my dreams could serve to hold some semblance of magic to the land."

"Is this why you had to come here?" Morgan asked, trying to understand the strange reunion taking place in front of her.

The king shook his head.

"No," he said, "although it gives me even more reason to be here." He held out the Waystone, offering it to Leigh. "The four stones are here, and so are the pair of Kithain who will open Silver's Gate, but it is my magic that will make the Isle of Dreams rise again from its place in the waters below us. You cannot open what is not before you," he said.

Morgan's mouth rounded in a silent "oh" of comprehension.

"That was so obvious, I'm surprised we didn't figure it out on our own," Rasputin muttered to Edmund. Tor gave the pooka a withering look. Rasputin shrugged and smiled apologetically. "Just being helpful," he said.

"How can we help?" Leigh asked the king, ignoring Yrtalien for the moment.

"First, you must decide which two of you will open Silver's Gate and distribute the gems accordingly,"

Meilseoir said.

"That decision has been made," Yrtalien snapped.
"Eleighanara and I are still bound by love and oath,
and we are the ones destined to open the gateway to
Arcadia."

"You are mistaken," Leigh said, turning to Valmont
and holding out her hand to the eshu knight. Valmont
took Leigh's hand and joined her in front of Yrtalien.
Clasping Valmont's hand, Leigh faced the Forsworn
Prince again.

"Our love died once and for all when you delivered
us into the hands of the Dauntain, and that betrayal
ended your oathbond to me," she said. "You are not
the only Unseelie prince in this place."

The eshu held out his other hand toward the
prince. "I have not yet reconciled all my differences
with the Seelie fae," he said, a wry expression on his
face, "and perhaps reconciliation is not necessary
where love exists. Leigh and I will open the gate."

Yrtalien looked away from them and down at the
stones in his hand.

"It is time, then," he said and, separating the
emerald from its ruby and opal companions, handed
it to Leigh. He deposited the two remaining gems in
Valmont's hand with a shrug and stepped carefully
back along the ridge.

"He has surrendered the stones," Glynnis said aloud.
She signaled the brothers. "It is time," she announced.

Donal and Dougal nodded grimly at one another.
Dougal turned to the army of Unseelie Kithain and
motioned them forward.

"Let's move," he snapped.

Glynnis put the piece of mirror back into the

pouch that hung around her waist, flinching slightly as her hand made inadvertent contact with the small sheathed dagger at her side. Joining the brothers at the head of the group, she began to make her way up the ridge to Achill head, still some distance away.

Stepping between Leigh and Valmont, taking each of them by a hand, King Meilseoir walked cautiously toward the tip of Achill Head, stopping only when there was no longer any room for more than three to stand abreast on the narrow piece of ground. Leigh looked down at the steep drop on either side of them and closed her eyes.

"We will not fall," the king said softly. She took courage from his quiet confidence and opened her eyes again to look outward toward the churning ocean.

Gazing westward, Meilseoir began a chant in a language that sounded familiar to Leigh's ears, though she could not remember having heard it before. *This is the pure tongue of the sidhe,* she realized. *It is the language we spoke long ago, before we gave our words to the mortals who changed them to fit their tongues.*

The gems she and Valmont held began to vibrate, each with a separate voice, forming a harmonic drone against the melody of the king's song. Below them, the waters started to roil as a deep rumbling sound began beneath the waves.

The shattered ruins of a once fabulous structure slowly began to reassemble themselves as the vibrations of compelling sound penetrated the ocean depths. Twin pillars that had crumbled into fragments of encrusted rock once again took their form, becoming lifelike stone images of faerie knights out of legend. Before them, a third figure felt the stirring of life within her begin to warm her frozen flesh, beginning with the delicate webbed membranes between her fingers and toes. Free to move at last, the queen of the selkies drew her sealskin cloak about her. Thrusting herself into the water away from the island, the graceful seal glided through the water, every movement a celebration of motion and release. With an agonized groan, the Isle of Dreams slowly drifted upward from its watery tomb.

In the air above the churning water, a misty shape began to form. The Bean Sidhe felt the pull of the magic below her and exulted in the anticipation of what was to come.

"Have we come in time for the show?" A cheery voice announced Liam's presence behind the four oathmates who stood as silent witnesses to the display of Glamour that danced above the face of the waters. Morgan jumped, clutching Tor as she lost her balance precariously close to the edge of the ridge.

"What are you doing here?" Tor asked, covering his own surprise with a gruff snort.

"This is an occasion that needs remembering," the clurichaun said. "And who better than a bard to tell the tale?"

"Did you have to bring him?" Edmund asked, pointing at Malacar, who stood grasping the clurichaun's arm.

"Of course I did," Liam said. "It was in my dream."

"Where are Lady Rowena and Sir Odhran?" Morgan asked. "Didn't they come with you?"

Liam shrugged. "I dunno," he replied. "When I woke, they were gone. Only my friend here was with me. I suppose they had their own dream to follow. Hush, now, and watch." He turned his attention toward the sea, just as the waters parted and a majestic island slowly surfaced, surrounded by a brilliant kaleidoscope of light that shimmered with the four colors of the Eyestones.

Morgan gasped as she watched the Isle of Dreams emerge from its long concealment.

"It's beautiful!" she breathed.

"It's green," Edmund commented beside her.

The Isle of Dreams sparkled atop the water, a verdant expanse of gently rising ground that culminated in a rounded hill in the island's center. Atop the hill, a faerie castle of crystal spires and prismic towers crowned the island's highest point. Before the gate of the castle stood a pair of stone statues, elegantly clad knights with long, flowing hair.

"Behold Silver's Gate and, beyond, the freehold where once sat the Court of All Kings," Meilseoir said, bringing his song to an end and gazing raptly at what he had helped to bring about.

"Um, this may be a stupid question," Edmund said, eyeing the distant island and gauging the distance from the ridge to the water below. "How are we gonna get from here to there?"

"Open your eyes and close your mouth and you might see something to answer your questions," Liam said, winking to soften his rebuke and pointing out to sea.

A bridge of silver latticework was spinning itself from the air between the island and the ridge, forming a graceful arched span that defied the rules of architecture and gravity with its ethereal beauty.

"We could always swim," Rasputin said, his soft brown eyes glowing with appreciation of the bridge's artistry.

Meilseoir took a step backward and, bringing his hands in front of him, released his grasp on Leigh's and Valmont's hands. Smiling, he motioned for the pair to join hands and proceed ahead of him across the bridge.

"Your part is still to come," he said. "Mine is almost over."

Leigh and Valmont led the way onto the silver bridge that crossed the ocean in a gentle downward slope to the Isle of Dreams. The king followed the small line of Kithain, a mixture of joy and sadness on his face. When Meilseoir was halfway across, Yrtalien began his own journey across the chimeric bridge.

For a moment, neither Leigh nor Valmont could concentrate on anything except the Glamour that infused the island, flavoring the air around them with a sweet freshness that bore traces of the king's forest and of other, still purer lands under other stars. Finally, Valmont squeezed Leigh's hand and pointed toward the twin pillars.

Leigh nodded, and began to walk with the eshu toward the statues that marked Silver's Gate.

With a stone in each hand, Leigh stepped forward to stand in front of one of the statues. She turned to face Valmont, opposite her in the place of the Unseelie brother.

"How do they know which is which?" Edmund asked in a loud whisper.

"They just do," Morgan said. "Maybe the stones told them," she suggested as an afterthought.

"That works," replied Edmund.

Valmont and Leigh faced each other across the gateway, their hands held out, palms upward as if in supplication. The four Eyestones seemed to burst into flames in their hands, as faerie magic exploded in a riot of color and taste and sound.

As they saw the gateway begin to open between them, they heard a childish shriek of pain from where their oathmates were standing halfway between the gate and the island's edge. Leigh turned her head just in time to see Morgan drop to the ground, an arrow buried in the back of her leg, just above the inside of the knee. Storming across the bridge, an army of howling Kithain, led by a pair of sidhe brothers and Glynnis, converged upon the oathmates. Standing to one side of the bridge, Yrtalien watched his troops swarm past him, then carefully made his way around the edge of the island toward the gateway to Arcadia.

The Battle for Silver's Gate had begun.

Screaming in wild abandon as she saw the battle erupt below her, the Bean Sidhe wrapped her cloak of dark energy around her and swooped down toward the island. Drawn to the pure essence of faerie unhampered by the trappings of mortal flesh, the tortured spirit of she who had once been Queen of Connaught launched herself at the one who had once been her lover and her rival. Her heretofore wordless wail shaped itself into a name.

"Ailill!" she groaned in ecstasy as she prepared to sate herself upon his naked Glamour.

Seeing Morgan fall wounded to the ground, Tor drew his battle axe and ran to stand over her as the first wave of attackers rushed down upon them. Liam turned in surprise and swore at the unexpected onslaught. With his foot, the clurichaun shoved Malacar to the ground.

"Stay there and play dead," he ordered the frightened satyr. "Maybe they won't bother with you." Drawing a slim chimeric blade from its sheath at his side, Liam stepped forward to stand beside Tor, the pair of them struggling to form a barrier against the oncoming horde.

"You take the left half, and I'll take the rest," the clurichaun quipped, his face set and grim.

Tor grunted, sparing his battle companion a momentary look of newfound respect.

"Don't forget about me!" Edmund called, kneeling down to cover Morgan with his body. "Don't you dare die!" he whispered to her.

"Just pull the arrow out of my leg!" Morgan cried, her voice a mixture of pain and anger.

"I'll do better than that," the redcap said, leaning down and grasping the shaft with his teeth. The arrow made a satisfying crunch as he snapped it off close to Morgan's skin. "Now it won't bleed all over the place," he announced triumphantly.

Rasputin saw the Bean Sidhe materialize above the king and heard Meilseoir's anguished cry of pain as his Glamour was ripped from him with each shriek of the forlorn faerie spirit. To his ears, it sounded like the crack of a belt against unprotected flesh.

"No!" the pooka screamed. "He's not good enough for you!" Without stopping to consider the consequences, he launched himself toward the crumpled figure of the king.

The gate was not yet fully opened, but her oathmates' cries spurred Leigh into action. Opposite her, Valmont, too, was leaving his place, one hand now clutching both his gems while the other reached for his scimitar. The newly forming gate began to shimmer and collapse as they started to abandon their posts.

"Give over the stones and we'll let you go rescue your friends," a clipped, nasal voice barked at the oathmates.

Donal and Dougal stood between Leigh and Valmont, swords already drawn and ready to strike. Behind them, Yrtalien stood waiting, a look of smug satisfaction on his face.

"When one plan goes astray, it is only sensible to have another one to hand," he remarked. "These twins are both as Unseelie as I am, but then, the old queen's curse only called for the inheritors of the original brothers' legacy, if your little redcap quisling is to be believed."

Leigh recalled Ondine's story and realized that Yrtalien spoke the truth.

"He's right," she whispered dully to Valmont. Fearful of wasting any more time, Leigh thrust her stones at one of the twins. Valmont dropped the ruby and the opal into the waiting palm of the other brother. Stepping into the spaces vacated by Leigh and Valmont, Donal and Dougal took their positions at the gate. Colors swirled wildly as the gate once more began to open.

"Sláinte," Donal said to his twin. Dougal nodded, unable to speak as the Glamour of the stones overwhelmed him.

Valmont hurried toward the battle. As Leigh started to follow him, Yrtalien reached out and grabbed her arm.

"He can go to war," the prince said. "You are

coming back to Arcadia with me. The rest of the army will follow when they've finished with your friends."

Leigh closed her eyes and nodded, letting her body slump in Yrtalien's grip. Feeling her capitulation, the prince started forward, his eyes on the shining gate in front of him, now almost fully opened. Seizing the opportunity she had created, Leigh continued to relax, dropping to the ground and pulling Yrtalien with her onto his back. Grasping her sword with both hands she raised it above her head and held it poised above Yrtalien's chest. The prince looked up at her in panic.

"I would have given you half of Arcadia," he said, his eyes glittering wildly.

"I don't want it," she said. "I want to bring the Dreaming back, not poison it by bringing a horde of ravaging bandits through its gates." She looked down at the prince she once loved and saw only a poor reflection of that shining noble, now lost in the madness of his own delusions. "I can't kill you with this sword," she said. "But I can make you forget who and what you are. Maybe you'll be better off for it." She gritted her teeth and plunged the chimeric blade into Yrtalien's body.

"You can't kill him," Glynnis' voice said, leaning down beside her. Her hand held a slim iron dagger to Yrtalien's throat. "But I can."

Helpless to prevent it, Leigh saw Sorcha reach forward to pull the steel weapon toward her neck. *Not again*, she thought. I won't be a party to another death if I can stop it.

"No!" Leigh cried out.

Glynnis paused. "You have not had to suffer his cruelties," she said. "He feeds on the pain of others to replenish his magic."

"He's not worth it," Leigh said. "Look at him." She watched as the prince's faerie essence began to slowly

fade, the noble lines of his sidhe heritage dissipating
from the chimeric wound to his heart. In place of the
Forsworn Prince of House Ailil, there lay only a
handsome, dark-haired young man.

"You're right," Glynnis said, gazing contemptuously
upon the unconscious form that would at some later
time awaken with only the haziest of mortal memories.
That is punishment enough, she thought. Impulsively,
she twisted her dagger around to cut the thong that
held the velvet pouch around Yrtalien's neck. Picking
up the small bag that once contained the Eyestones,
she hurled it behind her, not bothering to notice
where it landed.

At that moment, the sound of a hunting horn
echoed through the air. Leigh looked up to see the
Riders of the Silver Court thundering on horseback
across the bridge to join the battle. At the same time,
she sensed a second army of warriors rising up out of
the sea.

"This is not your fight anymore," Leigh said. She
stood up, pulling her sword, unblooded, from the
prince's form.

"You're right," Glynnis replied as a swarm of selkies
surrounded her, their eyes gleaming with menace.
Glynnis reversed her dagger and handed it, hilt first,
to the nearest selkie, who took it gingerly and,
spinning around, tossed it into the sea.

Smiling at Leigh, Emer stepped forward and
grasped Glynnis by the arm.

"I'll take charge of this one," she said. Leigh
nodded in stunned surprise, then turned and ran
toward her embattled friends. Ahead of her, she saw
Valmont gamely trying to intercept the Kithain who
had managed to evade Tor and Liam. She tried
without success to locate the others, but the island
had suddenly filled with the warriors of three armies.

She came to stand beside Valmont, thrusting her sword out to parry the spiked club of a troll that would have caught the eshu on his off side. Valmont nodded his thanks to Leigh and renewed his battle with the troll while she turned to face off against a pair of hungry looking redcaps.

"Help me stand!" Morgan told Edmund as the battle raged above the two childlings. "We're not doing any good down here!"

Edmund tugged at Morgan's arm until he had pulled her out from under Tor's protection. Leaning on the redcap, Morgan struggled to her feet, wincing as her weight sent a sharp pain through her wounded leg. She looked around at the battle and let out a small gasp as she saw Rasputin shielding the king from the Bean Sidhe's repeated attacks.

"We've got to help Rasputin!" she cried. "The Bean Sidhe will kill him!" Together, she and Edmund wove their way through the throng of battling Kithain.

In control of his memories for the first time since the Battle of the Redwoods, Tor wielded the flat of his axe blade as a bludgeon, letting its enchantment rather than its edge deal bloodless damage to the Kithain who struggled to fight their way past him. At his side, Liam's rapier flashed, lightning-swift, claiming its share of Glamour-draining blows. A pile of unconscious bodies was beginning to form around the pair as Tor suddenly became aware of the sound of music coming from the clurichaun's lips.

"What are you doing?" he snarled, catching his breath as a nocker slumped to the ground in front of him.

"Singing!" Liam replied, stopping his song long enough to answer the troll. "It's what bards used to do in battle. It helps my rhythm." He stabbed at a redcap, narrowly avoiding the Kithain's vicious bite.

"You made me miss a beat," he said, picking up his song in mid-verse.

"Just in time," Rasputin gasped weakly as Morgan and Edmund reached their oathmate. Kneeling over the king's motionless form, the pooka's face was haggard with pain, his Glamour nearly gone from him.

Morgan looked up at the Bean Sidhe, struggling to see the beautiful faerie queen inside her deadly shroud of Glamour-devouring blackness. "You promised!" she cried to the creature. "You promised you'd leave him alone."

The hunger is too much for me, the childling heard the honeyed voice cry inside her head. She turned around to Edmund, her face white with desperation. "She's starving for Glamour," she told the redcap. Her hand went for the locket she wore around her neck, along with the enchanted shell that was a gift from the menehune of Hawaii. "Maybe these will help a little," she said. "Have you got anything to feed her?"

Edmund started to shake his head, then remembered his chimeric sword, given him by Duke Aeon's herald, Sir Cumulus, before they left Goldengate. Drawing it out, he started to hand it to Morgan when he felt a tap on his shoulder. He whirled around.

"Mr. Dumpy!" he cried, his face breaking out into a grin.

The chimeric clown hung its head, a picture of shame as it stood before Edmund.

"Hey, it's okay," Edmund said, throwing his arms around the clown. "I figured out what was going on when Yrtalien showed up. You couldn't help it."

"What's that?" Morgan asked, as she saw the chimera from the Toybox for the first time. Her face lit up. "That's one of the creatures from the toy chest!"

"That's my friend, Mr. Dumpy!" Edmund said proudly, but his expression changed as he saw the look on Morgan's face. He stepped in front of the clown protectively. "No way!" he said. "He's not gonna feed that thing." He pointed upward at the Bean Sidhe.

"Rasputin and the king will die unless she has enough Glamour to satisfy her." Morgan said. "My locket and this seashell and even your sword will do some good, but what she really needs is a big dose of the stuff to make her leave them alone." The childling didn't stop to consider how she knew what the Bean Sidhe needed, but she trusted her instincts. "Please, Edmund," she said softly, looking away from her oathmate to Rasputin, now nearly unrecognizable as a faerie.

Mr. Dumpy slipped out from behind Edmund and gave the redcap a sad little smile. Edmund's throat grew tight. "You want to do this, don't you?" he whispered forlornly. The clown nodded.

Edmund sighed and looked from the chimera to Morgan.

"I guess if you can give up Tor's locket, I can give up Mr. Dumpy," he said. Morgan unfastened the locket from her neck and wound it around one arm of the clown, then wrapped the thong holding the seashell around the other wrist.

"I guess this is goodbye, huh?" Edmund said to the clown.

Mr. Dumpy nodded again and waved at the redcap. Edmund made a stirrup with his hands for the clown to step into. Before he could change his mind, he launched Mr. Dumpy into the air toward the Bean Sidhe, striking her squarely in the chest. The clown exploded in a chimeric fireball that engulfed the Bean Sidhe briefly before it disappeared into the creature's translucent form.

Her vicious hunger appeased, the ancient faerie spirit regained control of herself, overcoming the darkness that enshrouded her and gazing in horror at the damage she had wrought in her mindless frenzy. The king stirred and roused himself to look into the once-more beautiful form of the queen he once loved. He pointed toward the shining arch of Silver's Gate.

"That way lies your salvation," he whispered. "Go quickly, before the hunger overtakes you again."

"You're still alive!" Morgan said, kneeling down beside the king. Turning to Rasputin she searched the pooka's face carefully. "Are you going to be all right?" she asked.

Rasputin stood up shakily and brushed himself off. "Don't worry about me," he said, turning to look after the departing Bean Sidhe, now streaking through the air toward the open gateway. His eyes suddenly grew large and he darted off toward the gate, following the Bean Sidhe. Watching him run away from them, Morgan and Edmund both spotted what had caused his sudden panic.

"Malacar!" screamed Morgan. "He's going for the Eyestones!" She started to go after Rasputin, but her leg collapsed under her and she fell to the ground. "Stop him," she cried to Edmund. "He can't take them. The gate will collapse and who knows if it will ever open again?"

"Stay there," Edmund said. "I'll take care of this."

Even in his perpetual darkness, Malacar could feel the Glamour from the gateway. *The Court of All Kings lies just beyond the gate*, he thought, and began to pull himself slowly along the ground, allowing his faerie kenning to lead him in the direction of the strongest magic. His hand closed on an unmoving foot and he realized he had found one of the brothers. Quickly he pulled himself up, using the motionless brother's body to steady himself. His fingers scrabbled toward the frozen brother's hands seeking the gems. *I'll have them all*, he thought gleefully. *Two will serve as my eyes again and when the gate has opened I'll take the other stones and close it behind me.*

As he felt the raw heat of the gateway on his scarred face and started to close his hand over the first Eyestone, someone seized him by the shoulders and spun him away from the entranced twin.

"I've come to help you," Rasputin said in the satyr's ear. "You don't really want to take that, do you?"

With an enraged scream, the satyr shook himself free of the pooka's grasp, making a frantic dive toward where he knew the other brother must be. Rasputin thrust himself in front of Malacar and wrapped his arms around the satyr.

"I need to warn you," he whispered weakly, feeling his strength beginning to leave him, "physical combat happens to be my forte." He gasped as something sharp entered his side, just below his ribs.

"And dirty fighting is mine," Malacar said, twisting the steel dagger deeper into the pooka's chest before pulling it out and shoving the pooka away. Rasputin fell just in front of the gate, a pool of blood forming around him.

Malacar lurched forward again only to feel a searing pain in his ankle as his good leg gave out. Edmund spat out the foul-tasting flesh.

"You're not going anywhere!" he said. As he spoke, he grew aware that the noise of the battle had stopped. He looked up to find Leigh and Valmont standing over him, their faces looking tired and grim. Behind them, Tor carried Morgan, her arms wrapped around the troll's neck. Liam brought up the rear, supporting the frail figure of King Meilseoir. The Riders and the selkies, led by their rejuvenated queen, formed a distant line around the edge of the Isle of Dreams, a silent honor guard to the small group of Kithain gathered in front of Silver's Gate. Among their ranks stood those defeated Kithain who chose surrender over forgetfulness.

"Did we win?" Edmund asked.

Leigh nodded. Valmont looked at Rasputin and his face seemed to collapse. He dropped to his knees beside the pooka, who struggled for breath as bloody bubbles formed at the corners of his mouth. Leigh knelt down to join him, cradling Rasputin's head tenderly in her lap.

"I always knew I'd die alone in my bed," Rasputin gasped, barely able to form the words.

Leigh looked up at the king, her face wet with tears. "Don't tell us we can't save *him*!" she said, remembering Lady Rowena's words over Sorcha's dying body.

Meilseoir touched her tear-streaked face with his fingertips and shook his head sadly. Slowly, he leaned down and closed the pooka's gentle brown eyes.

"Not on this side of the Dreaming," he said, looking at her and past her to the gateway. "On the other side, anything is possible."

"How many sacrifices are left to make?" Leigh asked, her voice disconsolate.

"Only one," the king replied. He walked toward the gate and, without crossing its threshold, plucked the four Eyestones from the hands of the twins. "You have fulfilled the legacy of your ancestors," he told Donal and Dougal. "You can walk away from this now, if you choose. The gate is opened."

Freed from the hold of the stones, the Unseelie brothers stared at each other. Then they clasped arms and walked past the oathmates to take their place in the line of warriors.

The king lifted Leigh to her feet, helping her lower Rasputin's still form to the ground. He took her hand

and placed the emerald inside it, closing her fingers around the stone. "For the Summer Queen," he said.

Weeping shamelessly, Valmont rose of his own accord to face the king. Meilseoir handed him the opal Shadowstone. "And the Winter King."

He continued past them to stand before Edmund and placed the ruby in the redcap's already outstretched palm. "The Autumn Lad, who will grow into his role," he said, smiling. Finally he walked to Tor and Morgan.

"Put me down, please, Grandpa," Morgan said quietly in Tor's ear. "The last sacrifice is mine."

The troll eased his granddaughter to the ground and stepped away from her. Morgan winced as the wound in her leg throbbed.

The king passed over the childling to hand the sapphire Waystone to an astonished Tor. "And, finally, the Spring Warrior, who will recover his lost years across the gateway."

Tor looked at the sapphire and shook his head.

"It should go to Morgan," he said staunchly, turning to pass the stone on to his granddaughter.

"No, Grandpa," Morgan said, her voice firm. "I wish I could go with you, but I'm not finished here. In my dream, when we sailed to Hawaii and the sea monster tested us all, you told me that someday you would grow too old to remember who you were. Now it doesn't have to happen." She bit her lip to keep it from trembling as she stood on tiptoe to throw her arms around the troll. "It's not fair for you to suddenly remember everything only to forget it in a few years," she whispered. "I still have a lot of remembering ahead of me, and I have my diary to remind me of everything that's happened. Besides," she said wistfully, "I want to go home to my parents."

She kissed her grandfather's cheek and let go of him to stand beside the king.

Edmund looked at Morgan, his face agog at the enormity of her choice.

"You don't want this one, do you?" he asked, holding the Changestone partially out to her.

Morgan shook her head. "If anyone needs to go through the gate, you do," she said, grinning suddenly at the redcap.

Edmund sighed with relief.

Liam stepped away from the outer circle of Kithain and put his arms around Morgan.

"You've still got friends here," he said. "Some you don't even know about yet."

Trying to keep herself from reneging on her choice, Morgan nodded bravely and looking up at the clurichaun, gave him a shaky smile.

Leigh and Valmont came up to Morgan and embraced their oathmate in turn. "We won't forget you," Leigh said. "We will always be oathbound."

"Will you ever come back?" Morgan asked.

Valmont looked thoughtful, then nodded. "If there is a way, and if this is really the beginning of the union between this world and the Dreaming, I swear to you that we will return. Who knows what wonders we may bring back with us to replace what has been lost this day?"

Leigh and Valmont joined hands with each other and with Tor and Edmund.

"May your hearts be one with the Dreaming and may the love that you bear within you bridge the worlds of flesh and seeming, making them one within you forever and a day until the seasons cease their turning," Liam said softly as the four companions turned and walked slowly to the threshold of Silver's Gate. Just before they stepped across, Valmont let go of Leigh's hand and walked to where Rasputin's still form lay just outside the gateway. Leaning down, he gathered the pooka in his arms, cradling him like a sleeping child.

"If anything is possible, you will not be lost to those who love you," the eshu whispered. Taking his place once more at Leigh's side, he stepped with his three companions across the threshold.

Morgan watched until she could no longer see her oathmates, then turned around and buried her face in Liam's shoulder. Liam wrapped his arms around the childling and let her cry. After awhile, her sobs became quiet shudders.

Meilseoir gently touched the top of her head.

"It is time to go," he said quietly. "The selkies will resume their guardianship of Silver's Gate, protecting it from the harshness of the world but keeping it open for those whose paths lead them to it. Our way lies back across the bridge."

"If it please your Highness," Liam said, "there's one thing more that needs to be done." He touched Morgan's wounded leg, humming a soft tune as he did so. The childling could feel the Glamour from the clurichaun pour from his fingers into the place where the arrow had lodged. When he withdrew his hand, Liam held the arrowhead in his palm. Morgan flexed her leg.

"That's better!" she said. "Thank you!"

Liam gave her a wink and a smile before turning to King Meilseoir. "We're ready now," he said.

Walking between the king and the clurichaun, Morgan took one last look behind her at the shimmering gate. As the trio neared the bridge, the Riders who formed a guard of honor before the entry to the Isle of Dreams, Lady Rowena and Sir Odhran among them, dismounted and parted to let their king pass.

Meilseoir halted before Glynnis, who stood in the

custody of Emer and Kieran, not far from the edge of bridge.

"There is a place for you in my freehold," the king said to her. "There you may find respite from your troubled dreams. My Riders will bring you to me if you so decide."

Glynnis nodded, her impassive face suddenly softening with the unexpected show of mercy.

A pair of figures were waiting for Morgan as she crossed the bridge with Liam and the Hidden King to stand once more atop the ridge at Achill Head. She recognized Signe and shied back, uncertain about whether or not to trust the former Dauntain.

Signe held out her hands to the childling.

"I bring greetings from my oathmate, Sir Charles Fizzlewig," she said formally. "I have come to take you home to Goldengate, and to your mortal and Kithain families."

Behind her, Bridie gave Morgan a friendly smile. *She reminds me of Grandpa, just a little*, Morgan thought, feeling a little of her sorrow recede.

"I've always wanted to visit the new world," the troll said cheerfully.

"Where will you go now?" Morgan asked Liam.

The clurichaun winked at her and drew out a wood flute from his back pocket.

"I thought I'd pipe the king back to his castle before he fades away into thin air," the clurichaun replied. "After that, there's a small matter of returning some stolen Glamour to the places visited by the Forsworn Prince." Liam put the instrument to his lips and, arching an eyebrow at Morgan, began to strike up a slow march tune that made the air around him sparkle with Glamour.

Morgan looked from the king to Signe and back again. Meilseoir held his hand over her head.

all kings

"Your story is only just begun, child of the sea and daughter of the heart of Mac Lir. Your friends have entered the Dreaming, but it is through you that their dreams will find their way back to the world that cries out for wholeness." He turned to Signe. "May you, whose eyes look beyond the veil of time, lead her safely into the fullness of her future, and may you always find a road beneath your feet and a guide who will take you where you need to go."

His blessings given, Meilseoir put a hand on the clurichaun's shoulder and the pair stepped off the edge of the ridge and into the trod which had opened up at the king's approach.

As she saw the Riders begin to file across the bridge, leaving the Isle of Dreams in the care of its selkie queen and her subjects, Morgan took a deep breath and held out her hand for Signe to take. After only a moment's hesitation, she held out her other hand to Bridie.

"I'm ready to go home," she said.

As they began their journey down the slope of the ridge toward the eastern end of Achill Island and the Irish mainland, Morgan looked up at Signe.

"Do you know any stories?" she asked.

"That is the wisest question you could possibly ask an eshu," Signe replied. "Although yours is the best story I have heard in a long time. Why don't we start with that one?"

As Signe's voice wove its pictures, Morgan thought she heard the distant sound of a wooden flute traveling on the breeze from the sea.

all kings

biography

A native of Appalachia, Jackie Cassada has spent most of her life (with the exception of a ten-year sojourn in Boston) in the Blue Ridge Mountains. An avid reader, in college she majored in English with a specialty in Victorian literature. Her discovery of roleplaying games in 1978 resulted in rediscovering a talent for "let's pretend" and an appreciation for the art of oral storytelling.

She was the science fiction columnist for Library Journal from 1984-1995. In 1993, she began working as a freelance writer for White Wolf's **Wraith: The Oblivion** and other games in the Storyteller system, and her short stories have appeared in various White Wolf anthologies.

Besides writing, she has played in several rock, folk rock, and traditional folk bands, worked as a "techie" for local college and community theatres, and collaborated on the musical score for an adaption of Pinocchio for children's theatre. She currently works as a member of the administrative support staff for the Asheville-Buncombe Library System.

She shares a house in Asheville, NC with a long-time companion and five demanding cats. *Court of All Kings* is her third novel.

An exerpt from
Pomegranates Full and Fine
by Don Bassingthwaite

ISBN 156504-889-X
$5.99us / $7.99can
Paperback
Available Now

Chapter One

Sweet to tongue and sound to eye;
Come buy, come buy.

The big man glimpsed her movement and turned away from the fallen bouncer. *So much for the element of surprise*, Tango thought to herself. She crouched, waiting for the man to make his move on her. He would attack her, she was sure of that. There was unthinking rage on his face, and when he caught sight of the Pan's logo on her staff T-shirt, he bellowed like a bull in a ring. He lunged at her, maybe a little faster than she had expected. She slipped to one side, avoiding his arms and jabbing out with a blow to his kidneys. The man turned quickly, however. The blow glanced away. He snapped an elbow back, striking her on the side of the head hard enough to make her skip aside warily. He turned again. Tango dodged his fists this time, although a third bouncer, coming to her aid, wasn't so lucky. He received a crack to the face that sent blood flying from a split lip.

Enough of this. Tango brought the big man around with a few more blows to his side and back. Light blows, though, just meant to get his attention. He pulled one hand back and brought it around in a fast, heavy swing... then crumpled with a gasp and a squeak as Tango slipped in under his guard and kicked him hard in the testicles.

The watching men in the crowded nightclub drew in their breath in a collective wince.

Never go for the balls seemed to be one of the unspoken laws that connected men around the world. Maybe that was why they always seemed so surprised when a woman did it. The crowd was silent as Tango gestured for two more bouncers to carry the would-be troublemaker out of the club. The downed bouncer was getting up, with some assistance from the bouncer with the split lip. With the fight over, the crowd began to turn away, going back to the drinking and dancing that had brought them here. Jumping up on top of a table, Tango spotted the woman whose presence had started the fight. She pushed her way over to where she stood at the coat check. "Are you okay?" she asked over the club's pounding music.

"Yeah." The woman took her coat back from the attendant. "Messy break-up. Thank you."

"Where are the friends you were with?"

"They're staying. I..." She shrugged as she put on her coat, and for a moment Tango sensed something of the anxiety the woman was trying to hold back. "I think I'd better just go home."

Tango nodded and pulled half-a-dozen free passes out of her pocket. "Just as long as you come back again. I'm sorry you didn't have a better time."

A smile flickered across the woman's face. "Thanks." The smile vanished as she saw the bouncers walking her ex-boyfriend through the crowd. "I should go before he gets here."

"Just a second. Rick!" Tango grabbed the club's largest bouncer, who was acting as doorman. "Make sure she gets into a cab without any trouble."

"Got it."

The woman smiled again. "Thank you."

"Catch your cab." She handed the woman over to Rick, then turned to the man the bouncers were bringing to the door. She stopped them and put a hand on the man's chest. "I don't ever want to see you in here again."

He tried to focus on her and more or less succeeded. "You're history, bitch!" he slurred. "I want you fired. I want to see the manager."

Tango looked up at him. He was massively built, easily six foot five and at least two hundred and forty pounds. She was what dressmakers so politely called "petite," and a foot shorter than him, even in her boots. The man still went pale in front of the smile she gave him. "I am the manager, asshole." She glanced at the bouncers. "Make sure he lands hard."

She turned away. Running Pan's, one of San Francisco's newest and hottest nightclubs, wasn't easy, but it had its satisfying moments. That was why she insisted on being head bouncer as well as manager — the occasional turn on security was a great way to release stress. Tango pulled her headset from around her neck, disentangling it from her long, brown hair, and settled it back over her ears. "All clear, Alan?" she asked, adjusting the microphone.

Sometimes one fight would touch off a flurry of fights, a chain reaction of violence sweeping through the club. Not tonight, though. "All clear," crackled the tinny voice of Pan's assistant manager in her ear. "And you've got a visitor."

"Business or personal?"

"Personal. He came in just as you were asking our burly guest to dance. He said he'd wait over by the main bar."

"Thanks."

Tango kept herself alert, wondering who her visitor could be. She didn't have many friends, and the ones she did have seldom came to see her at work. At least Tango hoped it was a friend. She'd made a lot of enemies over the years — she knew it was a lot easier to piss her off than to please her, and she liked it that way. It meant that the friends she did have were good ones. And that her enemies were dangerous.

If the swirling hedonism of Pan's could be said to have a center, then the main bar was it. It had always impressed Tango far beyond the immense video wall or the soaring platforms and catwalks that took patrons up into the club's rafters and attracted most of the media's attention. The main bar was a bright oval of brushed steel, somehow managing to transcend the suburban space-cadet feel that bare metal so often had. Instead, the bar was like a movie star: sensual, begging for a caress, yet at the same time cold, aloof, haughty and untouchable. An ice queen. Dancers moved in a gleaming, chromed steel cage raised up over the bar, just as untouchable.

People swarmed around the bar as if that icy glamor could rub off on them. Tango shoved her way through the crowd, craning her neck in an effort to spot anyone she recognized. "Alan," she asked into the microphone, "did the person who was looking for me say he'd wait..."

Fingers dug into her ribs from behind.

Tango's voice cut off instantly. On pure instinct she grabbed her assailant's wrists and twisted hard. Not as hard as she might have, but hard enough to produce a yelp of pain. She flung one captured hand away and spun her assailant around, twisting his arm up behind his back so tightly his fingers were brushing his neck

— and his close-cropped, rusty-red hair. Tango blinked and cursed. "Riley?"

"Yes!" the trapped man hissed between clenched teeth. "Not very ticklish anymore, are you?"

"What's happening out there?" Alan's voice was sharp. "Tango? I've got bouncers heading toward you if you need help."

Tango turned Riley loose. "Tell them to forget about it, Alan. I just found my friend, that's all." She hesitated, then added, "I'm off-duty. Buzz me if you need me." She pulled off her headset, but left it hanging around her neck. "What are you doing here?"

Riley looked at her cautiously. "Do you greet all your friends like that, or just the ones you like?" He worked his shoulder gingerly as he bent down to pick up a ballcap from the floor. His hair was longer on top than on the sides and he wore an untucked shirt over a T-shirt and jeans. He looked about twenty, maybe ten years younger than her. In spite of his youth, though, his fox-red hair was already starting to thin. "Jesus, Tango, have you ever thought about switching to decaf?"

"You should have known better than to come up behind me."

"Winnipeg six years ago should have taught me that." Riley straightened his round wire-frame glasses. Looking around Pan's, he added, "Nice. I could stand to work in a place like this. I've got a great apartment in a building that's full of artists and musicians, but you know how artsy types are. Up at strange hours. Loud parties. Not that that's all bad, but it must be nice to be able to go home sometimes."

"Riley." Tango glared at the people who had turned to watch her initial conflict with him; they quickly looked away. "What the hell are you doing here?"

He grinned. "I heard you were working in Pan's, so I thought I'd check the place out while I was in San Francisco. You know we've heard about it all the way up in Toronto? There's this bar called Hopeful — they have a wall covered with club ads and the ads from Pan's...."

"I don't do the marketing."

"No," Riley added thoughtfully, "I don't suppose you do. You've never exactly been Miss Congeniality, have you?" Riley's eyes followed a knot of laughing people across the club. He inhaled deeply. "Damn." He turned to the bar and waved a bartender over. "Whiskey sour. Make it a double. You," he said to Tango, "are still just as nasty as you ever were. You know, I've never needed a picture to remind myself of you. All I have to do is go out and find a rock."

Tango's lips twitched.

Riley smirked.

Tango's dour face fell apart completely. "You doorknob!" She swatted playfully at Riley's bottom. This had become a game between the two. Each time they met — usually after a prolonged separation — Riley would try to make Tango laugh. Tango would resist as long as she could. That was usually about two minutes. The last time they had met, six years ago in Winnipeg, Riley had just looked at her and raised his eyebrows. She had broken down in seconds. Riley was one of her oldest friends. He might have looked twenty, but he was actually half again as old. And Tango was twice as old as that. "You're looking good. Except for the hair."

"That started about five years ago." Riley flushed and adjusted his ballcap self-consciously. A bracelet around his wrist caught Tango's eye. She grabbed his arm and took a closer look at it. It was heavy and silvery, with an intricate clasp worked in the shape of a dog's head.

"Nice. When did you start wearing jewelry?"

"Call it a midlife crisis."

"Twenty," Tango said firmly, "is not midlife."

Riley stuck his tongue out at her. "Spoken like a grump. You're acting older every time I see you. If you'd stop hanging around with hu—"

Tango made a face as the bartender returned with Riley's drink. Riley's voice cut off instantly and he took the drink, pulling several crumpled bills out of his pocket to pay for it. Tango caught his hand.

"On the house," she told the bartender. "Anything he wants, all night. Don't take his money."

"Spoilsport," muttered Riley as the bartender nodded and moved away. He dropped the money.

A handful of leaves fluttered down on top of the bar.

Tango gave him a tired look. Riley groaned. "I'm a pooka. I can't help it. You've been around humans too long, Tango. It's not good for you. You're getting..." he shuddered, "old."

"It's going to happen to you one day, Riley. It happens to all Kithain."

"But if you'd spend more time with your own kind...."

Tango sighed. *Our own kind.* This was another game that Riley played with her, and it was one she enjoyed a lot less.

Once there had been faeries in the world. Noble faeries and common faeries, highborn and low. The spirits of dreams and stories. There had been fabulous parades in the moonlight, and dancing under the stars.

Humans had tried to creep into faerie courts and spy on the magnificence of the Kithain. Some had been lucky and gotten away to spread tales of wonder. Others had been caught, pixie-led and pinched black and blue as punishment. A few had caught the eye of Kithain kings and queens and been spirited away to the faerieland of Arcadia as cherished guests and pretty prizes. Once there had been faeries — and then the splendor of that age had fallen. Now Arcadia was far away. There were no parades now and very little dancing, at least not the kind that the ancient faeries would have recognized. The Kithain who had been left behind in this gray, dull world had mingled with humans in order to survive. Tango and Riley were their descendants. Changelings, like the faerie children substituted for human as pranks so long ago. The last remnants of the Kithain were few.

"Give it up, Riley," Tango said wearily. "I'm not going back. I like humans."

"So do I."

"Only because you can play tricks on them so easily. There's no way I'm going back to Kithain society, so don't bother trying to talk me into it. Conversation over." She gestured to the bartender. He brought her a club soda. Riley just rolled his eyes. Tango knew that if something didn't have alcohol, caffeine, or at least sugar in it, he wouldn't drink it. "So if you came to Pan's to see me, what brought you to San Francisco?"

"An airplane." Tango gave him a nasty glance, and he amended hastily, "I'm here on business. A trip for the duke of Toronto."

"Worming our way into the duke's black heart, are we?"

Riley looked pained. "I've lived in Toronto for ten years. I'm not exactly worming my way anywhere."

"Is he as cold as they say?"

"Colder. If he were any more cold and stiff, he'd be a corpse. You wouldn't think an Unseelie Kithain would be so rigid and tradition-bound." Tango nodded. So much of the Kithain's heritage had changed over years of just trying to survive, but some things stayed the same. The Kithain loved pageantry. They loved the show of court — and, of course, there would always be those who were willing to rule the Kithain courts as dukes, duchesses, kings and queens. And even among the nobles of the dark, unruly Unseelie courts, there were those who held on to the chains of tradition. Especially when tradition supported their positions. "I've been appointed his Jester for the year."

"What happened to the last one?"

"He retired. It's harder to make Duke Michael laugh than it is to make you laugh. But there is a good side to the job." Riley smiled. "The Jester organizes the Highsummer Night party."

Tango spluttered into her club soda. "Nobody *organizes* Highsummer parties!" Even at the darkest times, the Kithain had clung to their festivals as the tattered banners of their faded glory. Highsummer Night, July 17th, was the biggest Kithain festival of the year, a night of enchantment, feasting and pranks. A wild free-for-all revel. Tango had been to Carnival in Rio once. It was a slumber party compared to Highsummer Night.

"They do in Toronto. Everything is organized. It's a strange city. You'll see."

He grinned at her expectantly. It took Tango a

moment to figure out the meaning behind that grin. "No."

"Please? Only for a visit? You'll have a blast. I'm here to get party favors from the Kithain court at Berkeley. They trade with a bunch of Cult of Ecstasy mages there. Do you know what the Cult of Ecstasy is?"

"I know more about mages than you do." Tango slammed her club soda down on the bar hard enough to make bubbles come fizzing out of the liquid. "But even if I wanted to visit a Kithain court again, I wouldn't do it during Highsummer. I *hate* Highsummer Night!"

"I can't believe that. It would do you good, Tango. I've seen grumps older than you frolicking like childlings...."

"No. Enough, Riley. I'm *not* going."

The finality in her voice made Riley turn to look at her. He was silent for a moment, then asked, "You're serious?"

"Why would you think I'd change my mind for a party? You know me." Tango spread her hands. "I haven't even set foot in a Kithain freehold in fifteen years!"

"And where has it gotten you? Older." Riley sipped slowly from his drink, then looked deep into the pale green liquid for a moment. "I was hoping you'd come for me." He sighed. "It's not every day that a pooka gets put in charge of something this big. Even so, do you think that anyone is really going to thank me for this? They'll all be too busy recovering from hangovers. I want someone there who's clearheaded enough to be able to say 'Good job, Riley.'" He looked at her again. "Please, Tango?"

"Don't make puppy eyes at me," she replied gruffly. "It's not going to work. I don't like Highsummer Night. You get drunk, you play a few pranks, then you find a human or another Kithain and screw like rabbits. And the next day everybody lies and says what a great time they had."

"There's more to Highsummer than that and you know it. Except for the pranks, you could be describing Pan's. You seem to like it well enough."

"I work here. I don't get drunk myself, and the last thing I did like a rabbit was have salad for dinner." Tango reached over the top of the bar and poured the rest of her club soda into a sink. "I'm sorry, Riley. Even if I wanted to, I can't. I have responsibilities here to think about. I have to work."

Riley's face went hard. "You are turning into a grump," he commented sourly. This time, Tango knew, he wasn't joking. She felt a little flush creep into her face. "You wouldn't have used work as an excuse six years ago."

"Riley..."

"Don't bother." He drained his drink and set the empty glass down on the bar. He pulled a pen and a piece of paper out of his packet. Writing something on the paper, he thrust it at her. "I'm flying Air Canada. This is my flight number and the hotel where I'm staying. I'm flying out of San Francisco International tomorrow night at 9:30." He looked into her eyes. "At least think about it, okay?" He took her hand and wrapped her fingers around the paper. "Give me a call. I'd really like to have you there."

Tango pulled her hand back. Riley looked disappointed, then sighed and walked away from her, disappearing into the crowd. For a moment, Tango considered calling him back. For a moment, she considered tearing up the paper and forgetting all about Toronto and his invitation. Instead, she slid Riley's paper into her pocket. She put her headset back in place and turned it on. "I'm on duty again, Alan. Anything to report?"

* * *

She looked at Riley's paper again a few hours later as she sat in her office. On the other side of the wall behind her, Pan's was closing up for the night. The staff was chasing the last few clubgoers out through the doors, cleaning up the dance floor and wiping down the bars. Another successful night at San Francisco's hottest club. Tango considered Riley's paper and wondered if Pan's couldn't manage without her for a week.

Highsummer Night was just a little more than a week away. And surely a weekend night flight to Toronto would still have seats available, even the day before. Taking time off work, in spite of what she had told Riley, wouldn't be a problem. Alan was good. She could leave the club in his hands. She drummed her fingers on the desk. Getting to Toronto wouldn't be a problem.

Going would.

Tango leaned back in her chair and stared up at the ceiling. She hadn't lied when she'd told Riley that she didn't like Highsummer Night. It was pointless, stupid, and childish. Like most Kithain celebrations, and like most Kithain themselves.

With the rare exception of Riley and a few other friends scattered around the world, Tango really did not enjoy the company of Kithain. They were too absorbed in the games that they played, too caught up in the pursuit of dreams and elusive wonder. Kithain were trapped between two worlds: the real world, where they lived, died, and ate greasy hamburgers, and a dream world, where they could still live as their immortal faerie ancestors had, amid pomp, adventures and raucous feasts. Kithain who lived with their minds floating in that dream world might stay young longer, but in Tango's opinion they also tended to be the next best thing to useless in the real world.

Maybe she was turning into a grump, one of the bitter, stubborn and dull older Kithain. If she was, then the change had been building for the last fifteen years. There was a small mirror in her drawer. Tango felt almost guilty as she took it out and looked into it. No wrinkles yet. No sagging. No gray hairs. She looked like any thirty-year-old woman. She didn't look like a grump. She didn't feel like a grump — at least not most of the time. A Kithain really was only as young or old as she looked and felt. And Tango felt about thirty most of the time, still energetic, but with experiences that were starting to become a heavy load. Some days that load felt heavier than others.

Like today. Tango had played the Kithain games of wild youth once, hopping from freehold to freehold, from the real world to dreams and back again. She had been fifteen, in both appearance and reality, when she had gone through the Chrysalis, the period of awakening to her faerie legacy and the existence of Kithain. She'd looked only twenty when games had become sour for her, thirty years later. Tired and disillusioned, she had walked away from a freehold in... she wasn't even sure where it had been now. Somewhere in Colorado, a freehold so lost in the Dreaming that it barely had a location in the real world. She had walked away, knowing that there must be more to the world than Kithain games. Two days later, she had been in Bangkok.

Traveling had done her good. She probably knew more about the other creatures and beings that shared the shadows of the world than most Kithain did. And she knew that she found most of them, and most humans, more interesting than most Kithain. She had met the owner of Pan's, a human playboy and mage named Aaron Barry, in Australia five years ago. They had become good friends, strong friends, almost instantly. But humans, mages or otherwise, weren't Kithain.

Tango worked a kenning, a tiny, simple enchantment that brought the fae seeming of people and things into focus for her. In the mirror, her reflection shifted. Her hair became wild and pale, her eyes dark and beady, her teeth crooked and her features rough, an exaggerated red sausage of a nose against apple cheeks. Her hands, holding the mirror, became tough and callused. Her arms and legs grew gnarled, and she became even shorter than she normally was. She grimaced at herself, almost sure that the mirror would break. This was her true face, the face of her kith or faerie race. Riley was a tricky pooka. Tango was a dour nocker.

But not even nockers were grim and grouchy all of the time. They were the descendants of earth faeries, the miners and smiths of the Kithain. In the modern age, their magic had also come to include machines, so much so that most nockers were more skilled with machines than they were with other Kithain. Still, they had their social moments. Kithain blood called to Kithain blood. And in spite of the way she felt about Kithain, Tango was more social than most nockers — maybe because her magic was weak and any knack for machinery almost nonexistent. She liked being around people. Her own crooked nocker face was, aside from Riley's, the only Kithain face she had seen in a long time. Seeing a few more for just a short while wouldn't hurt her, would it? It would be nice to spend more time with Riley.

Thirty years of Kithain life had left her with a lot of dark memories. Riley's offer was waking some of the brighter ones.

A stirring in one corner of the office drew her attention away from the mirror. The shadows in that corner were momentarily alight with a glow that only her kenning allowed her to see. Tango smiled. That was another reason to accept Riley's invitation. The glow was Glamour, the energy of magic and wonder — and lifeblood to the Kithain. Tango rose and walked over to the struggling shimmer. She dipped her hand into it, letting it tingle like saltwater across her skin. Stories said that Glamour had been everywhere once. Now it was rare, and clung to the real world in only a few places, like Riley's apartment building, filled with the creative energies of artists and musicians, or Pan's, enchanted by Aaron with his human magick but attracting a thin kind of Glamour as a side effect. The Glamour around Kithain freeholds and courts was usually thick, however. Part of Tango craved that density of Glamour, cried out to be submersed in it. Just as part of her craved the company of other Kithain for just a little while.

And she did have a few very fond memories of Highsummer Night.

Tango walked back to her desk and considered Riley's paper again. Maybe the pooka was right. Maybe it was time for her to go back to Kithain life, at least for a little while. It probably would do her good. She might even find that the years had taken away the disgust she felt for Kithain society and that she could stomach the company of other Kithain again.

If she didn't, at least Toronto had plenty of humans to hang around with.

She reached for the phone and dialed Riley's hotel. It was a good hotel; even at this early, early hour, there was a night clerk on duty. The giddy anticipation of Highsummer was already creeping up on her, and she briefly considered having the clerk ring Riley's room. She would enjoy waking him up. Instead, though, she just left a brief, anonymous message. *Let's tango in Toronto.* "He'll know what it means," she told the clerk.

* * *

Getting a ticket for the 9:30 flight to Toronto the next night was as easy as Tango had anticipated it would be. Riley had written down his seat number, and with a little smooth talking Tango even managed to get the seat beside his. There was no return call from Riley, but that was nothing unusual. Riley had never returned a call on time since she had known him. So Tango packed her bags, promised to call

Alan with Riley's number in Toronto as soon as she had it, and drove herself to the airport. She would rent a car in Toronto. There were very few lines at the airport. Not even the departure lounge was particularly crowded.

Which made it abundantly clear that there was no sign of Riley.

That wasn't especially unusual either. Riley was about as punctual as he was prompt in returning phone calls. To judge by the desire that he had expressed last night in Pan's to have her come to Toronto, though, she would have expected to see him waiting for her anxiously. But maybe not. Tango bought a cheap, trashy novel at a terminal convenience store and settled down to wait.

When preboarding was announced and Riley still had not appeared, she began to worry. Going to the desk, she caught the attention of one of the attendants. "I'm supposed to be traveling with someone. Can you tell me if he's checked in?"

"Certainly. His name?"

"Riley Stanton."

The attendant entered the name in his computer terminal, then shook his head. "I'm sorry."

"He hasn't checked in yet?"

"There isn't anyone by that name on this flight."

Tango bit her tongue. Riley could be traveling under a false name. The long-lived Kithain did that fairly frequently. She hesitated to ask any further questions in case he was. It could make things awkward for both of them, especially if Riley was carrying the kind of "party favors" that the mages of the Cult of Ecstasy usually made. "Thank you," she said politely. One of the other attendants called boarding for her row. Tango took out her boarding pass and got in line.

"Gate H," said the attendant mechanically.

Tango followed the other passengers almost numbly. There was late, and then there was Riley. And then there was *really* late. She could imagine him rushing through the airport as though he were a character in some travel comedy, the kind where tickets get left behind and overpacked luggage dumps clothing in the middle of the terminal. She hoped he made the flight. She had been looking forward to having a good talk with him during the trip. Once they got to Toronto, she was sure that she would lose him to his duties as organizer of the Highsummer party.

She found her seat, on the aisle, and stashed her carry-on in the overhead compartment. Just as she was settling into her seat, a tall woman with platinum-blond hair and an expensive jacket stopped in the aisle. "All right, Cheryl," she said to a small girl with her, "you have the window seat. If you need something, Mommy will be right behind you."

Tango glanced up. "I think there must be some mistake. I'm waiting for a friend." She touched the seat beside her. "This is his seat."

The woman glanced at the row numbers overhead, then at her daughter's boarding pass. "6A? No. It's ours." She flashed Tango a dazzling, perfect smile that spoke of long hours of adult orthodontics. "Excuse us."

"Yay!" squealed Cheryl, clambering around Tango.

"Wait!" Tango stood up. "Let's check with an attendant. There's been..."

"There's no mistake." The woman's mouth compressed into a hard line of displeasure. "I requested a seat reassignment when we checked in. This is the seat they gave my daughter."

Tango took a deep breath and resisted the urge to give the woman reason to spend even more money on corrective dentistry. "If you don't mind," she said smoothly, "I'd just like to check that myself." She flagged down an attendant and explained the situation.

The attendant disappeared toward the front of the plane, then reappeared a minute later. "I'm sorry," she reported with a smile, "but the seat assignment is correct."

The platinum-blond woman gave Tango a smug smile and settled into her own seat. Tango choked back a snarl. What kind of parent brought a kid on a night flight anyway? "What happened to the person who had the seat before? Has he been bumped?"

"No. The seat was never sold. If you will take your seat, we're ready to start taxiing to the runway."

Tango blinked and sat down in surprise. And an unpleasant thought occurred to her. A thought that made her hands itch to be around Riley's scrawny throat and squeezing.

Pookas took immense delight in playing pranks — one reason they loved Highsummer Night so much. Riley hadn't played a serious prank on her in years. She had thought their friendship was past that.

"Hi!" Cheryl said brightly. "This is my first time flying at night." She shoved her skinny little arm under Tango's nose. There was a gaudy gold charm bracelet around her wrist. Cheryl indicated a charm shaped like a star. "Mommy bought me a new charm. See?"

One of the plastic covers on the armrests cracked under Tango's grip. Cheryl glanced at the broken plastic, then up at Tango's face. Tango didn't look back at her. She was concentrating on breathing slowly and steadily, smoothing out her black anger at Riley.

You've read the stories.

Now live the adventure.

White Wolf Game Studio presents a trilogy of games to broaden your experience with the magical world of

Changeling: the Dreaming®.

White Wolf
Publishing

Immortal Eyes: the Toybox
Written by Sam Chupp with Keith Herber.

The first installment in the **Immortal Eyes** trilogy takes the characters to the city of San Francisco. Included is a complete setting for the City by the Bay as well as three mini stories. An excellent introduction to **Changeling** in the tradition of **Vampire's Chicago By Night**.

WW7200

ISBN
1-56504-703-6

$15.00 U.S.

immortal eyes:
shadows on the hill
Written by Bill Bridges, Jennifer Lindberg and
Angel Leigh McCoy. Art by Rebecca Guay.

WW7201

ISBN
1-56504-750-2

$15.00 U.S.

The second installment in the **Immortal
Eyes** trilogy, **Shadows on the Hill** picks up
where **The Toybox** leaves off. The
Immortal Eyes chronicle combines a trilogy
of novels with a series of game sourcebooks.
Shadows on the Hill takes the characters
to Hawaii, where they begin to learn the
full scope of the Unseelie conspiracy.

WORLD OF
DARKNESS

immortal eyes:
court of all kings
Written by Nicky Rea. Art by Rebecca Guay.

WW7202

ISBN
1-56504-713-3

$15.00 U.S.

The final chapter of the **Immortal Eyes**
trilogy takes the heroes to the Emerald Isle.
Learn the secrets of Silver's Gate, the last
gate to Arcadia, and explore the last
bastion of the fae — Ireland.

To order call 1-800-454-WOLF.